The Trick

A tap at the door made her stiffen briefly. Charlie quickly resettled the wig on her head and stood as the door opened, relaxing when her twin sister's head poked around it.

"Oh, good. You are alone." Slipping inside, Beth moved to Charlie's side as she stood. "It has occurred to me that London may be the better destination for us just now after all. We can make our way to our cousin's later . . . if we must."

Charlie's gaze narrowed at that. "What mean you by that?"

"Well . . . " Her sister pursed her lips slightly. "It does occur to me that we might like a coming out."

"Beth, we could not possibly! Uncle Henry—"

"He would not know if we do not give our true names," Beth pointed out simply.

Charlie rolled her eyes at that. "Oh, aye. I am sure that fake names would do the trick. Just exactly how many female twins do you think there are in England, Beth?"

"Why must we tell them we are twins?"

"You do not think they would notice?" she asked dryly.

"Not if we trick them . . . Charles."

By Lynsay Sands

Lynsay Sands

The Switch

AVON

An Imprint of HarperCollinsPublishers

This is a work of fiction. Names, characters, places, and incidents are products of the author's imagination or are used fictitiously and are not to be construed as real. Any resemblance to actual events, locales, organizations, or persons, living or dead, is entirely coincidental.

AVON BOOKS
An Imprint of HarperCollins*Publishers*
195 Broadway
New York, New York 10007

Copyright © 1999 by Lynsay Sands
ISBN 978-0-06-201982-0
www.avonromance.com

First Avon Books mass market printing: December 2013

Avon Trademark Reg. U.S. Pat. Off. and in Other Countries, Marca Registrada, Hecho en U.S.A.
HarperCollins® is a trademark of HarperCollins Publishers.

Printed in the U.S.A.

10 9 8 7 6 5 4 3 2

Dedicated to Sue Ross and Isabel Willan (Gran).

Thanks, Aunt Sue, for slogging through what I am sure are my sometimes incomprehensible first drafts. I appreciate your willingness to do so when no one else would, and will adore you eternally for stepping in to give the support I lost when I lost Mom.

Gran: Thank you. For your support. For being my communication and news depot, my emotional sounding board, and for reining me in when I'm doing something "silly"... which is quite often, but that can be our secret.

Chapter 1

$\mathcal{L}$ORD Radcliffe drew his horse to a halt and stared at the spectacle being played out before him. A young lad in the clothes of the gentry was standing under the front window of an inn, staring up the skirts of a girl hanging out of a second-floor window. The lad seemed to be speaking to the lass as he tried to grab at her feet, but Radcliffe was too far away to hear what was being said.

Deciding that they were probably trying to run out on their bill, Radcliffe started to urge his horse on to the stables, not really caring enough to get involved. But at that moment, the girl pushed herself off the ledge to dangle from her arms. Radcliffe slowed and stopped again, amused. The boy caught the girl's ankles to keep her from slamming into the building, then stepped under her to offer his aid the rest of the way down.

Unable to see what she was doing, the girl stepped on the lad's wig with one foot, setting it askew. She nearly lost her grip and tumbled backward to the ground when the obviously irate youth jerked her foot from his head to his shoulder. He then directed the other foot with about as much care.

Radcliffe chuckled under his breath as the woman suddenly dropped to sit on the boy's shoulders. Her skirts fell over the lad's head as she did, blinding him, and the shift in position unbalanced him enough so that he stumbled backward, then to the side as he fought to push the skirt out of his view. At this point, the woman clutched at his hair for balance, forgetting it was a wig. It lifted from his head with her hands, and her upper body swung backward. The lad, already off-balance, tumbled backward with her. They both hit the ground with soft thuds, hidden briefly in the shadow of the inn.

"Damn," Charlie muttered, staring up at the treetops above them until a pitiful moan from Beth stirred the cool night air. Sitting up, Charlie surveyed the prone girl with a worried frown. "Are you all right?"

Elizabeth sighed at the question. Her moan had been one of chagrin, but the concerned face suddenly leaning over her own told her that it had been misconstrued.

"Fine," she said dryly. She sat up to brush grass and dirt off of her dress.

Charlie started to help, but Beth waved the attempt away.

"Your wig is gone," she pointed out.

Sitting back, Charlie searched the shadows for the errant wig, then slapped it irritably against one leg to remove the grass clinging to it before slamming it back in place. "Is it straight?"

Beth glanced up long enough to nod, then struggled to her feet.

"Well. That wasn't so bad," Charlie murmured cheerfully, standing and moving to snatch up the bags they had thrown out the window before descending themselves.

Beth turned sharply, mouth open to give her own opinion of the debacle, but caught the twinkle of laughter in the coal black eyes that were so like her own. She relaxed, grinning back. "A ride in the park," she agreed dryly.

Laughing softly, Charlie handed her a bag, took the other one, and led the way to the stables.

"Is he unconscious?" Beth murmured as they entered the tottering old building and spied the stable lad slumped in a corner against a bale of hay. The bottle they had given him was still clasped to his chest.

"Seems to be. You did put the sleeping powder in there, did you not?"

Beth nodded silently, but held her breath as her twin carefully approached the boy, then lifted his head and let it drop back to his chest. He didn't even stir.

Shrugging, Charlie stepped back. "Out like a drunken sot."

Her breath rushing out in relief, Beth moved quickly along the stalls until she found the one where her mount had been settled for the night. Murmuring soothingly, she stepped inside to set about quickly saddling him while Charlie did the same for the mount in the next stall.

Several moments later, Beth was aware at once when her twin suddenly stiffened. Going still herself, she glanced up and about, her heart nearly freezing in her chest at the sight of a figure in the shadows by the

door. Charlie tossed her a warning look, then affected
the accent of the servant class and asked, "Some'ing I
can do fer ye, m'lord?"

One eyebrow rising at the boy's accent, Radcliffe
smiled slightly. "It is very bad manners to sneak out
without paying one's bill. And stealing horses is a
crime."

Charlie stiffened, eyes shooting to Beth's face. The
girl was as pale as the moon, her expression panicked
as their gazes met.

Radcliffe noted the silent exchange and wished for
better lighting in the stables. He'd bet a lot of money
that the girl was a beauty. His eyes were straining to
make out her features in the darkness when the lad
spoke up again.

"We are not stealing. The horses are ours."

The false accent was gone, he noted absently,
glancing at the boy. Obviously gentry, as he had suspected. "And your bill?"

"Taken care of."

Radcliffe raised one doubting eyebrow. "Then why
not leave by the door like most people?" he asked,
noting the couple again exchanging glances.

Charlie was trying to decide just what to tell the
snoopy hitch in their plans when Beth suddenly moved
out of the stall and into the stream of moonlight
coming through the stable doors.

Noting the look of appreciation that immediately
entered the stranger's eyes, Charlie peered at the girl
now too, curious to know what the man found so attractive. Beth was pretty enough. Straight nose, good
teeth. Her eyes were her best feature, large and blue-
black, while her hair was an unremarkable brown.

All of which described Charlie as well. Not surprising, since they were twins. But it was doubtful that the man had noticed that fact yet.

"We were forced to leave through the windows to escape my uncle," the girl said.

Radcliffe arched an eyebrow. "Why would you need to escape your uncle?"

Noting yet another exchange of glances between the young couple, Radcliffe smiled wryly. "Or need I ask?"

"I beg your pardon?" she murmured uncertainly.

"You need not explain. 'Tis obvious you are about to head for Gretna Green."

"Gretna Green?"

Charlie could have kicked Beth for her look of astonishment. If the saying were true that everyone loved a lover, they might have had a better chance of the man not interfering in their escape plans. He'd obviously thought they were eloping. Instead of leaving him with that mistaken impression, however, Beth gestured toward Charlie.

"Charlie is my twin—"

"Charles," Charlie corrected quickly, stepping forward to join her in the light.

Beth blinked, then nodded slowly. "Aye. Charles is my twin brother."

Radcliffe's eyebrows shot up as he looked the boy over. Except for the white wig, the two were identical. Well, of course there were the obvious physical differences. Where the girl's chest was ample, the boy's was not. After his initial surprise had passed, Radcliffe's eyes narrowed with some suspicion. "Why would the two of you need to flee your uncle in the dead of night?"

"Our parents died four years ago," the lad answered this time. "Our uncle took over our care. He has done his best to run the family estates into the ground, and now wishes to replenish his coffers by selling Beth off into marriage. To Lord Carland."

Radcliffe stiffened at that name, shocked. Carland was a brutal bastard. He had been through three wives already. The first had died in childbirth. It was said that a beating had sent her into labor, and may have had something to do with her death as well. The second wife had killed herself. The third had plunged to her death down the stairs of the family's country estate. There was much speculation as to whether she had had some assistance from her husband in that plunge.

Whatever the case, not one of his wives had lasted a year, and no one would even consider allowing their daughter to marry the bastard now. But from this pair's description, their uncle was more concerned with his coffers than his kin. Were they telling the truth?

"What are your names?" he asked abruptly.

There was a pause as the two exchanged glances once again.

"Charles and Elizabeth Westerly."

Radcliffe searched his memory briefly, then nodded as he recalled having heard of Nora and Robert Westerly. Happy couple. They'd had twins, though he had thought they were girls. The family members had spent most of their time on their country estate and hadn't cared much for town life. The parents had died four years ago in a carriage accident. Robert's brother Henry Westerly had supposedly taken over the care of the twins and the running of the estates. There had been some rumors of late that he was running through the money quickly in gambling, and from what the boy had just said, he had, and intended to make it up by selling his niece into a marriage that would likely result in her death.

Radcliffe wasn't at all surprised to hear that Carland was willing to pay for a bride. The man needed an heir, else his estate would be left to some distant nephew. His gaze slid over the girl and he sighed. She was a delicate little creature. Other than her over-endowed chest, she was thin to the point of frailty everywhere else. He did not think she would last a month with Carland.

"Where are you going?" he asked abruptly, gesturing impatiently when the boy stiffened at the question, suspicion tightening his mouth. "I am not going to tell on you. I would not wish to see your lovely sister in Carland's hands either. She would be dead in a week."

There was no doubting his sincerity. There was loathing in the man's eyes even as he said Carland's name. Still, Charlie hesitated to tell him the truth, that they were going to stay with their cousin Ralphy, a relative on their mother's side that Uncle Henry did not know existed. Lies were the only alternative. Oddly enough, the plan that came tripping out wasn't half-bad.

"London."

Radcliffe's eyebrows rose yet again. "Relatives there?"

"No."

"It takes money to live in London."

Charlie grinned. "Uncle Henry went through our father's family fortune, but our mother turned her fortune into jewels years ago. She left them to us in her will."

"And your uncle did not try to cash them in or—"

"He would have if he could have found them," the lad interrupted smugly. "But he couldn't. Mother and Father hid them years ago, in case of an emergency. Other than our parents, only Elizabeth and I knew where they were, and we conveniently forgot to mention that they had told us."

Radcliffe's mouth quirked at that; then he sobered. "He will find you in London."

"Eventually," Charlie agreed. "But by then Beth will be married off to someone in the ton."

"And you?"

"I shall be living well off of investments made once I have sold my share of the jewels," Charlie lied nonchalantly.

"You intend to give your sister a season by selling some of the jewels?"

The boy nodded.

Radcliffe frowned. "If you give her a season, your uncle shall hear about it and know where to find you."

"As I said, eventually, but he will not look in London first. He shall head back to the family estates, then check with relatives on my father's side."

"Why would he not look in London first?"

"Because that is where he was taking us. He would hardly think we had run off in the middle of the night to beat him there."

Radcliffe nodded at the sense in those words. Even Beth looked impressed with the reasoning, and Charlie grimaced at her slightly. She was supposed to already know of this plan. If she was not careful, Radcliffe would see it for the lie it was.

"What of Carland?" Radcliffe asked.

Charlie glanced toward the man. "Carland does not go to London. Most of the ton refuses him admittance. My uncle was taking us to London to purchase a trousseau for Beth, then we were to continue on to Carland's estates."

It was a sound plan for the most part, Radcliffe decided. What the boy lacked in brawn, he more than made up for in brains, it seemed. However, there were weak points in every plan and this one was no exception. For instance, if they planned on living off of a treasure of jewels, they obviously had the jewels with them. Probably in the bags, he decided, remembering the way they had carried them: one each, two-handed, as if they were heavy. All it took was a highway robbery to turn them into paupers at their uncle's mercy again, and he would guess the foolish boy was unarmed. Aside from that, there were all sorts of complications that could arise in London. Theft, of course, or a jeweler could cheat them if they went to the wrong one. And that was only the start of it.

Radcliffe tried to shrug away his growing concern for the pair, but it would not vanish. He would have to help them, he supposed, but couldn't for the life of him figure out why he felt the compulsion. His gaze rested on the girl briefly, but he mentally shook his head. No, it was not that he was enamored especially of this girl.

Oddly enough, he suspected he was going to do it because of the boy. There was a certain stiffness to the lad that spoke of fear, pride and courage all mixed in together as he stood protectively by his sister. He was taking a lot on himself to rescue her, trying very hard to be a man, though Radcliffe doubted that the pair was more than fifteen or sixteen.

"You had best finish saddling up. Time is passing. You will wish to be far and away from here come the morning." With that, the man turned and left the stables.

"Do you think he will tell?" Beth asked anxiously as they listened to his fading footsteps.

Shrugging, Charlie walked back into the stall to finish saddling the mount. "It does not matter. It might be good if he does, since the plan I gave him was a lie. But mount up quickly anyway. If he wakes everyone up, I do not wish to be here."

Nodding, Beth hurried back to her mount, then giggled nervously. "Where did you come up with those lies?"

"They were not all lies," Charlie pointed out grimly, and Beth's smile faded.

"No. The part about Uncle Henry losing all and trying to get it back through marriage was true enough. But I am not to marry Carland. I am to marry Seguin. Why—"

"He would hardly be sympathetic to the fact that you are being married off to a fat old goat," Charlie pointed out dryly. "That happens every day. Carland is another kettle of fish altogether."

"Aye. Besides, it was not really much of a lie, was

it? After all, Uncle Henry was selling *you* in marriage to Carland," Beth murmured quietly, her gaze moving over her twin sister. She still found it a little startling to see her in men's clothes. Especially with her breasts bound so tight they seemed nonexistent. She wondered suddenly if it hurt Charlie to have them all squashed up like that.

It had been Charlie's idea to dress as a man. A brother and sister traveling alone would not be noticed. Twin sisters traveling alone would have. She supposed they could have traveled as two boys, but Charlie had not mentioned the suggestion, and truth to tell, Beth had not even thought of it until now. Besides, twin brothers might have been just as memorable as twin sisters. Nay, she decided. 'Twas better this way. She as herself, and Charlie masquerading as her brother.

It was just the adventurous sort of thing Charlie liked to do. She was the braver, wilder of the two. Beth wasn't very adventurous at all. She was the sedate one. Well behaved, obedient, well mannered, she did what was expected. Until she'd found out about Seguin. But she probably would have obediently married the great cow if not for Charlie. Still, Charlie simply couldn't marry Carland. As the stranger had said, she'd be dead in a month, or in gaol for killing him in self-defense. That's why Charlie had decided to run away to Cousin Ralph to seek protection. And where Charlie went, Beth followed. They were twins, after all. They'd never been separated in all their twenty years, or not as far as Beth could remember.

"All set?"

Beth glanced up at her sister's question and nodded as she hooked the bag with her half of their mother's jewels onto the saddle.

"Good. Let us go." Charlie led her horse out of his stall and Beth followed suit, trailing her out of the stable. The pair walked their horses silently around the inn. Beth was staring at the darkened windows, wondering where the stranger had gone, when Charlie suddenly slowed and cursed. Glancing forward, she noted the man standing by a horse on the lane in front of the inn. "What do you think he is doing?"

Charlie was silent for a moment, then sighed. "I suppose we shall have to ask to find out."

Radcliffe smiled to himself as the pair approached. The girl wasn't bothering to hide her anxiety and confusion about his presence. The boy was hiding both staunchly behind a stiff exterior.

"I have decided to travel with you to London," he announced when they stopped before him, then nearly laughed at their blank expressions. They obviously hadn't thought to be so lucky. Deciding to give them a moment to recapture their thoughts so that they could thank him properly, he continued, "It is a three-day journey from here to London. The way is littered with highwaymen and perils of every nature. Since I am headed that way anyway, I thought to avail you of my protection."

Charlie glanced at Beth's nonplused expression, her own face stiff with fury. Why the devil hadn't she considered that the oaf might decide to join them? Why did he even want to? The jolthead was going to ruin everything. She did not for one moment think that he really wanted to help. So, what was he after, she wondered. The answer came to her almost immediately. It wasn't that hard to figure out, really. She should not have mentioned the jewels. He must have realized that they carried them with them and most likely, he intended to rob them somewhere down the road.

Straightening her shoulders, she glared at him coldly and announced, "Your offer is kind, I am sure, but I am quite capable of protecting my sister."

Radcliffe frowned at the boy's reaction, then realized that he had pinched his male pride. The pride of young men was a most fragile thing, and while Radcliffe normally would have done his most to protect such tender feelings, now was not the time for it. Not when the boy's pride might very well see him and his sister dead. "You are not even carrying a weapon, lad," he pointed out sternly. "If I had been a thief, I could have killed you both and taken your jewels in the stables."

Charlie blinked, wondering if the man had read her thoughts regarding his motives, then shrugged such worries aside. She had more important concerns. Such as finding some way to refuse his offer and avoid raising his suspicions at the same time. "Who are you?"

Radcliffe blinked. "What?"

"Your name, sirrah?"

He stiffened at the insulting address, then arched one eyebrow rather superciliously and reached into his pocket to withdraw a small card, which he presented to Charlie.

Stepping forward, she took the card and frowned

as she read the name out loud. "Lord Jeremy William Richards. The earl of Radcliffe." She looked up at him. "Lord Radcliffe."

He gave an ironic little bow, then relaxed as he saw the recognition on their faces and the way the brother and sister exchanged glances again. "You know the name."

"You knew our father," Charlie countered.

"I never met him," Radcliffe corrected. "But we did correspond on occasion. We were partners in several ventures."

Charlie nodded solemnly and did not correct Radcliffe's polite phrasing. *Partners* was a bit of an ambitious word to use for the investors who threw in with Radcliffe. The man was a genius, according to what her father had always told her. He had the Midas touch. Any investment he made paid back in at least triplicate. Everyone knew this and everyone wished to invest with him, but he was a choosy fellow. Very few people were invited to invest with him, and if one was not invited, one did not invest. As for it being a partnership, there really was none. The investors often had no idea where their money went, and fewer still really cared so long as it paid off. Radcliffe did all the thinking in the investments; those who he invited along simply rode on the coattails of his genius.

She turned the card over in her hand thoughtfully. Lord Radcliffe would hardly need the jewels they carried. While they were a small fortune, they were nothing compared to the wealth he enjoyed. "Why would you trouble yourself to help us?"

Radcliffe raised an eyebrow at the blunt question. "As I said before, you are not even carrying a weapon, lad. But, if I am right, you *are* carrying your mother's jewels." He grinned when Charlie stiffened. "As I thought. One highwayman and the two of you are paupers at your uncle's mercy."

Charlie winced considering that prospect, and Radcliffe's expression softened. "I am headed that way anyway. I see no harm in offering my company as a deterrent to thieves."

Charlie hesitated a moment, then grabbed Beth's hand and urged her a safe distance away, dragging their horses behind them.

"What are we going to do?" Beth hissed as Charlie stopped and faced her.

"We go with him."

"What? But—"

"He is right, Beth. We could be robbed on the road. I did not think of taking a pistol." Sighing, she shrugged. "He is protection. It is one thing to go to Ralphy with our inheritance. It would be quite another to show up penniless."

"But he is heading the wrong way," Beth pointed out after a hesitation.

"I know." Charlie thought for a moment, then grinned suddenly. "That might be to our advantage, though. As I pointed out earlier, our uncle will hardly look in London, or even in that direction for us." A soft laugh slipped from her lips. "We shall go that way with Radcliffe; then when he stops to rest, I shall steal his pistol and we will head for Ralphy's."

Beth looked uncertain. "But, Charlie, he is offering to help. I cannot like the idea of stealing his pistol as repayment. He—"

"I shall leave him one of Mother's bracelets. That

should pay for the pistol three times over." Her gaze slid back to the man in question. "He must have been on the road most of the day and this evening. He shall probably stop at the next inn, or the one after. There we will make our escape. And that will give us most of the night to travel."

Chapter 2

NOTHING in life is simple. Charlie came to that conclusion as the first faint fingers of dawn began to streak the sky. She had expected Radcliffe to lead them to the next inn and stop for the night. Instead, they had passed more inns than she would wish to count and they were still on the road.

Glancing at her sister, Charlie frowned and reached out to touch her arm gently. Beth had nodded off and was in great peril of tumbling from her horse. At Charlie's touch, she snapped awake and peered wearily around.

Charlie offered her a sympathetic smile, then turned to glare at the back of the man riding in front of them. They had ridden through the night without incident, not even catching sight of anyone on the road, let alone being confronted by highwaymen or ne'er-do-wells. Charlie was beginning to think that all that talk of the perils of the road was just a bunch of bunk, and that they should have conked the great goon over the head and set out in the direction they had originally intended, pistol or no. Now she was not sure what to do. The horses were fair done in from a whole day and night's travel and Charlie herself was having some difficulty staying awake in the saddle. Add to that the fact that they had now added an extra day's travels to their journey, and she fairly wanted to gnash her teeth in frustration.

When her mount suddenly drew to a halt, Charlie blinked and stopped glaring at the person she held wholly responsible for her misery, then peered about. Her eyes widened when she saw that they had turned a bend in the road and were now halted in front of an inn.

"We shall stop here to rest." Radcliffe dismounted, wincing. He, too must be feeling the stiffness in his legs and seat that Charlie was. He unhitched his traveling bag and walked to the horse where Beth sat half-asleep in the saddle. When she merely stared down at him in a kind of exhausted stupor, Radcliffe's features softened.

"Come along, little girl," he said gently, holding up his arms to assist her. "We shall have you tucked up in a nice warm bed in no time."

Beth roused herself enough to slide off of her mount, but gave a startled cry as her legs collapsed beneath her. Charlie moved forward, but her sister's fall was forestalled when Radcliffe caught the girl in his arms.

"See to the horses, Charles," he ordered, turning away. "I shall rent two rooms and see your sister settled in."

"'See to the horses, Charles,'" Charlie mimicked irritably as she watched the man carry her sister away. Sighing as they disappeared into the inn, she slid off her own mount, then gasped and gripped the saddle grimly as her own legs played her false. Leaning against her horse, she waited as the pain and weakness slowly ebbed, then took a shaky step away. Much to her relief, her legs held this time.

Letting her breath out on a sigh, she grabbed up the reins of all three horses and led them toward the stable beside the inn at a hobbling gait.

"His Lordship said ye'd be needin' me help."

Giving a start at those words, Charlie paused at the door of the stables and glanced back to see a boy approaching. He was no older than twelve. His hair was rumpled and his clothes a bit disheveled. It was obvious he had just awoken, and Charlie was briefly swamped with envy, until she realized that the sooner she finished with the horses, the sooner she could rest as well.

Offering him a weary smile, she handed over the reins of Radcliffe's mount, then led her own and Beth's mounts into the stables. She deposited Beth's horse in one stall, pausing long enough to unhook the bag of jewels from the saddle horn. It dropped to the ground with a crash, and she grimaced as she grabbed the handle in both hands and staggered out of the stall with it. Depositing it in the next stall, she then led her own mount into it and quickly unhooked the bag he carried as well. She then turned her attention to unsaddling him.

She watched the stableboy out of the corner of her eye as she worked. He was quick and efficient, unsaddling, brushing down, watering, and feeding Radcliffe's mount all before Charlie had even finished brushing down the first horse. Of course, she was so tired, she was clumsy and slow; she excused herself.

When the boy finished with Radcliffe's mount and then moved on to Beth's beast, Charlie sighed with relief that it would not be her chore. As it was, the boy finished tending the second horse just as she finished her own. Charlie bent then to grab up both her and Beth's bags, but groaned at their combined weight and let them drop. She could not carry them both; she simply could not.

Charlie was considering simply sinking to sleep in the straw with the bags as pillows when the boy approached her again.

"Need a hand, m'lord?"

Glancing up at those words, she sighed her defeat. "What is your name?"

"Will Sumner."

"Well, Will Sumner, truth to tell I am all in just now and I would appreciate a hand."

Grinning at the thought of the tip to come, he stepped into the stall and hefted one of the bags, eyes widening in shock at the weight of it. "Gor! What ha'e ye got in here, m'lord? Rocks?"

"Basically," Charlie muttered dryly, hefting the second bag and leading the way out of the stables.

Will followed her into the inn, waited patiently as she got directions, then followed her upstairs to the room the innkeeper had given her sister.

At the door to Beth's room, Charlie set down her bag and dug two coins out of her pocket.

"Just set that down there, Will," she murmured, holding out the coins. "And I thank you for your help."

Eyes widening at the generous tip, the boy thanked her brightly and disappeared back the way they had come. Charlie then opened the door before her, glancing at the bed where her sister lay in exhausted slumber. Sighing in pleasure at the thought of herself sleeping, she bent to pick up one of the bags. She was straightening with it in hand when the door to the neighboring room opened and Lord Radcliffe peered out.

"Ah. There you are. I was just coming to look for you." Stepping to Charlie's side, he picked up the other bag and turned away. "Come along. The innkeeper directed you to the wrong door. Our room is this one."

"Our room?" The words echoed through Charlie's brain like the crack of thunder. She stared at Radcliffe's back blankly for a moment, then followed him slowly into his chamber. "*Ours?*"

Radcliffe dropped the bag and pushed it under the bed with one foot, then turned to face Charles, who still stood, bemused, in the doorway. "Come in and close the door, lad. No need to hang about in the hall."

Charlie watched as Radcliffe slipped out of his frock coat, then set it aside. The man then glanced at the bed as he set to work at the buttons of his waistcoat. "You can have whichever side you want. I am not fussy. The innkeeper's wife is bringing up something for you to eat. Your sister and I ate while they fixed the rooms."

Tugging his waistcoat off, Radcliffe laid it over a chair, then sat on the bed to work on his jackboots.

Charlie froze, staring rather blankly at the man stripping before her. Who expected to share a bed with Charles Westerly, brother of Elizabeth Westerly. Which, of course, was only sensible. There were two men and one woman. The woman got one room. The men the other. *Only, I am not a man!* Charlie screamed silently.

A discreet cough behind her got Charlie's attention and she glanced over her shoulder to see a short little woman behind her, balancing a tray in her hands.

"Let her in, lad," Radcliffe ordered irritably, and Charlie stepped automatically into the room to let the woman pass. The innkeeper's wife smiled briefly as she walked over to set the tray on a table in front of the fireplace, then smiled once more as she silently left the room.

Charlie heard the door click shut, but her attention was now fixed on the tray of food. When her stomach rumbled loudly, announcing its hunger, she gave up her position by the door, dropped her bag on the floor, and hurried over to the table.

Out of the corner of her eye, Charlie saw Radcliffe smile wryly to himself as she dropped into a chair and attacked the bread and cheese the woman had brought.

Even as ravenous as she was, Charlie felt compelled to watch Radcliffe move about. Shaking his head, he set his boots aside, then moved over to grab up the bag she had thoughtlessly dropped by the door where anyone might reach in and grab it. Carrying it back to the bed, Radcliffe slid it under, next to the other one, then straightened himself and set to work on doffing his clothing.

Charlie froze in her seat by the fireplace. Her hand, holding a hunk of cheese, paused halfway to her mouth as Radcliffe shrugged out of his shirt.

The morning sun was still only half-visible as it crept up behind the trees outside the window. The room was still dim, the fire in the fireplace the only light from inside the room, but Charlie's shock quickly gave way to fascination as she watched the firelight reflect off Radcliffe's arms and chest. The man really was quite beautiful, she realized with surprise, watching the ripple and play of muscles in his arms and across his chest as he worked at the buttons of his breeches. But then they dropped to the floor and Charlie's eyes became round saucers of shock again before she jerked her face away several shades brighter.

God's fish! She could not sleep with this man. It was not proper. Whether he thought her a boy or not.

A rustling sound drew her gaze reluctantly back to him. He had turned his back to her and was slipping a nightshirt over his head. Charlie had a lovely view of firm buttocks and nicely shaped legs before the nightshirt dropped into place; then Radcliffe turned back toward her. Charlie's gaze shot studiously back to her plate.

"Almost done?" he asked, stretching tiredly.

Charlie nodded, gaze fixed grimly on the food before her.

"Any preference as to which side to sleep on?"

She shook her head.

"All right then. Good night." There was the rustle of bed-sheets, then silence.

Charlie hesitated, then glanced up. Radcliffe was settled comfortably beneath the covers, well on his way to sleep. Breath slipping through her teeth, she sank back in her seat with a sigh. She was not hungry anymore. And now that she had satisfied the worst of her hunger, exhaustion was creeping over her again.

Yawning, she rested her chin wearily in her hand and tried to think what to do. She could hardly sleep here with him. On the other hand, she could not think of a single excuse for why she could not that he might accept. And she was *so* tired.

Her gaze slid to the bed again and she sighed. After twenty-four hours without sleep, it was looking pretty inviting. . . . Even with Radcliffe in it.

Pushing herself away from the table, Charlie stumbled to the bed and stared down. It was a rather large bed. Very large. Lots of room. Why, she bet she could sleep in it quite easily without ever touching Radcliffe. Aye. She'd just sleep on top of the sheet, she decided, pulling the cover aside and slipping carefully beneath it. She'd sleep fully clothed too. . . . On top of the sheets and fully clothed. 'Twas proper enough.

Radcliffe was already up when Charlie awoke. He had donned his breeches and was just finishing washing out of the basin by the fireplace. Charlie watched the play of muscles in his back for a minute, then sat up, reaching up to check that her wig was still on straight. She probably would not have even thought to check it if it were not for the fact that her head was itchy. After so many hours of wearing it, the damn wig was becoming almost painful. . . . As was the binding around her chest, she realized, reaching down to scratch at that now, too.

"You are awake."

Giving up her efforts to scratch the bound flesh of her chest through her clothes, Charlie glanced up to see Radcliffe watching her as he donned his shirt. She stared back, taking in his facial features with some interest. Most of the time since they had met had been spent in near or complete darkness. She really had only managed to catch a glimpse of his shadowed face here and there. Even last night—well, early this morning, she supposed—in this room, the light had been dim, not lending itself to a true view of his features. She was interested to note now that he was quite an attractive man. His eyes were a rather striking pale gray and shone with intelligence and what appeared to be good humor this day. His nose was straight if a bit hawkish, and his lips were neither generous nor overly thin. His hair was dark, so dark as to be black, and fell off his face in short waves. He was not nearly as old as she had assumed the night before, and that made her frown somewhat as she slid her feet off the bed.

"You fell asleep in your clothes?" He seemed more amused than surprised.

Shrugging, Charlie stood, wincing as her muscles complained of the night's activities. She was not used to such long hours of riding. "We packed no clothes. There was no room, what with the jewels," she said by way of explanation, moving up to the second basin of water and washing her face.

"Hmm. I shall lend you a nightshirt for tonight, then," Radcliffe proclaimed, moving over to collect his boots from the side of the bed.

Charlie didn't respond to the offer. She had no intention of being there to accept it. If she was right, Radcliffe would decide not to travel today. It was already mid- to late-afternoon by her guess and there was no real need to set out before the next morning. It was safer to travel during the day anyway. Or so he had said. Tonight, once he was asleep, she would take his pistol, Beth, and the bags, and they would head for Ralphy's.

"We shall stay here tonight and set out in the morning," Radcliffe suddenly announced, verifying her thoughts. When Charlie's only answer was a quick nod as she dried her face, Radcliffe did not bother to explain further.

A light tapping came at the door. Charlie glanced at Radcliffe, then walked over to open it and find Beth standing there. The concerned expression on her face gave way to relief the minute she saw her sister.

Stepping into the hall, Charlie closed the door and urged Beth back toward her own room.

"The innkeeper's wife said that you two had shared a room," Beth whispered with concern as they went inside.

"It would have looked odd if I had not."

"Aye, but—"

"I slept fully clothed," Charlie quickly assured her. "And on top of the linens."

Beth nodded but bit her lip. "What are we going to do now?"

"Radcliffe plans on staying here until tomorrow. We shall leave in the middle of the night like last night."

"Not through the window again?" Beth did not even try to hide her distress at the idea. Charlie sighed and shook her head.

"Nay. We shall try the stairs this time."

"When?"

"I shall come for you as soon as he is asleep. Why do you not try to get some more rest? It is going to be a long night." She waited until Beth had moved to the bed, then slipped back out into the hall as Radcliffe left the room they had shared.

"Is she all right?" he asked with concern. "She seemed a bit pale."

Charlie shrugged. "She did not sleep very well last night. Worrying too much. I told her to get more rest."

Nodding, Radcliffe started down the stairs, Charlie right behind him. "She is very much like my sister," he said suddenly, bringing Charlie's gaze to curiously study his own.

"What is her name?"

He was silent for a moment, his expression brooding; then he shrugged. "Mary."

"Is she married?"

"She was."

"Was?"

"Still is, I guess, but she and her husband are both dead."

Charlie remained silent as she followed him into the inn's tavern. Once they were seated at a table, she glanced at his face. It looked as hard as granite now, not in the least approachable. No doubt he used that expression to let people know that no more questions were wished. With this realization, she began to relax for the first time since meeting this man. She felt some of her discomfort slip away and some control return.

It was only then that she realized that she had felt slightly out of control since the man had crept up on her and Beth in the stables. It had been a strange and uncomfortable sensation for her, but as she realized just how human Lord Jeremy Radcliffe was, she felt some control return. It was an odd thing about her and Beth. They looked alike, talked alike, and even shared a lot of tastes, but each of them had a different sort of talent when it came to dealing with people. Beth was good with handling illnesses of the body. She could look at a person, know what was physically ailing them, and what to give them to help. She had a certain flair for healing a body.

Charlie, on the other hand, had an instinct for people's motivations. She knew the pain they felt and what they needed to talk about. She could also tell when someone was hiding their true self. She'd taken an instant dislike to Uncle Henry, for instance, despite his seemingly kind and gentle nature when he had first arrived after their parents' death. Beth had been blinded by his facade and been taken in by him, until he had started to show his true self. And while Beth had been terribly hurt to find Charlie's instincts proven true about the man, Charlie hadn't been surprised at all. Now that instinct was attuned to Lord Radcliffe, and what she was sensing was that he never talked about his sister or her death. . . . And he needed to.

Her tone nonchalant, she asked, "How did they die?"

Radcliffe's face darkened. For a moment she thought he might tell her to go to hell and mind her own business, but then he answered, the words tumbling out as if they had been waiting a long time to escape. "They had come to visit me. They lived on the next estate and had ridden over on horseback for the day. A highwayman had been working the area, but no one had been hurt yet, just robbed, petty thefts really. My sister and her husband stayed for dinner. It was dark when they left. I suggested I have my carriage take them back. . . ." He paused. Something flickered over his face. Regret? Pain? Anger? "I should have in-sisted."

Guilt. Charlie sat back with a sigh, positive that it was guilt that Lord Radcliffe felt when he spoke of his sister. But why? "Was she younger than you?"

"Aye," he sighed and drank from his mug.

"What of your parents?"

"They died when we were both younger. I was eighteen then. Mary, twelve."

"You raised her? Took care of her until she was married?" Charlie guessed, and he glanced at her in surprise.

"Aye. How did you know?"

Charlie shrugged. "Who else would do it? You have mentioned no one else," she murmured absently, her thoughts on what she had learned. His guilt was because he had grown up taking care of his sister. He felt that he should have insisted more that they take his carriage. Mayhap he even thought that he should have accompanied them. He seemed to feel that he had failed them somehow. Such feelings were no doubt also behind his offering of protection to herself and her sister. After all, he had said himself that Beth re-minded him of Mary. Last night must have seemed similar to him to the situation that had seen his sis-ter's death. A man and a woman alone on the road. Traveling at night. Aye, now she understood his offer to help them.

Radcliffe frowned. He was likely irritated and em-barrassed with himself for revealing so much. Charlie could sense that she had elicited from him informa-tion he hadn't offered anyone in years. Suddenly impatient, Radcliffe glared into his drink briefly, then glanced up. "Can you shoot? Or has no one taught you?"

Charlie's hesitation was answer enough, and Radcliffe got to his feet. "No doubt your uncle wouldn't have bothered. Any man who would sell his niece to Carland would hardly be bothered with whether his nephew can defend himself." He gave Charlie a small smile. "Come along," he ordered gruffly.

Scrambling from behind the table, Charlie hurried after him.

"Where have you been?" Beth rushed forward as Charlie and Radcliffe entered the inn two hours later.

Charlie caught the concern on her sister's face and grinned, but it was Radcliffe who answered. "I was teaching your brother to shoot."

Beth's eyes widened incredulously. "Really? How did it go?"

Charlie began to chuckle when Radcliffe hesitated. She knew that she was not exactly what one would call a natural. She had not hit a single target. Surprisingly, Radcliffe had not lost his patience with her ineptitude. He had been terribly encouraging, telling her when they finally gave up that she would improve with practice. Lots of practice.

"What your brother lacks in accuracy, he makes up for in enthusiasm. He shall improve. He just needs practice," Radcliffe said finally, and Charlie's chuckles turned into all-out laughter at his attempt at diplomacy.

When Radcliffe smiled faintly at her amusement,

Charlie gave him a slightly mocking bow, then took Beth's arm and steered her toward the room they had dined in earlier, confiding cheerfully as they went, "I am a complete failure as a man, I fear. I could not hit the side of the inn at ten paces."

Beth blinked, then burst out laughing as they reached the table.

Radcliffe followed the pair, smiling like a benign monarch on his charges. Taking a seat across from them, he listened, his smile growing as Charles relayed the events of the afternoon, realizing as he listened that rather than be discouraged, the boy had found it all a great adventure.

The twins continued to chat during the meal, coaxing smiles from Radcliffe every so often. Then Beth excused herself and said she was going to rest. Radcliffe decided that the girl had a very delicate constitution if she must rest so often, but said nothing.

Charlie, on the other hand, watched her sister go with a sigh. Beth expected her to wait until Radcliffe was asleep, steal his pistol, then go to her. But she was beginning to dislike the idea. Radcliffe was . . . nice, and he had gone out of his way to help them. The idea of stealing his pistol, whether she left jewels in exchange for it or not, just did not sit well with her.

She glanced down at her ale and grimaced. On the other hand, they had to get to Cousin Ralphy, and having heard how Radcliffe's sister had died, she absolutely would not set out without a weapon. The perils of the road were suddenly very believable.

Pushing her ale away, Charlie stood and muttered

that she had to tell Beth something, then hurried up to her sister's room.

"I cannot steal his pistol," she announced, stepping inside and closing the door.

"Good." Beth finished stepping out of her gown and laid it across a chair by the bed, oblivious to Charlie's sudden frown.

"What do you mean, 'good'?"

"He is nice," Beth announced firmly, releasing her hair to fall in long waves around her shoulders. "And it would be stealing whether we left a bracelet or not."

Sighing, Charlie sank onto the side of the bed. "I know. Now what do we do?"

"You shall think of something," Beth said complacently, and Charlie was suddenly angry. It had always been that way. Were they in trouble and in need of a plan, Charlie was expected to come up with it and get them out of the hot water. Oddly enough, it had never bothered her before, but now it did. Before she could comment, Beth mused, "It is a shame that we are not in a town or something. We could simply buy one then."

Charlie stared at her blankly for a moment, then suddenly smiled. "Good idea."

Pausing in the act of crawling into bed, Beth glanced at her blankly. "What?"

"I shall see if the innkeeper has a flintlock. He is sure to have one. I shall buy it off him."

"What if he does not want to sell it?"

Charlie shrugged and walked to the door. "I shall offer him so much that he will not be able to refuse." She paused, raising a hand to silence Beth as she listened to footsteps come up the stairs. The door to the room she had shared with Radcliffe opened and closed, and Charlie smiled slightly. It meant that she could talk to the innkeeper without worrying that Radcliffe might overhear.

"Wake me if he sells it to you," Beth whispered as Charlie opened the door. Nodding, she closed the door behind her and headed below.

Chapter 3

THE innkeeper was a burly, rough-voiced man. Charlie took a seat at a table, accepted the ale the man brought over, then sipped at it as she considered how to approach him on the subject of a pistol. After a moment, she glanced about the room, empty but for her and the keeper, and waved him over.

"Is there something else you'd like, m'lord?"

"Company, if you do not mind, sir. Have a seat."

Eyes widening, the keeper hesitated a moment, then went to fetch a fresh pitcher and mug for himself. Returning, he took a seat across from Charlie, refilled her drink, then poured himself one and they drank in companionable silence for a while.

"I hear it can be dangerous on the roads," she commented finally.

"Aye." The innkeeper nodded solemnly. "I wouldn't worry none though, m'lord, what with His Lordship wit' ye. He handles hisself well."

Charlie nodded. "He was teaching me to shoot today."

The innkeeper grinned. He had seen the two of them out in the field. "Ye'll learn," he said sympathetically.

Charlie glanced up, then smiled wryly. "Aye."

Leaning forward, the innkeeper refilled her drink, and Charlie glanced down in surprise. She had not realized that she had been drinking so quickly. Determining to slow down her consumption, she asked, "Have you got a pistol?"

"Oh, aye. A fine piece, m'lord. Care to see it?"

Charlie nodded eagerly and the barrel-chested man maneuvered himself out from behind the table and hurried from the room. Charlie sipped at her drink as she waited, perking up when the man returned, pistol in hand.

"There." He set the flintlock pistol on the table with care, then poured more ale for them both as Charlie picked up the weapon. It seemed a fine piece; thirteen inches long with cut steel stock inlays. Her eyes widened as she noted the initials R. N. on the hand-carved stock, guessing correctly that an innkeeper would not be able to afford such a fine piece.

"Got it from a lord," he announced, noting her interest in the initials. "Couldn't pay his bill. Got caught up in a game of chance with some other customers at the inn. Lost all his money. Caught him trying to sneak out in the middle of the night. He gave me the pistol rather than find hisself arrested."

"Bad business, that. Sneaking out of an inn in the middle of the night."

Charlie nearly overturned her drink at those words and glanced up sharply to find Radcliffe standing over her, laughter in his eyes.

"I thought you had gone to bed, my lord," she commented irritably, shifting on her seat and handing the innkeeper the pistol back.

"We slept all day," Radcliffe pointed out, taking a seat at the table and waving the innkeeper back to his when he started to rise. "Do not leave on my account. I thought to join you both."

"I'll just get ye a glass, Yer Lordship," the innkeeper said happily, hurrying away from the table.

Charlie watched him go with a sigh. The man was overjoyed at this turn of events. It was not often, she supposed, that two members of the gentry sat to drink with him. It was a shame she could not share in his pleasure, but right that minute, Charlie wished Radcliffe anywhere but there.

"It is less than a day's travel to London from the next inn we shall stop at."

Charlie glanced at Radcliffe as he continued.

"I am going to send a messenger on from there to fetch my hack. It is enclosed, and I think it would be better if you and your sister are not seen arriving. You can stay at my townhouse and I shall introduce you as my cousins. That should give you a little bit of time before the lie is discovered and your uncle finds out your whereabouts. With any luck, we shall have her married off before then."

He was silent for a moment, then went on with his plans for them, "I shall take you to a jeweler I know the day after we arrive. He will give you a fair price for your mother's jewels. I would not recommend cashing them all in right away, though. Just enough to pay for wardrobes and make a few investments should do. I was heading to town myself to invest in a venture. You might want to consider it. It is a bit risky, but if all goes well, it might be very profitable."

Charlie merely sat blinking at the man, a little

stunned at all he was saying. He was offering a lot more than protection, and what he was offering was astounding. His home, protection, and aid. With his help, she could build a fortune and marry Beth off to a nice safe man that she liked. . . .

If she really were Charles and not Charlie, she reminded herself and sighed. Of the two of them, Beth was not the one who was really in peril. She would have been miserable married to Seguin, but she would have been well cared for. The real danger was to Charlie herself, and she could hardly find a husband as a man.

Sighing, she shook her head regretfully. It had been a nice thought, but she could not risk Beth having a coming out. Even with a fake name. Their safest option was to flee to Ralphy. That in mind, she determined to wait until Radcliffe went to bed, then to approach the innkeeper about his gun.

"The boy seems a bit under the weather, m'lord," the innkeeper commented with amusement. "Not used to strong drink, I'd be sayin'."

Radcliffe glanced at Charles' rather blank expression and smiled wryly. "And I would say you were right," he agreed dryly, reaching out quickly to catch the boy by the scruff of the neck when he suddenly lurched forward in his seat with every appearance of being about to slam face first into the table top.

"He's done gone and passed out," the innkeeper laughed.

"Aye." Sighing, Radcliffe straightened, still holding the boy's head up, then lifted him in his arms.

"A skinny little feller, isn't he?" the innkeeper

commented, glancing over the boy lying limply in the man's arms. "Looks a lot like his sister. Acts a lot like her too. He'll be a fine man once he's grown, though."

"Aye." Radcliffe headed for the stairs. "There will be extra coins when I pay tomorrow. Thank you for your company and the ale."

"Yer welcome, m'lord. My pleasure."

Radcliffe carried Charles up to their room, glancing curiously at the boy's face as he moved. The resemblance between the twins was rather amazing, and now that the innkeeper had mentioned it, they did act a lot alike. The boy could be almost missish on occasion. It was probably from spending so much time in Beth's company, he supposed, rearranging the boy in his arms to open the door to their room. He would shed those ways easily after some time in male company, no doubt. It had become obvious from the conversation at dinner that the brother and sister spent most, if not all, of their time together. That was unsurprising when the only other kin around was their uncle.

Kicking the door closed with one booted foot, Radcliffe walked to the bed and set the boy gently upon it, aware of an odd sense of relief as he did. He did not feel at all comfortable touching the lad. He had noticed it that afternoon while teaching him to shoot. An odd sense of awareness had fired through him at one point when he had positioned himself behind the boy, one hand on his shoulder, the other on his hand to help him aim. His mind now shied away from the memory, just as he had physically removed himself from the nearness to Charles at the time.

Radcliffe had a healthy sexual drive and had taken

many women to his bed, or theirs as the case had been. He really was quite taken aback by his reaction to this slim, young lad. It was probably the boy's resemblance to his sister, he decided suddenly, relieved at the simple explanation. It had been two weeks since he had broken off with his latest mistress. No doubt his abstinence of late, plus the boy's amazing resemblance to his sister, had caused a confused reaction inside him.

The convoluted explanation made perfect sense to him. Despite the fact that he had not noticed any such reaction to touching the girl when he had carried her into the inn upon their arrival, he decided that it was really Beth that he was attracted to. He had always had a weakness for soft curves, and the girl had an excess of those. She was who he truly was reacting to when he touched her brother.

He was so desperate to believe that, he might very well have taken the girl to his bed, except that he was not interested in marriage just yet and the girl was not the sort to be trifled with. Especially not when she was supposed to be under his protection. He supposed he would just have to make a visit to a brothel once they arrived in London. Everything would be all right then.

His gaze fell upon the boy sleeping in their bed and he nodded. He would take Charles with him. The lad would probably appreciate the initiation into manhood.

Radcliffe did not question how he knew that the boy was an innocent in matters of the flesh, he just accepted the knowledge. He also did not question why he was unwilling to strip the boy and prepare

him for sleep. He simply turned and walked to the
other side of the bed and began to undress himself.
He had removed his coat and shirt and was reaching
for the fastening of his breeches when he hesitated.
His gaze shifting to the sweet-faced boy in the bed, he
decided to leave his pants on and avoid a nightshirt
that night. He did not question that decision too closely
either as he put out the candle, then crawled into bed,
careful to arrange himself so that no part of him
touched the boy under the linens.

Radcliffe was dreaming of his last mistress, Lena.
They were cuddled up in bed, wrapped in each other's
arms. She was murmuring sweetly to him, her full lips
brushing kisses across his chest as she reached down
with one hand to cover and caress his manhood.

Sighing pleasantly, he opened his eyes and hugged
the woman a little closer, then stiffened. The woman
in his arms was not a woman at all. It was a sleeping
Charles Westerly. The hand he had dreamt was caressing him was actually the boy's knee thrown over
him with abandon as he slept. The lad was wrapped
about him like he was a warm whore on a cold night,
and worse yet, Radcliffe himself was responding to
the proximity in a way that no whore would. He was
as hard as a poker.

Cursing roundly, he struggled out from beneath
the boy in a fit of panic, gained his feet, and turned
back to glare at the lad as if it were his fault.

Startled awake by the jostling and bouncing, Charlie sat up abruptly, glancing about with alarm.

"What? What is it?" the boy cried. Charlie was
barely awake, but had apparently caught Radcliffe's

panic like a communicable disease and cast about for an explanation. The lad's first thought must have been that they had been robbed. Rolling onto his stomach, he leaned off the bed to peer under it, visibly relaxing when he spied the bags still there. Dragging one out, he yanked it open, then sighed as he saw that the jewels had not been stolen.

Closing his eyes, the boy took a couple of deep breaths, then turned back to glance at Radcliffe, who still stood by the bed, glaring down at him almost furiously. Bewilderment obvious on the boy's face, he rolled again onto his back, straightened the wig on his head, and sat up. "What?"

Blinking, Radcliffe stared at the boy for a moment, then glanced grimly away. The lad was totally oblivious to what had happened. One look at the lad's lap was enough to tell him that Charles had not been the least aroused by the encounter, asleep or no.

Turning his back to the boy, lest he notice Radcliffe's own arousal, he grabbed up his shirt and shrugged quickly into it, muttering, "Bad dream," by way of explanation.

He finished dressing quickly, though he could feel the boy's bewildered gaze boring into his back. Once finished, Radcliffe snatched his bag and headed for the door. "Wash up, then wake your sister. We leave as soon as we have eaten."

He closed the door behind him with a slam.

Shaking her head over the peculiarities of men, Charlie glanced down at the bag she had dragged out from beneath the bed. Closing it quickly, she moved to the washbasin to clean up, her mind going over the night before. She had been determined to outsit Radcliffe downstairs, then haggle with the innkeeper for the pistol. It would seem that she had failed miserably. She could not remember much of the later part of the night. The innkeeper had kept refilling her glass and she had kept drinking. She had not meant to, but somehow every time she had turned around she was swallowing more ale. She did not even remember coming up to bed last night. She supposed the fact that she had come to bed meant she had been unable to purchase the pistol.

Sighing, she glanced briefly at the closed door, then tugged the wig off of her head. Scratching at her scalp with both hands, she moved back to her bags to dig out a hairbrush. Seated on the side of the bed, she tugged her waist-length hair out of the back of her shirt, undid the tie that secured it in one long tail at her neck, then ran the brush through it. It felt greasy to the touch, and she imagined it looked even worse, but she was not surprised. She had worn that blasted wig for two days and two nights, her head sweating something fierce under it. Still, that had not been nearly as uncomfortable as the tight binding around her breasts, and her hair itching at her back beneath the shirt.

Charlie would have loved to release her breasts from their bondage. Even just long enough to take a really deep breath or two. She would have liked to wash her hair and enjoy a nice long bath as well. But any of the above options were far too risky to attempt. Radcliffe could return at any moment.

Thinking about the man made Charlie sigh unhappily. The fact that she had not managed to purchase the pistol or slip away with Beth had not really struck her on first awakening. Now it did. That meant another day's travel away from their intended destination.

Setting the brush aside, she retied her hair and pulled the collar away from her skin far enough that she could slip the braid of hair back into her shirt.

She could not say she was really sorry about being unable to escape. Radcliffe had been kind to them. She did not feel right about sneaking out on him in the middle of the night.

A tap at the door made her stiffen briefly, then Charlie quickly resettled the wig on her head and stood as the door opened, relaxing when Beth's head poked around it.

"Oh, good. You are alone." Slipping inside, she moved to Charlie's side as she stood.

"I was unable to obtain a pistol," Charlie began apologetically.

"Good," Beth said abruptly. When Charlie blinked in surprise, she shrugged. "I did not really wish to run out on Lord Radcliffe. Besides, it has occurred to me that London may be the better destination for us just now after all. Think on it. How much better would it be to arrive at Ralphy's with actual funds rather than just jewels? And with Radcliffe's assistance, we are sure to get a fair price for Mother's jewels. Later we can make our way to Ralphy's . . . if we must."

Charlie's gaze narrowed at that. "What mean you by 'if we must'?"

"Well . . ." She pursed her lips slightly. "It does occur to me that we might like a coming out."

"Beth, we could not possibly!" Charlie gasped in dismay.

"Why not?"

"What do you mean, why not? The answer is obvious. The moment Uncle Henry heard of our appearance in London, he would—"

"Why must he hear?"

"How could he not?" Charlie snapped impatiently.

"He would not hear if we did not give our true names," Beth pointed out simply.

Charlie rolled her eyes at that. "Oh, aye. I am sure that fake names would do the trick. Just exactly how many twins do you think there are in England, Beth? And how many of them do you believe are our age and likely to have a coming out this year? And how many have brown hair and midnight eyes?"

"Why must we tell them we are twins?"

"You do not think they would notice?" Charlie asked dryly.

"Nay. I do not . . . Charles."

Charlie stiffened at that, comprehension dawning over her. It was followed quickly by a pain that she hid by turning away. "I see. You would like me to continue this charade so that you might have a coming out," she murmured unhappily.

"Charlie," Beth whispered, reaching to touch her arm, but her twin jerked away.

" 'Tis all right."

"Nay. You misunderstood. I thought for us both to find a husband."

Charlie gave a harsh laugh at that. " 'Twould be hard for me to attract a husband as a man, sister."

"Not if we took turns at being one." When Charlie stared at her blankly, Beth explained, "We could switch back and forth. One night you be the brother and I will be the sister, and the next we'll switch. That way we can encourage whomsoever we choose. We can eventually tell the truth when we are sure of the men in question."

Charlie stilled at that and faced her. "You would take turns at being a boy?"

Beth nodded solemnly, her lips quirking slightly after a moment to ruin the effect. "Truly, it does seem that you get to have more fun as a boy, Charlie."

"Fun?" Her eyebrows shot up at that.

"Aye. Well, just look. Yesterday Lord Radcliffe took you shooting. Then last night, you got to stay up all night drinking until you passed out drunk."

"Passed out drunk?" Charlie stared at her sister, horrified.

"Aye. The innkeeper's wife told me all about it. Her husband told her that you drank near a gallon of his grog, then passed out like a fish. Lord Radcliffe had to carry you to bed."

"Oh, no." Charlie sank on to the side of the bed with dismay.

Beth watched her curiously for a moment, then commented, "You do not appear to be suffering for it today, though, do you?"

Charlie blinked at her words, then glanced at her with surprise. "Nay, I do not. I feel right as rain this morning."

"Hmm. Uncle Henry always complained of a pounding head the morning after overindulging."

"Aye," Charlie agreed with a grimace. The man had been bad enough to live with at the best of times, but he had been impossible while suffering a hangover.

"Father never suffered the morning after, though, did he?"

"Nay." Beth smiled brightly. "I do so want to try getting drunk."

"Beth," she chastised with more amusement than true reproach.

"Well, and why not? You always have all the fun." Beth said the words teasingly, then sighed suddenly and admitted. "I do grow tired of being the sensible one at times, you know."

Charlie started to protest at that, then recalled her annoyance of the other night when Beth had naturally expected her to come up with a plan that would solve all their problems. Those had been their natural roles. Charlie had always come up with one harebrained scheme after another, and Beth, with her sensible nature, had approved or disapproved. Should Beth disapprove, Charlie would scrap a plan. Should she approve, they had always carried it through. Charlie realized now that she had depended as much on Beth's sensibility as Beth had depended on her risk-taking and scheming. This was a nice change. "Everyone must try on a new pair of slippers once in a while," she murmured.

Beth blinked at that. "What?"

"Do you not recall the story that Mother told us when we were little? About the princess who had a lovely soft pair of slippers? Her cousin came to visit her one day with a pair of bright red hard shoes with shiny silver buckles. They were obviously too small for the princess. Still, she insisted on trying them out and wore them until her feet were blistered before giving them up to return gratefully to her lovely soft slippers. Mother said the moral of the story was that everyone must try on a new pair of shoes once in a while, if only to find that they prefer their own slippers in the end. I wonder if this is not exactly what she meant."

Beth smiled. "Mother was very clever, was she not?"

"Aye. So was Father." Charlie sighed. "I miss them both very much."

Sinking onto the bed beside her, Beth slipped her hand into hers and squeezed gently. "So do I."

They were silent for a moment, then Charlie stood abruptly. "Well. Then we shall go to London, turn our jewels into money, buy a new wardrobe, and find ourselves a couple of husbands." Smiling, she glanced at her sister. "My goodness, Beth. I do believe you have come up with your first hare-brained scheme. Think you it will work?"

Beth shrugged. "It cannot hurt to try. We can always flee to Ralphy if it does not."

"Hmm." Charlie nodded, then smiled. " 'Tis almost too perfect. Radcliffe offered to keep us and introduce us as cousins last night."

"Did he?" Beth's eyes widened in surprise. "That was nice."

"Aye."

"Do you think we should tell him that we are both girls?" Beth asked, looking worried.

"Not if you want to do any of those 'fun things' a man gets to do."

Beth nodded solemnly. "Then we must keep it a secret."

"So when did you wish to make this switch? Now?"

Beth hesitated, then shook her head and murmured, "Mayhap when we reach London."

Charlie's eyes lit up with amusement at that. "Afraid to share a bed with Lord Radcliffe? He is hardly likely to pounce upon you as a boy."

She smiled slightly at that, but shrugged. "Still, I am content to wait."

"As you wish, Beth."

The opening of the door brought them both around to peer at Radcliffe as he glared in at them. "What is taking you two so long? Come, we must eat and be on our way."

"Aye, my lord." Charlie smiled at him widely, then bent to retrieve one of their bags from beside the bed. Beth moved to take the other, but Radcliffe was there before her.

"I shall take that, child. Do not trouble yourself. 'Tis quite heavy. Come along, downstairs we go. The sooner you both breakfast, the sooner we can leave. Tomorrow you shall enjoy the comfort of a carriage ride into the city."

"It sounds lovely," Beth murmured on the way out the door, and Charlie smiled at her gentle words. Aye, it would be lovely to enjoy the comfort of a carriage after the days they had spent plodding along astride hard saddles, the dust kicking up in their faces. It would be heaven.

Chapter 4

CARRIAGES were the invention of the devil.

Charlie came to that conclusion within the first hour of the ride. She had never been far from home. Her parents had not been fond of travel and had preferred to spend their time at home with their daughters. Her parents had therefore only owned two carriages. The one they had been riding in the night they died had been destroyed in the accident that killed them. Uncle Henry had sold the other in this last year as the family's money had dwindled. Charlie was grateful for the sale of the carriage now, as they hit another rut in the road and she was nearly bounced to the floor. She would never own one of these infernal inventions.

Grabbing at the seat, she ground her teeth together and prayed they did not have much farther to go before London. They had been traveling for what seemed like days, and she was positive should they not reach the city soon, she was in dire peril of vomiting all over their esteemed host. She could not stand the airless little box the three of them were crammed into much longer.

Catching Beth's concerned expression, Charlie forced a reassuring smile for her sister's benefit, then closed her eyes and tried to imagine herself anywhere but inside this hard, airless hack, bumping and jostling along the rutted road. Surely no one got into one of these conveyances willingly, she thought desperately, opening her eyes again and grabbing frantically for the door handle.

Seeing her intent, Beth cried out in warning, drawing Lord Radcliffe's attention. Glimpsing the green tinge in Charlie's face and the way she was scrabbling at the door, Radcliffe shouted a warning to the driver, relieved when the carriage halted. Charlie got the door open and stumbled out of the cab. She knelt in the grass to the side of the carriage and tossed her breakfast out on the roadside. Radcliffe appeared behind her.

"Oh, my."

Glancing around at that dismayed gasp, Charlie saw Radcliffe take Beth's arm and urge her back toward the carriage, but her sister was having none of that. Opening the small bag she always carried dangling from her wrist, Beth slid out a small vial and knelt beside her. "Here, Charlie, take this. 'Twill settle your stomach."

Charlie took one look at the tonic her sister held out toward her, and turned to retch some more. Rather than be discouraged, Beth waited patiently for the course of vomiting to end, then pressed the vial on her sister again. This time, Charlie accepted the vial and even managed to swallow some of the concoction. She then got shakily to her feet and stumbled back to lean weakly against the carriage.

Charlie heard Radcliffe clear his throat. The man had turned away from the roadside and stood with his hands clasped behind his back as he waited for Charlie to regain herself. After a short time, he glanced at her questioningly. "Feeling better? Shall we get back in the carriage now?"

Charlie closed her eyes at that prospect, groaned, then pushed herself away from the carriage to kneel in the grass again. Beth was immediately beside her, murmuring soothingly as she held her sister's trembling shoulders as she was sick.

Radcliffe watched the brother and sister from beside the carriage and sighed. Things had not been going very well for the last two days. He had been suffering horribly from a hangover when he had finally managed to get the brother and sister to breakfast and then to depart the day before. Much to his disgust, despite the amount the boy had imbibed, Charles had not seemed to suffer the same problem. He had been grossly cheerful throughout yesterday's ride, smiling and happily chatting away to his sister, while Radcliffe had felt as if his head were splitting in half. He had been more than grateful when they had arrived at the inn at which they'd spent last night.

Radcliffe had immediately hired a messenger from the nearby village to ride into London and fetch back his carriage. He had then joined the twosome for supper before retiring early to bed to nurse his head, only to awaken in the middle of the night to find the lad once again wrapped around him like a second skin. Unfortunately, he had also found, much to his dismay, that he'd been quite enjoying the experience.

Disentangling himself, Radcliffe had slipped from the bed and spent the rest of the night sitting in a chair, gazing fretfully into the fire. The experience had only convinced him more than ever that he must visit a brothel the moment he arrived in London.

With dawn had come the arrival of his carriage. Unfortunately, the driver had hit a rut in the dark on his hurried journey and had only just managed to make it to the inn ere the front wheel had split. After making arrangements for it to be fixed and follow them to the city, Radcliffe had gone to the nearby village to hire a carriage. This small, rickety old trap had been all he had been able to come up with. Riding in it was tantamount to torture. He was sure his very teeth had been shaken loose after the first hour. Should he open his mouth, every tooth housed within was likely to tumble right out. Now he had a sick boy to contend with. Worse yet, the boy's violent reaction to the ride was raising a rather similar response within himself. Radcliffe was positive should he stand there another moment, he would be kneeling in the grass losing his own breakfast. Cursing abruptly, he whirled away and paced off along the road in search of fresh air.

"There, there," Beth cooed, smoothing her hand over her sister's back soothingly as Radcliffe marched away.

Charlie groaned as the last of her stomach's contents left her body, then collapsed backward away from the mess to lie on the ground miserably. After a moment, she opened her eyes to peer solemnly at her sister. "I am dying," she announced stoically.

Beth smiled faintly at the dramatic announcement and shook her head. "Nay, love. 'Tis merely the traveling sickness."

"Traveling sickness?" Charlie frowned. "What the devil is that?"

" 'Tis what Mother called it. Father had it too. He could not bear to ride in an enclosed conveyance. Why do you think they did not care to travel?"

Charlie's eyes widened, then narrowed on her sister. "Why are you not ill then?"

Beth shrugged. "I suppose I inherited mother's more stalwart constitution."

"We are twins, Beth. Identical in every way, no?"

"Apparently not so identical as all that."

Sighing, Charlie sat up slowly to glare at the carriage. " 'Tis that damned contraption. What a hellish invention it is."

"Aye. It is most uncomfortable," Beth murmured on a sigh, then glanced at her once more. "Do you think you could keep down the potion now?"

Charlie nodded and drank from the vial Beth lifted to her lips. Hoping the liquid would settle in her stomach, she did not rise then but remained where she sat, her gaze moving along the empty lane. "Where has Radcliffe got to?"

Beth shrugged mildly. "I suspect he has gone to find his own little patch along the road. He was looking rather green himself."

Surprised pleasure flooded Charlie at that. "Really?"

"You need not look so pleased at the prospect," Beth chastised dryly and Charlie grimaced.

"And why should I not? The man has been a perfect

beast to me for the past two days. Have you not noticed?"

"Aye, I have. I was wondering what it is you have done to the poor man to cause such irritation."

"Done to him? Why, I have done nothing," Charlie denied in surprise, but Beth's doubt showed and she frowned. "I have done nothing, I tell you. He woke up like that the morning after drinking with the innkeeper. I thought mayhap he reacts to drink like Uncle Henry does."

Beth considered that briefly. "That would explain his moodiness yesterday. But what of today?"

Charlie shrugged with a distinct lack of interest. "Mayhap his hangovers last two or three days."

"Hmm. He . . ." Beth began, pausing as a carriage came around the bend and rolled toward them. It came to a stop behind their own carriage and an elderly woman, a young girl, and a man some few years younger than Radcliffe himself stared at them curiously from inside for a moment before the door opened and the man got calmly out.

A sudden indrawn breath from Beth drew Charlie's gaze. Her sister's eyes had become wide and rather dazed. Eyebrows rising, Charlie got to her feet, offered a hand to her sister to help her rise, then turned to face the man now pausing before them.

"Is there some way I may be of service?" the stranger asked, offering Beth a charming smile.

Despite the fact that the question was addressed to Beth, Charlie was the one to answer. Her sister did not seem capable of responding just then. She was gazing at the man rather dreamily and Charlie could not for a minute understand why. He was attractive enough, she supposed, frowning at his sandy brown hair and strong features. Her gaze dropped to take in his figure. Long and lean. Not bad, but not her sort. "Kind of you to offer, but other than switching carriages with us, there is nothing you can do."

When the man blinked at that rather blankly and managed to tear his eyes away from her sister to toss a perplexed glance her way, Charlie grimaced and explained. "We are traveling with . . . our cousin," she said, stumbling over the words. "Unfortunately, his carriage broke down and we were forced to rent this conveyance to make the remainder of the journey."

The man peered dubiously at the rattletrap waiting at the side of the road, then took a step forward to glance inside, his eyebrows rising as he turned back. "Did your cousin remain behind with his carriage?"

"What? Oh. Nay. He wandered off up the road a ways for a breath of fresh air. He shall return directly, no doubt."

"Ah." He nodded solemnly, his eyes returning to Beth once again. He seemed to hesitate. Just as he would have opened his mouth to speak, the younger of the two women, a girl really, came stumbling out of the carriage and hurried forward to clutch at his arm.

"Goodness, Tomas, we must offer to share our carriage with them. They cannot rattle into town in that. It must be most uncomfortable. Do offer a lift to them, Tomas. Do." She ended her breathless little plea with a brilliant smile directed straight at Charlie. When she followed that up with a fluttering of the eyelashes that could only be called coquettish, Charlie shifted uncomfortably and suddenly found great interest in her shoes. The chit was flirting with her for gosh sakes. Amazing!

"Would you . . ." Tomas began, and Beth took an eager step forward.

"Oh, that would be lovely."

Charlie grimaced at the breathlessness in her sister's voice and glanced up to see her and Tomas grinning widely at each other like a couple of star-struck fools. A sudden clamp of fingers around her arm then drew Charlie's attention to the young girl who was suddenly pressed close to her side, smiling up at her from beneath long eyelashes.

"Shall we walk up the road a ways and find your cousin?"

There was a definite predatory look in those eyes, Charlie decided grimly, raising her hand immediately to disengage the claws clutching at her. "I would not think to trouble you so. I shall fetch him back myself."

"That will not be necessary."

They all turned as the man in question made his return known.

"Radcliffe!" Tomas's surprise was obvious. "I did not realize that you were this pair's cousin." Stepping forward, he held his hand out in greeting. Radcliffe accepted that hand and nodded pleasantly back.

"Mowbray. Good to see you."

"Aye. We came across your conveyance and stopped to see if aught was wrong. Your cousins explained that your carriage had broken down and you were forced to rent this rattletrap." He gestured toward the carriage in question. "We offered to share our carriage with you for the remainder of the trip, if that is acceptable?"

Radcliffe hesitated. His gaze slid to Charles, then to the girl who was even now slipping her hand persistently back onto the lad's arm. Noting Charles's annoyance and the way he seemed to be trying to tell him by his expression that the ride should be refused, he nodded solemnly. "That would be most appreciated," he answered, deciding it would be good for the boy to enjoy a bit of female attention. Whether he liked it or not.

"And so Maman had a whole new wardrobe made for my coming out. She thinks I should be engaged in no time. What do you think, Charles?"

Charlie blinked at the tug at her arm and glanced at the girl rather blankly. Clarissa Mowbray was a slender, sweet-faced, and sandy-haired girl, but she had not stopped babbling since Radcliffe had accepted her brother's offer of a ride. She had rattled on about sundry unimportant trivial things all throughout the transfer of luggage from the rented conveyance to the Mowbray carriage, pausing only long enough to make the seating arrangements. She had managed so that she was crowded onto the one bench seat between Charlie and Radcliffe, while her brother was seated between Beth and the older woman on the other side.

The older woman, as it turned out, was Lady Gladys Mowbray, the widowed mother of Tomas and Clarissa. The woman was hard of hearing, which had become obvious as Clarissa had shouted the introductions. It also explained why she did not rein in her daughter's chatter. Charlie was just miserable enough at that point to decide that Lady Mowbray had most likely gone deaf in defense against the girl's prattle. Charlie normally would have been ashamed of such catty thoughts, but she was finding it hard enough to breathe with all of them crammed into that small space, without the silly chit hogging all the air inside the stifling carriage to propel her witless gibberish. Charlie was positive that she was going to faint from lack of oxygen.

"I am sure he agrees with your mother's prediction," Beth murmured now, glaring at her sister for not answering immediately. "Is that not right, brother?"

"Oh, aye. No doubt," Charlie muttered dryly, glaring out the window.

"I do not recall ever having heard that you had cousins."

There was a brief electric silence at Lady Mowbray's words. The woman had been silent as a stone for the past several hours of the journey, and Charlie would not have minded had she remained so. The woman's comment sent a shock of fear running down her neck. Turning sharply, she glanced at Radcliffe to see how he would respond to the question. Much to her relief, he looked completely unruffled and even managed a small smile and shrug.

"Elizabeth and Charles are second cousins to me by marriage."

"I see." The way Lady Mowbray was peering from Radcliffe to herself made Charlie shift uncomfortably. She remained that way throughout the rest of the journey, fighting off the effects of traveling sickness and avoiding Lady Mowbray's speculative gaze as Clarissa babbled on about nothing. It was a great relief when they finally reached London and were dropped off at Radcliffe's townhouse.

They were greeted at the door by a tall, slender, gray-haired man who exuded an impermeable air of dignity. Radcliffe introduced him as Stokes, asked him to show Beth to a room and arrange a bath for her, then gestured for Charlie to follow him. He led her into the library, saw her seated, then spent several minutes outlining what he had decided they should do to prepare for Beth's coming out.

Charlie listened impatiently, her mind distracted by thoughts of finally removing the horrid wig, stripping off her clothes, unwinding the torturous binds, and sinking into a tub of warm, soothing water. When Radcliffe finally finished, she agreed to his suggestions with alacrity and escaped the room to find Stokes waiting to lead her upstairs. He showed her to a room, informed her that her sister was in the adjoining one, and left her alone with a brimming tub of hot water.

Charlie had just finally removed the last of her boy's clothes and stepped into the tub of water when the door suddenly opened. Gasping, she dropped under the water, submerging herself in an attempt to hide from whomever it was, only to come springing up, splashing water everywhere a moment later when someone tapped on her head. She was wiping her eyes and casting frantically about for an explanation when she recognized Beth's soft laughter. Irritation was Charlie's immediate reaction.

"Do not do that," she hissed, glaring at her twin

angrily. "I near to had a heart attack. I thought it was—"

"I am sorry, dear," Beth managed to murmur through her chuckles.

Sighing, Charlie relaxed in the water, her gaze moving over her sister's clean pink cheeks and nearly dry hair. "You were quick about your bath."

"Hmm," she murmured, sinking onto the end of the bed. "I was so tired, I feared I might fall asleep in the tub. I rather rushed through it."

Charlie nodded in understanding. She herself thought she might sleep in the warm, silky water if given half a chance.

"Shall I help you with your hair?"

"Aye. Please," Charlie murmured, sitting up slightly as her sister knelt by the tub.

They were both silent for a while as Beth worked on her hair and Charlie worked on the rest of herself, removing the dust and filth from their days of travel. Then Beth asked what Radcliffe had wanted to speak to her about.

Lowering her leg back into the water to rinse the soap off it, Charlie sighed. "He wished to tell me of his plans for us."

"Which are?"

"He sent a message to a dressmaker in town. A Madame Decalle, requesting her presence tomorrow to fit us for dresses."

"Us?"

"Well, you or me. Whoever is the sister tomorrow." She sensed rather than saw her sister nod in response to that.

"What else has he planned?"

"He intends on taking Charles, whomsoever of us that is tomorrow, to a jeweler to cash in some of our inheritance, then to a tailor to be fitted for new vestments."

They were both silent for a moment, then Charlie glanced over her shoulder at her sister and told her, "He also wishes to take Charles somewhere tonight. I thought, as you wish to take turns at being the brother, you would like to go tonight rather than myself."

"Tonight?" Beth's hands stilled in her hair, then pushed gently on Charlie's shoulders, urging her to lean back farther in the water to rinse her hair. Both of them were silent as they rinsed all of the soap out; then Beth stood and moved to fetch a linen for her.

Standing in the tub, Charlie took in her sister's frown as she returned with the linen and raised an eyebrow as she accepted it. "I thought you wished to take a turn at being the brother."

"Aye, but—" Shrugging, Beth moved back to the bed to finger the clothes Charlie had dropped there. "Not tonight, Charlie," she said finally. "I am ever so tired. 'Tis all the traveling, I think. I am not accustomed to it. Could you go tonight?"

"If you wish," Charlie agreed, though she had really rather hoped it would be the other way around. She, too, was rather exhausted from their journey. Resigning herself to a night of carousing with Radcliffe, Charlie began to unfold the linen she held, only to stiffen and glance over her shoulder in shock when the bedroom door suddenly burst open.

Radcliffe had taken his own bath, dressed, then gone back to the library to await Charles, but the boy seemed to be taking an inordinate amount of time at his bath. Deciding to hurry the lad along, he jogged upstairs, then along the hallway to the door of the room Charles had been given. He was so impatient, he entirely forgot his manners and burst into the room, mouth open to harry the boy into hurrying. The sight that befell him stole the words from his mouth and left him gaping blankly, for it was apparently not Charles he came upon in the room but Elizabeth.

Naked as the day she was born. Water dripping from her generous figure. She stood half-turned away, glancing back over her shoulder toward him, frozen in place, shock on her face, and a half-open linen in her hands.

For a moment, all Radcliffe could do was stare. She was Aphrodite rising from the foamy sea. Astarte in all her glory. She was beauty incarnate. His eyes slid over the bend of her shoulder and paused at the sweet fullness of one breast as it peeked out from around her arm. Then his gaze dropped along the curve of her back where beads of water sparkled in the candlelight like jewels on rosy velvet next to the dark mystery of the hair that lay damp and smooth down the center of her back, framed between her shoulder blades. Following the length of it down to the delectable curves of her behind, he took in the rivulets of water dripping from her damp hair and rushing down over those curves and along the backs of her thighs before returning to join the water in the tub.

It was a path his hands suddenly itched to take, he realized, and recognizing the dark area his thoughts were taking him to, he quickly regained himself enough to turn away and face the hallway he was blocking.

Muttering an apology, he pulled the door closed behind him and leaned against the wall beside it, amazed to find himself trembling.

Charlie turned wide eyes to her sister. Beth stood frozen beside the bed, shock and dismay on her face. Muttering under her breath, Charlie stepped quickly out of the tub and wrapped the linen around herself as she hurried to her sister's side. "Quickly, help me dress," she ordered tersely, giving the girl a push to wake her from her frozen state.

"Dress? But he saw—"

"He saw you."

Beth blinked at that as Charlie tossed the damp linen aside and snatched the hose from the bed to begin dragging them on. "Nay, I do not think he noticed me at all. He was too busy ogling you."

"He was busy ogling *you*," Charlie corrected grimly, donning the breeches now, then turning to grab the binding to secure her chest. When a glance at her sister showed her looking confused, Charlie pointed out impatiently, "He will think it was you in the tub, Beth."

Her sister blushed with embarrassment as she started to help her bind Charlie's breasts once more. "But how will we explain what I was doing in your tub?"

Charlie considered the problem as she tied her hair at the nape of her neck, then catching the end of the long ponytail, she slid it into the back of her breeches before tugging her shirt on and quickly doing it up.

"We switched rooms," she announced, grabbing the wig and slamming it on top of her damp hair before grabbing the jacket and hurrying for the connecting door between their bedrooms. "This is your room now."

"But—" Beth began, but was cut off as the connecting door closed behind her sister.

It took several minutes for Radcliffe to calm himself enough that he felt ready to face anyone. It was not seeing Beth naked that had affected him so. It was his reaction to her. During the last three days since encountering Charles and his sister, Radcliffe had felt nothing more than an avuncular affection for the girl. His feelings and reactions to the boy had been something else altogether. His body had responded to the closeness of the boy in his sleep. That had been distressing. And then of course he had begun to analyze every little reaction he had to the lad, picking apart every little increase in heartbeat and every little tingle the boy aroused in him.

Now he supposed his own fears had been the problem. For the sight of Beth standing so gloriously nude had raised nothing but good, clean, unadulterated lust in him. The woman was as luscious as a mouth-watering roast duck all dressed on the table. Radcliffe was beyond relieved. He was joyous. He was not turning to the more unusual proclivities of some of the nobles who, having grown bored with their lives and a never-ending stream of wine, women, and song, looked for new avenues of excitement. While he had always considered what a person did behind closed doors to be his own affair, he had never had any inkling of such feelings in himself. Now, he knew he was fine.

Smiling wryly at his own foolishness, Radcliffe straightened away from the wall and tugged at his cuffs. He had been so long without allowing himself to feel affection for anyone, he had quite mistaken his affection for the boy as something else entirely. It was most embarrassing, really. He was grateful he was the only one to be aware of his own foolishness.

Shaking his head, he turned down the hall and walked to the next door. He started to reach for the doorknob, then caught himself and raised his hand to knock instead. The knock never fell. Even as his knuckles would have rapped wood, the door was pulled open to reveal a slightly out of breath Charles standing there, blinking at him in surprise.

"Radcliffe."

"Charles." Relief still riding high within him, Radcliffe graced the lad with a more than warm smile. "I was just coming to see what had held you up."

"Oh . . . So sorry, I, er. . . . Well, I did have to talk to Beth before I bathed and changed. Tell her of tomorrow's doings and all."

"Of course." His smile did not fade in the least. "She was not happy with her room?"

"What? Oh . . . Well . . . She preferred the other room. Blue is her favorite color." The boy paused. "Why? Did you go there first looking for me?"

"I am afraid so. In fact, I fear, thinking it was your room, I did not even bother to knock but merely walked right in. Most rude."

Despite his words, he could not manage to look the least upset by the incident, though he knew the brother of the girl would be scandalized. Instead, the boy looked at him dryly and pulled the door closed behind him. "Well, I am sure there was no harm done. Was she asleep?"

Still grinning, Radcliffe shook his head. "Nay. In fact I fear I caught her stepping out of the bath." When Charlie arched an eyebrow at his tone of voice, he grimaced slightly. "I shall, of course, apologize at the first opportunity."

The boy shook his head and followed Radcliffe as he led the way down the hall. Well, Radcliffe thought, the embarrassment of his having walked in on the boy's sister in the bath would quickly fade with the night ahead. It would be the boy's first real adventure as a man. They were about to go out on the town in London. Radcliffe wondered if Charlie had any inkling of where he would be taken. Mayhap he thought Radcliffe would take him to a gaming hall. Or the theater. Or one of the men's clubs he had surely heard about.

Charles had a surprise coming. They were going to a brothel.

Chapter 5

*T*HE trip had been relatively short, but Radcliffe had insisted on their destination being a surprise. Charles had tried guessing as they rode through the dark London streets, hoping that should he hit on where they were headed, he might confirm his guess, but Radcliffe had merely smiled mysteriously and shaken his head at each guess he'd given.

The boy had been beyond frustration and well on the way to expiring from curiosity when the carriage had finally stopped. Radcliffe stepped out of the conveyance and found himself standing on a cobbled street in front of a rather uninteresting house.

His confusion showing on his face, Charles had turned to Radcliffe. "Where are we?"

"Aggie's," had been his unruffled answer as he'd started up the path to the front door.

"Aggie's," Charles had echoed unhappily. Radcliffe smiled as he realized the boy had never heard of the place. The boy had thought they were going to carouse with London's young bloods. Now, he thought they were going visiting, that this was the house of one of his friends. How incredibly boring! Radcliffe chuckled.

"Come along. Do not dally." Radcliffe waited until the boy reached his side, then rapped at the door. He didn't know if that was the usual approach to gaining entrance to the establishment. He'd never visited Aggie's before. He had only heard of it. It was doubtful if there was another male in London who had not heard of Aggie's, though he himself had never favored such places. He preferred the slightly less tawdry habit of taking a mistress and keeping her in style throughout the length of their relationship, to enjoying the variation though less choice quality of Aggie's girls. He could have hardly taken Charles to his mistress, though, had he had one at the moment. He was between them, in any case.

The corpulent woman who answered the door could be none other than the infamous Aggie. Her hair was a brassy red, her face a map of the London streets with all its lines, and her body best resembled an overripe tomato ready to burst at the seams. Dismayed at such a presence, Radcliffe barely managed to conceal his shock and present a somewhat uncomfortable smile.

"Well, now, what ha'e we here? Two fine gen'lemen's come to call on old Aggie. No need to loiter about on the step, m'lords. Come on in. Aggie's open for business."

Radcliffe was trying to decide if he really wished to go through with this when Charles shifted beside him, drawing his gaze. Remembering the reason behind this excursion, he straightened his shoulders and nodded. It was for the lad, after all. Best to get the chore done.

* * *

Charlie gawked at the woman before them in amazement. She had never seen her like before. She was wearing a gown of bright red silk, though "wearing" was not exactly an apt description. It was more as if she had been poured into the material.

Surely Radcliffe had made a mistake? This could not possibly be where he had meant to bring them. The driver must have got the directions wrong. Movement in the room beyond Aggie caught her attention and she tried to peer past the woman. An impossibility. She filled the doorway like pudding filled a bowl, spilling out sideways toward the door-frame.

As if sensing the attempt to see past her, the woman suddenly shifted, allowing Charlie a glimpse into the lit room beyond. What was revealed to her then was even more shocking than the woman herself. There were anywhere from ten to twelve women beyond, and equally as many men. They were all moving about, laughing and drinking and—good God—the women were near to nude! They were also of obviously loose morals. What else could one say about a woman who allowed a man to grope about down the front of a see-through gown as if he were looking for a monocle that had popped out and right down her top?

They were most obviously in the wrong place, she assured herself, then gaped at Radcliffe as the woman moved aside and he suddenly made as if to enter.

"Come along, lad. You shall find this edifying." Not leaving her much choice, Radcliffe took her arm and dragged her in with him.

Charlie felt rather like partridge pie at a party. The moment she was propelled into the room, half of the women suddenly swooped upon her. They were all cooing and murmuring sweetly about what a fine young lad she was and how she would grow into a strapping and handsome man. They were also rather free with their hands, running them across her cheeks, over her shoulders, and down her bound chest. One even pinched her buttocks and commented on what a tight package she came in.

The pinch was the impetus to knock Charlie out of her stunned state. Turning abruptly, she made for the door, only to have Radcliffe grab her by the collar and draw her up short.

"Relax," he ordered, seemingly vaguely amused by the panicked expression on her face as she made an attempt at escape. He seemed a bit overwhelmed himself, but Charlie hardly noticed. With the women pouncing on her rather like a pack of wolves on a leg of lamb, she was looking for any exit. Radcliffe pointed to an empty couch along the wall, and dragged Charlie over to it. He had barely pushed her into it when one of the women handed him a glass of some drink or other. Radcliffe immediately handed it to Charlie, then straightened. "Sit here and relax. I wish a word with Aggie."

Before Charlie could protest at being abandoned, Radcliffe was gone and the wolves had closed in. The two younger ones were fastest. Charlie would have placed them as younger than herself had she any interest in guessing. She did not, though, as they hurried forward and dropped to sit on either side of her on the couch, each clutching at one of her arms and drawing it against their chests. She was frowning and concentrating on keeping her drink from spilling when a third woman dropped to sit in her lap.

"There now," the woman on her lap cooed, wrapping her arms firmly about Charlie's neck. "I'm thinkin' you and I could be fine friends."

"Yer thinkin' wrong then," the girl on Charlie's right muttered bitterly. "Ye know Aggie likes to keep all the little virgin boys for herself."

"Aggie's a nasty old cow," the woman on her lap snapped irritably, then smiled sweetly at Charlie and cooed. "You'd rather have me than that paunchy old harpy, wouldn't ye? Look what I've got for ye. Aggie doesn't have anything as tasty as these." The woman tugged her almost-see-through top downward with one hand, baring her breasts as she began to exert a gentle but inexorable pressure on the back of Charlie's neck with her other hand.

Charlie stared horrified at the woman's breasts as they drew closer. To her they appeared as two swollen, pale pink orbs bent on suffocating her as they neared her face.

"Yer not the only one around here with something to offer." Before Charlie could be smothered by those massive breasts, she felt the hand of the woman on her left slip between her and the woman on her lap. The hand slid down toward her crotch.

Crying out in dismay, Charlie leapt abruptly to her feet, depositing Miss Bared-Breasts on the floor just as Radcliffe appeared before her.

"Thank God," she gasped, completely forgetting the charade she was playing at and throwing herself against the man's chest. "Get me out of here, Radcliffe. Now."

Radcliffe's first reaction was to wrap his arms protectively around her. Then, frowning, he pushed her away instead. "Act your age, Charles. They are naught but a bunch of women. Do you not find any of them attractive?"

"Attractive! They are she-wolves." Charlie glared at him coldly. "I want to go home. Now."

Grunting, Radcliffe frowned, his gaze moving to the women in question. He seemed to consider her words, then murmured something about Aggie being right and it being worth a gamble.

Upset as she was, when Radcliffe said "Come along," relief rushed through her. She followed him out of the room to where the old whore Aggie waited by the stairs with a younger female. They were going to pass up the establishment's more lascivious offerings for some gambling, was her conclusion. She was so relieved by this realization that she followed eagerly when the older woman turned and led her up the stairs. Radcliffe and the other woman followed.

At the top of the stairs, Aggie took a right and led them down a long hallway, then directly into the third room along the hall.

Charlie followed her in and stepped past the waiting woman to peer around the room. A huge bed screamed for attention as she entered. Its covers and drapes were a brilliant bloodred. It looked rather vulgar to Charlie. Other than that there was a chest, a chair, and a wardrobe. There were no tables with men seated playing cards, no baccarat tables, nothing in the way of gambling at all.

The slam of the door behind her drew her head around to see that Radcliffe was no longer with them. She was alone with the old crone who had answered the door.

"Here we are, luvy. Let's get to it then."

Charlie's eyes widened and she took an abrupt step backward, quickly catching the other woman's hands as she reached out to undo her cravat.

"What do you think you are doing?"

"Helping ye to undress, son."

"Why on earth would you think to do a thing like that?" she asked shortly, redoing the difficult tie.

The woman's lips quirked in amusement. " 'Tis difficult to do with yer clothes on, lad."

"There is nothing we are like to do that I need remove my clothes for," Charlie assured her, stepping stiffly toward the door. She had barely taken a step when Aggie caught her arm and whirled her back around.

"Oh, ye like it like that, do ye? Quick and with yer clothes still on," she murmured insinuatingly, reaching down to cup Charlie at the juncture between her legs.

Gasping in horror, Charlie jumped back from the touch, but that was as far as she got. The woman was still holding her arm.

"My, you are a small one, are ye no'. I did not e'en feel ye," she exclaimed, turning her attention and hands back to removing Charlie's cravat. "Well, 'tis a handicap that, but not insurmountable. Ol' Aggie'll show ye how to overcome it."

"Overcome it?" Scowling, Charlie tried to push her hands away and refasten her tie.

"Aye. Trust me. The saying is true, 'tis not the size o' sail, but the way you handle the jib that decides the ride. Ye feelin' a'right, boy? Yer lookin' peaked all of a sudden."

"Oh, dear Lord!" Whirling, Charlie ran for the door, but before she could open it, she was caught by the arm and dragged backward toward the bed.

"Now, now, lad. No need to panic. Aggie'll be gentle."

"I do not want you to be gentle," she managed, tugging desperately at her arm. Much to her relief, Aggie stopped at that and turned to arch one eyebrow at her.

"Ye don't?"

"Nay." She shook her head frantically. "I do not—"

"Well, why did ye no' say something? Well, that explains everything. I was starting to worry ... Ye were actin' so odd." Shaking her head, she moved toward the wardrobe beside the door to riffle through, muttering, "Well, now. Lord Radcliffe, he said ye were inexperienced, but 'tis obvious yer not and ye know what ye want—Ah, ha!"

Charlie was still blinking over the first part of her statement when the woman grunted in satisfaction, withdrew from the wardrobe, and turned toward her, rope in one hand and a long, evil-looking whip in the other.

"There. Now that I ken what ye like, we can get down to business." Smiling sweetly, she cracked the whip.

Charlie bolted for the door. She had barely taken two steps, however, when the snap of the whip preceded something tangling around her feet and drawing tight. Crying out, she threw her hands out to break her fall as she stumbled forward onto her stomach.

"Now there's a naughty boy for ye," the hag crooned, catching her by the collar and dragging her back toward the bed. "We'll have to spank that naughtiness out, I think."

Charlie thought not and began to struggle in earnest as the woman sank onto the side of the bed and tried to draw her over her knee. Breaking loose, she turned away, only to be caught about the waist and thrust onto the bed on her back. Before she could move, the woman had crawled to sit upon her chest.

Snatching up the rope she had tossed onto the bed earlier, the woman quickly tied Charlie down; each wrist to its own bedpost.

"There!" The woman gave a sigh of satisfaction, then blew the hair that had come loose on her forehead out of her face. She eyed Charlie with a bit of exasperation. "Yer a lively one, you are. I'm getting too old fer these games. I'd best get a huge tip out of this."

When Charlie merely stared at her dumbly, she sighed and leaned to the side. "Here now." Her smile was sprightly as she straightened again, whip in hand, fondling the grip suggestively. "Is it just the threat o' pain ye like, or will ye be wantin' the real thing?"

"Tell me more about this Aggie. She will be gentle with the boy, will she not?"

The strumpet's hair almost hid the way she rolled her eyes at his question. She was likely frustrated, too. Radcliffe had been fretting over the boy ever since they had entered the room. It was most annoying. He was entirely too preoccupied with that damn boy. She had been cooing and petting him for several moments now and he was not even hard. He couldn't concentrate.

"Aggie will be most gentle, my lord," the woman murmured huskily, raising her eyes to cast him an alluring look as she continued working on the buttons of his shirt. "She has been in the business a long time. She'll break him in proper and with care."

"Aye, of course she will." Radcliffe forced a smile and tried to concentrate on the woman's attentions as she finished with the buttons of his shirt and slid her hands across his chest. Still, it was most difficult. He could not get the boy out of his head. It was rather like an annoying hangnail, irritating and nagging.

Grimacing at his own foolishness, he raised his hands to her shoulders and drew the woman up for a kiss, trying to work up some enthusiasm.

A loud scream brought an end to his efforts, making his head whip toward the wall. There was no mistaking the panic and pain in that shriek as belonging to Charles. Cursing, Radcliffe pushed the woman away from him and hurried for the door.

He was crashing through the door of the room Charles was in before that first shriek ended, but came to an abrupt halt in the doorway at the sight before him. Charles was staked out and tied down to the bed as if on the rack, his whole body stiff with terror, his head raised off the bed, his wig somewhat askew, his mouth wide open in a second shriek. That was only half of the picture, however. The second half, the one that made Radcliffe goggle somewhat, was that the aging Aggie was seated astride the lad's thin chest, with what looked very much like a whip in her hand.

"What the devil is going on here?"

Mouth snapping shut, Charles swiveled his head

toward the door, relief swelling across his face when he spied the man standing there. "Radcliffe." That breath of sound was soaked with relief. Pausing, he swallowed to regain his breath somewhat, then roared, "Get this hag off of me!"

Radcliffe was across the room in a trice. "Madam, I suggest you remove yourself, else I shall be forced to do it for you."

Aggie scowled from the lad she sat on to the man looming above them menacingly. "Is this more game-playing?" she asked uncertainly.

Unable to restrain himself further, Radcliffe lifted her bodily from the lad, then set her away from the bed. She began to protest at once.

"Here now, what're ye doin'? The lad asked fer it! He was wantin' me to do such 'n the like to 'im."

Radcliffe paused to arch one eyebrow at Charles.

"The silly old strumpet misunderstood everything," the boy informed him with apparent disgust. "Hurry up and untie me. I want out of this den of iniquity."

"Oh, no!" the old bawd fluttered behind Radcliffe helplessly. "Now don't be untyin' him, he's a slippery little eel an' it took me forever to be trussin' him up in the first place."

Ignoring her whining complaint, Radcliffe untied Charles, then turned to face the now irate Aggie. She was protesting still, but had added threats to her words, wanting to be paid for this fiasco. The boy had kept her jogging about like a horse at the races, she said, and she was deserving payment for it.

Charles scooted off the bed, sidling around to the bottom of it as Radcliffe faced the old cow and the younger woman who now joined in the complaining.

Silencing the harping women at last, Radcliffe shook his head. "I shall pay you both as soon as I fetch my jacket from the other room," he assured them rather coldly, then started toward the door, the two women hard on his heels.

Charlie sagged with relief the moment she was alone. This whole night had been something of a nightmare. Not at all what she had expected.

Sighing, she glanced around the room with distaste and moved quickly toward the door, suddenly eager to remain as close to Radcliffe as possible until she was free of this place. A brothel. Good God, the man had brought her to a brothel! This was his idea of a good time? Pausing at the door, she peered cautiously out into the hall, relaxing when she saw that it was empty. She would just die of shame were anyone she knew to discover she had visited such a place.

Charlie had just stepped out into the hall when a burst of rather familiar laughter made her step closer to the rail and peer down at a man and woman ascending the stairs. It took her but a moment to recognize Lord Seguin, Beth's affianced. At first she was so horrified that she could not move, for truly the man had seemed the epitome of propriety, the last person she would have thought to run into here. But then as the couple reached the top step and began to turn toward her, she whirled and fled back into the room she had just exited. Reaching for the door, she started to push it closed, then merely slid behind it instead, afraid to attract attention by closing it. She realized her mistake a moment later.

"Here we are then, this room is empty."

Charlie could feel the skin shrivel on her face, the blood rushing from it as the twosome entered.

"Fine, fine," Lord Seguin thrummed cheerfully.

Seeing his fingers come around the door as he grasped it to push it closed, Charlie covered her face with her hands in dismay and awaited discovery.

Chapter 6

"What would ye be liking tonight, guv?"

Blinking, Charlie lowered her hands slightly until she could peek over her fingertips. It seemed that neither Seguin, nor the voluptuous female with him, had bothered to glance behind as he pushed the door closed. Neither of them had spotted her . . . yet.

Swallowing, she glanced frantically about. The door to the room was right beside her, but the handle was on the opposite side from her. That meant she would have to sidle several feet to the right, undetected. It seemed like miles just then, when Seguin or the prostitute might glance in her direction at any moment. On the other hand, she was standing directly in front of the wardrobe, leaning against its closed door, next to the one Aggie had left open earlier when she had gone in search of the whip. It was merely a step for her to slide into the concealing wardrobe and tug the door closed.

"I think I should like Indians tonight, Maisey." Charlie heard Seguin's response as she slid into the wardrobe, but hadn't a clue what it meant. A glance toward the couple as she tugged the door closed showed the rotund little man smiling with an odd sort of excitement as Maisey opened the chest at the foot of the bed and began to rifle through it.

Once she had pulled the wardrobe door closed, Charlie noticed that there was a sliver of space between the two connecting doors, enough to give her a slightly limited view of the room beyond. At an exclamation from Maisey, Charlie put her eye to the gap and peered out. The woman was straightening up, some sort of large feather in one hand and a strip of cloth in the other. These she gave to Lord Seguin, then returned to rifling through the chest. Charlie glanced toward Seguin, but when he began to remove his knee breeches, she turned her attention quickly back to Maisey. The woman had fetched a second feather from the chest. Setting it aside, the woman promptly removed all of her clothes except for a chemise, then placed the feather in her hair, added a couple of bracelets to her arms, and turned to present herself to Lord Seguin.

Glancing back to the man, Charlie nearly gasped aloud. He had removed every stitch of clothing he had entered in and now stood wearing the strip of material as a loincloth. The feather perched rather precariously in his wig was the only other thing he was wearing at the moment, she saw, her gaze moving with dismay over his blotchy, bulgy little body. The man was no taller than Charlie herself, but must have weighed at least twice as much. And every pound of that weight seemed to have been deposited in the belly which hung ponderously over the makeshift loincloth. Everywhere else the man seemed a scarecrow. His legs were as spindly as a crane's, his arms not much better. He looked quite ridiculous.

"Lovely," he pronounced with a decidedly lascivious gleam in his eyes as he surveyed Maisey. "Come here, my little Indian princess."

A wicked smile coming to her lips, Maisey shook her head and took a step away. Seguin, rather than appear distressed at her refusal to obey him, grinned back just as wickedly, then set out after her. What followed was the most absurd game of catch to which Charlie had ever been made witness. Maisey was giggling and rushing about. Lord Seguin, that icon of dignity and diplomacy, was slapping his fingers to his mouth and whooping in what she presumed was supposed to be the Indian fashion, as he chased after her. He could have easily caught her had he wished, Charlie was sure, for truly Maisey was giggling too hard to be able to move very quickly, but that did not appear to be the object of the game. It seemed the chase was the fun.

Charlie was seeing Seguin in an entirely new light, and one she could have done quite well without ever having known about. All she could think was that it was a good thing Beth had decided to flee with her rather than marry the man. She simply could not see her sister being willing to indulge in such foolishness.

The game finally came to an end with the "Indian princess" pausing beside the bed and turning to face her pursuer with arms outstretched as if to hold him off. "Oh, mighty Indian warrior! Mercy!" she cried dramatically.

Seguin staggered to a halt and took a moment to catch his breath before gathering the girl's slender form into his arms. "Now you will be mine," he panted, pushing her back onto the bed.

Charlie could not help but notice that the woman landed with legs splayed, her chemise sliding up to her hips as if this scene had been played repeatedly and she knew what to expect. She caught a glimpse of Seguin tugging his loincloth upward, then drew her eye quickly away from the opening as he stepped between the woman's legs.

Deciding that now would be a most propitious time to leave, Charlie slid out of the wardrobe and slunk to the door. The couple on the bed were far too busy to notice when she backed out of the room and eased the door closed. Turning, Charlie heaved a sigh as she saw that the hallway was as empty as it had been before the arrival of Seguin and Maisey. Radcliffe was nowhere in sight. She had not really noticed which direction he had taken when he and the women had left the room. Now she wished she had.

Shrugging inwardly, Charlie started down the hallway to the left, sure she would run into him soon enough. That, or he would find her, she was sure. The first door she passed was closed. Soft moans and giggles came from inside. Charlie listened until a man spoke. Once assured it was not Radcliffe, she moved on. The next door was closed, too, and there was a key in the lock, but no sounds reached her through the door.

She was about to continue on when the sound of a door opening made her glance anxiously back. Maisey, now wearing a nearly see-through blue robe, appeared in the door and glanced back into the room. For a moment, Charlie was too stunned by the speed of her appearance to do anything. Goodness, it had only been a moment ago that Seguin had been commencing to . . .

er . . . commence with the woman. Surely it could not be over so quickly? she thought with dismay, then stiffened as Seguin's voice drifted down the hallway toward her.

Afraid that he would step out of the room next, Charlie reached for the knob of the door she stood before. She began to panic when it did not budge under her efforts, then recalled the key in the lock and quickly turned it, opened the door, and slid into the room, taking the key with her. Pushing the door closed, she locked it and pressed her ear against it to listen.

"I shan't be a moment," she heard the woman say, then there was the click of a door softly closing, followed by silence.

Charlie was just beginning to relax when a sound behind her made her stiffen and whirl to peer blindly about. All she could see were vague shadows. Then a shuffling step sent a small shiver of apprehension down her back.

"Who's there?" she asked anxiously.

A whimper was the only response and she frowned slightly, some of the tension leaving her. " 'Tis all right," she assured the darkness. "I am leaving. I am sorry to have disturbed you."

Turning back to the door, she unlocked and drew it cautiously open. Once assured that the hall was empty, she opened the door wide, then glanced curiously back. Even with the light now streaming into the room, it took her a moment to spot the girl. She was barely more than a child really, perhaps sixteen or so, and wore the plain rough dress of a country lass. She could have been any number of the young girls from the village near her family home, Charlie realized, then noticed that the lass was shivering with fear.

Spying a candle on a table near the door, Charlie stepped over, took it in hand, then moved into the hall to light it from one of the oil lamps there. Returning to the room, she smiled reassuringly at the terrified girl as she set it on the table, then hesitated and peered at her uncertainly. "Are you all right?"

When the girl remained silent, Charlie shifted uncomfortably, then took a sideways step toward the door. "I am sorry to have bothered you. I was simply trying to avoid someone in the hall. I thought the room was empty," she explained as she moved, discomfited by the girl's accusing eyes.

"Who are ye?" the girl blurted out just as she reached the door.

Pausing, Charlie peered at her curiously. This slip of a girl was nothing at all like the other women here. Her clothes were plain and worn, her hair pulled tightly back from her pale face. And the door had been locked from the outside, her brain reminded her suddenly.

"Who are ye?" the girl repeated, her fearful tone pulling Charlie away from her thoughts.

"Lord Charles Radcliffe," she lied blandly with a small bow. "And you are?"

"Bessie," the girl murmured hesitantly, then in a stronger voice, "Are ye . . . Yer not workin' fer *her*, are ye? Aggie, I mean."

Charlie gave a start. "Certainly not!" At that, she noticed, some of the tension left the girl. Casting a watchful glance toward the door, she grimaced and turned back to ask, "What are you doing here?"

"She won't let me leave."

Charlie nodded with resignation. It was what she had begun to suspect, of course, but having her suspicions verified created something of a problem. She was not the sort who could say, "Dear me, that is a shame," then leave the girl to her fate. "What does she want with you?"

"She's wantin' me to . . . work fer 'er."

The shame that accompanied that admission was almost palpable. It was obvious the girl was not up to the idea. Still, Charlie had to be sure before she made any rash decisions. "Do you wish to?"

"Nay!" The feeling behind the word was most emphatic.

Nodding abruptly, Charlie closed the door, locked it, then turned to the young woman, sighing when she saw that fear once again pinched the lass's expression. "It is all right. I have already told you I will not harm you. I simply thought it better if no one saw that you were not alone. The last thing we need is company just now."

The girl did not seem much relieved by that explanation, but Charlie did not know what else to say to calm her, so she did not try. Instead, her gaze slid to the draped windows.

"Where are you from?" she asked to distract the girl as she moved toward the nearer window.

"Woodstock, me lord."

Charlie grunted at that as she tugged the heavy drapes covering the window aside. They had passed by the little Oxfordshire town on their way into the city. "What are you doing in London?"

"I came lookin' fer work—respectable work," she added hurriedly. "A position as a maid. There was nothin' available in Woodstock and . . ."

Charlie glanced over to see her shrug unhappily. "How did you end up here at Aggie's?" she asked.

"The coach. The driver's a friend o' me father's and let me ride alongside him fer free. When we got to the post . . . That was where I met Lady Roughweather."

Charlie glanced around again at that. "Lady Roughweather."

"Aggie," the girl explained with a grimace. "She was callin' hersel' by the name Roughweather at the time."

Charlie rolled her eyes at that and turned back to peering out the window. The room faced an alley. They were on the second floor, of course, and it was quite a drop to the hard cobbled stone below, but . . .

" 'Twill have to do."

"What will have to do?" Bessie asked curiously, taking a cautious step closer.

Glancing at her, Charlie took in her size and thinness. "Finish explaining about Mrs. Roughweather," she instructed, then turned back, placed her hands on the upper portion of the window and pressed upward, relieved when it immediately began to raise. It seemed "Aggie" did not believe the girl could be ingenious enough to try to escape through it. Which she supposed was true, since the girl was still here. Satisfied, she eased the window back down, then turned to listen to the end of her story.

"Well . . . she seemed ever so nice then. Pretended great concern for me, she did. Said it wasn't safe for a pretty young girl like me to be walkin' the streets alone." She blushed as she admitted that, then frowned as she added, "She said she ran a home for runaway girls and asked if I had a place to stay and if I wasn't hungry. When I said no, I hadn't a place to stay, and that I was ever so hungry, she suggested I come back to her home and eat a meal. Then she would see if she could not find me someplace to stay until I found a position. I came back here with her, but we came in the back door, through the kitchens. It was there she fed me. Afterward I was ever so tired and she suggested I rest and led me up here to this room."

"Did you not wonder what sort of place this was when you saw the other women here?" Charlie asked with exasperation.

"I saw no girls. It was early morning when I arrived and silent as a tomb in here. I imagine they were all still abed." She made a face. "I know *I* was tired. By the time I finished the porridge she gave me, I was so tired I didn't think I would even make it up the stairs. I don't recall enterin' the room and gettin' mesel' to bed."

"She most likely drugged you," Charlie decided with disgust, then managed a reassuring smile when she saw the dismay on the girl's face.

"What happened when you awoke?" Turning back to the window, she opened it. This time she slid it all the way up and held it there so that she could lean out and get a better look at the wall itself to see if it might offer any purchase, or if there was another window beneath them they need worry about passing. There was a window, but its drapes were closed. The wall offered no purchase.

"That was just a little while ago," Bessie murmured in response to her question. "The door was locked when I tried to leave. I began to knock and yell. Mrs. Roughweather came. She was still bein' nice at first. Said as how I should call her Aggie, not Mrs. Rough-weather, and askin' me how I was feelin' . . . . But I was on to the fact that something was wrong. I was by the door when she opened it and there was a couple going past. The woman was dressed rather scanty-like and laughin' vulgar-like and the man . . . why, he had his hand so far down her top he was like to find her—" She paused and blushed slightly, then shrugged. "That and the sounds coming from the next room told me this was no house for runaways. I thanked Mrs.—Aggie, but told her as how I was wantin' to leave now. She said that was fine, so long as I paid her the coins I was owin' her."

"What coins?"

"That's exactly what *I* said!" Bessie nodded firmly, her mouth twisting with displeasure. "She says the coins for me meal and sleepin' in this fine room. Said this ain't no house of charity and either I'd be payin' her the money or I'd be workin' it off. I don't have no money," she ended forlornly.

"She expects you to become a prostitute in exchange for a bit of food and a bed for a night?"

When Bessie nodded solemnly, Charlie shook her head with disgust.

"Criminal," she muttered, glancing about for something to hold the window open with. "Fetch me that candle over there."

Bessie hesitated, then seemed to decide to trust this would-be knight-errant and glanced about. Spotting the object in question, she hurried over to tug it out of its holder.

"No, the holder too," Charlie exclaimed and Bessie gave up trying to separate the two objects and brought both over. Holding the window up with one hand, Charlie took the candle in her other, set it on the sill as close to the wall as possible, then gently lowered the window until it was jammed in place. "There, that should do."

Turning back to the room, she glanced about. "Do you have any belongings you wish to take with you?"

Bessie hurried over to the bed, knelt, and dragged a small battered traveling bag out from beneath it. Straightening, she saw the way Charlie was holding a hand out to take it and briefly clutched it to her chest as if all the wealth in the world were in it. Which was probably true. At least to the girl. The small satchel probably held everything the chit owned. "Come, come, we haven't all night."

Sighing, Bessie reluctantly gave up the bag, then gasped in horror when, after shaking it to be sure there was nothing breakable in it, Charlie dropped it out the window.

"What're ye doin'?" The girl rushed forward, nearly knocking Charlie out the window as she tried to spot her bag below.

"We are leaving," Charlie explained simply, turning sideways to the window and lifting one leg over the sill.

"Through the window?" Her dismay was more than obvious.

Straddling the ledge, Charlie faced her calmly. "Well, I would pay Aggie for your stay here, but I haven't a pence on me just now. I shall have some tomorrow. Shall I leave you here and return for you when I have the proper funds?"

The girl's expression was answer enough.

"Right. Then the window it is. I shall go first. Once I am below, sit on the ledge here as I am doing, then lower yourself until you hang by your hands as far as you can and let go. I shall endeavor to assist you from below. Understand?"

"Aye, but . . ." She glanced down at her gown and Charlie could almost read her thoughts. She wasn't happy with the idea of a man looking up her skirts, no matter the purpose. Well, Charlie could sympathize, but she wasn't about to confess her sex to put the girl's anxieties at ease.

"Did you wish to try the stairs?" she asked a bit archly, impatient to get it over with. As she expected, Bessie's mouth snapped closed on any further protest.

"Charles!"

Both of them jumped at that hiss from outside. Charlie peered down at the alley below, aware of the suddenly stiff girl leaning forward to peer past her. It was Radcliffe, of course. What the devil he was doing in the alley was a question she did not have the answer for. That he was furious was obvious, however, and she sighed with resignation. Charlie had rather been hoping to keep this little episode to herself. Rescue the lass, send her on her way, and go wait in the carriage for his return—that had rather been her plan.

Ah well, the best laid plans and all that, she thought philosophically with another sigh.

"Who is that?" Bessie asked anxiously.

"Who is that?" Radcliffe hissed up at the same moment as he spotted Bessie peering out the window beside her.

Rolling her eyes, Charlie glanced from one to the other, but was saved from deciding who to answer first by a sound from the door. It was a muttered curse coming from the hallway. Charlie recognized the colorful comment as being from Aggie, and grasped the window ledge for balance as Bessie suddenly clutched her arm with claw-like fingers, her face blanching.

"Oh, God." The girl barely breathed the word.

"What the devil did I—" came the irritated murmur from the other side of the door, then in a much louder voice: "Glory! Get over here! Did ye see a key in this door earlier? I'm sure I left it in the lock."

"Can't say as I noticed," came a young prostitute's bored voice.

"Charles." Radcliffe's hiss came to them clearly from below.

Charlie released the window ledge to wave Radcliffe to silence as Aggie muttered again from outside the door. "Well, it's not in any of my pockets. What the devil could I have done with it?"

"Maybe ye lost it during that tussle ye had with the boy," the other voice murmured with amusement, and Aggie spat a most unladylike curse.

"Damn lad. Yer probably right. I'd best go check the room."

"Maisey's in there with Lord Seguin."

"Oh, aye." A sigh heaved outside the door. "Lord Seguin and his odd games. It's to be his last visit before he leaves town, too. He wouldn't appreciate my interrupting."

"Wait 'til he's left then." Charlie could almost hear the shrug in the younger woman's voice, then there was a knock at the door.

"Bessie?" The voice was sweet, sickeningly so, with an underlying note of malice. "He's here. And as soon as I find the key I'm coming to prepare ye for him. And don't get yer hopes up that I won't find it neither. 'Cause I'll just have one o' the men break down the door if I don't. He's paying me enough to replace a thousand doors."

Silence greeted those words. When it drew out with no response from inside the room, all sweetness left Aggie's voice.

"Bessie! Did ye hear me, girl?"

"A-aye," Bessie gasped in reply when Charlie nudged her.

Grunting in satisfaction at what sounded like fear in the quavering voice, Aggie muttered, "Maybe I should interrupt Maisey and Lord Seguin after all. Himself doesn't like to be kept waiting, and I doubt the chit is like to cooperate."

"Do as ye like, but he's been in there with Maisey for five minutes or so already. A couple more minutes and he'll be coming out on his own anyway."

"Aye." Aggie gave a harsh chuckle. "Maisey says he's faster than a cook crackin' eggs."

The voices faded as they moved off, and Charlie and Bessie both sighed in relief.

"Charles!"

Muttering under her breath, Charlie turned and peered out the window. "What?!" she hissed back.

"What the devil are you doing?!"

"I shall explain later. Go fetch the carriage to the mouth of the alley."

Radcliffe hesitated, then opened his mouth to say something, but Charlie interrupted him. "Please," she hissed.

Sighing, the man turned away and moved up the alley muttering to himself.

"Who is he?"

Charlie shook her head at the would-be-maid's question. "Later," was all she said, then she tossed the girl a reassuring smile, slid her second leg out the window to join the first, turned so that she lay on her stomach across the ledge, and lowered herself carefully out. Once she was hanging by her hands only, she let go and dropped to the ground, wincing at the jolting of her bones as she landed.

The grass outside the inn window several days previous had made for a much softer landing than the cobblestone here. The drop also hadn't been quite as far, she saw as she peered up through the darkness at the oval that was Bessie's pale face. She was already seated on the ledge.

Offering her a reassuring smile, Charlie stepped forward to stand directly beneath the window and waved at her, telling her to get a move on. However, the girl either forgot the instructions or misunderstood the wave, for rather than turn and rest on her tummy to lower herself carefully out, she suddenly plunged off the ledge, plummeting straight at the horrified Charlie.

Before she could get out of the way or even move, the full impact of the girl's body was clobbering her over the head and tumbling them both to the ground.

Chapter 7

O H, Lord! I'm ever so sorry!"
Charlie heard those words through a sort of haze and a ringing in her ears. Not only had she broken Bessie's fall with her body, she had also conked her head rather nastily on the cobblestone ground as she had collapsed beneath the girl's weight. Most painful. Horrendous really. Was she seeing double?

"Oh, gad! Oh, please say yer a'right? I'm sorry. I slipped. I was turnin' to lower mesel' out the window just like ye said, but my hand slipped and I fell and I hit you and—"

"Shhh," Charlie hissed, pressing her hands to either side of her head a bit desperately.

"Oh, o' course. I'll be drawin' attention I will and we'll be caught am I not quiet."

Charlie grimaced. She had not even considered being overheard. Her shushing had more to do with the way the girl's voice was adding to her pain than any other concerns she should have. Shifting her legs carefully, Charlie began to rise, grateful for Bessie's efforts to assist as the young girl caught her arm.

"Yer none too steady on yer feet, me lord," Bessie

murmured with concern, dragging Charlie's arm over her shoulder and taking most of her weight as she steered her to the wall. Leaning her there, the girl peered at her worriedly. "Yer pale as a ghost too. Ye took a nasty knock."

"Aye," Charlie sighed, raising a hand to probe tentatively at the back of her head. "There is a bump but no blood," she announced as she found the area.

The other girl's face relaxed somewhat. "Thank goodness for that."

"Aye," Charlie murmured, the clip-clop of horses hooves drawing her gaze to the mouth of the alley in time to see Radcliffe's carriage pull up. Straightening her shoulders determinedly, she eased away from the wall. "We had better go."

Nodding, Bessie rushed off to collect her bag from where it had landed when Charlie had thrown it out the window. When she returned, Charlie took her arm and they made a mad dash for the carriage.

Radcliffe threw the door open as they reached it, and Charlie nearly stuffed the poor girl inside. Clambering in behind her, she tugged the door closed with a snap and collapsed onto the bench seat beside Bessie with a relieved sigh. When several moments passed in silence without the carriage moving, she opened one eye to peer at Radcliffe.

"Can we go now, please?" she asked politely.

Radcliffe's response was to cast a suspicious glance toward Bessie, then turn back to arch an eyebrow at Charlie.

Sighing, she sat up and murmured politely, "Bessie, this is Lord Radcliffe. Radcliffe, this is Bessie . . . Beth's lady's maid," the last came on an inspiration.

She and Beth did need a lady's maid. They also needed one they could be sure would not give away their secret should it accidentally be uncovered. And Charlie was pretty sure that Bessie was grateful enough for her assistance this night that she would keep the secret should she accidentally discover it. It seemed a perfect arrangement.

Radcliffe didn't seem quite as enthusiastic with this orchestration of events, however. "Lady's maid?" he asked archly.

Charlie turned wary at his tone. "Aye."

"Charles, I brought you here tonight to sample some of Aggie's offerings. Here. On the premises. Not to drag one of her girls home to sample her at your leisure."

"It is nothing like that," Charlie snapped, aware of the way Bessie had stiffened beside her in suspicion.

"She is one of Aggie's girls, is she not?"

"Nay."

"Charles," he growled in a warning tone, and Charlie shifted impatiently.

"Does she look like a prostitute to you?"

Radcliffe glanced reluctantly at the girl, taking in her plain dress, fresh face, and long, undressed hair.

"She is a country girl," Charlie said when he remained silent. "She is from Oxfordshire. She came to London to find a job as a lady's maid."

"How did she end up at Aggie's, then?"

"Because your dear friend Aggie lured her back to that brothel of hers under the pretext that it was a home for runaways. She fed her, offered her a bed for the night, then locked her up in a room to force her to work for her."

Radcliffe frowned at that but had the good grace not to claim that Aggie would not do such a thing. Instead, he rapped on the roof of the carriage, signaling the driver that he was ready to leave. Charlie and Bessie both relaxed somewhat as the carriage started to move, taking them away from the possibility of the carriage door suddenly opening to reveal a furious Aggie, eager to snatch back her victim.

Charlie cast one last reassuring smile at the girl, then leaned her head back on the carriage seat and turned her face to the window to peer out at the passing night. They had ridden in silence for some time when Radcliffe finally shifted and muttered, "She is not my friend."

Charlie sniffed at that. "You could have fooled me."

"She is not. I have never even been in that establishment before," he said irritably. "Though I don't know why I'm bothering to say so."

She glared at him. "Well, then why the devil would you go there tonight? And why drag me along with you?"

"I thought you would enjoy it," he snapped.

Charlie snorted. "Oh, aye. I have always fancied the idea of being tied to a bed and whipped." When Bessie gasped, her eyes going round, Charlie managed a stiff smile and reassured her quickly, "It did not go so far. She tied me to the bed, but Radcliffe came ere she used her whip."

"Oh, blessed saint, she is a wicked woman."

"She is a spongy, swag-bellied bawd," Charlie replied with disgust, then bent a glare on Radcliffe. "I notice that while you stuck me with her, you managed to lance yourself a lovely little bit of fluff. I suppose that Glory person was just your way of passing the time while I enjoyed myself?"

Before he could deny it she went on, "Next time you wish to take me somewhere I might enjoy myself, my lord, might I suggest you try one of the clubs or coffee houses? I only tell you this so that I do not find myself somewhere equally enjoyable next time, like . . . oh, I do not know . . . say a castle dungeon or bedlam."

"I take your point," Radcliffe growled.

Grunting in response, Charlie turned to peer out the window again, determined not to say another word to the man tonight. A brothel for God's sake! Wait until Beth heard about this. Her eyes were slipping closed, her mind beginning to drift as she heard Radcliffe ask Bessie where she came from. Already knowing the answer, Charlie allowed their voices to combine with the gentle jostling of the carriage to lull her to sleep.

"Wake up, Charles. We are here."

Opening her eyes, Charlie peered dully at Radcliffe. Her brain was throbbing painfully and it took her a moment to recall even who Charles was. Sighing wearily as recollection returned, she waited as Radcliffe disembarked, then helped Bessie out of the carriage, before stumbling after them and up the path to the front door, which was even now opening to reveal Radcliffe's butler. "Good evening, m'lords. You had a good night, I hope?"

"Barrels of fun, Stokes. Just barrels," Charlie commented dryly when Radcliffe merely grunted at the question. Ignoring the man's obvious curiosity, she gestured toward the young maid, preparing to explain her presence, but Radcliffe beat her to it.

"This is Bessie, Stokes. She is—" He hesitated, a frown tugging at his lips as he debated what to say, then finished simply with, "Lady Elizabeth's maid."

When the old man raised one questioning eyebrow at the girl's sudden and late arrival, Radcliffe added, "She came in by carriage today, and had some difficulty on the journey. No doubt she is hungry and tired. See that she has a nice meal and give her a comfortable room."

Nodding, the old servant turned away, leading Bessie down the hall as the door to the library opened and Beth stepped out.

"I thought you would be asleep by now," Charlie murmured with surprise.

"I *was* asleep," Beth admitted wryly, then held up a book. "I fell asleep reading." Lowering the book, she glanced curiously about the hall. "Did I hear something about a maid?"

"Aye." Charlie glanced at Radcliffe, then whispered, "I shall explain as I walk you to your room."

Nodding, Beth closed the library door and crossed the hall to lead the way upstairs with Charlie trailing behind her.

"Charles."

They both paused on the steps to turn back at Radcliffe's weary voice.

"I apologize for giving you grief over Bessie. You showed great compassion in involving yourself in her troubles. You . . . er . . . your father would be proud of you, I am sure." On that note, he turned and strode into the library, closing the door quietly behind him.

Beth managed to contain her curiosity all the way up the stairs and along the hall to Charles's room. Once in the bedchamber, however, she turned on her questioningly. Charlie dropped onto the bed and told her everything. The tale sounded somehow more amusing and less frightful as she told it, so much so that they were both rolling on the bed with laughter as she regaled her with her tussle with the whip-wielding Aggie. Beth showed some dismay over Lord Seguin's behavior, however, then anger at Aggie's attempt to force Bessie into such a dishonorable business.

Once Charlie fell silent, Beth sighed and rolled onto her stomach upon the bed to prop her chin in her hands. "You always seem to be the one to have the adventures."

"You could have gone," Charlie reminded her unsympathetically, relaxing upon her back, her hands beneath her head. "I did make the offer."

"Aye, well . . . in truth, I am glad it was you. I should have been terrified in your position." When Charlie remained silent, she asked, "You do not think he really did anything with that girl, do you?"

"Radcliffe? And that prostitute?" Charlie frowned at the thought, finding the very idea troublesome. "Nay," she said at last. "He would not have had the chance."

"Hmm." Beth began to pluck at the coverlet of the bed. "Do you think he was telling the truth when he claimed never to have been there before?"

Charlie shifted irritably and sat up. This was an uncomfortable subject. "I do not know. Are you going to be Charles tomorrow, or am I?"

"Me, please," Beth answered at once, then sat up

as Charlie nodded and moved toward the connecting door between bedrooms. "What are you doing?"

"Going to bed."

"But you should sleep in here tonight. You are to be me tomorrow, after all."

"Aye. And we have switched rooms, remember?"

"Oh, yes," she smiled wryly. "I moved my things into your room and yours into here, but forgot about it while I was in the library." Her expression became curious. "What did he say about walking in on your bath?"

"Nothing much. Just that he would apologize," Charlie murmured as she opened the door. "I suppose he forgot tonight."

"No doubt. Good night, Charlie."

"Beth."

"Aye?"

"Nay," Charlie murmured with a sigh. "I meant, I am Beth now. As of now I am Beth and you are Charles."

Her sister smiled slightly at that. "Then should we not switch clothes?"

"Oh, yes." Pulling the door closed, Charlie began to remove her clothes. When she got to her braies, she suddenly suggested. "You had best roll up one of our stockings and tuck it in your braies on the morrow . . . Just so the tailor does not notice anything amiss."

"Hmm." Beth sighed as she removed her gown. "It will be nice when we have more than one set of clothes each."

"Tomorrow should take care of that," Charlie agreed dryly. There was nothing more annoying in this life than a fitting. Prior to now, she had always managed to avoid those boring hours of being poked and jabbed at with pins. Usually she would show up late, then claim that since she and Beth were the same size and Beth was already being measured for it, there was no sense in wasting time measuring her as well. Beth could see them both fitted out. That argument had worked wonderfully for years now. In this case it would not. If she was to be Elizabeth on the morrow she alone would have to suffer the dressmaker's attention. Perhaps she would get lucky and it would go quickly.

Charlie should have realized by now that Lady Luck was not exactly feeling generous towards her. After all, had she not found herself engaged to a murderous brute, at the mercy of a whip-wielding harridan, and clobbered over the head by a falling lady's maid all within the last week?

She supposed she should not be surprised then that the seamstress kept her all the day through, tucking, measuring, pinning, and prodding. By the time the woman announced her chore finished and gathered her cloths and workers together to depart, Charlie was nearly ready to break down in tears of relief. She considered lying down for a nap, for as boring as her day had been she could not help but be wearied by it, but decided to relax in the library with a book and a cup of tea. After asking Bessie to fetch her some of the soothing liquid, she retired to the library and walked idly along the rows of books, pulling one from the shelves, leafing through it in a desultory fashion, then slipping it back and moving to find another. Charlie was not big on reading. She was more a doer than a reader of others' doings. In the end, nothing really tickled her fancy and she was relieved when Bessie arrived with the tea to distract her.

Moving to sit in the chair by the fire, she watched Bessie pour her a cup from the service she had brought. The girl was wearing a plain gray gown that had seen better days but was clean and serviceable. She was also looking far more cheerful today and less as if the world could be coming to an end at any moment. When the maid straightened and offered her a warm smile before heading for the door, Charlie forestalled her leaving with a quick question. "Have you settled in nicely?"

Bessie paused and turned back, smiling widely. "Oh, aye. Thank ye, miss. Mr. Stokes is most kind, as is the rest of the staff. Well, except for cook, but Joan, the housekeeper, she told me he is the, er, temporarital— No, that's not it." Pausing, her brow puckered slightly and she hesitated, then tried again. "Tempermeanal?"

"Temperamental?" Charlie suggested, and the girl's face brightened at once.

"Aye, that's it. He's the temperamental sort, she said. Though I think he's just mean. Everyone seems scared stiff o' him. Even Stokes steps lightly around him, if ye know what I mean." She tilted her head to the side thoughtfully and murmured, "He's like Lord Kentley's valet where me mum works at Woodstock. He's a nasty old sot 'cause he knows he can be. No one would dare dress him down fer it. . . . Except perhaps Lord Kentley himself, but then the valet would ne'er be, er, tempermeanal with him."

Charlie frowned slightly at that news. She had heard quite a bit of banging and shouting coming from the kitchens earlier, mere moments after Beth and Radcliffe had left, in fact, and had wondered what was about. The answer seemed to be that the cook had been having some sort of outburst. She wondered if Radcliffe realized that his cook behaved so when he was not about. The man's meals were passable at best; he was hardly in a position to make harassing the staff acceptable behavior. She would have said as much to Bessie, but just then they both heard the front door open.

Turning, the maid moved to open the library door, allowing Beth's excited voice to float in to Charlie moments before her flurried footsteps echoed up the stairs. Bessie closed the door, then and turned back to beam at her. "Lord Charles is home."

Eyebrows rising slightly, Charlie nodded. "So he is."

"He is such a nice man and ever so handsome," Bessie went on, adoration obvious in her eyes. "I'll be forever grateful for his saving me from Aggie's. I don't know what I would have done had he not."

"Aye, well," Charlie began uncomfortably, but paused when Radcliffe entered the room.

"Oh!" He halted in the doorway upon spotting them. "I am sorry, I did not realize anyone was in here."

Relief adding warmth to her smile, Charlie beamed at him. " 'Tis all right, I was just about to have a cup of tea. Would you care for some?"

Radcliffe hesitated, then nodded.

"I shall fetch another cup," Bessie murmured, hurrying from the room.

Radcliffe watched her go, then moved to join Charlie. "She seems a nice enough lass. How is she working out?"

"Very well. She is quite competent as a lady's maid."

"Good," he murmured, settling into the seat across from her before actually looking at her. When he did, his gaze seemed suddenly arrested.

Charlie shifted uncomfortably under his sudden intense stare. "Is something wrong?"

"Wrong?" he murmured faintly, then seemed to snap out of his almost dazed state and smiled brilliantly. "Nay. Nothing is wrong. You look quite lovely today."

"Thank you, my lord," she murmured self-consciously.

"There is something different about you somehow."

Charlie stilled in surprise at that comment. Could he tell the difference between her and Beth? she wondered a bit frantically. Nay, he could not. Only their mother and father had ever been able to tell them apart. To everyone else they were identical. Her gaze dropped to her lap under his continued stare, and she blinked at the lavender material, understanding making her relax. "It is simply the new gown. I have worn the same one for days now."

"The gown," he murmured, his gaze dropping to it now. The gown she wore was a plain lavender frock with white piping. It was simple, but clean and fresh and a nice change from the yellow muslim she had been forced to wear for the last few days.

"Hmm. It is a lovely gown. But . . ." He was silent for a moment as his eyes slid back to her face taking in her features, aware of the small changes taking place within his body. He had waited for days for just these blessed reactions to overtake him, terrified each time these tingles had attacked him while with the brother, despairing when he had felt nothing but lukewarm admiration when with the sister. Now, today, everything had switched. He had just spent hours with Charles, silently marveling at the easy amusement and even almost affection that were all he had felt toward the lad that day. And now, alone with the sister, he felt the tingles of awareness, the slight increase of his heart rate, and the shallow breathing that he had heretofore experienced only around the brother . . . and upon espying the girl leaving her bath. This seemed to prove his earlier theory true. He was really attracted to the girl.

Thank God, he thought, grinning suddenly as he peered at her in the new gown, his mind casting back to the night before when he had barged into Charles's room only to find Beth standing naked in a tub of water. He was having much the same reaction to her now as he had had then.

"Madame Decalle sent back to her shop for it when she realized that I had only the one gown," she blurted out as his eyes roved slowly over every detail of her figure in the gown. "She was making it for a duchess someone or other who was of a size with me."

Catching the confusion and discomfort on the girl's face now, he managed to dim his smile slightly as the memory of the bathing vision prompted him to murmur, "I must apolo—"

The opening of the door as Bessie returned made him halt and he waited patiently, smiling at the maid as she set another cup on the tray and poured tea into it. She then smiled at them both and slipped quietly from the room.

Charlie took a sip of her tea, then asked, "Did you and my brother accomplish all you wished today?"

Nodding, he picked up his cup. "We visited the jewelers to transfer some of the jewels into cash, stopped in at the tailor's for a quick fitting, then dropped in at the club." He raised an eyebrow at her. "Did your fittings go well?"

Charlie's mouth twisted wryly. "Not as well as my brother's, I can see. Lady Decalle arrived directly after you left and was not finished with me until just moments ere you returned. I spent the entire day being poked and prodded by the woman."

"Oh, dear. It sounds trying." She appeared somewhat irritated when he sounded more amused than sympathetic.

Charles's sister smiled sweetly, then tilted her head to the side, asking innocently, "Did you not start to say something about having to apologize?"

His amusement faded at once. "Ah, yes," he sighed. "I did. Yesterday, when I burst into the room while you were . . ."

She arched one eyebrow at his hesitation, but could not help a slow blush that crept up her neck as she recalled her nudity when he had burst in on her bath.

"Well, I fear I was rude in not knocking. I had not realized that you and Charles had switched rooms and I . . . It was most rude of me to barge right in like that. I am terribly sorry for catching you in such a state."

"Aye, well," she interrupted him at last and set her cup on the table. She was as embarrassed as he by this apology and the memory of his seeing her so. Standing, she made to skirt the table between them, suddenly almost eager to slip from the room. Gentleman that he was, Radcliffe stood at once, and when she caught the toe of her slipper on the base of a table leg in her rush and stumbled, he stepped quickly forward to catch her against his chest.

Flushing even darker and feeling rather foolish, Charlie straightened away from his chest. She peered up at him, her breath catching briefly as she took in the expression on his face and the naked hunger in his eyes as they dipped over the mounds of her breasts where the corset she wore and the cut of the gown pushed them together and up like a pair of ripe melons about to tumble from a basket. Aware of little prickles of awareness tingling along the back of her neck and across the bare flesh of her chest, Charlie swallowed and started to take a step backward, only to bump up against the side of the chair she had just left and nearly fell once again. Radcliffe grabbed for her arm once more to steady her, then—quite without conscious intent—found himself tugging her gently forward, his lips dropping to cover hers.

Chapter 8

CHARLIE went still as Radcliffe covered her mouth with his. At first her stillness was due to surprise, but she remained that way out of curiosity. She had spent her whole life in the country, with Beth as her only playmate and friend. In truth, other than her father and her uncle, Radcliffe was the first man she and Beth had spent any time around. . . . He seemed a decent enough fellow. Staid. Masterly. Trustworthy. And she had always wondered about kissing a man. Who safer, then, to do a little experimenting with than Radcliffe?

She was just getting the hang of this business of kissing, she thought, when Radcliffe suddenly changed the rules on her. One moment their lips were swimming across each other's, the next she felt his tongue licking at her lips like a cat at his paw. When she opened her mouth in protest, the kiss changed tune entirely. It went from the sweet, warm embers of a banked fire as their lips first meshed, to the roar of a full-blown blaze as his tongue invaded her mouth and he began almost to devour her.

Charlie liked it. A lot. There was no thought in her

head of stopping him; all she wanted was to get closer. Clutching at his shoulders as his arms went around her, she pressed against him, opening her mouth further under the onslaught of his kiss. It was marvelous. She never wanted it to end and certainly would not have asked that it should. Until he breathed the name "Beth" against her lips.

It was as if someone had opened the front door and the door to the library at the same time, allowing a cold stiff breeze to rush into the room and up her spine. Radcliffe wasn't kissing *her*, he was kissing Beth. A jumble of emotions crashed down on her. Disappointment, jealousy, resentment. Had he kissed the real Beth before? Like this? She stiffened in his arms, preparing to pull away, but before she could, a sound near the door made Radcliffe himself pull back.

"Yes, Stokes?"

Flushing with embarrassment, Charlie glanced at the butler's expressionless face, muttered her excuses, and fled the room, running upstairs without encountering anyone. She paused in the upper hallway, leaning against the wall and closing her eyes. Her heart was thundering in her chest, her breath coming in gasps, and she had no wish to explain herself to her sister.

Beth. Radcliffe's moan echoed in her head. Had he kissed her just so before? Nay. Surely her sister would have said something had that been the case. Wouldn't she have? Charlie frowned at the thought. Mayhap Beth would not. They had shared all their secrets through their lives, howbeit this one—Well, Charlie had no desire to share this experience with Beth, so perhaps her sister in turn would not have wished to share it with her. *Had* he kissed Beth just so?

"There you are!"

Charlie straightened guiltily as her sister appeared suddenly before her.

"Goodness, I was about to search the house for you," she announced, grabbing Charlie by the wrist and dragging her into the room that was "Elizabeth's."

"You would not believe the fun I had today," Beth exclaimed excitedly, pausing to push the bedroom door closed before dragging Charlie to the bed. "We went to the jeweler's. A Mr. Silverpot. Can you imagine? What a funny little man he was. I swear his stomach was as large and round as a pot. And his hair was silver, too. Not white or gray, but silver. Is that not amusing? But he was very nice and he gave us loads of money for Mother's diamond and emerald set. See?" She whipped a bag of coins out as she spoke, a very heavy bag that jingled merrily.

"Radcliffe wanted to lock it away, but I convinced him to let me show you first," she announced as she opened the bag and tipped its contents onto the bed.

When Charlie's eyes widened at the number of coins, Beth laughed and hugged her. "Is it not wonderful? We are rich. Mr. Silverpot said that the stones were the finest quality he had ever seen and he would be most grateful to buy more of Mother's jewels if they were of similar quality. We shall have the finest gowns in all of London with this."

Charlie smiled at her enthusiasm, then helped her collect the coins and return them to the bag as Beth continued, "We went to the tailor's from there. What a fancy-pants *he* was. Goodness! Were his nose stuck any higher in the air, he would be sure to bump it against the doors he walked through. And he had the most dreadful habit of nudging my stocking every time he measured my inseam. . . . Which he insisted on doing *three* times."

Charlie glanced automatically toward the crotch of Beth's braies, her eyes widening in shock. "Beth!"

"What?"

"What is that?" She pointed at the lump in the girl's pants and Beth followed the gesture, then frowned in confusion.

" 'Tis a stocking. You said to roll one up and put it down my braies."

"Aye, but—Good Lord, 'tis a perfectly round ball. It looks like you have a grapefruit in your drawers," Charlie said with exasperation. "Could you not have—I don't know—shaped it to look a bit more natural?"

"Well, how was I to know what would look natural? 'Tis not as if I walk about gaping at a man's nether regions."

Charlie sighed, then gave a burble of laughter. At Beth's questioning glance, she shook her head. " 'Tis no wonder the tailor kept nudging you. He was most like trying to figure out whether you were deformed, or just sporting a melon down there."

When Beth didn't join in her laughter, but merely looked dejected over her mistake, Charlie quickly changed the subject. "What did you do after you left the tailor's?"

"We went to Radcliffe's club," she murmured, brightening at once.

"His club!" Charlie exclaimed jealously and Beth nodded.

"Oh, aye! It was. . . . Well, it was just marvelous. All these men looking important and officious, servants everywhere and . . . Goodness, Charlie, men do not act nearly so stiff and polite when women are not around. Why, they were positively boyish! Joking, and laughing and having a jolly good time. I met all sorts of nice young men. Radcliffe made a point of acquainting me with as many of the fellows our age as possible. He said it would be good for me to make some chums. He left me with a bunch of them while he spoke with some business acquaintances. It was jolly fun and a good opportunity to size them up. Oh, that reminds me, should you meet a dark-haired fellow named Jimmy or a blond named Freddy, give them a wide birth. They are having some sort of competition to see who can seduce the most young women of the ton this season and are taking wagers on it. From what was said this afternoon, they have ruined nearly half this season's females already."

She nodded firmly when Charlie gaped at her, then lay back on the bed with a sigh. "I am positively exhausted, yes indeed, what a day." She stretched, smothered a yawn, then glanced at Charlie to ask politely, "How was your day?"

"My day?" Charlie reached behind her to grasp the corner of a pillow. "Well, my day was just great. While you were gallivanting about having a *marvelous* time, I was being poked and prodded by a Madame Decalle. Does that not sound amusing?" she asked sweetly, then clobbered the grinning girl over the head with the pillow and slid off the bed with disgust.

Laughing, Beth pushed the pillow aside and rolled onto her stomach to prop her chin on the heels of her hands. "It serves you right for all those years of allowing me to serve as dressmaker's doll," she announced unsympathetically. Then her eyes widened as she finally actually looked at her sister. Sitting up abruptly, she slid her feet off the bed and stood to rush forward. "You are wearing a different gown! Do not tell me this Decalle woman finished a dress already?"

"No, of course not," Charlie murmured as her sister moved around her in a circle. "I promised her extra money if she worked quickly, but even so she could only promise a gown a day, starting tomorrow if she hired another couple of workers."

"Then where—"

"She was preparing this for someone who had similar measurements to us. When she realized that 'Elizabeth' only had one dress, she sent for it immediately."

"Is that not marvelous?" Beth tugged here and there at the material. "This person does have the same measurements. It fits you perfectly."

"Aye, well, actually the lady was a bit taller and larger in the waist, but Madame had one of the girls take it in as we plodded through her book of designs."

"Book of designs?" Beth frowned at that. "What did you choose?"

Charlie's eyebrows rose. "Why the sudden interest? You were not the least concerned when you left this morning."

"Well, in my excitement I fear I forgot you have no experience at such tasks."

Charlie smiled slowly at the other girl's obvious trepidation. "Aye, well, never fear, dear sister. Beth shall love her gowns; after all, she chose them. Though I must confess, Madame Decalle was a bit dismayed at one or two of the choices." On that note, she turned on her heel and quickly left the room, hurrying down the hall toward the stairs. She actually made it half-way there before Beth regained herself enough to come after her.

"What do you mean, *dismayed*? What did you choose?" she asked anxiously, grabbing her arm to stop her.

"You shall see," Charlie murmured, slipping free and continuing forward.

"But—Oh, wait! I forgot to tell you. We have been invited to the theater tonight."

"We have?" Charlie paused to face her sister, her gown swirling about her legs as she did. "By whom?"

"Tommy." When Charlie stared blankly, Beth colored and clarified, "Tomas Mowbray. He invited us to share his box with him and his sister Clarissa."

"Hmm." Charlie glanced at her in the newly tailored men's clothes. The outfit was rather sharp. Radcliffe's doing, no doubt. The man had impeccable taste.

"Well?"

Charlie's eyebrows flew up. "Well, what?"

"Well, do you not think we should go? I told him I was not sure at the time because we only had the one gown and he had already seen me in it, but now that Madame Decalle has provided a second gown ... well, it does seem the thing to do. To meet other prospective husbands," she pointed out hopefully.

"Aye, of course we must go. The idea is to get married, after all, and we cannot manage that should we not go out and about. Besides, I have been bored to tears all day. It will be nice to get out for a bit."

"Good." Beth's relief was obvious as she suddenly snatched Charlie's arm up and turned her back toward the bedroom, dragging her along. "Come along then."

"Why?"

"We must change," Beth explained, dragging her into the bedroom.

"Into what? I told you this was the only gown Madame Ducalle had available. Do you not think this will suit?"

"Oh, it will suit. I meant switch clothes back to my being Beth and your being—"

"Now just a minute, Beth. I am not going to the theater as Charles. I thought you wished to be the brother for the day."

"Well, I did, aye, I did."

"I thought you had fun at the club and the—"

"I did, but I . . ." She looked uncomfortable, and Charlie's gaze narrowed.

"Why do you not tell me more about Tomas Mowbray?" Her sister's flush was answer enough and Charlie sighed. "I see," she murmured. It seemed her sister had taken a liking to the man and wished to be Elizabeth around him.

"I am sorry," Beth began unhappily. "If you wish to continue as Beth for the evening, then surely you should. The full day was the agreement, after all."

"Do not be silly," Charlie chided, reaching up to begin undoing the dress she wore. " 'Tis just the theater."

"Thank you, Charlie," Beth murmured gratefully.

" 'Tis all right," she responded, then sighed slightly as she realized she would now suffer several hours of Clarissa's tender mercies.

* * *

"Charles!"

Charlie sighed as she recognized the voice moments before she spotted Clarissa Mowbray making her way toward where she, Beth, and Radcliffe stood. Tomas Mowbray was hard on the girl's heels, doing his damnedest to keep up with her as she charged through the mob.

"Tom said you were coming tonight. I was so happy at the news," Clarissa gasped as she latched her hands onto Charlie's arm.

"Aye, well, I'm sure," Charlie murmured uncomfortably, doing her best to escape the girl's clutches, but finding the task extraordinarily difficult.

"Mowbray," Radcliffe greeted Clarissa's brother with amusement as the breathless man reached them.

"Lord Radcliffe." Tomas smiled wryly at the man, then grabbed his sister's arm to tug her away from Charlie. Between that and Charlie's own efforts, they managed to remove her grasp. "For God's sake, Clarissa, leave the fellow alone," he muttered irritably, then tossed an apologetic smile Charlie's way. "Sorry, friend. She's always been rather like a bull terrier. I expect it's from competing for attention with Mother's dogs." Ignoring Clarissa's irate gasp at that, Tomas turned his gaze to Beth, his smile widening as it fell on her in the lavender gown. "Lady Beth. You look a sight."

"Thank you, my lord," Beth murmured shyly. "And thank you for inviting us to join you tonight."

"My pleasure." He grinned widely, seemingly oblivious to the frantic tugging Clarissa was trying in an attempt to free herself.

Charlie glanced curiously at Radcliffe, wondering

how he was responding to the other couple's behavior after having shared that kiss with who he thought was Beth in the library. But he appeared not even to notice; his gaze instead was watching Charlie herself with amusement as she sidled cautiously away from the amorous Clarissa.

"Shall we go in?"

Charlie glanced around to see her sister smile sweetly at Tomas and place her hand on the free arm he now raised toward her. Mowbray then reached up to clasp that small hand, dropping the hold he had on his sister as he walked Beth to the doors.

Stifling a sigh of disappointment, Charlie managed not to wince as Clarissa's claws closed around her arm again, drawing her forward. "Come, you will enjoy the show."

"Somehow I doubt that very much," Charlie muttered, then glared at a laughing Radcliffe. "Come along, Radcliffe. You would not wish to miss the show."

"No indeed, I wouldn't," he agreed with amusement, following slowly behind and peering from Beth to Charles as he went. He had noticed the attraction between Beth and Tomas and had awaited a sense of disappointment or jealousy, but there was none forthcoming. In fact, despite that passionate embrace in the library, he found his attention once again being dragged back to the brother. For instance, just now he had noticed the sweet upside-down heart that his behind made in the breeches he wore.

Charles did not have a man's behind, he realized, glancing around at the other male patrons with a frown. Not one of the other men present had as nice a behind. None of them made him want to keep looking, or drew his eye the way Charlie's pert little bottom did. He did not know whether to be relieved by that or further distressed. What the devil was the matter with him? He had never even *looked* at another man's body before, not really. Certainly not like this. Yet now, this boy . . . this stripling, drew his attention and desire like no woman ever had.

There, he had said it. He desired the boy. Good God, he *was* losing his mind, he realized with dismay. He had no desire to be with a man. He did, however, fervently wish that Charles were a woman. His gaze slid to Beth. She was, for all intents and purposes, a female version of Charles, and he had felt incredible passion with her in the library. But he did not now. It was all very confusing.

Radcliffe pushed such thoughts away as he overheard Tom inviting them on a picnic the next day. "A small affair," he was saying. "But we would love to have you there."

"Is it not lovely?" Beth breathed happily.

"Charming," Charlie muttered, disgruntled, not even bothering to glance about the grassy glen they had disembarked upon. The theater the night before had been a hellish experience thanks to one Clarissa Mowbray and her calf-like infatuation. Today was going no better, since she had once again found herself finagled into being Charles.

"Oh, Charlie, do not be such a grump. It is a lovely day for a picnic and—"

"Aye, well, if Clarissa paws me one more time I swear I shall—" Her words came to an abrupt halt as Beth gave a tinkling laugh.

Catching sight of Charlie's narrowed eyes, Beth stifled her laughter and tried for an apologetic look that fell decidedly short of sincerity. Sighing, she shook her head in wry amusement, then murmured, "She does seem quite taken with you."

"Taken with me?" Charlie harrumphed in disgust. "She is like a particularly virulent branch of ivy. She clings to me at every opportunity. Truly the chit is— Oh, drat," she muttered as she spied the girl in question making her way determinedly toward them. Charlie had spent the better part of the hour-long journey doing her best to avoid Clarissa Mowbray. An impossible feat when trapped on a barge with a hundred other people. Still, Charlie had given it a go, repeatedly disengaging the hands that clawed at her sleeve and fleeing with little concern for politeness.

Clarissa had neither seemed to notice nor care that Charlie was showing a distinct lack of interest in her charms. Truly, the girl seemed to have no self-esteem at all. She was certainly lacking in dignity. She had literally chased Charlie about the ship like a puppy chasing its master. It was all rather embarrassing as far as Charlie was concerned. And terribly wearing as well. If Clarissa ever did find a husband, Charlie suspected the man would be brought down by sheer lack of energy. The girl would wear him down until it seemed easier to give in than fight any longer. Charlie decided she had best do something about the determined lady or she was going to spend a decidedly uncomfortable afternoon.

"There you are!" Clarissa exclaimed as if they had not been playing hide-and-seek for the last hour. Latching firmly onto Charlie's arm, she positively beamed with triumph. "Goodness, you are as slippery as a fish. I wanted to show you a spot a little further along the river, but you slipped away."

Charlie remained silent as she was dragged off, sparing merely a glare for her laughing sister, then concentrated on negotiating her way through the crowds of people as Clarissa led her away from the still disembarking guests.

The Mowbrays' idea of a small picnic was piling sixty people on a barge along with nearly as many servants, then transporting them downstream to a suitably grassy spot for a light luncheon at temporary tables and chairs. Had Charlie realized it was to be such a hullabaloo, she would have politely declined and spent the day at home. Well, perhaps not; as boring as she found this outing, pacing about Radcliffe's townhouse seemed worse. At least this way she could see how Radcliffe and Beth interacted with each other. Not that today's adventure was disclosing anything of interest. Radcliffe had been greeted and drawn into a crowd of rather staunch looking older men the moment they had arrived, while Beth and Charlie had been swallowed up by the younger set.

Her gaze slid to Radcliffe now. He was still standing with the older men. Not one of them was less than twenty years older than him, and she frowned as she recalled Beth telling her that he had done the same thing the day before at the club, leaving her in the company of the young bucks and wandering off to discuss business matters with his elders. She was coming to the conclusion that he had quite forgotten how young he was.

How young was he? she wondered suddenly and

frowned as she peered at him. He did not yet look thirty. She would put him at twenty-eight or so. That made him eight years older than herself and Beth. Yet he acted at least twice that. Sad, really. A shame.

A gasp drew her attention back to Clarissa as the girl stumbled over an uneven patch of land. Charlie steadied her with a hand at her elbow that the girl quickly clutched and squeezed warmly.

"Thank you, my lord." Clarissa half-whispered the words of gratitude, her gaze adoring until Charlie shook her hand free and indicated that she should lead the way.

It didn't take long for her to realize that Clarissa didn't have a clue where she was going. There was no path to follow and they were stumbling through the woods like two lost bulls. It was obvious there was no "spot" Clarissa wanted to show her, or actually Charles. She had just wanted to get him alone and it did not take much thought to figure out why. Charlie had to give the girl credit, she was a bold bit of fluff. Still, her boldness was likely to get them in trouble.

"Clarissa," she said at last, catching the girl's arm and drawing her to a halt. "We should head back."

"Oh no, the spot is just ahead," Clarissa murmured almost urgently, and Charlie shook her head with irritation. The girl was a worse liar than Beth.

"Enough," she snapped, turning back the way they had come. "It is obvious you do not know where you are going, and I have no wish to get lost in the woods today."

"Oh, but—" Clarissa caught her arm desperately, drawing her to a halt, pleading naked on her face until she glimpsed the irritation in Charlie's expression.

Once she did, she dropped her hold at once and peered down at the ground, unhappiness falling about her like a cloak. "I am sorry, Charles. 'Tis obvious you had no desire to walk with me."

Charlie shifted uncomfortably. Clarissa looked so pitiful. It was obvious she was desperate to be liked. Unfortunately, she seemed to have no idea how to go about it. Feeling most of her irritation slip away, Charlie sighed. "It is not that I would not enjoy a walk with you, Clarissa. But it is not proper for a young girl to be alone with a ... er ... young man," she explained uncomfortably, wondering how she got herself into these situations. "The man might take advantage. That is why parents insist on chaperones. As your mother should have," she added dryly.

"My mother couldn't be bothered," Clarissa muttered, then added earnestly, "And I was rather hoping you might take advantage. I would not mind. Really."

"What?" Charlie gasped, scandalized, and Clarissa blushed but nodded anyway.

"Truly. If you wish to kiss me I would not mind. I was rather hoping you might like to." On that note, she closed her eyes and tipped her head up in anticipation.

Charlie stared at the girl in dismay for a moment, then shook her head and started walking back through the woods toward the other picnickers. She had taken a mere few steps when Clarissa opened her eyes to see her escaping. Like a bulldog with a bone, she was after her at once.

"Wait, you cannot go back. Are you not going to kiss me? I—" Her words shuddered to a halt when Charlie whirled on her in a temper, her patience spent.

"Stop hounding me, you silly little girl. Whatever is the matter with you? Have you no pride at all? Or has that gone the way of the wind along with your sense? You shall be ruined ere you even have your coming out at this rate. Hoping I would take advantage of you, indeed! You are lucky I am not one of those fellows that are taking bets on seeing how many girls they can ruin this season, or you would be ruined already."

When Clarissa paled, tears springing to her eyes, Charlie suddenly felt an idiot. The silly chit was annoying, but she was also innocent and young and . . . Well, hell, that was reason enough for her foolishness. Truly, Charlie supposed most girls in the first bloom of womanhood were equally silly, it was just that usually they had someone to look out for them. Clarissa seemed sadly lacking in that area. Which, Charlie supposed, explained her seeming desperation for someone to pay attention to her.

Shifting uncomfortably as one big fat tear after another rolled down the girl's pale face, Charlie sighed and reached out to pat her awkwardly on the shoulder. "Do not cry, you are safe with me. I am not taking bets on ruining girls this season," she murmured a bit laconically, sighing when Clarissa suddenly threw herself against her chest, weeping copiously all over the new waistcoat the tailor had delivered only that morning.

"I am an idiot," Clarissa cried in self-loathing, and Charlie frowned.

"Nay. Nay, you are not an idiot, Clarissa. 'Tis just that you must be more careful; all men are not gentlemen. And you certainly must never suggest they take advantage of you." She shuddered inwardly at the thought of what would have happened if the girl had thrown herself at someone like the Jimmy and Freddy that Beth had been telling her about.

"That was stupid of me," Clarissa admitted with a sniffle. "I am always doing stupid things. It is why no one likes me."

Charlie scowled. "You are not stupid, Clarissa, and I am sure a great many people like you."

"Do you think so?" she asked hopefully.

"Well, certainly."

"Do you like me?"

Charlie forced a smile when Clarissa pulled away to peer up at her. "Of course."

"Then you may kiss me." So saying, she tipped her head up once more, lips puckered and eyes squinted closed.

Charlie pushed her away at once. "You have not heard a word I said!"

Clarissa's eyes blinked open at once. "Aye, I did, and you said I was safe with you, so why can you not kiss me? You said you liked me, Charles!"

Charlie sighed at her reasoning unhappily, then, for want of a better excuse, muttered, "There is such a thing as being too enthusiastic, you know."

Clarissa peered at her uncertainly, but Charlie wasn't too concerned. It seemed to her that she had struck on a way to help keep Clarissa safe and get the girl to leave her alone at the same time. "Truly," she averred, nodding her head. "Think of a fox hunt. The fox is released to run and hide and the hunters chase after him. The hunters chase because the fox runs. Sometimes they will chase for hours and hours.

The longer the chase, the more exciting the victory when the animal is caught. Is this not so?"

"Aye," she agreed uncertainly.

"And were the fox not to run at all, but to simply stand there and allow itself to be caught, where would be the sense in the hunt? It would be no fun, would it?"

"No, I suppose not."

"Well, there you are then." She nodded firmly, sure she had explained it so that the girl understood.

"So, you are saying that you refuse to kiss me and do your best to avoid me to keep me chasing you?"

Charlie blinked at that, her mouth dropping open briefly before she gasped, "Nay! Good Lord, you are impossible. *You* are the fox."

"But I am not running."

Charlie rolled her eyes and took a deep breath before gritting out, "That is the point. If you wish people to chase you, you should be running in the other direction."

"But I do not wish for people to chase me. I just want *you* to *like* me."

Charlie sighed at that, wondering what unlucky fates had decided she should be Charles today and not Beth. "Clarissa, my dear. Men, such as . . . er . . . myself, prefer a chase. It is more interesting and . . . er . . . exciting. We like to"—she shrugged helplessly—"chase."

Clarissa hesitated, then asked, "You mean to say that were I to run, you would give chase?"

"Aye."

"And you would like that?'

"Aye."

"Well . . ." She shook her head unhappily, then

straightened her shoulders and sighed resolutely. "If 'tis what you wish, Charles." Pausing, she glanced consideringly at the bush that surrounded them, then glanced back. "Which direction shall I run in?"

Charlie rolled her eyes and groaned. "Clarissa. I was using a metaphor."

"A metaphor?"

"An example," Charlie explained impatiently. "I do not truly wish to dash about the woods after you. I am saying you must pretend that you do not care for me."

She blinked in dismay. "But I *do* like you."

"I know that, but you should pretend that you do not. You should ignore me, give me the cut direct, do whatever you think necessary to convince me you are not the least bit interested in me."

"But what will you be doing while I am ignoring you?"

"Me? I—Well, I shall be admiring you from afar."

"From afar?"

She did not look the least pleased with the idea and seemed about to protest, so Charlie blurted out, " 'Tis all the rage. It's considered most romantic."

"Romantic?" She perked up at that.

"Aye, I shall write love poetry about my broken heart."

"And send them to me?" she asked excitedly, bringing a frown to Charlie's face.

"Nay. I am no good at poetry. They shall be horrible and morbid, so I shall crumple them up, throw them into the fire, and suffer most horribly."

"Suffer?" she asked in alarm. "Oh, Charles I do not wish you to suffer."

"Our parish priest says suffering is good for the soul," Charlie told her firmly, taking the girl's arm to lead her back in the direction from which they had come.

"Oh," she murmured as they paused on the edge of the woods. "Well, if you think this is for the best."

"It is definitely for the best," Charlie assured her laconically, then added, "And you must promise me that you shall stay away from anyone named Jimmy or Freddy."

"As you wish, Charles," she murmured dutifully.

"Good girl," Charlie muttered, peering through the bushes at the people beyond. "No one appears to be looking now. You go on back to the picnic. I shall wait a moment, then follow so as not to attract talk."

"Yes, Charles." Turning, she stepped into the clearing.

Charlie watched her go with a sigh of relief, then moved to lean against the trunk of a tree and wait the appropriate amount of time necessary before returning herself.

Chapter 9

RADCLIFFE moved through the picnickers, his gaze searching the laughing, chatting people for Charles. He had not seen the boy for quite some time and was beginning to worry. More than he really should, he realized on a sigh and shook his head at his own behavior.

As much as he told himself he should concentrate on the sister and avoid the boy altogether, he could not help himself. The moment Charles had traipsed into the breakfast room that morning and beamed a cheerful smile at him, he had realized how impossible the task would be. There was just something magnetic about the boy. Endearing even. He had enjoyed a rousing conversation with the lad at the table about the current political situation and laughed heartily at his wit. That was not so bad, but when their hands had met as they both reached for the marmalade at the same time, Radcliffe had felt a shock of awareness run through him that had sat him back in his seat with dismay.

It was most distressing. One day he found himself taking advantage of the sister who was supposed to be under his protection and the next he was feeling things for the brother that he had never felt for any member of the male sex in his life. It was all beyond his understanding, and he had decided that it would simply be best if he kept his distance as much as he could from the twins. And he truly would have given both brother and sister a wide berth today had he not already agreed to take them on this picnic. Still, he had managed to avoid them nicely up until now, leaving them in the company of the other young men and women that had been invited on this picnic and placing himself with the older set. He would still be there, talking economics and politics, had Charles not gone missing, he thought with irritation as he reached the spot where Beth stood chatting amicably with Tomas and Clarissa Mowbray.

"Where is Charles?" he asked without preamble, and the threesome turned in surprise at his interruption.

"Charles?" Beth repeated blankly, then glanced about. "Oh, well . . . He was here not long ago, he must have—"

"He went for a walk in the woods."

Radcliffe glanced sharply at the young Mowbray girl when she blurted out that answer, and she immediately blushed guiltily under his gaze. "Where?" he demanded.

"In the woods. He . . . umm, wished to get away from the crowd for a bit. No doubt he shall return shortly."

Radcliffe frowned, considering whether it was necessary for him to hunt the boy down, then sighed unhappily. It seemed the wiser thing to do. The lad was in his care, after all. Besides, after the fiasco at Aggie's he did not trust the boy to have the sense of a gnat. No one else he knew could have ended up tied to the bedposts by a whip-brandishing old whore. The boy, he thought to himself, may very well be lost.

Charlie cursed and grabbed at the wig on her head as another branch caught at it, then released her hold on the item to swat at a bug buzzing near her face. She had never been much of an outdoors sort. Truly, as boring as the picnic had proven to be up to now, she would much rather be back in the clearing, seated at a temporary table, dining on squab and pigeon pie than struggling her way through this thick under-brush headed for heaven knew where. And she certainly would have been, had she not heard a distressed cry just as she'd been about to reenter the clearing. Charlie could not ignore such obvious fear, even when it was that of an animal, and when the cry came again, she had given up the idea of returning to the picnic and started in the direction from which the cries appeared to be coming. They had led her away from the picnic, but closer to the river's edge, she realized as she set her foot down and found it sinking in spongy, damp ground.

Pausing, she stepped back, frowning at the damage to her shoe, then glared at the branches of the bush before her and continued forward once more as the whining became a panicked sort of squealing, whim-pering, and mewling. After a moment the frantic cries were suddenly muffled and Charlie stiffened, the si-lencing of the sound alarming her more than the ac-tual squeals had. Her throat tight with anxiety,

Charlie lunged through the brush and nearly stumbled to her knees in surprise when the undergrowth gave way abruptly to another clearing. This one was much smaller than the first and held a leathery-faced farmer who was in the process of tossing a squirming sack into the river.

"Nay!" she cried in alarm, but it was too late, the sack was already tumbling through the air toward the water. Without thinking about it, Charlie sped forward, hurtling into the water after the bag. She was quick on land, but the water seemed to drag at her feet, making each step an effort. Still she continued determinedly forward, a frustrated curse slipping from her lips as the sack dropped into the water some ten feet in front of her and immediately sank below the surface, the river swallowing it up, silencing the crazed mewlings the sack emitted.

It seemed like hours to Charlie, but was probably only seconds as she waded to where the sack had landed. Unconcerned that she was soaking herself and ruining a brand-new suit, she bent forward to feel about for it. Relief coursed through her as the top of the sack brushed against her fingers and she was able to grasp it, tugging it quickly out of the water. Holding it aloft, she turned and began to wade out of the water, chanting a prayer under her breath that she had been quick enough.

Reaching the shore, she dropped to her knees on the soft turf, ignoring the farmer who was moving closer as she quickly worked at the knot holding the top of the sack closed until it gave. She tugged the bag open and peered fearfully inside, gasping at the handful of soaking, silky, dark brown puppies that lay inside. She reached quickly in for the top pup, catching him by his back paws and lifting him out of the sack. She had barely moved him clear of the sack when his upside-down position moved him to retch up the water he had swallowed.

Murmuring soothingly, Charlie laid him on the grass and quickly grabbed up the next pup, this time giving a little pat and shake to help urge him on when the pup did not immediately toss up the river water as the first had. Once her urgings had worked, she set the pup aside and reached for the next in the sack. She repeated the action six more times and managed to save six of the eight puppies. The last two were beyond help and no amount of effort on her part would revive them. Giving up on the last pup, Charlie set him by the first one that had died and sighed unhappily. She stiffened when the farmer, who had stood silently by throughout, shifted and spat on the ground near the two corpses.

"Aye, well, them two's beyond help, but 'twas a fine attempt jest the same, m'lord."

Eyes narrowing to slits, she raised her head slowly and glared at the man, taking in his sun-baked skin, jowly cheeks, and the gray peppering his red hair.

"An' sure enef it was, m'lord. A fine effort. A mighty fine rescue iffen I do say so. Ye saved six out o' the eight of 'em. Now, let's see, that'd be . . . Well, I guess a groat would about cover it, seeing as how there's only six of 'em."

Charlie shook her head in bewilderment. "What?" she asked, glancing distractedly down as one of the six pups she had been able to save struggled weakly to its feet and shifted closer to her before collapsing onto its belly and settling down to some serious licking of her fingers as if in gratitude.

"For the pups," he explained as if to a simpleton, drawing her gaze back to his solemn face. "You rescuing them an' all, I figured on yer wantin' to buy 'em."

"Buy them?" she repeated in disbelief. "Are you mad?"

One rust and gray eyebrow arched at that. "Yer not wantin' to buy them?"

When Charlie merely glared at him, fury and indignation making it impossible to speak, he shrugged and stooped to snatch up the bag she had discarded. "Well, what'd ye go to all this trouble fer then? Ye jest made more work fer me. Now I'll be havin' to drown 'em again." So saying, he scooped up the pup who had been licking her fingers and plopped him back in the bag.

"The devil you will!" Charlie roared and made a grab for the bag.

Radcliffe had gone quite a distance with no sign of Charles and had just decided Clarissa had been mistaken when a string of curses and shouts broke out from the woods ahead. He picked up his pace and soon found himself stepping into a clearing where a startling sight met his eyes. At first he merely stood gaping at Charles and a burly farmer playing tug of war with a squirming sack. The size of the farmer foretold who the winner of the battle would be, and Radcliffe wasn't the least surprised when the lad's hands lost their grip on the sack and he tumbled onto his behind in the damp grass. Radcliffe's mild amusement turned to shock when the farmer then bent to grab up some puppies, and Charles regained his feet and launched himself onto the man's back.

Roaring in surprise and pain as Charles grabbed up handfuls of the man's hair and tugged viciously, the farmer dropped the bag and the pups and straightened abruptly, swatting at the boy as if he were a swarm of bees on his back. Charles deftly avoided the first hand that swatted at him, but the second one caught him upside of his head. The boy released a shriek of pain, but held determinedly on to his position.

The blow had more effect on Radcliffe, however, who launched forward, bellowing, "What the devil goes on here?"

The twosome froze. The farmer stilled in mid-blow and glanced guiltily toward him, while Charles heaved a sigh of relief and swiftly slid from the man's back.

"Radcliffe," the lad gasped and took a step toward him, his relief obvious. He seemed to catch himself then, and glanced from Radcliffe to the farmer, then down at the squirming bag at his feet. Distressed yowls came muffled from inside it.

"What is going on here, Charles?" Radcliffe asked as the lad bent to open the sack and scoop out a furry bundle from inside.

"Leave my dogs alone," the farmer growled as Charles quickly began snatching up the pups nearest.

"Yours!" he snapped back. "You threw them away."

"Aye. And I'll be doing so again should ye not pay for 'em!"

"The devil you will!" Charles snarled and glared at the man.

"The devil I *won't!*" The brute moved toward the lad then and the boy danced quickly behind Radcliffe, struggling to hold on to the four squirming bodies he had managed to gather. The farmer stopped at once, apparently unwilling to accost a member of the nobility that was not attacking him. Suddenly, frustration crested on the man's face, and he whirled and moved to snatch up one of the two remaining pups. Lifting the animal, he held the body in one beefy hand and took the head with the other.

"No!" Charles shrieked, stepping out from behind Radcliffe when the farmer made as if to break the poor animal's neck. The man paused and arched an eyebrow in enquiry, and Charles turned to glare at Radcliffe, pleading, "Do something!"

Sighing, Radcliffe glanced from his annoying charge to the farmer, then back. "How can I do anything when I do not know what is happening?"

"Can you not tell? Good God! This, this *man*—"

Radcliffe's eyebrows rose at the way the word was said and nearly laughed since the boy was insulting his own sex, but managed to restrain himself as the lad continued.

"—tied these poor creatures in a sack and tossed them into the river to drown. I rescued them and managed to revive six out of the eight of them. Now he expects me to pay for the six who lived or he will throw them back into the water. Tell him he cannot do that. Tell him." Charles turned to glare at the farmer with an obvious combination of satisfaction and spite, nodding with grim triumph as he awaited Radcliffe's proclamation. That triumph died, transformed into dismay when Radcliffe finally spoke.

"I am afraid he can."

"What?"

"They are his dogs," he answered solemnly.

"His? But he threw them away . . . to drown. He tried to kill them. They would be dead now but for me. I—I found them."

"They are still his to do with as he wishes," Radcliffe sighed, feeling as if he were letting the lad down by admitting such, and not liking it very much at all.

"There ye are, then." The farmer's barrel chest puffed up with importance. "So, either ye'll be paying me sixpence for the beasties or I'll be breaking this one here's neck and drowning the rest."

"Sixpence! A minute ago it was a groat."

"That was afore ye attacked me."

The boy glared at the man briefly, then set the squirming mass of puppies down and began digging through the pockets of his jacket, frowning when they came up empty. "I must have lost my money in the water. Pay the man, Radcliffe."

He raised his eyebrows at the order, and the boy grimaced. "You know I am good for it."

Heaving a sigh, Radcliffe dug out a small sack of coins and withdrew a silver one which he handed to the man. The farmer's fierce scowl gave way to a beaming smile as he accepted it. Then he handed Radcliffe the pup he had been holding, gave a slight nod, bent to snatch up the sack still holding the two dead pups, and turned to saunter away.

Radcliffe watched the man swagger off into the trees with distaste, then saw Charles sigh and glance down at the damp puppies that were presently climbing all over each other in an attempt to crawl up his sodden pant legs and gain his attention.

"Poor darlings," Charles murmured, bending to scoop up two more of them. " 'Tis all right. That nasty old man won't hurt you anymore," the lad assured them, cuddling them close to his face, then he caught the raised eyebrows Radcliffe was giving him. Frowning at him slightly as if his behavior were all Radcliffe's fault, Charles glanced toward the two pups still on the ground, then back to him with arched eyebrows. "Do you suppose you could pick up those two?"

Radcliffe blinked at that. "Whatever for?"

"Well, I can hardly carry all six of them by myself, can I?"

His eyebrows drew down with unpleasant suspicion. "Why would you want to, anyway? You do not plan to keep those mutts, do you?"

"What else did you think I would do?" the boy asked with open amazement. "I can hardly leave them here for that farmer to kill later."

"Well, you are certainly not bringing them back to my home," Radcliffe said with a snort.

"My lord." Stokes's smile of greeting as he hurried down the hall toward the open front door two hours later turned into a gasp of surprise as six little brown fur-balls suddenly erupted around his feet. Yipping excitedly, they flew past Radcliffe, dashing wildly if a bit clumsily every which way into the entry, legs flying out from beneath them on the polished marble floor as they tried to sniff everything at once.

His mouth was still agape a moment later as each

and every one of the creatures suddenly froze. Tails stiff and quivering excitedly, they lifted their noses upward and sniffed the air briefly, then made a mad dash down the hall toward the kitchens.

"Oh, no you don't!" Charlie cried, leaping past a pained looking Radcliffe and charging after the pups, scooping one after another up into her arms. She grabbed up the last one just as it reached the kitchen door. Turning then with the squirming bundle of bodies caught awkwardly in her arms, she started back down the hall, relieved when a laughing Beth hurried into the house and to Charlie's side to assist her with them.

"Poor darlings." Beth laughed, taking three of them and cuddling them against her chest. "They must be hungry again."

"I do not know how that is possible," Radcliffe sniffed, irritation marring his expression as he pushed the door closed with a decided crash. "They acted more like pigs than puppies at the picnic. After all the food they ate there, they should be full for a week."

Charlie rolled her eyes at that and Beth laughed. "Hardly, my lord. They were adorable at the picnic. Quite a hit. Why, every woman in attendance descended on you and Charlie when you came out of the woods with the little wonders. They considered both of you to be quite the heroes, once the story of how you rescued them unfolded."

Charlie's lips quirked at Radcliffe's disgruntled expression as he finished removing his gloves and slapped them against his butler's chest. The action finally startled the servant out of his stunned state. He closed his mouth and quickly caught the gloves, then accepted the hat Radcliffe shoved at him.

Radcliffe had not stuck long to his refusal to take the pups home with them. What else could he do? They could hardly leave them there in the clearing to be killed. When Charlie had pointed that out to him and left the problem as to what to do with the animals up to him, he had quickly realized there was little other solution but to return home with them . . . temporarily. He had made that as clear as glass. This was a temporary situation and one he did not appreciate. Charlie was to find a home for the beasts as quickly as possible. And they were not to be allowed to make a nuisance of themselves.

Charlie had promised to keep the pups in her room and out of the way until she found them homes, then happily helped him cart the little fur-balls back through the woods to the picnic. As Beth said, the women in the party had descended on them at once when they had reappeared with the pups, cooing and sighing over the furry little monsters. Charlie had been more than aware of Radcliffe's discomfort under the avalanche of attention and had not been surprised when he had extricated himself from the crowd and slipped off to join a group of older men to watch the foofaraw from a safe distance, leaving Charlie to deal with the attention and the puppies both.

Not that she'd had much difficulty with the puppies. She'd had more than enough volunteers to aid in minding and feeding the little creatures. In fact, the other "ladies" had nearly come to blows as they'd fought over who got to hold, pet, and feed them. The pups had been fed the choicest bits of squab and dishes of pigeon pie by every female there. Still, they were puppies. Energetic, happy, bounding everywhere to the delight of the picnic guests, and they now appeared already to be eager for more food.

"Come along, Beth. Let us take them upstairs, then raid the kitchen for them."

Shaking his head in disgust, Radcliffe turned on his heel and strode into the library, no doubt headed for the bottle of port that waited there, Charlie thought with amusement. She led Beth upstairs.

"Oh, my lady. Just look at the gown Madame Decalle sent today," Bessie cried excitedly, holding up the gown she had just unpacked as Beth led Charlie into "Elizabeth's" room. "It arrived only moments ago. Is it not lovely?"

Beth paused in the door, three puppies in her arms and her eyes wide with a combination of dismay and alarm as she stared at the gossamer gown.

Shoving the door closed with one foot, Charlie pushed past her stunned sister and set the puppies she held on the floor before walking over to survey the dress with a smile. "It *is* lovely, is it not, Bessie?" she murmured, smugly, then glanced toward Beth with amusement. "Faith, Beth, you have amazing taste," she complimented, laughter in her eyes as her sister stared at the burgundy gown.

Beth had a preference for prim pastels and classic cuts. And as Beth had always been the one to stand as model for their gowns, Charlie had allowed her to choose the styles. They had spent the past several years dressed in pink, baby blue, white, and cream gowns with necklines that could be called nothing less than respectable.

Charlie's taste, in comparison, was much more

dramatic. Had she been concerned with fashion and the like through those years, she would have leaned more toward deeper, more vibrant colors, and far more daring styles. Of course, she had not been concerned. Now that they were on the marriage market, however, it seemed to her that it was time to "dress the window." The gown she had chosen was in the height of fashion, as low a décolletage as could be worn and still be thought respectable, and a jaunty little hat to top it off. Simple, stylish and sexy as the devil, she hoped. It was obvious to her that Beth was taken aback at the gown.

"Charlie! How could you—"

"Bessie?" Charlie interrupted. "Please go down and see if cook has anything for the puppies to eat. And a bowl of milk for them, too," she added as the maid set the gown down and moved to leave the room.

"What have you done?" Beth whispered once the door had closed behind the girl, moving to stand by the bed to gape down at the gown.

Charlie shrugged with unconcern. "I chose clothes."

"Are they all like this?"

"Of course not. They are all different styles and colors."

"What colors?"

Charlie's eyebrows rose at the menace in Beth's voice. "Emerald green, crimson—"

"Crimson!" Beth dropped onto the bed, her hands raising to cover her face. "Oh, God!" She pulled her hands away to stare at her sister in horror. "Is this punishment for making you stand for the measuring?"

"No, of course not!" Charlie threw her sister a dirty look, then spread the gown out. "Really, Beth. Just look at it. It is lovely. How can you think it a punishment? Why, 'tis a beautiful cut, the color vibrant, the sheen to the material lovely."

" 'Tis loud."

"Nonsense!" Charlie glowered at her for the insult to her taste, then sighed. "Look, if you must know, I have always found your taste in gowns rather . . . well, to be honest, quite dull."

"Dull!" Beth stood up, dismay on her face.

"Yes. All those pale pastels that melt into nothingness and high décolletage." She wrinkled her nose. "They were all rather tedious, you know."

Her sister's mouth worked briefly, then snapped shut and she suddenly stood straight and tall, her expression cold. "I see. Well. I am sorry to have burdened you with my *tedious* taste all these years."

Charlie smiled faintly. "It was not a burden, Beth. Had that been so, I would have chosen my own gowns long ago."

"Why did you not?"

Shrugging, Charlie touched the burgundy gown reverently, a pleased smile touching her lips at how well her choice had turned out. She answered distractedly, "There seemed little reason to bother. It was not as if anyone actually saw me in them out in the country."

At her sister's outraged gasp, she glanced at her sharply, suddenly recognizing the insult she had dealt. She shook her head at once. "Now, Beth, do not take it so. 'Tis just that our tastes differ somewhat."

"You are right, of course. I just never realized how

much." Her mouth firming, Beth peered at the gown. "I cannot wear this, Charlie. I would not feel comfortable."

"Whyever not? Our coloring is perfect for burgundy."

"Perhaps in your opinion, but I prefer the pastels. Besides, I can tell from just looking at it that the neckline is indecently low."

" 'Tis not indecent. 'Tis all the rage."

"Mayhap, but I could not possibly wear it. I would feel uncomfortable. On display. I prefer a more understated style with nice—"

"Pastels," Charlie finished for her dryly. "Beth, you are on the marriage market now. 'Tis no time to play the shrinking violet, unless you wish to be a wallflower. You must display your wares."

"I cannot do it. 'Tis not my style. I will not wear it."

Before Charlie could think of what to say to that, Bessie returned carrying a silver salver. The excitement on the young girl's face distracted both sisters from their discussion.

"You will never believe it," the girl cried, setting the tray down and grabbing a handful of paper scraps off of it to rush to them. "Look, just look! They are invitations to balls and such. Master Stokes says that a couple of them came this morning, but that the door knocker has been banging nonstop since ye returned from the picnic."

"This one is for a ball at the Hardings'. Tonight!" Beth cried, opening one. "They were at the theater last night, Charlie. Tomas pointed them out to me."

Smiling at her sister's excitement, Charlie took out one of the invitations to read. "The Seawoods are having a ball tomorrow evening and we are invited," Charlie murmured with a small perplexed frown. "Who are the Seawoods?"

"They were at the picnic today. Their daughter, Lily, was one of the women helping you with the dogs," Beth answered distractedly as she read another invitation. "Oh look, the Wullcotts! They were at the picnic too. And here is one from the Fetterleys. Oh, Charlie, we are a success! We shall be married in no time."

"*You* shall," Charlie corrected quickly.

"Oh, aye." Beth glanced self-consciously at Bessie, then away.

Picking up another invitation, Charlie opened it, then froze.

"What is it?" Beth asked, aware of her reaction at once.

"Bessie, please arrange for a bath to be brought up for each of us, and ask cook to prepare an early dinner."

"Aye, sir." Bobbing, the girl left the room and Charlie handed the note she had opened to Beth.

"'I know who you are,'" Beth read with dismay. "'If you do not want me to tell, you will have to pay. Bring—' My God!" She lifted horrified eyes to Charlie. "What are we going to do?"

Standing, Charlie paced to the window and peered blindly out. She stayed like that for a moment, then suddenly turned back. "We are going to the Hardings' ball tonight. Then tomorrow, I shall see Mr. Silverpot to cash in some more of Mother's jewels. Tomorrow night you shall have Radcliffe escort you to the Seawoods' ball. I shall claim to be too tired to attend and will meet this person to pay them off."

Beth bit her lip. "Charlie, I do not like the idea of your meeting this person alone. It could be dangerous."

"Aye, but one of us has to keep Radcliffe busy," Charlie pointed out with a sigh.

"Well . . ." Standing, Beth moved to the connecting door of the rooms. "I suppose I should start getting ready. You said the tailor sent some new clothes around?"

Charlie's eyebrows rose. "Aye. Did you not wish to be Elizabeth tonight?"

Beth shrugged, but her gaze was annoyed as it fell upon the burgundy gown. "Nay. You have to be Charles tomorrow night, so you should be Elizabeth this evening."

Chapter 10

CHARLIE sank back into the carriage seat with a weary sigh. This night had been an unmitigated disaster. The Hardings' ball, her first actual social event as a female, had gone over like a stone. She had not danced with anyone but Radcliffe and Tomas Mowbray. She had not even had a chance to meet prospective husbands. Tomas had hovered over her like a love-sick calf, and Radcliffe had behaved like some dowager aunt guarding her virginity and glowering at any male who came near her, including an oblivious Tomas. Meanwhile, Beth/Charles had fluttered about anxiously, babbling away to Tomas.

Charlie had suffered the ridiculous charade until her head and feet both ached. And that was the excuse she had used to end the farce: her aching feet and head. Immediately solicitous, Radcliffe had insisted on taking her home. Beth/Charles had shown enough reluctance to leave that Tomas had suggested that she stay and he would drop her off later. Nodding, Radcliffe had ushered the woman he thought was Elizabeth out of the ballroom.

The carriage hit a rut in the road, and Charlie

grabbed for something to hold on to as she was jostled against Radcliffe's side.

"Are you all right?"

Charlie glanced up at him through the dim interior of the carriage, slightly startled by the husky sound of his voice. She was even more startled by the sudden intensity of his eyes as he looked down at her. Swallowing, she licked her lips nervously and began to nod, only to pause self-consciously when his gaze dropped to her lips with interest.

Dropping her head shyly, she peered blindly at her hand for a moment, then realized that it was clutching his thigh. She pulled it away with dismay. "Oh! I am sorry, my lord. I did not mean to—"

" 'Tis all right," he assured her gently. "I know it was not on purpose. How is your head?"

"Muzzy," she murmured distractedly, wondering why her hand had begun to tingle the moment she'd realized where she had placed it while searching for something sturdy to hold on to.

"Muzzy?" Concern filling his voice, he slid a finger beneath her chin to lift her face up for his inspection. "Is your headache worse?"

"Nay," she admitted on a sigh, then asked plaintively, "Is it hot in here?"

"Nay. 'Tis a cool evening." He was beginning to frown now, anxiety drawing small lines on his forehead as he raised a hand to feel hers. "Mayhap you are coming down with something."

Charlie was beginning to suspect her problem had nothing to do with a true illness. She seemed to be one huge ball of sensitivity. She was very aware of his nearness, could feel the pressure of his leg along her own, his breath on her face, the scent of him in her nose, and the memory of their shared kiss when last she'd played Beth was now crowding her mind. Feeling herself sway slightly toward him, she drew herself up and pulled back as far as the carriage wall would allow.

"These carriages are very small, are they not?" she asked in a high, strained voice.

Radcliffe blinked, dragging his gaze away from her chest where it had dropped when she had suddenly leaned back.

"Small?" He glanced around the dark interior of the hack. They hit another rut, and Charlie would have bounced right onto the floor if Radcliffe had not caught her and drawn her protectively against his chest. When she raised her head to peer at him, he bent to kiss her.

Charlie sighed as his mouth claimed hers. Her headache was suddenly gone, her feet no longer hurt. The entire night seemed somehow less of a miserable failure than it had been as his mouth opened passionately over hers. Slipping her arms up around his neck, she pressed eagerly forward, her mouth opening in welcome, her toes curling inside her slippers. Little shivers and shudders of pleasure ran through her as his hands slid down her back, molding her to him. His lips left hers to search out her ear, and she gave a keening cry of surprised excitement before his attention and lips slid down to her neck.

"Oh, Radcliffe, please," she whispered, her hands sliding from his head where she had been clutching his hair, down to clasp his shoulders convulsively as he caught and cupped her breasts through her gown.

His response was to shift her so that she straddled him on the bench seat. She was now slightly above him, her breasts at face level, and he took advantage of that, nibbling the flesh that was revealed by the low-cut gown, nudging the gown lower until his teeth could gently graze one nipple.

Charlie gave a start, her body jerking slightly at the unbearable sensation, a moan slipping from her lips as she arched in his arms. She was just becoming aware of his hands sliding up her legs beneath her skirt when the carriage came to a shuddering halt. Unprepared for the small jolt, Charlie found herself tumbling from his lap. She landed on the opposite bench with a grunt of surprise. They both stared at each other blankly, then Radcliffe peered out the window and cursed. Charlie knew at once that they were home. She also became aware suddenly of the sight she must be with her clothing in disarray and one bare breast peeking out from her gown. Shuddering with embarrassment now, she quickly straightened her gown, studiously avoiding looking at Radcliffe as she did. She had just finished putting herself back in order when he reached out and caught her hand.

Charlie glanced up guiltily, surprised to see that same expression on his face. "I am sorry, Elizabeth. I have behaved abominably. You are under my protection and I have taken advantage of my position. I do not know what came over me."

Charlie would have felt better at once, thought him sweet, and taken her share of the blame . . . had he not called her Beth. That just managed to put the icing on the cake of her humiliation. She was reminded that he really had not been kissing her at all.

It was Beth he had thought he was kissing. It was Beth he wanted.

Closing her eyes briefly, she drew herself up, nodded stiffly, then hurried out of the carriage. She was in the house and racing up the stairs before Radcliffe had even managed to get out and close the carriage door.

It was a sloppy lick of her cheek that awoke Charlie in the morning. Blinking, she peered at the grinning puppy perched with his front paws on her cheek and his back paws on her chest, a gurgling laugh slipping from her lips as he lost his purchase and tumbled into the curve of her neck and shoulder. Reaching her hand up awkwardly, she gave him a pat, then glanced down the length of her body to see the other five furballs scampering and playing over the blanket across her legs.

Chuckling softly, Charlie sat up, slid her feet out from under them, and shifted to sit on the edge of the bed, petting the half-dozen darlings as they converged on her, yipping and licking at her hands and wrists.

"Good morning to all of you, too," she murmured, then stood and moved to the adjoining door to "Charles's" room. "Let's go see if Beth is up yet."

Opening the door, she watched the six little bodies scamper through, then followed, reaching the bedside as they leapt onto it and threw themselves excitedly onto a sleeping Beth. The other girl came awake with a miserable groan.

"Oh no, not yet. It cannot be morning yet." Beth clasped her head desperately between her hands and turned her face into the pillow.

"I take it you got in late last night," Charlie laughed, crawling into bed beside her sister and sitting with her back against the headboard. When Beth's only response was an unintelligible mumble, Charlie nudged her shoulder.

"Just let me die," Beth begged into the pillow. "I think I broke my head."

Charlie blinked at that. "Broke your head?" Grabbing her arm, she pulled her sister onto her back, eyebrows rising at the sight she made. Her face was pale, her eyes red-rimmed. "Did you drink a lot last night?"

"Aye. And stop yelling."

Charlie's eyebrows rose. She had not been yelling, but she was beginning to gather that while she herself had apparently inherited her father's ability to drink to excess without paying for it the next day, Beth had inherited Uncle Henry's nasty problem of hangovers.

"What else did you do?" she asked in an almost-whisper.

"Ask me later," Beth groused, dragging the pillow over her head again.

Charlie scowled impatiently at her back. "How much later?"

"This afternoon. I shall get up at noon, I promise. But, I did not get in until dawn. Let me sleep now."

Charlie hesitated for a moment, then sighed and took the pillow away. "I am afraid I cannot wait that long," she said regretfully. "I am to be Charles today. Remember? I shall need to know what I did last night in case Radcliffe asks, or I run into Tomas on the way to see Mr. Silverpot."

Beth stiffened at the jeweler's name, then sat up

with a grimace of mingled pain and resignation. "I had quite managed to put that out of my head," she admitted sadly, waiting until Charlie finished arranging her pillow against the headboard for her, then leaning back on it wearily. "Ask me what you need to know."

"How long did you stay at the Hardings' after we left?"

"We left right after you and went to the Kit Kat Club."

Charlie sucked in her breath. The Kit Kat Club? It seemed Beth had all the luck.

"We drank quite a bit and Tom told me that he was falling in love with you."

"Me?" Charlie gaped at her.

"Elizabeth," she clarified with a sigh.

"Oh, Beth! That's wonderful," Charlie cried, hugging her, then pulled back uncertainly at her sister's lack of response. "Is it not?"

"I do not know. I love him, but—" She gave her sister a tortured look. "But is it me he is falling in love with, or you?"

Charlie gave a laugh and hugged her again. "You goose! 'Tis you he loves. Last night was the first time that I have been Elizabeth around Tomas. You were Elizabeth in the carriage to London, at the theater, and at the picnic. And the two of you spent each occasion deep in conversation. Why, I hardly said two words to the man last night. It must be you he loves."

Beth brightened considerably at that, then sobered again. "He was quite jealous of Radcliffe last night, you know. I think he sensed that something was not quite right, but not knowing what else it could be, he blamed it on Radcliffe's attitude."

Charlie stilled. "You mean, you think he knew that I was not you?"

She nodded solemnly. "He said you were not yourself—I mean I was not—"

"I know what you mean," Charlie interrupted, a smile tugging at her lips. "Well, then it must be love."

"Do you think so?" she asked hopefully.

Charlie shrugged. "Mother and Father were the only ones who could ever tell us apart. No one else has ever been able to. Do you remember what Maman said when we asked her that time how it was that they always knew who was who?"

"Hmm. She said it was because they looked at us through the eyes of love, and the eyes of love never lie."

"Exactly. So Tomas must be looking through the eyes of love."

Beth fairly beamed at that. "Thank goodness Radcliffe acted so oddly last night. Otherwise Tomas might have delved deeper into the matter. Do you know why he behaved as he did?"

Charlie avoided her gaze for a moment, then sighed. "I think he was jealous."

Beth's eyes widened incredulously. "Jealous? Of what?"

"Over the way Tomas was fawning over you . . . me . . . Elizabeth. Beth, I think that he is falling in love with you, too."

When Beth merely stared at her blankly, Charlie shifted impatiently. "Well, surely you must have realized? I mean, he has been kissing you, too, has he not?"

"Nay!" She nearly shouted the word and Charlie blinked in surprise.

"He has not?"

"Nay. Never once. He has been a perfect gentleman with me. Why, almost uncle-ish in his attentions. He—" Her gaze zeroed in on Charlie. "He kissed you?"

She nodded slowly, her heart filling with glee that he had not kissed Beth.

"When? Last night?" Charlie's blush was answer enough for Beth, and her eyes widened. "Is that the only time?"

"Nay, he also kissed me the first time you played Charles."

"But Radcliffe was with me that day."

"It was when you came home. He joined me in the library and . . . kissed me."

"So both times that you have been me, he kissed you." Beth considered that briefly, then smiled. "Then he must be kissing *you*."

"I just said so, did I not?" Charlie muttered indignantly.

"Nay. I mean, he is only attracted to Elizabeth when *you* are her," she explained, and Charlie stiffened.

"Why do you say that?"

"Well, goodness, sister. He has had a dozen opportunities to kiss me as Elizabeth, and he has not even tried. And last night was the first time that he showed any sign of jealousy over Tomas. It must be you he is attracted to."

Charlie sucked her lower lip into her mouth and contemplated the matter briefly, then shook her head, afraid to believe something she was only now realizing that she wanted. Radcliffe. She had convinced herself that her feelings for him were amused indifference because she'd feared he was beyond her reach. Too sophisticated. Too handsome. Too marvelous. He would never be interested in a country bumpkin, and that was what she was. A member of the nobility, but a country-bumpkin member of nobility with a gambling drunk for an uncle who would sell her to her death for a couple of coins.

"You are wrong," Charlie said at last. "'Tis you, Beth. He loves you."

Beth frowned, opened her mouth to argue, then paused and crawled out of bed with a determined expression. "Well, I suppose we shall see soon enough."

Charlie eyed her warily. "And how will we see?"

"By how he reacts to me this morning." She crossed the room as she spoke, but paused at the door to peer back. "Do you need any help with your bindings?" When Charlie shook her head, she nodded. "Good, then I shall go ring Bessie and get dressed."

Charlie watched her go, then glanced at the moving blanket on the bed. Leaning down, she tugged it aside, freeing the dogs Beth had covered when she had tossed the blanket aside to get up. They immediately bounded around her with excited yips, and, despite herself, Charlie felt a smile tug at her lips. Then she forced herself to rise and begin to don the clothes of Charles.

Beth was dressed and securing her hair on top of her head when Charlie rejoined her, the puppies scampering about her feet as she went.

"I told Bessie we would take the puppies downstairs to her so that she could take them outside for a few moments," Beth commented, finishing with her hair.

"Good idea." Charlie scooped three of the mutts up, then waited as her sister gathered the other three.

"They are adorable, are they not?" Beth laughed as they all tried to climb up her bosom to lick her face as she followed Charlie into the hall.

"Aye," Charlie agreed, starting down the stairs. She was on the second last step when a gasp from Beth made her glance back. With her hands full of puppies, the girl had been unable to hold her skirt out of the way while traversing the stairs. Her foot had apparently tangled in her skirts and she was now tee-tering on the sixth step, alarmed.

Dropping the three puppies she held, Charlie started up the steps even as Beth dropped her three and reached wildly for something to save herself. Charlie was just in time to catch Beth as she tumbled forward. Grunting under the sudden impact, Charlie stumbled back, her foot coming down on nothing but air. Cry-ing out in alarm now herself, Charlie braced herself as they crashed to the floor . . . at Radcliffe's feet.

"Are you all right?" he asked, kneeling beside them with concern as Beth rolled off her sibling.

"Aye," Beth assured him quickly, then turned to her twin. "Oh, Charles. Are you all right? You did not hurt yourself, did you? I am so sorry. Thank you for catching me. You are not hurt, are you?"

"I am fine," Charlie murmured with a grimace, forcing herself to sit up. "Do not fuss. What about the puppies? We did not land on any of them, did we?"

They all glanced around now at the empty entry.

"Where did they—" Radcliffe's question died as cursing, shouting, and banging erupted from the kitchen.

"Oh, dear," Charlie muttered, jumping to her feet and rushing down the hallway with Beth and Radcliffe hard on her heels. The minute Charlie pushed the kitchen door open, six dark blurs whizzed past her, yipping for all they were worth as they raced down the hall. Cook was the next through the door, nearly knocking Charlie on her back again as he charged past, face purple with rage, a meat cleaver in hand, and cursing a blue streak as he hunted his quarry.

Grabbing for the door to keep her balance, Charlie glanced at Bessie as the girl hurried forward, followed by Stokes.

"I am sorry, my lord. 'Tis all my fault. I heard a cry from the hallway and started out of the kitchen to see what was amiss, but when I opened the door, the dogs came charging in. Cook tried to kick one and fell, sending breakfast flying everywhere. Then he grabbed the cleaver and started after them before Stokes or I could do anything to stop him." She gave this explanation as she and Stokes chased after Charlie, who had taken one look at the mess on the kitchen floor and headed after the furious cook. She found him in the salon, chasing the puppies around the sofa and waving his cleaver madly.

"Cook!" Radcliffe snapped, coming up behind Charles.

The man slid to a stop at once, but his furious expression remained as he whirled to face his employer. "They have ruined my breakfast! They are a nuisance. I will not have such goings-on." Pausing, he drew himself up staunchly. "Either they go . . . or I do!"

"Oh!" Beth cried, turning a pleading look to

Radcliffe as her twin moved forward to shepherd the pups a safe distance away before turning to peer at Radcliffe pleadingly as well.

Scowling, Radcliffe glanced from Charlie to the cook. "An ultimatum? Then 'tis you who goes, master cook," he announced firmly, eliciting a shocked gasp from the man.

"But, my lord, I have served you faithfully for several years now."

"You have served me *poorly* for several years now," Radcliffe corrected dryly. "You are the worst cook I have ever had. The only reason I put up with you for this long was because I was not here often enough to care and did not have the time to trouble with hiring a replacement. Howbeit, sirrah, your meals are bland, generally cold, and unsuitable to serve my guests. It has become obvious to me that you cannot perform your job. Good day to you."

Charlie watched wide-eyed as the man sputtered briefly, then turned and stormed down the hallway. She felt a brief pang of guilt, then caught the satisfied gleam in Stokes's eye as he watched the man go. She began to relax a little. The man was a rotten cook. And he had treated the staff horribly. This was for the best.

Holding her skirt out like a basket, Bessie began scooping puppies up into it, and Charlie moved quickly to help her.

"I am ever so sorry, my lord," the maid murmured, taking the two puppies Charlie had gathered and adding them to the other three in her skirt. " 'Tis all my fault."

"Nay, it is not," Charlie assured the girl firmly.

"Charles is right," Beth announced, collecting the

last puppy and joining them. "It sounds as if cook was a thoroughly nasty man. Besides, he would not have ruined breakfast had he not tried to kick one of the precious creatures. He got what he deserved. His meals really were rather bland. Radcliffe will do better with another cook."

They all glanced toward the doorway where the man had been, but he had slipped silently away. The click of the front door closing drew Charlie to the window in time to see him climb into his carriage. When she turned back to the room, Bessie was gone, taking the puppies with her.

"Was that Radcliffe leaving?" Beth asked.

"Aye," Charlie said thoughtfully, then headed for the door.

"Where are you going?"

Pausing at the door, she glanced about to be sure that no one was around to hear, then said, "Now seems the perfect time to accomplish that little *task* we talked about."

"Mr. Silverpot?" Beth whispered, eyes round as she hurried forward to clasp her hand anxiously. "Do you wish me to come with you?"

Charlie hesitated, then shook her head. "You look all done in. Why do you not return to bed and rest a while longer? I shan't be long."

Chapter 11

CHARLIE watched from her window as Radcliffe helped Beth into the carriage. She waited until he got in and it pulled away before dropping the curtain closed again and gathering the sack of coins Mr. Silverpot had given her that afternoon for a couple of her mother's jewels. The transaction had gone without a hitch. She had hired a hack to take her to the jeweler's, had been greeted warmly as "Charles," and been paid far more for the gems than she had expected.

Thanking the man, Charlie had headed right back to the townhouse to find Beth entertaining Tomas Mowbray in the salon. Radcliffe had arrived almost directly behind her and taken them all out to lunch. It was after lunch, while they had been walking in the park, that Charlie had begun to complain of weariness. When they had returned to the townhouse, she had announced herself far too weary to be bothered attending a ball that evening. She had waited just long enough to see Radcliffe accept that news and assure Beth that he would escort her, then Charlie had fled to her room to pace until Beth joined her.

She had spent the rest of the time between then and now helping Beth prepare for the ball and convincing her that all would be well. She would not get hurt during this endeavor. She would convince the blackmailer to leave them alone, at least until they had both found husbands and were safe. She would be careful.

Now, she repeated those same reassurances to herself as she sneaked out the front door of Radcliffe's townhouse and hired a hack.

Charlie alit from the carriage several streets later, paid the driver, then glanced about a bit nervously. This was not exactly a good area. The street was poorly lit, the people walking it unsavory.

Slipping her hand into her pocket, she clutched the sack of coins, hunched her shoulders, and started up the street. The instructions had said that she was to go to an alley next to a Madame Claude's confectionery. Charlie had had the driver drop her off a block before the place so that she might scout the area. She was not eager to enter a dark alley on her own and had hoped that the walk there would reassure her.

She was not reassured. If anything, having a closer look at the menacing, shabbily dressed men she was passing and the dilapidated state of the shops she walked by was making her extremely edgy.

Passing Madame Claude's, she reached the mouth of the alley and hesitated. It was extremely dark in there. And there was a most unpleasant odor emanating from it.

Biting her lip, Charlie peered into the darkness nervously, then took a deep breath, straightened her shoulders, and plunged into the alley. The first thing that overwhelmed her was the odor. It smelled as if something had crawled into one of the alley's dark corners and died. Covering her nose with distaste, she continued forward, peering carefully into the shadows, trying to ensure that she was not passing anyone who might come out from behind and jump her. She might as well not have bothered. It was impossible to penetrate the inky blackness around her.

"Hurry up, damn you."

Charlie stiffened at that husky whisper from ahead, eyes widening as she searched the black wall she faced. She had just spotted a slightly darker shape among the blackness when the voice hissed impatiently again. "Come on. Come on. We don't have all night."

Swallowing, she took several steps toward the shape, then paused to ask warily, "Is that you?"

There was no mistaking his disgust as the shape shifted impatiently. "Who else would it be, Charlotte? Now give me the damn money."

Charlie grimaced at her proper name. "How do I know you will not demand more? Or tell on us?"

"You do not. You will just have to take your chances."

Charlie scowled at the shape. He sounded educated. One of the nobility. A gentleman, she guessed, even though blackmailing and forcing a lady to meet him in this alley were hardly the actions of a gentleman. He was probably one of her uncle's mates. Which was worrisome. The last thing she and Beth needed was his informing their uncle of their whereabouts. She was trying to come up with a way to elicit a promise that he would not do so when the blackmailer suddenly shrank back into the darkness, whispering angrily, "I told you to come alone."

"I did," Charlie said with some surprise.

"Charles! Is that you?"

Gasping, she whirled toward the mouth of the alley, recognizing Radcliffe's backlit form at once. "What are you doing here?" she cried with alarm.

"More to the point, what are *you* doing here?" he snapped, starting up the alley toward her. "You are suppose to be at home resting."

"Get him out of here," the blackmailer hissed behind her.

"Good Lord! This alley smells." Pausing, Radcliffe tugged a handkerchief from his pocket, covered his nose, and continued forward.

"Go!" the voice from the darkness hissed, giving Charlie a shove forward.

Radcliffe grabbed her by the collar as she stumbled forward, then turned to drag her back out of the alley. "This is deplorable. Hanging about in alleyways. What did you do, spot me following you and duck in here to try to lose me?"

"Of course not," Charlie snapped, pulling free and straightening her collar before turning to glare at him. "And what are you doing following me?"

"Trying to keep you out of trouble."

"I am not *in* trouble."

An inelegant snort was his only response.

"My lord," Charlie got out between clenched teeth. "I am a full grown wo . . . er . . . man. I do not need a keeper."

"I fully agree, and if it were not for your sister, I would leave you to ruin yourself."

"What has my sister to do with this?"

"Did you really think I would allow you to gamble her money away?" When the lad stopped walking to peer at him blankly, Radcliffe stopped as well. "I saw Mr. Silverpot this afternoon, Charles. I know about the jewels you sold. I wasn't sure if Elizabeth knew what you were up to, so I wanted to confront you alone about it but did not get the chance. When you said you were feeling weary and wished to stay in and rest this evening, I decided our talk could wait until tomorrow."

Charlie arched one eyebrow at this. "What changed your mind?"

"Elizabeth."

Charlie stiffened. "Beth told you—"

"Nay. Nay. But she was so distracted and anxious on the way to the ball, I realized that something was amiss. I hurried home just in time to see you hail the hack. I had my driver follow you. As soon as I saw the hack drop you off, I realized what your plans were, and I will not allow it."

"Allow what exactly?" she asked curiously.

"I will not allow you to gamble away yours and Elizabeth's money," he snapped impatiently. "Now give them to me."

"Gamble the money away?" she murmured with bewilderment, ignoring the hand he held out for the coins. "How did you come to the conclusion that that was my intent?"

Radcliffe heaved a sigh of exasperation. "Charles, you had the driver drop you off right in front of a gaming hall."

"I did?" she asked with surprise. Charlie had not

been paying close attention to where she'd been dropped off, she'd been too busy watching the riffraff on the street.

"You know you did," Radcliffe snapped.

"But I did not go in," she argued.

"You must have seen the Radcliffe coach pull up as you alit," he said with a shrug.

"Ah . . . aye. I must have." A slow grin began to spread across her face. His explanation for this night's jaunt was far preferable to the truth, and while she could no longer pay the blackmailer tonight, she had no doubt he would arrange another meeting. The scoundrel could hardly hold *her* accountable for this night's failure. Especially since she was sure he had overheard every word of the discussion she and Radcliffe had just had.

"Well, you have found me out," she confessed eagerly now. "I suppose gambling is in my blood. Runs in the family. Ah, well, 'tis for the best that you stopped me, I suppose. . . . Let's go." Grabbing his arm, she urged him toward the mouth of the alley, eager to escape the fetid atmosphere.

"Just a moment." Radcliffe turned on her grimly and held out his hand.

"What?" She glanced warily from his hand to his face and back.

"The money."

"Oh." Her lips twisted with displeasure. "There is no need for that. I will not gamble it away now."

"The money, Charles," he repeated firmly and Charlie shifted impatiently.

"It is mine, Radcliffe."

"Yours and Beth's. Were you the only one involved,

I would let you gamble the coins away. But they are yours *and Elizabeth's*. Now, give them to me."

Her teeth ground together in frustration. "I shall give them to Beth."

"*I* shall give them to Beth." He pushed his hand out until it nearly touched her bound and vested chest.

Charlie glared at him resentfully, but dropped the sack of coins into his hand. "There. Can we go now?"

"Not quite," he announced calmly, bringing her to a halt when she would have whirled on her heel and stormed out of the alley. Reaching into the sack, Radcliffe retrieved a couple of coins and handed them to Charles, then stowed the sack in his pocket.

"What are these for?" she asked dryly.

"For you to use in the gaming hall. Since you are so determined to go, I shall take you. But," he added when her eyes widened in surprise, "that is all you shall play with. Once those are lost, you are done. I only hope this will teach you what a foolish venture gambling really is and dissuade you from frittering your inheritance away in such a manner."

Charlie gaped at him as he turned to leave the alley, then hurried after him. "You are taking me to a gaming hall?"

"Much against my better judgment, aye."

Charlie sighed at this news. She had failed to pay the blackmailer, so still had that to worry about. Worse yet, Radcliffe had confiscated the payoff and she would have to replace it. Obviously, Mr. Silverpot could not be trusted to keep his mouth shut, so they would have to find another jeweler. Which was risky. The new jeweler could rob them blind. On top of that, she had been tense and anxious since receiving the blackmailer's letter, then terrified and nervous to-night on her escapade, and simply wasn't in the mood for a gaming hall tonight. But she could hardly say all that and did not wish to make Radcliffe suspicious, so she would have to humor him and go.

Radcliffe paused suddenly and Charlie glanced up to see that they had retraced her route along the block and now stood at the entrance to the hall. Their way was blocked by a rather large, bald, muscular looking man. Arms crossed, he was shaking his head at a tall woman in rather poor quality but clean, plain clothes who stood before him, holding hands with a small boy on one side and a young girl on the other. "Yer not get-tin' in, I tell ye."

"But—" the woman began desperately, pausing when she realized that he was no longer paying atten-tion and was glancing from Radcliffe to Charles.

"Evenin', me lords," he murmured, opening the door, then moved the woman and her children aside not ungently to clear the path for them. "In ye go and good luck to ye."

Radcliffe nodded and strode inside. Charlie, dis-mayed that the woman would even consider taking her children into such a place, followed more slowly, her gaze taking in the tear-stained face of the woman, along with the exhausted and hungry expressions of the children. They should have been home in bed, not standing outside a gambling den while their mother begged for entrance. Gambling was truly a sickness, she thought grimly as the doorman firmly shut the door behind them. And one she did not wish to ac-quire.

Sighing with sudden depression, she turned to peer

at the room she now stood in. It was brightly lit. Candles and lanterns sat on every surface, the smoke rising from them to join the smoke from the cigars and pipes at least half of the patrons had clamped between their teeth. The combination created a solid cloud that hovered at ceiling-level.

"Why is it so bright in here?" she asked with dismay, peering about at the gamblers and garishly dressed women in the room.

"To reduce the chance of cheating."

"Oh." Lifting a hand, she fanned her face briefly. It was at least twenty degrees hotter in here than it had been outside. Between the smoke, candle flames, and heat, she decided she now knew why some called these establishments gaming *hells*.

"Come." Radcliffe moved farther into the room and Charlie followed with a grimace. Truly, she would rather have turned around and left. Between her uncle and the little scene at the door, she had been cured of any desire to gamble, and she had seen enough to satisfy any curiosity she may have had. The gamblers seemed to be made up of two types of men, those who played their games with indifference, and those who hovered with a sort of desperation at the tables. There was only one sort of woman present: cheap, made-up, there to coax winners to make larger bets. Not one bothered to comfort the losers.

"Shall we try 'Laugh and Lie Down' first, or 'Noddy'?"

Charlie wrinkled her nose at the mention of the card games. Then, spotting a table where several gentlemen were playing dice, she drew his attention to it. "I think I would prefer that game."

"Hazard?" When she nodded, he led her silently to the table.

Hazard appeared a relatively simple game. The man who held the two dice threw them, and lost or took another roll depending on the results. It appeared that anything under five or over nine on the first roll made you a loser, whereas a five to nine let you roll again. If you were fortunate enough to roll the same sum once more, you won outright; if not, depending on what you did roll, you either lost, won, or were able to roll yet again. Once she'd gathered all that, Charlie turned her attention to the players.

The fellow presently controlling the dice played with an air of bored unconcern. That, combined with his expensive clothes and the jeweled baubles he wore, told her that this was all just entertainment to him and that the king's ransom in coins he was throwing away meant nothing. His supercilious smile as he paid out his losses and handed the dice to the man on his left spoke to the fact that he knew the same was not true for that man.

Charlie felt her teeth clench in offense for the new caster as he accepted the dice. Not that he seemed to even notice the other gambler's slight. Tall and thin to the point of emaciation, he wiped sweaty palms on his frock coat before taking the dice. His concentration was intense, his expression desperate as he clutched the small cubes tightly to his chest and bowed his head. After moving his lips in apparent prayer, he cast them on the table, almost sagging with relief when he rolled a nine.

A hopeful smile touched his lips as he accepted the comments of the others around the table and listened to them lay their bets, then he picked up the dice again. Tension suddenly gripping him again, he repeated the earlier ritual. This time his prayer went unanswered. His second roll came up a three. Shoulders slumping, he paid out to those around the table who had bet, then held the dice out to the man on his left.

His loss, however, did not stop his gaming, Charlie saw with a frown a moment later as the man laid a bet on the caster following him. Disgust claiming her briefly, she watched the new caster roll. Like the first man, this one could obviously afford to lose. Short, tubby, and with more hair on his chin than on his head, he wore a doublet made from a cloth woven with gold. Jewels flashed on his fingers. He tumbled the dice with a certain flair, then took the time to slide a coin down the top of the tall, brassy woman on his left as he kissed her, turning to do the same to the dark-haired woman on his right before taking up the dice again. He had quite a long winning streak. Charlie felt sure his lips must be sore from so much kissing by the time he lost and leaned past the brunette to offer the dice to Charlie.

She stared at the dice as if he were offering her a live snake until Radcliffe nudged her impatiently, hissing, "Go ahead. You wanted to play this game."

Sighing, she accepted the dice, tossing them at once, flinching when they came up a four and two.

"Six," Radcliffe muttered, frowning with irritation.

Charlie supposed that he had hoped she would lose right away. She had been rather hoping for that as well, she admitted to herself wryly as the other players began placing their bets. Once they were finished, she rolled again. Two threes this time. Six again.

Charlie listened impatiently to the mingled crowing and groans of those around her as they settled up and laid new bets. Radcliffe was the only person besides herself who was silent, and he radiated displeasure. She had more than doubled her money. It meant a delay in being able to leave.

"Go ahead," he murmured impatiently as soon as the last bet was placed and Charlie tossed the dice.

"Nine," he muttered as the bettors broke into excited chatter. Charlie barely waited for them to finish placing their bets before casting again. "Five."

It meant she would roll again and she did.

"Five again!" Radcliffe's irritation was obviously mounting. She knew that he had brought her here to teach her a lesson. Winning was not part of that lesson. Charlie felt Radcliffe sag beside her, then tense as she snatched up the dice and cast them again . . . and again . . . and again. Her pile of coins grew at an alarming rate. Her arm began to ache from the constant repetitiveness of the game. And her attention began to drift to the other players again.

The young fellow's mask of indifference was starting to slip. Excitement was glittering in his eyes and giving his mouth a hard edge. Mr. Fat-and-Happy was raking in coins by the handful, dispensing a good portion of them down the blouses of his two companions. And Mr. Tall, Thin, and Desperate was starting to sweat as his coins dwindled. He had started out betting for Charlie, and had originally increased his small pile of coins, but then, several rolls ago, he had started to bet against her. Presumably he had decided to go with the odds. Unfortunately, Charlie seemed to be immune to the odds.

"Charles!"

Glancing to Radcliffe, she saw that he was holding the dice out to her. While she had been contemplating the other players, they had finished with their bets and were waiting impatiently for her to roll again.

Radcliffe frowned at her reprovingly, and as the dice flew through the air and tumbled end over end atop the table, he found himself clenching his hands and silently chanting in his head, *lose, lose, lose.*

"Damn!"

Charlie snatched up the winning dice again.

"Just a moment." Radcliffe caught her arm to prevent the toss. "What are you doing?" He pointed to her bet. "You should keep some of that back. You have got a hefty sum there."

Charlie merely shrugged. "You play your way. I shall play mine."

Biting back anything else he would have said, Radcliffe watched the game play out, shaking his head with bewilderment as Charlie's winnings grew once again.

"Amazing," Radcliffe breathed, then nudged Charlie and stated the obvious. "You have won again. Shall I take half the money and—"

"Leave it there," Charlie murmured distractedly, watching Mr. Tall-and-Desperate lay yet another bet against her. He was almost out of coins, she noticed unhappily. Why did he not simply quit?

"What?"

Sighing, she faced Radcliffe. "I said, leave it there."

"But you will lose all that money."

" 'Twas only a couple of coins."

"It was at the start. But now"—he gestured toward

the pile—"it is almost as much money as you originally brought with you."

"But only a couple of coins are really mine," Charlie pointed out.

"But—" Radcliffe began, then sighed. She knew that he had wanted her to lose and learn a lesson. Still, he obviously now felt uncomfortable at her losing such a large amount. The game rolled on anxiously, and Charlie noticed the tension stiffening Radcliffe's body and making him sag quietly against the table as she won again. She had won a small fortune. She was beginning to attract the attention of gamblers from other tables.

"Leave the money again?" Radcliffe asked, then glanced up when she gave no answer. She'd hardly been paying attention. "Charles?"

Her answer was to toss the dice again, her gaze fixed on Mr. Tall-and-Desperate as she did. The way he sagged told her that she had won again. And he had lost another coin. He was down to only two coins. Surely he would quit now, she thought, and was mentally willing him to do so. Apparently, he was beyond reason, however. He placed one of his last two pence on the table and waited, hands clenched, face pale, sweat dripping down his forehead as the others laid their bets.

"Charles!"

"What?" Charlie turned around.

"Roll the damn dice!"

She blinked in surprise at Radcliffe. Something had changed. He was no longer stiff and disapproving. Excitement was gleaming in his eyes. Energy was rolling off of him in waves. Frowning, she cast the dice, noting the way he leaned against the table, hands grasping the edges tightly as he watched the dice tumbled end over end.

"Eleven!" he crowed jubilantly as the dice settled. "You won again!"

Charlie's gaze narrowed suspiciously as she caught a whiff of whiskey fumes as he grinned at her. "How much have you had to drink?"

Radcliffe blinked at her question, then glanced at the table, eyes widening at the four empty glasses that stood in a row. "Surely I didn't drink all of those," he began. "There was that redhead waitress and then . . ." His gaze slid back to the table and the mountain of coins Charles had won. The question of how much he had drunk was apparently forgotten. "Hurry and roll again," he said.

Charlie shook her head and glanced toward Mr. Tall-and-Desperate as he fingered his last coin. *Nay. Enough. Not again. Do not bet a*—"Damn!" she cursed with disgust as he pushed his last pence forward.

"Dammit, Charles, will you roll those dice?"

"Nay." Turning suddenly, she began raking up her coins, shoving them into her hat for want of a better place. Good God, she had won a small fortune!

"What?" Radcliffe seemed horrified. "You cannot quit now."

"Of course I can."

"But you are on a winning streak. You have made more money at the table than you got for cashing in your jewels. You cannot quit now!" he wailed.

Charlie rounded on him with disgust. "Have you not had enough? Really, Radcliffe, your behavior is shocking. I would think that you, of all people, would know better than to waste time and money on gambling. Just look at these people. 'Tis a sickness. Come, let us go home."

When he merely stared at her rather blankly, she took his arm with her free hand and turned him firmly toward the door. "I would suggest that you not risk entering such an establishment again," she said. " 'Tis obvious you get too caught up in the game. I would not wish to see you ruin yourself in one of these places."

Radcliffe allowed her to drag him away, and Charlie heard groans from the people behind them who had been winning by betting on her and had hoped to win more. Radcliffe had the decency to look somewhat contrite. Charlie shook her head as they exited the establishment.

"Oh, my lord!" a voice pleaded, "Please. If you could? They won't let me in to find my husband. If you could just nip back in and fetch him out for me? I'd be ever so grateful."

Charlie glanced around at that soft, imploring voice as they stepped out of the gaming hall. It was the woman who had been begging entrance on their arrival. "Your husband?" Charlie glanced from the boy who clung to the woman's skirt, to the girl who held her hand firmly and looked so solemn.

"Aye. He . . ." She hesitated, lip trembling, then shook her head in despair. "He's in there gambling our lives away. He don't mean to do it. Don't even want to, I don't think, but he just can't help hisself. We lost our inn to his debts six months ago, and we moved to the city. He took a job as a driver, and I found one as a half-time cook in an inn here, and we've been hobbling along, I thought. I'd buy groceries and he'd pay the rent. Or at least he was supposed to, only I found out today he hasn't been paying the rent. I came home to find the landlord barring the way. My husband hasn't paid rent for three months and 'til he pays up we are out. We cannot even collect our things. And today is payday. I know he has the rent money with him and is even now losing it. Please. Please," she begged. "If ye'd jest fetch him out so I can tell him about the landlord. He'd stop then, I know he would."

Charlie gazed at the woman, taking in her clean, plain gown and the children in clean but poor quality clothes and scrubbed faces with a sinking heart and asked, "Is he very tall and thin?"

"Aye. You saw him in there?" she asked hopefully, and Charlie felt her heart constrict. She suspected the woman's husband was Mr. Tall-and-Desperate, the man who had gambled every last coin away; the weary woman's troubles were about to increase. The woman's gaze dropped to the hatful of coins Charlie clutched and she frowned slightly. Charlie could easily give the woman her rent money, but if her husband was Mr. Tall-and-Desperate he would be out any moment, and should he get his hands on it, it would go the way of the money she had watched him lose tonight. Mayhap she should just follow them home and pay their rent or—

"There he is! Papa. Papa!"

Charlie gave a start at the boy's sudden happy

cries and turned to see the man now exiting the gaming hall. As she had suspected, it was Mr. Tall-and-Desperate. He looked even worse now than he had inside. His eyes were empty, his skin sickly white as he gazed at his family. Nodding slowly, he walked toward them.

Charlie stepped back as the woman anxiously blurted out the news about the landlord. "Do ye have the rent money?" she asked.

Seeming not to hear her, he hugged and murmured something to each of his children. When she repeated the question, he straightened, and Charlie felt the hairs on the back of her neck stand on end at the man's expression as he faced his wife.

Taking the anxious woman's face between his hands, he kissed her almost reverently.

"I'm sorry. I love you," he murmured, then released her and stepped back. He gave her a queer smile, then turned and walked into the street, directly into the path of a passing carriage and four.

Chapter 12

"PAPA!"

Charlie caught that heart-wrenching cry and glanced down at the children with dismay as she realized that this was the last image they would have of their father. A curse choking her, she shoved her hat into her pocket and turned the children away, hiding their faces against her waistcoat and shielding them from the sight. She couldn't prevent their hearing, however, and felt them shudder in horror, then begin to sob as the air filled with the panicked screams of horses and men.

Radcliffe had hurried after the man in an attempt to draw him back, but had not been able to reach him before the horses did. Now he knelt, examining the broken body before straightening. His ashen face was enough to tell Charlie what she needed to know, and she glanced worriedly at the silent woman beside her. Obviously in shock, the wife waited tensely as Radcliffe approached, probably knowing what he would tell her, but hoping against hope that she was wrong.

"I am sorry. There is nothing to be done for him. He is dead."

The woman slumped at those words, her head drooping like a limp daisy, silent tears coursing down her cheeks. Radcliffe watched her with concern for a moment, then turned and let loose a piercing whistle that brought his carriage forward at once.

"Help them into the carriage, Charles," he instructed. "I shall only be a moment."

Nodding, Charlie ushered the children forward as the driver leapt down to open the carriage door. She lifted first one child, then the other into the carriage before glancing around to see that the mother still stood where she'd been. Even as Charlie started back for her, Radcliffe shoved some money into the hand of a man he had taken aside, then moved to assist the woman. Taking her arm, he gently urged her toward the carriage, speaking to her softly as he did.

Swallowing a sudden lump in her throat at the gentle concern he was showing, Charlie turned and got into the carriage, smiling at the weeping children reassuringly. The widow followed at once, with Radcliffe right behind her. He murmured something to the driver, the door closed, the carriage rocked as the driver regained his seat, and they moved off at a funereal pace. The silence inside the carriage was thick and stifling, but there was little Charlie could think to say as she eyed the trio on the opposite bench. They were like clothes in a wardrobe. Slack and empty. Turning away from their hollow eyes and expressionless faces, she stared blindly out the window at the passing buildings.

It was not until the carriage came to a halt outside a dilapidated boarding house that the woman suddenly regained some expression, and that was panic.

Her gaze shot to her children helplessly, tears welling in her eyes.

" 'Tis all right," Charlie reassured her quietly. She knew the woman was terrified of being turned away, but she had every intention of putting her winnings to good use by helping this family.

"I shall see them to the door," she murmured to Radcliffe as the driver opened the door. Stepping down, she waited as the driver assisted the widow out, then lifted down first the daughter, then the son to the street. Casting another reassuring smile at the mother, Charlie started toward the front door of the establishment, pausing when it suddenly flew open and an odious little fellow in a filthy and tattered shirt and pants stepped out to bar the way.

"Back are ye, Mrs. Hartshair? Well, yer still not comin' in. I told ye. I'm wantin' my money. Ye owe me fer three months and ye'll pay it or kiss yer belongin's goodbye."

"Please, Mr. Wickman," the woman murmured painfully, clasping her children close. "My husband . . . he's *dead*." She shuddered over the word, but forced herself to continue. "We've nowhere else to go. I'll pay the rent the best I can, but my children—"

"Dead?" the man interrupted, a startled look on his bull-dog face that became calculating as the woman nodded. "Well, that there puts a whole different picture on things, don't it?" His gaze slid up and down her consideringly. "A woman shouldn't be on her own. Not safe. Mayhap we can be coming to an agreement."

His expression left no doubt as to what kind of agreement he was considering, and Charlie felt herself bristle like a hedgehog. "The only agreement will be her paying the rent she owes you and collecting their things. She will not be staying here."

His beady eyes swiveled to Charlie, taking in her gentleman's outfit with an arched eyebrow. "So that's the way of it? Already found herself a protector?"

Charlie stiffened at his words, then turned to the woman he had addressed as Mrs. Hartshair. "You said it was three months' rent you owed?"

She nodded uncertainly.

"How much a month?"

When the woman hesitated, the landlord spat out an amount that made her eyes widen incredulously. " 'Tis barely half that!"

"Aye, but it's late, so I'm charging you interest," he announced smugly.

"I am afraid interest is out of the question."

Charlie glanced around with surprise at Radcliffe's steely words. She had not heard him approach.

"You shall take the correct amount and allow them to collect their things. Or you shall be paid nothing and we shall use the money to replace whatever they are forced to leave behind. Which shall it be?"

Charlie turned back to see the landlord scowl briefly. His gaze moved from Radcliffe's tall, erect form to the crumpled hatful of coins that she had pulled from her pocket; then he gave a surly nod. "Deal."

Charlie counted out the necessary coins and held them out. The man snatched them so swiftly she almost missed the action.

"Take them inside, Charles, and assist them in gathering their things. Mr. Wickman and I shall wait out here for you."

Mr. Wickman obviously did not care for the arrangement but could do little about it. He stepped reluctantly aside, glaring as the Hartshairs hurried past. Charlie followed them into the dim, smelly interior of the building and up two flights of rickety stairs to a small room that had made up the entire living space of the Hartshairs. One end of the room was taken up with a bed; a length of string strung alongside it told her that a sheet or some such thing had probably been slung over it at night for privacy. Two pallets in the opposite corner were where the children had obviously slept, leaving a small spot around a fireplace that held a chair with a broken and mended leg, and rough tools for cooking.

Charlie felt a lump develop in her throat at such penury and was grateful that it didn't take long for them to gather what little they had. She had never been inside such a dismal dwelling, nor had she ever known anyone who'd had so few possessions. A couple of ragged items of clothing. A tattered little doll of the girl's. A clumsily carved wooden figure that was the boy's. One pot and one pan for cooking. They all fit into a small bundle, then Mrs. Hartshair turned to face Charlie with determination.

"I'm wishing to thank you for what yer doin', payin' our rent and all, but . . ." She swallowed and drew herself up proudly. "I'll pay ye back somehow, but—"

"I am not truly doing you a favor so much as you are doing me one. Or at least I hope you will," Charlie interrupted her.

When the woman peered at her a bit suspiciously, Charlie explained, "Radcliffe—the gentleman downstairs?" At her nod, Charlie continued, "Well, I fear his cook quit just this morning. He has not had an opportunity to look for a replacement just yet and . . . Well, it does seem as if you need a home and a more substantial job just now."

"A job?" she echoed with an expression of combined hope and fear.

"Aye." Charlie offered her a bolstering smile. " 'Tis a live-in position, so the problem of your being without a home just now would be solved."

"But what of the children?" she asked anxiously. "They would not be underfoot?"

"Nay. I am sure all will be fine. Why, your daughter could help out Bessie, my sister's maid. 'Twould be good training for her. And I am sure they could always use a hand in the stables when your son is old enough."

"Oh, my." She dropped onto the edge of the bed, looking suddenly overcome. Charlie eyed her uncertainly.

"Are you all right?"

"I . . . it is just . . ." She shook her head weakly and tears began to course down her face. Her children were at her side at once, confusion and fear on their faces even as they sought to comfort her. She drew them into her embrace, kissing the top of first one head, then the other before raising her face to peer at Charlie with blind gratitude and adoration. "Things have been so bad for so long. My husband, God love him, he did not mean to gamble, to make things so hard. He tried to stop, constantly promised to. But—" She shook her head wearily. "He was a good man when I married him, then he took to gaming, then the drink. He neglected business and began to sleep the day away. When we lost the inn, I thought that he must see how much damage all of this was causing. I thought sure he would change. But when Mr. Wickman told me about the unpaid rent, then—"

She paused and her eyes became glassy with horror. Charlie was sure she was recalling her husband's death. The woman's expression cleared and she whispered, "God forgive me. I never wished him dead, but right now I see more hope for the future than I have in years." She raised slightly shocked eyes to Charlie. "I'm an awful woman to feel that way, aren't I?"

Charlie shook her head solemnly. "Nay. You are a woman with two children to raise, clothe, and feed. And you have been trying to do so alone for quite some time while your husband stole the roof from over your head and gambled it away. Now you are free of the sickness he had and the hold it had over your life. You can start fresh. There is hope. There is no shame in embracing it."

The woman considered that silently, then nodded. "You are a good man, my lord. I have been praying for help for a long time. I think surely God must have sent you to me in answer to those prayers. I will be the best cook I can be."

"I am sure you will do fine," Charlie murmured, uncomfortable with her gratitude. "Now, we had best go below before your Mr. Wickman comes looking for us."

Moving to the door, she held it open and ushered the threesome out and back downstairs. Radcliffe and Wickman were still on the front stoop. At Radcliffe's questioning glance, Charlie merely shook her head and followed Mrs. Hartshair and her children into the carriage.

Radcliffe entered after Charlie, then sat to eye the woman and her two children seated on the opposite bench seat. He experienced a definite sense of déjà vu, only the memory mixing with this reality was of Bessie seated fearfully on the bench. Sighing inwardly, he shook his head and sat silently for the duration of the ride home.

"It would seem we have guests, Stokes," Radcliffe announced, slapping his gloves and hat into the butler's waiting hand as the man gaped at the woman and children who trailed him into the house.

"Not exactly guests," Charlie corrected gently as she followed the family into the house and pushed the door closed.

"Oh?" Radcliffe arched one supercilious eyebrow at the lad. "Pray tell?"

"You are in need of a cook, as I recall. Unless you have already made arrangements?"

Radcliffe grimaced. "You know I have hardly had the opportunity for that."

Charlie breathed a small sigh of relief. She had not thought he had done so yet, but if he had, that would have been a complication indeed. "Well, now you need not bother. You need a cook. Mrs. Hartshair is a cook."

Radcliffe blinked at the simple announcement, then glanced toward the woman for verification. "You are a cook?"

"Aye." She swallowed nervously as her gaze slid around the luxurious foyer before she added unhappily, "Aye, I am a cook, but I—I'm a fair hand at buns and such, but the sort o' food I can cook is . . ." She glanced at Charlie, who gave her an encouraging smile. Straightening slightly, the woman murmured, "'Tis tasty, hearty food, my lord. But I know naught about fancies and pastries and the like."

"That will not be a problem," Charlie assured her quickly. "His Lordship never entertains. Besides, his last cook could not even boast tasty or hearty fare, and you shall learn anything necessary over time. Is that not right, Radcliffe?"

There was a moment of silence, just long enough to make Charlie glance at him in reprimand, at which he nodded solemnly. "Aye. 'Tis quite true. I am sure you will do very well." His gaze went to the weary and bedraggled children hanging onto their mother's skirts, and he murmured, "Your children look as if they are all in. Stokes will show you to your room."

"Thank you, my lord," the woman gasped, her face blossoming into near beauty with her relief. "Thank you."

Nodding, Radcliffe glanced toward Stokes expectantly, frowning at the servant's stunned expression and the way he gazed, unmoving, upon the widow. "Stokes?" he prompted, drawing the man's attention. "Show them to a room."

"Of course, my lord."

The servant had actually blushed slightly, Charlie noticed. Radcliffe grunted and turned to her. "In the library, Charles."

She grimaced at the autocratic tone, but paused to suggest to Stokes that he offer the Hartshairs some food before seeing them to bed. The three looked pale and thin to her. They could use some meat on their bones, and she doubted they had eaten that day. When the man assured her he would see to it, she turned resignedly and followed Radcliffe's trail to the library.

He was standing at the sideboard pouring himself a drink when she entered. A stiff drink, she could not help but notice as she settled in a seat before the desk to await the lecture she knew would come. She did not have long to wait.

"My home is not a refuge for runaways and waifs, Charles."

"Runaways?" Her eyes widened innocently as she watched him cross the room to take his seat at the desk. "I have brought no runaways here, my lord."

His brows drew together in displeasure. "You know what I mean, Charles."

"Aye, well," she sighed briefly, then shook her head. "Actually, no, I do not. I am hardly using your home as some sort of charity workshop, Radcliffe. Beth needed a maid and I found her a maid. You needed a cook and I have found you a cook. The fact that both women were in untenable situations when I found them is merely coincidental."

This fine argument, one she was rather proud of, was blown to the four winds by a child's sudden squeal of "Puppies!" from the hallway, followed by a shout from Stokes and the scampering of little feet. Charlie could picture what was happening in the hall. Stokes had led the Hartshairs to the kitchens to feed them, unthinkingly opening the kitchen door, only to have the puppies make a grand escape. All no doubt to the children's glee. They were now surely chasing the little creatures about, attempting to recapture them. Charlie almost smiled at the pictures running through her head, but she managed to restrain herself when she caught the expression on Radcliffe's face.

"As I said," he muttered grimly, "you must stop collecting people and puppies."

"Of course, Radcliffe. You are right. I shall refrain from rescuing any more wayward strays," she murmured soberly.

Radcliffe sighed heavily. "I wish I believed that."

"Oh, you can. After all, there are no more positions in the house to fill, are there?"

"I did not have a position for the puppies," he pointed out.

"Aye, well . . . he was going to kill them," she said helplessly, and Radcliffe dropped his head into his hands and began massaging his scalp, making her ask sympathetically, "Does your head ache? Mayhap you should take yourself off to bed."

"Aye." Standing wearily, he gestured for Charles to lead the way, then followed her to the door.

Charlie felt a sense of relief that the lecture was over . . . until she opened the library door. The puppies were gone, apparently having been recaptured and taken away. However, Beth and Tomas Mowbray were in a clinch just inside the front door. Slamming the door, she whirled to face a wincing Radcliffe. "I just had a thought. Mayhap a nice massage would ease your ache. You just sit yourself down right over here and I shall see what I can do."

Charlie started to urge him toward the desk, but Radcliffe dug his heels in halfway across the room. "Thank you for the offer, Charles. However, I think you had it right the first time. Bed will cure what ails me."

"Oh, but—" Charlie hurried after him as he started back across the room, throwing herself in front of the door when he would have opened it. "What about tomorrow?"

He stared at her blankly. "Tomorrow?"

"Do we have any plans?"

He shifted impatiently. "We can discuss that at breakfast, Charles."

"But—"

"I have a headache, Charles. Please get out of the way so that I can go lie down and be rid of it."

Shoulders drooping, Charlie stepped aside, opened the door, and followed him into the hall. The empty hall. Much to her relief, neither Beth nor Tomas Mowbray were anywhere in sight. She followed Radcliffe silently up the stairs, pausing at the top when he suddenly stopped. She glanced at him questioningly.

"I forgot all about Elizabeth." When she raised an eyebrow questioningly, he explained, "I left her at the ball with the Mowbrays. They promised to see her home. I suppose I had better check and see that she has returned and all is well."

"I shall do that," she volunteered quickly. "You go ahead and lie down."

When he hesitated, she hurried past him to "Elizabeth's" door and knocked briefly. The minute it started to open, she turned to offer Radcliffe a reassuring smile, then gasped as she was grabbed by her arm and tugged quickly inside the room.

"Charlie! You wouldn't believe what a wonderful time I had. It was marvelous! Fantastic! Amazing!"

Pushing the door closed, Beth whirled Charlie around the room gleefully, then released her and collapsed backward on the bed with a huge sigh to hug herself. "What a stupendous night."

"So I saw," Charlie murmured dryly, seating herself on the bed beside her as the girl colored prettily.

"Was that you in the library?" she asked, her nose wrinkling. "I did wonder."

"Wonder? Are you mad? If Radcliffe had caught you at your antics—"

"But he did not," she laughed and dropped back upon the bed, only to sit up abruptly again. "Did you pay off the blackmailer? Radcliffe did not find you, did he?"

"Nay. And aye," Charlie answered in order, then went on to explain the night's adventures, running through them quite briefly since it was obvious that her sister was not paying much attention. When she fell silent, Beth immediately began to regale her with her own evening, which seemed incredibly dull in comparison. She had danced with Tomas, talked with Lady Mowbray, danced with Tomas, discussed fashion with Lady So-and-So. Then she'd danced with Tomas again, and so her evening had seemed to have gone. Compared to her own night, Beth's evening seemed terribly tame. Her mind had begun to wander when she caught her sister's last words.

"So, you may be Elizabeth during the day. But I should like to be me in the evening again at the Wulcotts' ball. You do not mind, do you?"

Charlie sat still for a moment, her heart seeming to have dropped into her stomach somewhere. Then she shook her head and rose wearily. "Nay, of course not."

"Oh, thank you, Charlie. I knew you would not let me down."

Nodding, she moved to the connecting door and started out of the room, then turned back. "I suppose you should sleep in "Charles's" room tonight, then."

"Oh, aye." Bouncing off the bed, Beth moved cheerfully across the room, kissing her sister's cheek affectionately before closing the door behind her with a cheery "Good night."

Charlie stared at that door for several moments, feeling vaguely cheated. She had to find a husband, too. Her own need for one was even more pressing than Beth's, really. After all, while Seguin may not be every girl's dream come true, at least he was not dangerous like Carland. And there was the source of her upset, she realized glumly. They were supposed to be taking turns here at being the girl. Both of them were supposed to have their chance at finding a husband. Yet it seemed that Charlie was spending most of her time playing Charles. And most of her time was spent in the company of Radcliffe. She would never find a husband that way. Straightening her shoulders grimly, she marched into "Charles's" room, startling Beth as she started to crawl under the bed covers. "Charlie. What is it? Is something wrong?"

"I am afraid I disagree with your playing Elizabeth tomorrow night. To date, the Hardings' ball is the only event at which I have been the sister and allowed to hunt up a husband, and then Mowbray and Radcliffe clung to me like limpets the whole time. If we are to take turns at this as you suggested, then take turns we shall. Tomorrow evening is my turn to be a girl and look for a husband. If you wish, I shall be Charles during the day tomorrow, but in the evening, I *will* be Elizabeth."

Beth opened her mouth to complain at the switch, then paused, shame covering her expression. "I am sorry," she said at last. "You are absolutely right. 'Tis your turn. Besides, your need for a husband is more pressing than mine, and I do already at least have my eye on someone. Of course, you must be Elizabeth tomorrow night. And during the day, too," she added firmly. "I shall even endeavor to keep Tom and Radcliffe away from you tomorrow evening so that you might find someone you are interested in without their interference."

Charlie's shoulders sagged suddenly in relief and weariness.

"Charlie," Beth murmured when she started to turn away.

"Aye?"

"This was a good thing, I think."

She stared at her blankly. "What?"

"All of this." She waved vaguely around the room, then explained, "Having to escape, meeting up with Radcliffe, ending up in London, fending for ourselves. . . . Well, with a little help from Radcliffe, of course."

Charlie shook her head. "I do not think I understand—"

"It is changing us. I have always been terribly shy. You know that. But here I am learning to deal with social situations better. And you, you have never really stood up for yourself or what you want, yet twice now you have done it here."

Charlie blinked at that. "What on earth do you

mean, I have never stood up for myself before? I am forever standing up for myself, rebelling and such. My God, Beth, you make me sound like a coward."

"Nay. Never a coward. You have a great deal of courage. You have always been a grand champion for others. But only for others. You never stand up for what you want." Seeing the bewilderment on her face, Beth explained, "The dresses, for instance. For years you have put up with my choices, never complaining once, let alone demanding—"

Charlie waved that away impatiently. "Dresses. What did they matter in the country? Besides, you were going through all the fittings, you had every right to choose."

"But I did not mind the fittings, and while I was doing those, you were doing something else. Something I disliked doing, like mucking out the stables."

"Well, after Uncle Henry let go all of his staff, 'Old' Ben had a rough time keeping up with things. He needed help."

"Aye. I know. But I detested working in the stables. You did not mind it so much, so you did it while I went for the fittings. 'Twas an equal trade and you should have had a say in what gowns you wore as much as me. You never said a word. Until now. Just as with everything else you let me have my way. Until now, you would have let me attend the ball as Elizabeth. In fact, your first instinct was to let me, but then you stood up for yourself and said it was your turn."

"Well, aye, but this is a matter of my life. Do I not find a husband, I shall have to marry Carland and he would kill me. I must find a husband. I must have my equal turns."

"I see, so you are saying that you are only doing this because your life is more important than my pleasure?"

Charlie blinked in amazement that she would even ask the question. "Well, aye, of course my life is more important than your pleasure!"

Beth nodded solemnly. "Yet your pleasure is less important than mine."

Charlie frowned. "How do you come to that conclusion?"

"That is what you have said. You are not letting me have my way this time because your life is at stake. You let me have my way with the dresses because it was simply a matter of taste. Yours versus mine. Mine was more important."

"You are twisting things," Charlie muttered impatiently.

"Am I? Then what of our birthday dinners?"

"What are you talking about now?"

"Cook always asked what we would wish for our birthday dinner and I always chose roast duckling and blueberry torte."

"So?"

"You detest duck. And blueberries, while you like them, are not your favorite flavor of torte."

"Please get to your point, Beth."

"But that *is* my point. Had things been fair, we would have had roast duckling and blueberry torte one year and a meal of your choice the next. Or we would have had roast duckling and your choice of dessert one year, then your choice of meal and blueberry torte the next. But, nay, for the past several years, we had roast duckling and blueberry torte on our birthday."

Seeing that what she was saying was sinking in, Beth murmured, "You did things like that all the time, Charlie. You stood up for everyone from the village drunk to me. Everyone but yourself. And you always put others' wants before your own. 'Twas as if you thought everyone else was better than yourself. I bet that if Uncle Henry had arranged marriages between myself and Seguin and between you and someone similarly disgusting but harmless, you would have gone ahead and married the old coot."

Charlie grimaced but did not deny it.

"And I blame Uncle Henry."

She gave a laugh at that. "Something else to blame him for?"

Beth's chin rose. "Well, he was constantly criticizing you. He was forever calling you stupid and cheap and—" Her shoulders slumped. "And 'twas all *my* fault," she finished miserably.

Charlie's head shot up. "Your fault? Good Lord, Beth!"

"Well, it *was* sometimes. The times he would start out picking at me for something and you would jump to my defense. He would turn his anger on you then and leave me alone." She sighed. "Mayhap had I returned the favor and defended you back, he may have left us both alone, but I—" She raised stark eyes to her sister. "I was so afraid of his temper."

Charlie moved to her side at once, placing a comforting arm around her. "I know. 'Tis all right."

"Nay. 'Tis not. I am ashamed of myself. You were not afraid."

"Of course I was."

Beth stilled at that, eyes wide and incredulous. "You were?"

"Of course. Uncle Henry has a terrible temper. I was terrified every time I faced him. So you see, there is nothing for you to be ashamed of. I was afraid too."

"Oh, but this is worse," Beth breathed with dismay. "Do you not see? You were afraid like I was, but you stood up to him anyway. That is true courage, Charlie. While my allowing my fear to hold me back was cowardice."

"Beth." Charlie shook her impatiently. "Stop it. For heaven's sake. As if we do not have enough to worry about. Anyone with any sense would have kept their mouth shut and let his criticisms run their course, ignoring everything that man said. Now, why do you not go to your room and get some sleep?"

"I am in my room. Charles sleeps here and I am to be Charles tomorrow."

"I thought you might wish to be Elizabeth during the day, since I am going to be—"

"Nay. I shall be Charles all day and night."

Chapter 13

THE Fetterleys' ballroom was filled to capacity with men and women all asparkle in their finery. It was also unbearably hot, and the fact that she had been dancing non-stop since arriving wasn't helping much, Charlie thought, fanning her face with one hand as she followed the steps of the dance.

"I did not realize that Radcliffe had any cousins, Lady Elizabeth."

Charlie glanced sharply at her dance partner, Lord Nor-Something-or-Other. She hadn't really caught the name. She hadn't caught the names of most of the men she had danced with this evening. But then, none of them had been all that memorable anyway. This one at least was taller than she was, had all his teeth, and hadn't stepped on her toes yet.

Actually, he was rather attractive too, she realized with some surprise, peering at his face for the first time since he had cut in on her dance with Lord Whoever. He had blue eyes, nice features, and light blond hair. He was also nearly as tall as Radcliffe, with shoulders almost as wide as his.

"Is there something on my nose?"

Realizing that she had been staring, Charlie flushed and dropped her gaze. "Nay, my lord," she murmured, her mind returning to the comment he had made.

"Do you know Lord Radcliffe well?" she asked cautiously after a moment.

"As well as anyone, I would wager. His sister was married to my brother."

"Mary." She whispered the name sadly, then tilted her head to look at her dance partner. "You met B– Charles at Radcliffe's club," she recalled Beth telling her.

"Aye. A charming lad. Though not as charming as his sister."

Flushing at the compliment, she glanced away, wondering how she was to feel him out to see if he was possible husband material. He was the first likely candidate she had met so far. The fact that he was tall, confident, attractive, and a good dancer already put him far above the other men she had met that night. And he came from a good family. It had to be good if Radcliffe had let his sister marry into it. "Are you married?"

"Considering me as husband material, my lady?" he teased.

Charlie flushed, but managed an unconcerned shrug. "Is that not what these balls are all about?"

"Aye. But usually the ladies are more subtle about it. I am single," he added gently, then teased, "No diseases that I know of and quite capable of producing heirs." Charlie flushed again and he laughed softly. "How charming you are. Blunt and to the point, yet you blush deliciously. Does that blush go all the way down, I wonder?"

When her eyes went round and she stumbled slightly, he pulled her against his chest to steady her, his hand sliding to the base of her spine and applying gentle pressure.

Charlie swallowed, confused by her responses as his body caressed hers through their clothes. There was the excitement she had experienced with Radcliffe, and yet it was different. With Radcliffe it had been pure, unadulterated pleasure. Her heart had leapt and she had followed it, reveling in the sensations. With this man there was an edge to the excitement. Where she trusted Radcliffe not to hurt her, she instinctively knew this man did not worry overmuch about any consequences. He could ruin a woman without regret. Radcliffe would never do so. His sense of right and wrong was too strong.

"*Does* the blush go all the way down?" he whispered seductively in her ear, and Charlie swallowed as a shiver convulsed her.

Feeling out of her depth, she cast her eyes about in search of Beth and Radcliffe. Her gaze was halfway around the room when she caught a glimpse of a man that made her stumble again, hard. Ralphy!

"Are you all right?" he murmured with concern, steadying her.

"I . . . Nay." She managed an apologetic smile. "I fear I have overdone the dancing, my lord. Would you mind terribly if I cried off the rest of this dance?"

"I am shattered. But I should not wish you to faint from overexertion," he murmured gallantly. Taking her arm, he led her off the floor, his gaze sweeping over the ice blue gown she wore with its needlelace trim and silk-lined sashes in a darker blue. "I noticed you had not sat out a single dance since arriving. Mayhap a cool beverage would revive you," he suggested solicitously as he saw her seated in one of the few empty chairs lining the wall. "Shall I fetch you one?"

"Please," Charlie murmured, her gaze drifting around the room as soon as he moved away. She wasn't sure, but she thought Ralphy had seen her and might approach her now that she was alone.

"There you are!" Beth appeared before her suddenly in the new fawn breeches and coat that had arrived that afternoon. "You are a difficult one to keep track of."

Charlie nearly smiled at that complaint. She knew Beth had known exactly where she was all evening, but had been misdirecting Radcliffe as promised. Tom had made her job easier by not showing up to need distracting.

"We saw you dancing with Norwich." Radcliffe's disapproval was obvious.

"Norwich?" It took her a moment to realize that he meant her dance partner. "Oh, aye. The heat was affecting me adversely so he went to fetch me a beverage."

"It was more likely the fact that he was holding you too damn close that was affecting you adversely," Radcliffe snapped, then forced a smile. "Come. I think some fresh air may do more to revive you than a beverage and his presence."

"Oh, but—" she began, grimacing when he raised an eyebrow at her in question. "Well, I really would like a drink. Besides, is it not rude to just disappear on him?"

"I shall fetch you a drink in a moment," he promised, urging her toward the doors to the terrace. "As for being rude, it was rude of him to hold you so closely on the dance floor."

"Still, Radcliffe, it does seem unconscionably ill-mannered to simply leave like this," Beth murmured, following them.

"Then, Charles, you should probably stay behind to explain that Elizabeth was feeling faint, needed some air, and is now in my care."

Beth's eyes widened, her footsteps faltering. "Oh, but—"

Whatever she wanted to say was lost to them as Radcliffe drew Charlie onto the terrace and closed the doors with a decided snap.

"Self-absorbed, spoiled little whelp," he muttered, leading her to the railing that ran the length of the terrace.

"Are we still talking about Norwich?" Charlie asked with amusement. She had never seen Radcliffe so upset. He was acting almost jealous.

"He should not have risked subjecting you to possible scandal that way."

"Scandal! We were not dancing *that* closely," Charlie argued with exasperation.

"Had the two of you been unclothed, you would have been making love."

"But I do not love him, and we were not unclothed, and we were no closer than this." The last came out a bit breathlessly as she realized how close they were. They had gravitated toward each other with each word they had spoken. Now she smiled at him, unaware of the hunger in her eyes or the seductive quality of her voice as she murmured, "Does that mean if we were unclothed, we would be making love?"

"Elizabeth." Her name was a groan on his lips as he took her in his arms and kissed her with all the pent-up frustration he had experienced that evening as he had watched her flit from the arms of one man to another.

Charlie melted in his arms like chocolate over the fire. Her arms slid up around his neck her hands gliding into his hair, her lips opening hungrily beneath his. It was hot, sweet, and over quickly. It seemed to her that it had just begun and he was gently setting her away with a groan.

Charlie opened her eyes slowly, disappointment and hunger plain in her eyes. Seeing it, Radcliffe released a pent-up sigh, then offered her a regretful smile. "Perhaps I should fetch you that punch now," he murmured huskily, then moved away, slipping through the partially open doors they had come through moments earlier.

Charlie watched him go with a sigh of her own. Her body was humming, desire thrumming through her veins like a living thing. She could still taste him on her lips, she realized unhappily as she stared blindly at the dancers swirling by the doors. In comparison, Norwich's effect on her when he had pressed her close on the dance floor had been rather tepid.

Groaning inwardly, she turned away from the windows, only to pause as a movement from the shadows caught her eye. She was tensing in anxiety when a figure suddenly moved into the light from the terrace doors.

"Tomas!" she greeted him with a strangled voice, her eyes shifting instinctively toward the door that Radcliffe had just stepped through. The door that had been open when they'd stopped kissing, but that he had closed behind them when they'd come out. How long had he been standing there watching them?

A hard grasp on her upper arm drew her gaze reluctantly around to see that he now stood before her. And he was furious.

"You did not mention that you and Radcliffe were *kissing* cousins."

"I . . . he was just. . . ." she stammered, her mind searching for and discarding explanation after explanation. Not that Tomas seemed in the mood to listen anyway, she decided with a sigh as he drew her closer in a mockery of an embrace.

"Or is it just that you share your kisses with everyone?"

"Now, Tomas," Charlie tried a soothing tone as she pressed her palms flat against his chest, attempting to ease some space between them. He was neither willing to be soothed nor held at bay. A growl of what Charlie presumed was strangled rage sounded from his throat, then his head suddenly swooped down to cover her lips with his own.

Charlie was too stunned to react at first, and then she was too disappointed. She felt absolutely nothing. His lips were firm and warm and moved across her own with obvious skill, and yet he might as well have kissed a post for all the response he managed to wring from her. The contrast between her lack of response to him and her weak-kneed, fluttery-tummy response to Radcliffe was terrifying to her. What if Radcliffe was the only one who could stir her in that way? What if no one else could raise her passions?

Recognizing her lack of response, Tomas redoubled his efforts, his tongue sweeping over her lips and pushing into her mouth. Charlie remained pliant in his arms and simply waited, her body remaining stubbornly uninterested. This was *horrible!*

A gasp finally brought the tepid embrace to an end. Pulling apart, they turned as one to see Radcliffe standing frozen in the door, a drink in hand. He looked shocked. Frozen even. But no more so than Beth, who stood beside him.

Groaning inwardly, Charlie fatalistically awaited the outburst of rage that was burning in Radcliffe's eyes. There was none, however. As quick as a blink he forced the rage from his face, stepped forward, handed her the drink with a cold, courtly bow, then turned and walked back into the ball.

Sighing, she looked down into the drink briefly, then glanced at Tomas who, taking a page from Radcliffe's book, suddenly bowed toward her with stiff dignity, then walked into the building as well. It figures, Charlie thought wryly. Just like a man. Kiss a girl, then blame her for it. She hadn't asked either man to kiss her, had she? Yet here they were, both of them storming off as if discovering she were some sort of tart. Men!

Her gaze slid to Beth to find her glaring daggers. "Oh, for heaven's sake," Charlie snapped. "You do not think I asked him to kiss me, do you?" When Beth's anger wavered, she added, "He came out to see Radcliffe kissing me and—"

"Radcliffe kissed you again?"

Charlie waved the question away impatiently. "Aye, and Tomas saw it, waited in the shadows until he left, then gave me a furious kiss of his own. And it was awful."

Beth straightened in offense at that. "Tomas is a very good kisser."

"I am sure he is. But not for me. I did not feel a thing when he kissed me. What is more, it seemed pretty obvious that he was disappointed in the kiss as well."

Eyes widening, Beth turned and glanced back into the ballroom. "Oh, no," she gasped. "He is leaving."

She raced off to chase after him, leaving Charlie alone on the balcony to brood over Tom's lack of effect on her, and her all-too-heated response to Radcliffe. Surely it was just a fluke? she thought hopefully. Surely Radcliffe was not the only one who could stir a response in her? Perhaps her lack of reaction to Tomas was merely because she'd thought of him as Beth's. Perhaps she already thought of him as a possible brother-in-law?

That possibility gave her great hope. She had quite enjoyed the passion Radcliffe had wrung from her with his kisses. The marital bed would be quite an enjoyable place if it contained anything like those kisses. But if Radcliffe were the only one who could raise those passions, she had a problem.

"Lady Elizabeth."

Charlie turned at that surprised greeting and forced a smile as Lord Norwich stepped out onto the terrace. "My lord."

"Whatever are you doing out here on your own?" he asked with concern.

"I was just thinking, my lord," she answered evasively, and found herself studying him curiously. He was a handsome man and he had raised some response from her earlier. Of course, he wasn't nearly as striking as Radcliffe, but—

Scowling, she forced the other man's image from her mind. "Would you kiss me?"

If he was shocked at her question, it was no more so than Charlie herself. The words popped out before she had even realized that the thought had occurred to her. She wanted to convince herself that Radcliffe was not the only one who could gain a response from her. And, that her lack of response to Tomas was because he was Beth's love interest and therefore almost a brother-in-law. To that end, it did seem she needed to kiss at least one more man. Hopefully, Norwich would be able to soothe her fears.

A moment of silence passed as he contemplated her, and quite suddenly Charlie was embarrassed by her forward behavior. Shifting uncomfortably, she cleared her throat. "I am sorry. Please forget that I—"

Her words died in her throat as he caught her arm and swept her against his chest in an embrace. Then his lips were on hers, firm and forceful, pressing her head back. Clutching at his shoulders, Charlie gasped in surprise and he took immediate advantage of that, his tongue sweeping in to conquer. He was most masterful, and Charlie felt relief slide over her as she felt the first faint stirrings of a response awaken within her.

It was a short-lived relief. The faint stirring was as much as he could muster from her, and Charlie's heart sank slowly as the embrace continued. Even his caresses did not help. They were pleasant, but did little more than capture her attention. They raised no fire. Fanned no flames. Left her lukewarm, not feverish. It was most distressing. Not that Norwich seemed to notice. While her response was tepid, his was more heated. She could feel how affected he was by the bulge pressing against her stomach.

"Elizabeth!"

Norwich released her so abruptly that Charlie stumbled a step or two before regaining her balance and turning in resignation to face the owner of that voice. It figured that Radcliffe would show up again at another inconvenient moment. Really, the man had to work on his timing.

Charlie watched Radcliffe pace the floor with growing irritation. After snapping her name on the balcony, there had been a tense moment as everyone had merely stared at each other; then Radcliffe had snarled that it was time to leave.

Embarrassed at being caught—once again—in a man's embrace, Charlie had rushed silently back into the ballroom. Radcliffe had whirled to follow, then taken her arm in hand and steered her firmly out of the ballroom, the house, and into his carriage, then had sat in contemptuous silence all the way back to the townhouse. It was that contempt that had slowly worn away Charlie's embarrassment and guilt and begun to awaken a responding anger in herself. An anger that had only grown as he had marched her tight-lipped into the townhouse, straight to the library where he had slammed the door shut, left her standing before his desk, and begun to pace irately before her.

He had been pacing for a good ten minutes, and aside from being angry Charlie was impatient now as well. It was partially his fault, after all. If he had not kissed her, she never would have realized how important that part of marriage could be. She would not have—Her thoughts died as he suddenly stopped pacing and whirled to face her.

"I do not know what has come over you. Twice tonight I caught you kissing men out on the balcony."

"And once you kissed me yourself," she snapped back, her face flushing with embarrassment despite her anger.

"Aye. Did you think then that meant you could run about kissing everyone?"

"I hardly did that!" Charlie fought the guilty flush that wanted to color her cheeks. "I did not even kiss Tomas. He kissed me. It was unexpected, and if it makes you any happier, I did not enjoy it in the least."

That seemed to bring him up short. His gaze narrowed. "And Norwich?"

He *would* ask that, she thought, but admitted, "I asked him to kiss me."

Radcliffe seemed to deflate with disappointment. "Why?"

She debated whether to lie, but he looked so miserable. . . . "Because I did not care for Tom's kisses."

He blinked in confusion. "Tom's kisses?"

"Aye. He is a skilled kisser, I can tell, but his kisses did not affect me at all."

Radcliffe shook his head as if trying to scatter a fog clouding his brain. "You asked Norwich to kiss you because Tom's kisses did not affect you?" When she nodded solemnly, he was silent for a moment, then, "And did you like Norwich's kisses?"

Charlie hesitated. "They were nice."

"Nice?"

"Aye. They were pleasant enough, but they did not make my knees go all weak and my stomach quiver as if it were full of butterflies," she admitted, then glanced up with surprise when he was suddenly standing before her. A hair's-breadth away.

"And whose kisses do that to you?" he asked huskily.

Charlie swallowed. Her breathing had turned shallow at his proximity, the blood roaring in her ears like rushing water.

"Hmm?" he breathed, raising a hand to the pulse fluttering at the base of her throat. It immediately began to race. "Do my kisses affect you that way?"

Charlie swallowed again to keep from groaning as his finger slid down to trace the neckline of her gown across the swells of her breasts. His other hand slid to her neck, rising until his fingers curved around the base of her skull, his thumb resting before her ear and caressing gently.

Charlie's eyes closed, her face pressing into his palm like a cat nuzzling its owner.

"Do they?" he whispered, his head lowering until his lips were inches away from her own, his breath a warm caress across her mouth.

"Aye," she moaned in defeat as the finger at her neckline feathered over her breast, brushing one painfully erect nipple through the cloth of her gown. "Radcliffe?"

His breath catching at that plea, he finally dropped

his lips to hers. It was as if he had poured whiskey on embers. The flame exploded within her, her body arching violently, pressing her breasts hungrily against his chest. Head falling back, she opened her mouth for his invasion and clung desperately to his shoulders.

For a few moments it seemed more a battle than a kiss. Both of them were fighting for more, demanding it. There was no tenderness, just burning need as they devoured each other, bodies thrusting and hands grasping. Then Radcliffe broke free of the kiss, to worship her chin, cheek, then her earlobe with his mouth.

Charlie shuddered wildly as his tongue laved her. His hand slid to cup her breast through her gown and she cried out as he squeezed it frenziedly. When he released her at once, she nearly wept with disappointment until she felt his hand at the neckline of her gown tugging at it until he had freed her breast to his uninhibited touch.

"Oh, God," he breathed into her ear as his hand closed over the warm swell of flesh, and Charlie gasped as his thumb brushed over her puckered nipple. When the weakness she had spoken of suddenly hit her knees and she sagged in his arms, he slid one leg between hers, his thigh rubbing against her pelvis through the cloth of their apparel.

"Please," she breathed into his ear, nipping at the succulent lobe, then sucking hungrily until he pulled his head away and pushed her back against one arm to drop his mouth to the breast he had revealed.

Hands catching in his hair, she twisted her head feverishly, shaking her hair loose from its pins. But then she wanted his kisses again, needed them, and she tugged at his hair until he released her breast and claimed her lips once more. Running her hands over his chest, she suddenly pushed his coat off of his shoulders, and he helped her, shrugging out of one sleeve, then the other. It wasn't enough for Charlie, though; she wanted his bare flesh against her own, and she began tugging at the buttons of his shirt.

Releasing a half-chuckle, half-growl at her frustrated whimper as she struggled with the buttons, Radcliffe tugged the shirt out of his breeches and slipped button after button free of its hole until the shirt hung loose. Charlie immediately pressed her hands to his chest, marveling over the hard strength of him, the width, the curly dark hairs that brushed her fingers making them tingle.

She bent to press a kiss to the very center of his chest, then shifted her lips to one small pebble-like nipple. Closing her lips around it as he had done to her, she grazed it with her teeth, then gasped in surprise as Radcliffe suddenly stiffened and pushed her away. Her eyes shot to his face in hurt surprise until she recognized the intent look he had acquired. Then she heard Beth's voice sing out, vibrant with excitement. "Ch–Elizabeth! Beth!" Her footsteps pounded up the stairs and faded.

She saw the passion fade from Radcliffe's eyes to be replaced with regret, and felt her anger stir. "Do not even consider apologizing for what just happened," she warned icily. "It was as much my fault as yours and I enjoyed it too much to be sorry."

Radcliffe's eyebrows shot up even as his jaw dropped.

Charlie felt at least a smidgen of satisfaction at that fact as she rucked her neckline back up, smoothed her skirt, lifted her chin, and sailed out of the room before he could regain his voice.

"There you are!" Rushing down the stairs, Beth grabbed her arm excitedly. "You will not believe it. I am so happy. Tomas has asked me to—"

When Beth closed her mouth abruptly, Charlie glanced over her shoulder, not in the least surprised to see Radcliffe standing in the door to the library. No one looking at him now would believe he had been in flagrante delicto just moments ago—unlike herself she supposed with a sigh, running a self-conscious hand through her hair.

"Tomas asked you to what?" Radcliffe queried when Beth stared at him blankly.

"He . . . er . . . to . . ." Panic began to color her face, then it cleared. "Go hunting with him. In the country. For a couple of days." She was positively beaming with a happiness Charlie very much doubted had anything to do with hunting, but it had been a good save and Charlie could not resist smiling in return, until Radcliffe said, "I am afraid that is impossible."

"What?" Beth and Charlie both cried the word at once, turning to glare at him.

"I am sorry. You cannot go." He did not sound sorry. "How would it look?"

"How would what look?" Beth asked warily, her gaze shooting to Charlie, who had also stiffened at his words. Did he know? Did he know they were both girls? And if he did, how long had he known?

"Your running off to go hunting and leaving your sister alone here with me . . . Unchaperoned."

"Unchaperoned?" Charlie relaxed. He did not know.

"Radcliffe, everyone thinks you are our cousin. I have no need of a chaperone."

"Everyone thinks we are cousins *now*, but what happens when it comes out that we are not related? What then? There would be whispers about the fact that at some point during the charade Charles had run off leaving you here unchaperoned. Besides, our supposedly being cousins does not make us above scandal. Cousins marry all the time."

"But—" Beth began desperately.

"'Tis all right," Charlie murmured, drawing her sister's reluctant gaze. "Come. You can tell me all about your night." Taking her arm, she urged her up the stairs and Beth allowed herself to be led to "Elizabeth's" room. Once there, however, she tugged her arm free and turned on Charlie defiantly. "I told Tom everything. All about us."

"I am not surprised. He seemed very upset when he left the ball."

Beth grimaced. "He was furious. He was also confused. He said that kissing you was like kissing Clarissa. He could not figure out what was going on. But he wasn't happy seeing you, I mean me, in Radcliffe's arms. Well, who he thought was me."

Charlie nodded solemnly. "So, you told him everything and . . . ?"

Happiness exploded on her face. "And he asked me to marry him."

"I thought as much," Charlie admitted with a grin and hurried forward to hug her, truly happy for her sister. "Congratulations."

"Oh, Charlie." Beth squeezed her desperately. "I love him *so*. What am I to do?"

"Do?" Charlie pulled back to look at her with surprise. "Why, you shall marry him, of course."

"But Tomas wants to elope to Gretna Green at once. He is waiting out front."

"Then you had best hurry and get ready, hadn't you?" Releasing her, Charlie rushed into the dressing room.

"Why?" Beth asked miserably, following to find her searching through the gowns they had received so far from the dressmaker. "Radcliffe is not going to let me out the door. He is afraid for Elizabeth's reputation."

"And he is right," Charlie said absently as she packed the lavender gown in a satchel. "Elizabeth should not be here alone. Aside from our reputations, there is the blackmailer to consider. Radcliffe would never let Elizabeth out alone at night, and criminals do seem to like to arrange their meetings at night."

Beth watched her pack away various toiletries, her confusion slowly turning to understanding. "So Elizabeth will rush off to elope with Tomas, and Charles will remain here," she reasoned out slowly, beginning to glow with happiness.

"Nay."

Beth's glow died an abrupt death. "Nay?"

"Nay, of course not. How on earth can I find a husband for myself as Charles? Impossible. Ridiculous. Completely hopeless."

"Then why are you packing a case?" Beth wailed.

Charlie peered at her with surprise. "Why, so that you can elope, of course."

"But you just said—"

"*You*, Beth," Charlie interrupted patiently. "*You*

are going to elope. In the meantime, Charles will be terribly under the weather and spend most of his time in his room. That way, Elizabeth's reputation is safe, Charles is available if the blackmailer arranges another meeting, and I can be Elizabeth almost full-time to search for a husband."

"You will play both roles!" Beth gasped with understanding, following when Charlie snapped the satchel closed and led her from the dressing room.

"Only for a couple of days. Do make sure Tom hurries you back."

Beth bit her lip. "Tom said it would take a full day, a night, and almost another half day to reach Gretna Green if we ride without stopping," she admitted reluctantly.

"A day and a half there, and a day and a half back." Charlie began to shake her head. "You will have to stop to rest the night. That means you will be gone almost four—"

"Nay. We will head right back," Beth interrupted to assure her, afraid Charlie was about to change her mind about all this. "It will only be three days."

"Beth, you cannot ride three days straight without rest, and even if you could, his horse could not."

"We are taking the carriage. Tom and the driver can take turns at the whip, one driving while the other rests. And we can change horses regularly," she added as Charlie began to look hopeful.

"Do you think Tomas will agree to all this?"

"He loves me," was Beth's simple answer.

Smiling wryly, Charlie nodded. "Very well. And once you get back, you can play Charles full time. It will give you a chance to spend as much time alone with your new husband as possible until I find one, too. If I have not found one by the time you return," she added on a sigh, turning to hold the satchel out.

Beth grabbed the bag in one hand, then pulled her sister into an enthusiastic hug. "Oh, Charlie, you are brilliant! Magnificent! Incredible!"

"I love you, too," Charlie murmured, holding her close briefly. Then she pushed her away and turned to open the window. "Now, you had best get going."

Beth glanced at the window, her smile fading somewhat. "Out the window?"

Charlie arched an eyebrow. "Would you care to try walking right out the front door under Radcliffe's nose? If he catches you, the jig will be up."

"Aye, but . . ." she hesitated, recollections of her encounter with the window at the inn filling her mind. What a dreadful experience that had been.

Leaving her to her thoughts, Charlie peered out the window. They were on the second floor above the salon, facing the road, and there was a bush directly beneath the window, offering a cushion should Beth fall. Her gaze slid to the street to see Tomas pacing anxiously beside the Mowbray carriage. Placing two fingers in her mouth, Charlie used the whistle the stablemaster at home had taught her while working with the horses.

The piercing sound drew Tom's head around at once. Spying her at the window, he rushed forward to stand by the bushes beneath the window. Gesturing for him to stay put and remain quiet, Charlie turned back to Beth and took the bag she had packed. She dropped it into the bushes, waiting until Tom scrambled to remove it before turning back to her sister.

"He is waiting for you," she said gently.

"Tom?" Startled from her thoughts, Beth leaned out the window to wave at her husband-to-be before straightening again. "I can do this."

She didn't sound at all certain. Smiling, Charlie hugged her one last time. "We have already escaped unwanted marriages, fled inns in the middle of the night, made our way to London, and fooled the entire ton into thinking we are brother and sister. Beth, I think we can do anything we set our minds to."

Grinning, Beth stepped back. "We are rather daring, are we not?"

"Bold as brass," she agreed cheerfully.

Straightening her shoulders, Beth turned and crawled out to sit on the window ledge before glancing back. "Three days."

"Three days." Charlie agreed, then gasped in alarm when Beth pushed herself off the ledge. Leaning forward, she peered down to see Tomas holding her cradled in his arms, having caught her. Releasing her legs, he let her stand. The couple kissed briefly, then glanced up, waved, and hurried through the darkness to the waiting carriage.

Charlie watched them ride out of sight, then closed the window with a sigh. "Three days."

Chapter 14

CHARLIE had never imagined that time could pass so slowly. These past three days had seemed more like a week to her. She had played Charles each evening since Beth's leaving, donning the wig, jumping into bed, and pulling the linens up to cover her gown as Bessie delivered "Charles's" tray at dinnertime. Dressed as Elizabeth, she had taken up the morning and afternoon trays herself, much to Bessie's relief. The girl was quite busy with the puppies, taking them for walks, then fussing over the fact that they seemed to be off their food. Little did she know that the reason for this sudden drop in their voracious appetites was that they were snacking on the food meant for Charles.

Pacing to the salon window, Charlie peered out. There was still no sign of Radcliffe's carriage. They were supposed to have left for the Sommervilles' ball four hours ago, but Radcliffe had never arrived home to take her. She had gone from irritation, to anger, to anxiety, and now she was worried silly that something had happened to him.

The sound of the front door closing drew her

glance out the window again to see that Radcliffe's carriage had returned. Turning smartly, she hurried into the hall in time to see Stokes disappearing with his master's gloves, cape, and hat. "You are home."

About to step into the library, Radcliffe paused and glanced at her with surprise, then changed direction and moved toward the room she had just exited. "Oh, good evening, Elizabeth."

"Did you have a good day?" she asked sweetly, following him into the salon and watching as he poured himself a drink from a carafe on the table.

"Very good, actually. That investment I made—the one I included you and Charles in—has paid out. We tripled our money," he murmured with satisfaction, then swallowed some of his drink. "That is where I have been, actually."

Charlie's tension eased, her anger dissipating quickly. He had been tending to business. That was why he had not arrived home to take her to the Sommervilles' ball. She could hardly be angry at him for that. She could not expect the man to give up his life or shirk his business to aid her in finding a husband, she thought. And then he added, "I was out celebrating with some of the other investors."

Radcliffe had raised the glass to his lips again when a missile flew at him. Catching it out of the corner of his eye, he dodged it automatically, sloshing port all over the place as he did. It smashed against the wall behind him and he stared at it with amazement, then turned in time to see Elizabeth's skirts disappear through the door. "What the deuce?"

Setting his glass down, he hurried after her. She was halfway up the stairs when he stepped into the hall. "What the devil was that all about?" he shouted after her, taking to the stairs himself.

Not having anything close to hand to hurl at him, Charlie did not deign to stop and answer him. Instead, she picked up her pace in an effort to avoid him. Unfortunately, the constricting farthingale that women were forced to wear to be fashionable, tended to make little things like breathing difficult, and running was out of the question without air, which was why Radcliffe caught her on the landing.

"I want an answer." Catching her arm, he dragged her around to face him. "What was that all about?"

Pressing a hand to her chest, Charlie made a determined effort to regain her breath, then offered him a perplexed look. "What, my lord?"

"In the salon," he snapped. "You threw something at me."

"Did I?" she murmured. "I must have been terribly angry."

"Aye, but about what?"

"Do you know, my lord, I think I have forgotten."

"Forgotten?" He stared at her dumbfounded, and she nodded solemnly.

"Aye. Just like you obviously forgot about the Sommervilles' ball." Turning on that note, she headed down the hall toward "Elizabeth's" room.

"Oh, damn," Radcliffe breathed, squeezing his eyes closed for a moment, then blinking them open again as she reached the door to her room. "Elizabeth, I am sorry. I meant only to have one, maybe two drinks, then head home, but I—"

She whirled on him coldly. "You are not sorry, my lord. Pray do not pretend that you are."

"But I am!"

"Is that right? Well, pray forgive me if I find that hard to believe in light of your recent behavior." His head came up at that, and he hurried forward as she opened the door to her room.

"What do you mean? What recent behavior?" he demanded, barging into the room behind her as she would have closed the door in his face.

Charlie stared at him briefly, then shook her head and crossed the room to peer out the window. Her expression when she turned back was solemn. "Radcliffe, you know that I must find a husband. This is not a question of what I want, it is what I need. If I am not married ere my uncle and Carland find me, I will be forced to marry him. And if that happens, I can guarantee you I shall be dead within a week."

"I would not let that happen."

"Would not *let*? You are practically *guaranteeing* that outcome," she cried.

"Do not be ridiculous."

"Ridiculous? My lord, you took me to the Halthams' ball the night before last."

"There! You see? I am trying to aid you."

"The Halthams are eighty years old if they are a day."

He looked uncomfortable. "Well, that does not mean—"

"There were exactly three men at that ball under sixty years of age, and when one or another of them even looked my way, you glowered at them so ferociously that they immediately turned away."

"Well, not one of them was much of a man if a little frown scares them off."

"My lord, next to Carland, Mr. Haltham himself looks like a prince."

Flushing guiltily, he shook his head. "All right, the night before last was a failure and it was all my fault."

"Last night you took me to the Whitmans' ball."

"Alice Whitman isn't a day over nineteen," he pointed out quickly.

"But Lord Whitman is ninety if he is a day. He is also deaf as a post and blind as a bat and uses these frailties as excuses to literally drool down every single woman's bodice as he supposedly listens to them speak. This is why, as I learned last night, no one who is anyone attends his balls, and *why* there was not one single available male in attendance. Or female, for that matter. Oh, other than myself, I mean," she added dryly. "But am I to believe that tonight was not another attempt to sabotage my efforts at saving myself? Fine. The Sommervilles' ball slipped your mind. My need to find a husband *to save my life* slipped your mind. *I* apparently slipped your mind!"

Radcliffe stood silent before her, shame covering him like a cloak. She was right, of course, though he had not even realized it himself until now. He *had* deliberately sabotaged her efforts to gain a husband. And he could not even explain why. All he knew was that the last three days had been hell as he had tried to keep his distance and behave appropriately while all the young bucks in London sniffed about her. Oh, he had noticed the way they looked at her. And had found it damned annoying. Every gleaming eye that was cast her way had made him clench his teeth in fury.

She was too good for them. Too good for them all. The thought of any of them having the right to take her to his bed, to touch her body, taste the sweetness he had experienced . . . The very idea made him furious. Impossible. Never. Over his dead body. He would marry her himself first.

Radcliffe went still. Marry her? His gaze slid over her in the royal blue gown, caressing the mounds of her breasts, remembering the weight and feel of them in his hands. An ache started immediately in his groin, and he swallowed thickly. If he married her he would have the right to feel them again . . . And much more. He could have her in his bed every night. Face her across the table every morning . . . She would be safe. More importantly, she would be his.

Then he thought of Charles and the odd reaction he'd had to the lad sometimes, and Radcliffe frowned. To marry the sister meant having to be around the brother a great deal. A prospect that made him extremely uncomfortable.

"I need your assistance, not your interference, Radcliffe."

He glanced down with a start to see that she had moved to stand directly in front of him, close enough for him to smell. Close enough for him to touch. His heart rate picked up just at her nearness, his body responding with definite enthusiasm. Mayhap Charles would be interested in a Grand Tour. "I must speak to your brother."

Charlie's eyes widened in shocked dismay at Radcliffe's announcement. She leapt forward, grabbing his arm in panic as he turned to exit the room. "Oh, nay. Please, you mustn't disturb Charles. You know he is unwell just now."

"Aye, and I promise I will not disturb him for any longer than I have to, but I must have a word with him."

"But he—" Seeing the determination on his face, Charlie slid between him and the door, caught him by the ears, and dragged his head down to her own. Radcliffe went stiff as a board as her lips mashed his. Realizing that her play was not working, she released his ears, slid her fingers into his hair, and eased her lips until they were rubbing and nibbling at his. She sensed his hesitation then and slid her tongue out to lick his lips, in what she hoped was a provocative manner.

Much to her relief it seemed to work. Giving in to temptation, Radcliffe slid his arms around her waist, his lips opening and his own tongue coming out to master hers. The result was shattering. They had been playing with fire too long, dancing with arousal, then leaving it unfed too many times. Both of them went up in flames.

Continuing to kiss her, Radcliffe swept her up in his arms and carried her to the side of the bed. When he set her down again, Charlie found that someone had stolen her strength and her legs were shaking with her need. Breaking the kiss, he straightened suddenly, caught her at the waist, and turned her away from him. Then she felt his hands at her lacings, and she held her breath, releasing it with a sigh when the top of her gown loosened, then slid off her shoulders and down her arms to pool at her feet. Her chemise quickly followed, and before her nipples could pucker defensively against the sudden chill of vulnerability, Radcliffe's hands replaced the material, cupping her breasts and pressing her back to lean against him.

"You are so lovely," he breathed into her ear, peering down her body from behind.

Charlie glanced down, seeing what he saw; smooth ivory skin and the curve of her breasts held in his darker hands. It was an erotic sight, and she shuddered against him as he caught her nipples between each thumb and forefinger to roll them teasingly.

Moaning, Charlie dropped her head back onto his shoulder as he kissed and nipped at her neck, then stiffened in his arms, quivering as he slid one hand down between her thighs. Gasping, she twisted her head abruptly, searching for and finding his lips and kissing him with a violence that startled her. But Radcliffe merely chuckled deep in his throat and tugged his lips away to shift her around to face him once more. Charlie immediately took that opportunity to push his dress coat and waistcoat off, then commenced with undoing his shirt buttons, kissing every inch of skin she could reach as it was exposed. She had run out of shirt and started to work at his breeches when he caught her by the shoulders and pushed her back to sit on the bed. Following her, he kissed her feverishly, then trailed his lips to her ear, then down her throat to a spot between her breasts. Catching her breasts in his hands, he turned his head to kiss first one, then the other and continued his trail downward.

Swallowing, Charlie knotted her hands in his hair and clenched her stomach against the quivers that shot through her as he licked a path along it. Then she stilled, even her breathing seeming to halt as she felt his hands clasp her ankles and draw her legs farther apart, then slide slowly, deliciously upward, over her calves, her knees, her thighs. Lifting his head, he caught her lips in another passionate kiss, then pulled away and kissed the inside of first one knee, then the other. A gasp tore from her throat and she nearly leapt off the bed when he then pressed a kiss to the very core of her, his tongue whipping out to tease the center of all her sensation, his teeth grazing her tender flesh. Throwing her head back, Charlie released a high, piercing cry of need that died on a whimper as he gently inserted one finger inside, slowly stretching her.

"Oh God, oh God, please," she sobbed breathlessly, not even sure what she was begging for.

Radcliffe knew, however, and he continued his tender ministrations until she found it, the release she needed. It came with a thundering of blood in her ears, a rush of sensation, then Radcliffe was straightening before her, catching her beneath the knees to pull her to the edge of the bed. Clasping her buttocks in hand, he lifted her slightly and eased into her still shuddering body, groaning as she closed around his engorged flesh. Plunging forward, he took her innocence swiftly and painlessly as she pulled his head down and kissed him demandingly. Radcliffe kissed her back, his tongue thrusting into her mouth as he drove into her body.

It was the closing of the door that woke Charlie. Blinking sleepily, she peered at the empty bed beside her, then slowly sat up. Sunlight was peeking through the closed drapes. Radcliffe had slipped out while she slept. She was just wondering if she should be upset when she heard the knock at the door.

Glancing toward it, she frowned slightly, wondering why it sounded so faint, then realized it was because the knocking was not at that door but next door, in Charles's room. She'd taken to leaving the interconnecting door open, in case of just such an occurrence. Sighing, she shoved the blankets aside, grabbed the wrap to cover her nakedness, and stumbled wearily between the bedrooms. She covered a sleepy yawn, then paused in the center of Charles's room, cleared her throat, and called out, "Who is it?"

"Lord Radcliffe. I know it is early, but I need to speak with you."

Charlie's eyebrows rose at the almost hushed sound to his voice, but she sighed, "Fine. I shall be down directly."

"Nay. I would speak with you now."

She frowned at that, her gaze dropping to the robe she wore and the unbound breasts pressing eagerly out from beneath it. "Now? Can it not wait until—"

"*Now.*"

Hearing the firmness in his voice, Charlie shifted irritably. "Just a moment then," she snapped, and began searching for the cloth to bind her breasts. Spotting it trailing toward the connecting door of the bedrooms, she grabbed it up, shrugged out of her robe, and began the binding.

"It is about your sister."

"What about her?" Charlie asked, wincing as she tightened the cloth around her breasts. Good Lord, it was uncomfortable to be trussed up thusly. Had she really spent days strapped so? Amazing what women were forced to do to—

"I cannot speak of it through the door. May I come in?"

"No!" she cried, dragging her shirt on over the binding, then, realizing how sharp she had sounded, added more calmly, "I am not dressed. I shall let you in directly."

There was silence for a moment as she found and began to tug on her stockings, then his impatient voice came again. "It is quite important."

"Fine, fine. Just a moment." Tying her hair quickly, she stuffed the strands down her back, plopped the wig on top, and peered about for the knee breeches. Spying them sticking out from beneath the bed, she hurried over and knelt to retrieve them.

Hearing the soft tread of someone moving up the stairs, Radcliffe stiffened and stepped toward the rail to peer down. Bessie was coming up, no doubt headed to awaken her mistress. He was just sighing in relief that he had left Elizabeth's room ere the woman's arrival and thus had avoided an embarrassing scene, when he realized that he was still wearing last night's evening clothes. Panicking, he opened the door to Charles's room and stepped inside, closing the door just as the maid reached the top of the landing.

"I am sorry, Bessie was coming and I—" he began, only to pause and gape at the bare behind directed toward him. Charles was on his hands and knees at the side of the bed, apparently attempting to drag something out. He was dressed only in stockings that reached to his thighs and a shirt that had risen up to reveal his derriere as he searched. And what a shapely derriere it was, Radcliffe noticed with dismay. Good God! It was almost an exact replica of Elizabeth's. He supposed he should not be surprised at that. After all, they were twins. Then again, perhaps his shock was not so much at that as at the fact that his body was reacting to the sight of it in about the same way as it had reacted to the sight of Charles's sister's. So much for last night clearing up his sexual confusion.

Cursing, he turned around abruptly. It seemed to help little, however; the pink upside-down heart that was both Charles's and Elizabeth's derriere seemed etched on his brain.

Hearing his curse, Charlie straightened abruptly, knee breeches in hands as she glanced around to see Radcliffe standing with his back to her. Flushing with embarrassment despite the fact that he had seen every inch of her nude the night before, she leapt to her feet and began tugging on the breeches. "Dammit, Radcliffe, I did say to wait a moment."

"Yes, well, I . . . er . . . Bessie was coming up the hall," he explained lamely.

"So?" Charlie asked irritably, tucking her shirt into the breeches.

"So I did not wish her to see me like this."

She glanced at him curiously. "Why not? You look fine."

"These are the same clothes I was wearing last evening." Glancing over his shoulder, Radcliffe saw that the lad was dressed now and turned to face him. "Which is part of the reason I wished to speak with you."

Charlie blinked at that. "You wished to speak with me because you are wearing last evening's clothes still?"

"Nay," he snapped impatiently. "Because of the reason that I am still wearing last evening's clothes."

Understanding struck Charlie then and she nearly smiled. This was what one might call the big confession scene. He thought to tell her that he had ruined her sister last night. Of course, he had really not ruined Beth at all, but *her* playing Beth. Well, she had not really been playing Beth last night, because Beth loved Tomas and so would not have slept with Radcliffe, so she supposed she had really been Charlie last night, but Charlie the girl, not Charles the brother. Goodness, what a tangle things were getting into.

Radcliffe cleared his throat, drawing her attention again as he began to pace before her. "Charles, it has occurred to me that perhaps you would care to take a Grand Tour?"

When he quit his pacing to peer at her hopefully, she frowned with bewilderment. "What has that to do with the fact that you have not changed your clothes?"

"Ahh . . . yes . . . well, you see . . . I thought perhaps . . . If we married, you see—"

Charlie gaped at him. "Excuse me?"

"I said, I am going to marry your sister," he repeated grimly.

Charlie frowned at that, for she was absolutely positive that there had been no mention of marriage to her. Not to her as Elizabeth at least. Then the fact that Radcliffe did not exactly sound pleased at the notion struck her. "Why?"

Radcliffe shifted uncomfortably. "Why?"

"Why do you wish to marry her?"

"I . . . well . . . last night we . . . er . . ."

"Last night you '*er*'?" she repeated grimly, taking great offense at the description. "Er" seemed to reduce what had been a beautiful experience to a rather tawdry little episode. Fury raising in her, she snapped, "You '*er*'d her?"

"I realize this is a poor showing on my part."

"A poor showing?" she repeated, incredulous.

"I had offered the two of you my protection and I have behaved badly," Radcliffe continued as if Charlie had not interrupted. "I am terribly sorry for my slip, but . . ." Frustration crossed his face. This was not at all the way he had meant for things to go. He didn't even know why he had brought up last night except that it was looming large in his mind just now . . . Along with the fact that he could repeat it should he marry Elizabeth. Good Lord! He realized with dismay that he was allowing his manly parts to make decisions now.

Nay, he corrected himself at once. He was *not* marrying Elizabeth simply to bed her. And he had decided on marrying her ere bedding her. Last night merely meant that they would have to be married at once to avoid the possibility of having a child too soon after the wedding. Marrying quickly was a necessity anyway, thanks to Carland.

"You were saying?"

Radcliffe cleared his throat, then frowned. "What *was* I saying?"

"You were sorry for your slip and . . . ?"

"Oh." He frowned. "Well, really, that part was not very important."

"You '*er*'d my sister and it is not important?"

Radcliffe eyed the lad warily. There was something

rather threatening about his attitude. "It is important, of course," he tried to explain. "But it really has nothing to do with why I am prepared to marry your sister."

"So, the fact that you '*er*'d her is not important, but you wish to marry her because . . . ?" The lad was waiting.

"So that no one else can." Oh dear, that didn't sound very good at all. "I mean, I am willing to suffer the consequences of my actions and marry her at the first opportunity."

"Suffer the consequences?" The boy was nearly foaming at the mouth, but visibly forced himself to calm down. "What of love?"

"Love?" Radcliffe was nonplussed by the question. "Well, I do not—" He paused there, frowning slightly, for he had been about to say that he did not think it an issue at the moment, besides his feelings were most confused on the subject. One moment he would look at Elizabeth and feel heat and desire and she seemed the most exciting creature he had ever met. Then the next time he saw her she would seem quiet and reticent, and he would feel nothing but a slight avuncular affection. His reactions to the boy before him were just as confusing. "I do not—"

The boy turned away at those words, paling.

Shaking his head, Radcliffe gave up attempting to sort out his feelings. "My feelings are not at issue here. What happened last night is. Should I not marry her, your sister will be ruined . . . or forced to marry Carland. Do I have your permission to marry her, or not?"

"Oh, by all means," Charlie sighed, sounding almost

bitter. "Marry my sister . . . If she will have you. I couldn't care less."

Frowning at his tone of voice, Radcliffe hesitated, then turned toward the door. Now he would have to talk to Elizabeth. Mayhap he should go collect the engagement ring first. Aye, a capital idea. This had to be done properly. He would collect the ring, have Mrs. Hartshair make a special dinner. . . . "I have something I must do. Do not tell your sister. I wish to tell her myself."

"As you wish," Charlie murmured as the door closed behind Radcliffe, then whipped off the wig furiously with one hand, using the other to half-shrug, half-tug off her shirt as she turned away from the door. Radcliffe had not left a moment too soon, she saw. Her bindings—as sloppily as she had donned them in her haste—were half-undone and quickly unraveling.

Grimacing, she tugged the last of the bindings away and tossed them after the robe, only to stiffen as a gasp sounded. Lifting her gaze slowly, she stared at the girl frozen in the connecting door between rooms, her wide eyes taking in Charlie half-in and half-out of her disguise.

"Bessie." Charlie took a step toward her and the girl turned and fled. Cursing, she was after her at once, following her into "Elizabeth's" room. Seeing that she was fleeing for the door, Charlie charged forward, leaping onto the bed and running right over it in an effort to reach the door first. She slammed against the door just as Bessie started to tug it open, her weight forcing it closed with a crack like thunder. Bessie fell away at once, shock and fear on her face as she stumbled backward across the room.

" 'Tis all right, Bessie. I am not going to hurt you," Charlie murmured reassuringly, her gaze dancing between the girl and the room until she spied Elizabeth's robe lying across the foot of the bed. She moved quickly to grab it, and Bessie danced skittishly away from her, her eyes darting nervously around for some escape. Sighing impatiently, Charlie donned the robe and ripped at the ribbon that held her hair at her back, then brushed some of it forward before facing the girl once more. " 'Tis all right, Bessie," she repeated on a sigh. "See?"

"Nay, I'm not seein'," Bessie cried unhappily, but she stopped moving and focused on Charlie now. "What's going on? Which are ye? The brother or the sister?"

"Both," Charlie answered truthfully with a wry smile, then sighed again as she saw she had only confused the girl further. "I am Charlie."

As impossible as it seemed, the girl's eyes widened more and she shook her head a bit wildly. "Nay. Yer not. Ye've bosoms. I saw them."

"Aye, well, that is because I am a girl. Charlie is short for Charlotte. I was just pretending to be a boy to—" She paused and took a step to the side, blocking the path to the door when Bessie started in that direction again. Bessie paused at once, but it was obvious she would flee at any moment. "Bessie, I am the same Charlie that rescued you from that room at Aggie's. Do you not think you at least owe me the chance to explain?"

The girl swallowed at that, uncertainty covering

her face as she peered longingly at the door; then she sighed unhappily and gave one small nod.

"Good." Charlie offered her a gentle smile, then gestured to the small table by the window. "Why do we not sit down so that I can explain everything?"

Bessie looked doubtful, but moved to perch on one of the two seats at the table, eyeing Charlie warily as she followed and claimed the other seat.

"You see," Charlie began promptly, not surprised when as her story progressed, Bessie's suspicious expression was replaced by surprise, concern, then sympathetic murmurings. She told the servant everything. Well, almost everything. She kept back any mention of the blackmailer and her less respectable moments with Radcliffe. By the time she was finished, the girl was eyeing her with admiration.

"Yer so brave. To have dressed up as a lad and fled your uncle." She shook her head in wonder, but Charlie smiled wryly and reached out to pat her hand.

"No more brave than you, Bessie. You may not have dressed up as a lad, but you did travel all the way to the city alone to seek employment."

"Oh, aye. But just look how that turned out. Aggie fooling me in to—" She paused suddenly, her eyes wide with realization. "You were in a brothel! Oh, my lord. A lady in a brothel!"

"Shh," Charlie hissed nervously, afraid of their being overheard. "That was Radcliffe's idea. He thought I was too . . . umm . . . feminine and thought to make a 'man' out of me." Amusement tugged at her lips as she admitted that.

Bessie's eyes widened further. "Lord Radcliffe doesn't know that yer a girl?"

"Nay. No one knows but you." She sighed, then added under her breath to herself, "And the black-mailer."

"Blackmailer!" Bessie nearly screeched the word, her face a picture of horror, and Charlie grimaced. The girl's hearing was amazing.

"Aye. Well," she murmured, then quickly explained about the letters they had received, the botched pay-off attempt, and the last letter that had warned them to get the money together and be prepared, that they would hear from the blackmailer again today. "I did not tell Beth before she left. She would just worry."

"Aye, she would have," Bessie agreed, then glanced nervously toward a tray on the table, murmuring, "Today, ye say?"

"Aye." Charlie followed her gaze, eyebrows rising at the rolled-up scroll that lay on the tray. It was secured with a blood-red ribbon. "What is that?" she asked warily. "Where did it come from?"

"It arrived just ere I came upstairs," Bessie admitted anxiously. "A young street urchin delivered it. He said it was urgent one o' ye get it right away."

Charlie stared at the scroll, suddenly torn. Part of her wanted to snatch up the scroll, read the instructions, and follow them to get the whole thing finally over with. Another part was suddenly flooded with foreboding. Shrugging the dark feeling away, she reached for the scroll and silently undid the ribbon, very aware of Bessie's worried gaze as she read it.

"What is it?" Bessie asked when she suddenly cursed.

Tossing the scroll impatiently on the table, Charlie stood and began to pace. "His plan requires the two of us to be there."

"You and I?" Bessie asked with shock, and Charlie shook her head impatiently.

"Nay, Elizabeth and I. We have to—" She paused suddenly and turned to stare at the maid, her mind working furiously.

Bessie sat back, her expression wary. "Why are ye looking at me that way?"

Chapter 15

"My, you make a lovely lady," Mrs. Hartshair murmured, stepping back from her handiwork with pride. "Doesn't she, m'lord? I mean, m'lady."

Charlie smiled slightly at the woman's expression. The cook had even more trouble accepting the fact that Charles was really a Charlotte than Bessie had.

It had taken Charlie an hour to convince Bessie to assist her. The girl really had a horrid aversion to the idea of impersonating a lady. In the end it was guilt that had got her to agree. Desperate by that point, Charlie had shaken her head in feigned sadness and murmured that she could not believe what an ungrateful wretch she was . . . and after all she, Charlie, had done for her. Miserable, Bessie had caved in and agreed to do what was necessary. By that time, however, they had been left with only moments to prepare, and Charlie had reluctantly decided the cook had to be taken into confidence and put upon to help them.

"Aye," Charlie murmured now in response to the cook's comment. "She is quite lovely. 'Tis no wonder Aggie wanted her to work for her." Bessie made a face at that, and Charlie grinned as she tied off the thread she had used to sew a veil to one of "Elizabeth's" hats, then broke the thread and set the needle aside as she stood. "Here you are. The final touch to your disguise."

Taking the hat, Bessie donned it while Charlie moved to the table and slid the paper with the address into her pocket.

"How is this?" Bessie asked, drawing her attention again.

"Perfect." Charlie grinned with relief at the way the hat and veil completely disguised Bessie's hair color and facial features. "And now we have to go."

Turning, she opened the door and started out, Bessie on her heels, but Ms. Hartshair chased after them anxiously. "How long shall you be?"

Charlie paused on the landing and frowned over the question. "I am not sure," she admitted, then sighed impatiently. "We should not be long. We will be back within the hour, before noon at the latest."

The Cock and Bull was a decidedly seedy establishment. Charlie and Bessie eyed it from the confines of the carriage, then glanced at each other. At least Charlie thought Bessie was looking at her. It was hard to see her eyes through the veil she wore.

"You are sure this is where the note said to go?" Bessie asked unhappily.

"Aye," Charlie sighed.

"What are we supposed to do now?"

"We are to go in and book a room under the name"—Charlie pulled the note out of her pocket and checked it—"Pigeon," she muttered wryly, then glanced back out the window at the shabby exterior of the building. "I suppose we had best get this over with."

"Aye." Bessie sounded less than enthusiastic about it, and Charlie gave her a reassuring smile.

" 'Twill all be over in a jiffy, and when it is, I shall buy you a fine new gown of your own as a thank you."

"That won't be necessary, my lady. As you pointed out earlier, you have done quite a lot for me already and I would hate to have any more to have to pay you back for."

Charlie glanced away guiltily, then sighed. "I am sorry, Bessie. I never should have blackmailed you so. If–if you do not wish to accompany me inside, you could just wait in the carriage and—" She paused at a disgusted snort from the girl.

"And waste all that primping and poking for nothing? Nay. Someone shall see me dressed up so ere I remove all this fancy finery, thank you. Besides, it is the least I can do," she added more gently. "And I am sorry if I sounded a bit touchy just now."

Charlie hesitated another moment, nodded with relief, pushed the carriage door open, then stepped out and turned to help Bessie down.

If the exterior of the Cock and Bull had looked seedy, the inside was positively depressing. The heavy stench of smoke and stale ale were the first things to hit Charlie. Nose wrinkling, she blinked several times in an effort to adjust to the dim interior after the bright sunlight outside. When she could see clearly, she had to wonder why she had bothered. There wasn't much to see. Scarred wooden tables. A dirty wooden floor littered with various bits of debris.

Brown walls which may have started out cream or white but were now stained from decades of smoke. Unkempt people with stained, shabby clothes filled every cranny, despite the fact that it was not yet noon.

Taking Bessie's arm, Charlie led her quickly through the noisy crowd to the bar. The innkeeper noticed them at once. Flashing a set of teeth as stained as his brown walls, he continued to wipe a mug with a filthy cloth as he nodded in greeting. "What'll it be?"

"A room please. For Lord and Lady . . . er . . . Pigeon."

His hands slowed in their wiping as he glanced over them curiously, then he nodded slowly. "That'll just take a minute. One of the girls'll prepare the room. Why don'tcha sit over there at that corner table and have an ale while ye wait."

It wasn't a question. Charlie followed the man's gaze toward the table indicated, noting that there was a lone man seated at it. Short and stout, his head was sunk deep on his chest as he studied his drink with an air of boredom. Realizing that this must be the man she was to meet, Charlie nodded and started to turn away, but paused when the innkeeper suddenly grabbed her arm.

"Ye'll be paying for the room and ale in advance, won't ye."

That wasn't a question either, Charlie noted as she grimly reached into her pocket and withdrew a couple of coins. Tossing them at the man a bit impatiently, she hurried Bessie toward the table they had been directed to, eager to have the ordeal done with.

The stranger lifted his head when Charlie and Bessie stopped at the table. His eyes skimmed them both, noting their matching height and slender frames. "Yer late."

Charlie stiffened at the belligerent tone, her eyes scanning his face. She frowned over his bulbous nose, thick lips, and pockmarked face. He was not someone one was likely to forget meeting, and she was positive she had never met him before. Which meant he probably wasn't the actual blackmailer but an agent for him. She had been rather hoping to have a discussion with the blackmailer himself, to discern whether he intended to try to extort more money later. It seemed she wasn't going to get the chance. Which meant they would be left to wonder and worry for a while longer.

"A couple more minutes and I would have left," the man added, obviously displeased with her silence in response to his complaint.

Shrugging impatiently, Charlie reached into her pocket to retrieve the sack of coins that was the payoff, eager to get this meeting over with.

"Put that away," he snapped, adding with disgust when she did, "D'ye want to get us killed or something? Gawd!" Rising abruptly, he gestured for them to follow and headed for the back of the establishment, leading them through a door that opened into a small, filthy kitchen, then on through that to another door. This one led into an alley behind the inn. An alley that positively reeked of rotting meat and human excrement.

Covering their noses with distaste, Charlie and Bessie followed the man several feet away from the door before he stopped to face them, grinning with obvious pleasure over their discomfort. He didn't seem to be affected by the odors at all. Apparently his nose was all show, and not very useful otherwise. Years of boozing had probably killed any ability it had once had to smell, Charlie thought nastily as she once again reached for the sack of coins. This time he did not stop her. Dropping the sack into the hand he held out, she waited while he opened it and peered at the coins inside. When he nodded in satisfaction, she shifted, drawing his attention once again. "If our business is concluded . . . ?"

"Not quite."

Stilling, she glanced around when he gestured as if to someone behind her. With a sinking heart she saw two men moving toward them from the back door of the inn, and whirled angrily back to the man she had just handed the coins to. "What is this?"

"Well, now, it seems that my boss thinks that if you will pay this well to keep your whereabouts a secret, your uncle will pay even more to have you back."

Before Charlie could do or say anything in response to that, a cry from Bessie brought her around to see that the men had reached them. One had grabbed her upper arms from behind and was attempting to subdue her as she began struggling and kicking. Charlie moved at once to try to help, but had barely taken a step when she found herself facing the second man. He was a behemoth. As tall as a tree and as broad as a barn. His presence before her blocked out the sun and cast her in shadow.

Charlie swallowed grimly, fear leaving her frozen until another cry from Bessie made her move. Stomping on the man's foot, she ran around him and launched herself at the back of the other man as he forced Bessie up the alley toward a carriage that suddenly appeared there. This man wasn't quite as tall as the other, but he was as brawny. He gave a grunt when she attached herself to his back, one arm around his neck, the other hand caught in his hair and pulling furiously. Her feet and knees dug into the flesh of his hips as she scrambled for purchase. Then she was grasped about the waist, and her upper body was pulled away from the man.

"Here now, don't hurt her," the man with the nose muttered. It was the last thing Charlie heard. The fellow who had grabbed her released her at once, and Charlie—whose legs were still wrapped around the other man's hips—had no time to grab at anything to stop her fall as her upper body suddenly plummeted downward, her head crashing onto the cobbled street.

"Good day, my lord. I trust your expedition was successful?"

"Most successful, Stokes," Radcliffe murmured, handing over his frock coat, hat, and gloves before reaching down instinctively to pat his pocket, feeling for the jeweler's package there. "Is Lady Elizabeth in the salon?"

"Nay, my lord. She is still out."

"Out?" He stilled at that. "Out where?"

"With her brother, my lord. Lord Charles asked me to procure them a carriage shortly after you left this morning."

"And they have not returned yet? Where did they go?"

Before Stokes could answer either question, a tap at the front door drew him forward to answer it.

"Elizabeth!" Radcliffe hurried forward as he spied the woman on the doorstep, his smile turning to a scowl when he noticed Tomas a step behind her. Taking her arm, he drew her into the house and away from the other man. "Stokes said you left with Charles this morning. Where did you go? And where is Charles?"

"Charlie is not here?" Worry pulled at her brow as she asked Stokes that.

"Nay, my lady. He has not returned since the two of you departed this morning."

"The two of us?"

"Aye, my lady." His confusion was obvious.

Elizabeth frowned at his words, then seemed to come to a conclusion that soothed her. "But not at the same time. First one left, then the other, is that not right?" she guessed. Stokes blinked.

"Nay, my lady. You both walked out together. You were wearing a different gown, though."

This news seemed to simply confuse the woman, Radcliffe saw with irritation as Elizabeth turned worriedly to Tomas Mowbray, whispering his name in confusion.

"And a veiled hat," Stokes added suddenly, which brought a spark of what seemed to be understanding to Mowbray's eye.

"You are saying Charlie and a woman in a veiled hat left the house this morning, but they have not returned yet?"

Stokes nodded slowly, his expression becoming thoughtful as he recognized the distinction being made. "Aye, my lord."

Beth's frown deepened. "Who could the woman have been?"

Radcliffe was frowning now, too. "Are you saying it was not you?"

"It was not me," Beth confirmed.

Radcliffe glanced at Stokes' confused face, then asked, "Then when and how did you leave the house today?"

"I did not leave the house today."

He shifted impatiently. "Do not be ridiculous. You must have left. You have just returned with Mowbray in tow."

Beth shook her head. "Nay, my lord. I never left the house today. I have not been here for the past three days. I left the night of the Fetterleys' ball. Charlie pretended to be me to hide the fact that I was gone."

"That is rot, madam and you know I know it is!" Grabbing her wrist, Radcliffe turned toward the library. "I do not know what game you are playing, madam," he snapped as he moved. "But you shall explain yourself."

"Hang on there," Mowbray said as he hurried after them and caught Beth's free hand, tugging her away from Radcliffe.

"Let go of her, Mowbray, this is none of your concern." Radcliffe dragged her back a step so that Beth stood between the two men, caught in the middle of a tug of war.

"It certainly is my concern, man. She is my wife."

"What?" Radcliffe blanched.

Tomas nodded with satisfaction. "'Tis where we have been for the last few days. Gretna Green. We rode there by carriage, married, and I brought her directly back."

Radcliffe laughed his relief at that. "Do you take

me for a fool? You could not have possibly taken her there. She was here."

"Nay, my lord. That was Charlie," Elizabeth said. "Charlie has been covering for my absence," she repeated gently.

Rather than being soothed by her gentle words, Radcliffe grew more angry, his mouth tightening grimly. "You know you cannot fool me with that nonsense, Elizabeth. Why would you even try?"

"But 'tis true, my lord," she insisted, merely managing to annoy him further.

"Charles in a dress? And with long dark tresses?" he queried sarcastically.

"Aye."

Radcliffe shook his head. "Even if it were true that Charles could pass himself off as a woman in a dress, you and I both know that I know that it was not him. Do I really have to state how I know it was not Charles in front of this young buck, or will you confess this a poor joke and give it up?"

"But Charlie *did* pretend to be me while I was gone," she insisted once more.

"Madam, the body I held in my arms and *made love* to last night was a woman's. It definitely was not your brother, Charles."

"You made love to Charlie?" the girl asked with some shock.

"I made love to you!" Radcliffe snapped back.

"The devil you did," Tom muttered. "Even I have not had that honor yet. There was no opportunity what with having to rush back here to save Charlotte."

"Charlotte? Who the deuce is Charlotte?"

"Charlie!" Beth and Tomas answered as one. When Radcliffe merely stared at them blankly, Tomas explained. "Beth and Charlotte are twin *sisters*."

"Charlie only pretended to be a boy so that we might travel safely," Beth added quickly. "Are you all right, my lord? You have gone quite pale."

Radcliffe shook his head. "I think you had best explain this to me. . . . slowly."

Beth bit her lip and glanced at her husband, then back to Radcliffe. "Well, it is really very simple. You see, Uncle Henry had arranged our marriages to Carland and Seguin, and Charlie and I—Well, really, my lord, you yourself said Carland has seen three wives to the grave. As for Seguin, I fear he has some peculiar predilections. Though I must confess I did not know that until you took Charlie to the brothel."

Radcliffe gave a start at that, horror passing across his face even as Tomas turned on him accusingly. "You took her to a brothel?"

Grimacing now, Radcliffe shook his head. "I took Charles. The boy was missish. I thought to make a man of him."

"I fear that would be quite impossible," Beth murmured with amusement, then hurried on with her explanations when he glared at her. "At any rate, we decided Carland and Seguin were unsuitable and that we would flee to our cousin Ralphy's."

Radcliffe gave another start. "Ralphy? I thought you were headed to London."

She smiled apologetically. "Well, no, not really. Charlie simply told you that in case you should run into Uncle Henry and give us away. We were really headed to Ralph. He is our cousin on our mother's side, and Uncle Henry did not know about him as far as we knew. It seemed the best place to go, but it is not safe for a woman to travel alone. . . . Nor even for two women, so Charlie decided to dress as a man. She thought it would keep us safe from ne'er-do-wells, as well as make it harder for Uncle Henry to track us. He would have been looking for two women, you see?"

"I see," he said dryly, recalling the slim youth facing him in the stables. His fear had been obvious, but equally obvious had been the boy's determination to protect his . . . *her* sister. "Why did the two of you not tell me the truth?"

"Well, we did not know you then, my lord."

"Nay, at first you did not," he conceded. "But after, when I offered my aid—"

"We never really meant to accept your assistance. In fact, we did try to refuse it, if you will recall, but you seemed unwilling to leave us to our own devices. So we were forced to start out for London with you, but planned to sneak off in the middle of the night and head back for Ralphy's alone."

His eyebrows rose at that. "And why did you not do so?"

"You did not stop," she pointed out dryly. "We expected you simply to lead us to the next inn to rest for the night ere continuing on the next day, but you rode us through the night, stopping only at dawn. We were too exhausted to be able to leave then."

Radcliffe smiled wryly, recalling Charles's stumbling wearily about their room that first morning as dawn had crept into the sky. She had taken a grave risk in sharing that room. She could have been ruined had she been discovered. He suddenly recalled waking up with her wrapped around his body and his own shock and horror at his physical response to the boy's proximity and grimaced. If he had known then what he knew now . . . Pushing such thoughts aside, he asked, "Why did you not leave the next night, then?"

She shrugged. "You had pointed out the necessity of having a firing arm and we did not have one. Then, too, as time passed and we got to know you, my lord, we came to quite like you. It did not seem right to run off in the middle of the night when you had been so kind. So we decided mayhap London would be the better destination for us. You had offered to help change our jewels for us and . . ." Flushing guiltily, she glanced at Tomas. "Well, we did rather hope that we might find alternative husbands, saving us from having to hide at our cousin's country estate and spend our lives as spinsters," she admitted self-consciously.

Smiling, Tomas placed his arm around her comfortingly. "And so you did, my dear, and I am grateful for it."

"As am I. I was attracted to you from the first, but I knew you were the man for me that day at Radcliffe's club," Beth murmured back, hugging him close so that she missed Radcliffe giving a start again.

"My club? When were you at my club?"

"The day after we arrived, my lord," Beth answered, glancing at him with surprise. "Do you not recall?"

"I took Charles there, not you."

"I was Charles that day," she admitted, blushing furiously.

"That day?" He looked nonplused. "What do you

mean, that day? I thought Charlie . . ." He was looking bewildered again and Beth hurried to explain.

"Well, Charlie seemed to be having so much fun that I thought to try it. After all, you had taken her to learn to shoot, to a brothel, sat up all night drinking with her . . ." She frowned as he seemed to pale further with each example of the "fun" he had shown Charlotte. "I thought I should like to try being a man for a day. So the morning after we arrived, we switched. Charlie played me, and I played Charles."

"I see," he murmured faintly and thought he actually might be beginning to. He vividly recalled the trip to his club that she spoke of. How could he not? It had been the first time that he had been with Charles and not found himself reluctantly attracted to the boy. Thinking on it now, he realized that that afternoon had also been the first time he had found himself attracted to who he had thought was Beth. It had actually been Charlotte. He had kissed her there for the first time, then they had gone to the theater that night and she had flirted horrifically with— "But you were Beth again that night when we went to the theater?"

"Aye."

"And the next day?"

"Aye."

"But not that night?"

"Nay." She looked surprised that he could tell when she had been herself and when not, but he was not about to explain that it was not actually him but his body that had known the difference. Every time Charlotte—what a horrendous name—had played Beth, he had been drawn to her like a moth to a flame.

Just as he had been drawn to Charles only when Charlie was the one wearing the breeches. It was damned relieving, that. At least he knew there was nothing peculiar about him. He was suddenly quite happy with himself and the world around him. His feelings were all sorted out now. It was Charlie. Charlie he had desired, Charlie he had wanted, Charlie he found charming, and Charlie he had loved. The wicked little femme had really pulled one over on him. She looked damned good in breeches. Mayhap he should have her wear them once in a while to—

"—realized Carland was headed here, we headed directly back."

Radcliffe blinked his less than sterling thoughts aside as he caught the end of Beth's explanations. He had missed quite a bit of them while imagining the things he would like to do with Charlie. The important parts, he suspected with irritation as he turned to her now. "What did you say?"

"I said we headed directly back."

"No, before that."

"Oh." She frowned. "About Carland?" When he nodded, she explained, "Well, he and Uncle Henry were in the same inn as us last night. He didn't see me, luckily, but Tomas overheard them talking. From what they said, we gathered that they knew we were in London and some plans were afoot to bring us to them. Tomas and I did not even stay the night in the end. We left right away and returned."

"Why did you rush right back? If you and Mowbray are married, all is well. Your uncle cannot force you to marry Carland if you are already married."

"Nay. Not me. Charlie."

"Charlie?" He paled at that. "But you two said—"

"We could hardly tell you that Charles was to marry Carland," she pointed out logically. "And we feared that had we told you I was to marry Seguin, you may have been less than sympathetic. After all, at the time, we'd heard nothing derogatory about him except that he was old. You may have stopped our attempted escape. You may even have turned us in to our uncle."

"Charlie with Carland?" His horror was obvious. "My God, he would never put up with her sass. She would be dead within the day!"

Beth nodded solemnly. "That is why we returned. To help her flee."

"Flee?" He looked as if the word were alien to him, then stood up suddenly. "Nay. There is no need for her to flee. We are to marry."

Beth blinked at that. "You are?"

"Aye. I told her this morning."

"You *told* her?" She frowned with concern.

"Aye," he answered distractedly, his thoughts on all she had said. Charles was really Charlotte, and she had gone somewhere with Bessie this morning and had not returned. Did her uncle already have her? Cursing, he jumped to his feet and moved to the door of the library. He tugged it open, then paused, his eyebrows raised. Stokes, whom he had been about to call, was standing right there, looking as dignified as a butler could when caught with his ear to the door.

"Aye, my lord?" the man murmured calmly, straightening.

"Did Charles have anything with him when he left?"

Stokes cleared his throat. "I presume you mean besides the young lady?"

"I mean something such as baggage," Radcliffe bit out impatiently.

"Nay, my lord. They had no baggage."

Radcliffe relaxed slightly at that. "Did he mention where they were going?"

"Nay, my lord. *She* did not tell me where *she* was headed. But . . ."

"But?" Radcliffe coaxed when the older man hesitated.

"Well, my lord, cook helped Lady Charles and the young woman dress. Perhaps she overheard something of use."

"Cook? Why was Bessie not assisting him?"

"I suspect that may be because Bessie was the veiled woman with *Lady* Charles."

"Of course," Elizabeth exclaimed. "It must have been Bessie."

Radcliffe nodded solemnly, then ordered, "Fetch cook to me."

"There's no need to fetch me, m'lord, I'm here." Those anxious words made Stokes turn sideways to reveal the woman in question standing a foot or so behind him, wringing a cloth between her work-worn hands fretfully. "I was comin' to tell ye as how I was worried about the lady and Bessie. Lady Charlie said as how they shouldn't be any later than noon and it's well nigh supper now. I've been frettin' and stewin' all day over the two of 'em. I knew somethin' was afoot."

"Where did they go? Did she tell you?"

"Nay. But—" Sighing, she grimaced and confessed,

"There was a piece of paper on the table and I kept sneakin' peeks at it, trying to find out where they was going."

"And?" Radcliffe snapped, unintentionally intimidating the woman with his ferocious expression.

"And—" She paused, frowned, licked her lips, then shook her head with irritation. "It was an address in Change Alley."

"Change Alley?" Elizabeth murmured blankly.

"By the docks," Tomas explained while Radcliffe cursed under his breath. "Where the brokers go to invest in ships."

"Where in Change Alley?" Radcliffe asked.

"It was an inn," she murmured unhappily.

"Which inn?"

Her brow furrowed in concentration and she tipped her head back to squint at the ceiling as if expecting it to be written there, but finally she shook her head unhappily. "It's on the tip of my tongue, but—" She shook her head again helplessly.

"Think, woman!" Radcliffe snapped, too worried to be patient.

"You are scaring her, my lord," Stokes pointed out. "That will hardly help her recall." Nudging his master out of the way, he clasped her shoulders gently and bestowed a sweet smile on her. "Now, just relax, love, and concentrate. The paper was on the table. You peeked at it and read . . . ?"

"I peeked at it and read"—she was squinting again—"I read something-something inn, Change Alley. What was it now . . . ?"

Radcliffe shifted in frustration. "We do not have time for this."

"Give her a minute, my lord. She will remember." Stokes gave her an encouraging smile and nod as he added, "Won't you, love?"

Her smile in response was confident. "Oh, aye. I'll remember. I made a special note to myself to remember, so I'll remember . . . eventually. Now, if I were to see the name, 'twould spark my memory fer sure. Mayhap if we just rode down there—"

When Radcliffe went still at the suggestion, Tomas murmured, "Mayhap that would be a good idea, Radcliffe."

Before he could agree, Elizabeth suddenly murmured, "Mayhap the note is still upstairs." Turning to the cook, she asked, "What was Charles wearing this morn?"

"Black breeches, a white shirt, and a dove gray waistcoat. She said as how it was solemn and blackmail was a solemn business."

"Aye. I shall see if the letter was left behind," she announced and whirled about, her skirts flying as she hurried from the room.

Chapter 16

CHARLIE's head was throbbing, her brain slipping and crashing about inside her skull like loose livers in a bowl. It was a most uncomfortable sensation. Opening her eyes slowly, she grimaced as the light assaulted her, and squinted them closed briefly before trying again.

"Yer awake!" That relieved gasp from somewhere above her head was enough to send her eyes flying shut with a moan once again. "My lord? I mean, my lady? Are you all right?"

"I am alive," Charlie muttered grimly, not sure if it was a good thing or a bad one at that point. Or even if it was a state that was likely to remain. Her head was positively killing her. Reaching up tentatively to prod the area, she was dismayed to find her skull still intact and a bump all she had to show for her pain. There wasn't even a drop of dried blood to show for the agony she had suffered. "Amazing."

"What is, my lady?" Bessie asked curiously at the thready word from Charlie.

"Nothing," she murmured on a sigh and forced her eyes open once again. She was lying on the floor of a carriage, her head resting in Bessie's lap. The girl was curled up on the floor with her, unconcerned for the care of the gown she wore.

"How long have I been unconscious?" she asked, easing to a sitting position.

"I am not sure. Two, mayhap three hours."

"Two or three hours?" Charlie gasped in dismay, then dragged herself up to sit on the bench seat and peer out of the window. Bucolic scenes of country life were passing by the window. Trees, cows, and sheep, along with the occasional hut all whizzed by under a bright blue sky clear of all but the fluffiest of pure white clouds. They were definitely far and away from the smog and stench of the city.

Cursing under her breath, she glanced at the worried girl beside her. Bessie had discarded her hat, her long red hair had given up its tight bun and now hung down her back in a tumble. "Did you overhear anything about where we are headed?"

"Nay. They merely picked you up and bundled us both into the carriage. I was so worried about you, I did not pay much attention to them once the door closed. I am sorry."

Charlie waved her apology away. How could she be upset that the girl was more concerned about her health than about their destination? "Are we locked in?"

Biting her lip, Bessie glanced toward the door, then back helplessly. "I am not sure, but I do not think so."

Charlie started to nod at that, then caught herself before committing the undoubtedly painful movement and sighed. "You do not know if all of them came with us then either, I suppose?"

"Nay," the girl admitted with a disheartened sigh.

" 'Tis all right," Charlie assured her quickly. " 'Tis easy enough to find out."

Bessie raised an eyebrow at that, then bit her lip anxiously when Charlie shifted closer to the window and stuck her head out.

The breeze that hit her face was soothing. Charlie inhaled deeply, her eyes closed, then opened them again and leaned farther out to peer toward the front of the carriage. From this angle, she could just see an arm and the back of a hip. She couldn't even tell if it was the driver's hip or someone else's, but judging by how close that hip was to the edge of the driver's wide bench seat, she would guess that the driver was not alone up there.

"Get your head in or I'll knock it off!"

At that, Charlie whipped her head around to peer toward the back of the carriage, her eyes widening in amazement when she spied the man hanging from the back left footman's stand. It was the behemoth who had attacked her. She pulled her head in at once and sank back onto the seat. She had her answer now. At least two of the three attackers now rode the carriage with them and the driver. What good that information was, she didn't know quite yet.

"She must have taken the note with her," Beth said as she hurried back into the room, slightly out of breath from rushing about.

Radcliffe blinked, not from the news, but from her transformation. Gone was the dress and fancy, up-swept hairstyle. Even her breasts were gone. Beth was now "Charles," her hair covered by another of those awful wigs Charlie had been sporting since Radcliffe had first met the pair, her breasts hidden somewhere beneath the gray overcoat she now wore with black pants.

"Amazing," Stokes murmured, drawing Radcliffe's gaze.

Taking in the older man's bemused expression, Radcliffe grimaced and sighed, knowing that his own expression was not much different. He did not know which was more amazing, the fact that the two sisters were most definitely identical, how different yet similar Elizabeth looked as each character, or the fact that everyone had been fooled for so long. Her stride, though a little longer and more confident, was definitely still a feminine stride, and her hand gestures were as well. How had they neglected to figure out that the pair were twins—and girls?

"I thought being in a male garb might be more practical," Beth explained.

"But Charlie is 'Charles' right now," Tomas pointed out and she nodded.

"Aye. Trust me. I have the sense that my pretending to be her may come in handy at some point." Turning to cook, she asked, "Have you recalled the inn's name?" When Mrs. Hartshair gave an apologetic shake of her head, Beth patted her arm reassuringly. "I am sure that once we get there you shall recall." She glanced toward the men questioningly. "Shall we go?"

"Aye." Radcliffe strode forward. "We shall have to take your carriage, Mowbray. I sent my driver on an errand with my carriage. He will not be back for hours."

"Oh, no!" Tomas said.

Radcliffe peered from Beth's horrified face to Mowbray's grim one. "What?"

"I sent my driver home to bed," Tomas admitted unhappily. "He had driven for two days and a night straight without a wink of rest. He was falling asleep on his bench. I thought sure we could get a ride home with your driver."

"Mayhap Fred has not yet left," Stokes murmured hopefully of Radcliffe's driver. He rushed off to check.

"All will be well."

Charlie roused herself from her anxious thoughts at that calm announcement from Bessie. She had been searching her mind for a way out of this mess. Unfortunately, she wasn't coming up with any brilliant notions just yet. Of course, she wasn't planning to tell Bessie that. She had got the girl into this and was determined to get her out. Preferably in one piece. Not that the other girl appeared worried. The maid was looking as serene as a cow, Charlie noted with some irritation. Didn't she know the fix they were in? For God's sake, they had been kidnapped!

"Is there something you know that I do not?" Charlie asked suspiciously, and the other girl's eyebrows rose slightly at the question.

"Nay."

"Oh." Charlie glanced away, then back, a frown tugging at her lips as she continued to study the young woman's calm countenance. "Then why do you say all will be well like that?"

Bessie smiled. "I have said a prayer to Saint Sebastian."

"Saint Sebastian? Is he not the saint for the plague?"

"Aye, well, there are no plagues about just now so I thought he might be the least busy. Besides, it worked when I was locked in at Aggie's. He sent me you."

Charlie simply nodded. She was all for prayers and such, but had found in her life that it was always good to help prayers along a bit with some effort of one's own. After all, plague or no plague, saints were awfully busy fellows. They couldn't be expected to be everywhere and do everything asked of them. Clearing her throat, she offered a reassuring smile. "There is little we can do at the moment but rest. When we see our chance, we shall make our escape."

"Aye. Besides, Lord Radcliffe is no doubt charging after us right now." At Charlie's blank look, she pointed out, "'Tis well past noon. No doubt Mrs. Hartshair has realized something is amiss and fetched the blackmailer's letter to give to him. He will go to the inn and force that nasty old barkeep to tell him where we are being taken, then he shall follow and rescue us." She said it as if she had the deepest faith in the matter. Charlie didn't have the heart to tell her that the letter in question was presently lining the inside of her pocket.

"Slow down, Stokes. We must read the inn names for Mrs. Hartshair," Radcliffe shouted out the window as the carriage turned into Change Alley.

Fred had already left with the carriage when Stokes had gone in search of him. The fastest option at that point had been to hire a hack and Stokes had left promptly to do so. As soon as he had left, Beth had rushed upstairs to fetch some things that they may need. She had returned with the large sack Tomas now held on his lap, just as Stokes had arrived back at the helm of a rickety old coach.

It seemed that all the drivers had been out on fares when he'd reached the stables, and that he had only managed to gain the hack he had at an exorbitant fee. Assuring Radcliffe that he had served in a stable in his youth and could well handle driving the contraption, Stokes had pointed out that speed was of the essence and urged him to fetch the household. And—much to Radcliffe's dismay—in the end it had been the *entire* household. Beth and Tomas had insisted on going, of course, and Mrs. Hartshair was needed for the name of the inn. But Radcliffe had not counted on having to take her two children as well. Unfortunately, after learning that the cook next door— the only woman friend Mrs. Hartshair had managed to make since taking over the cooking at Radcliffe's— was laid up in bed with pneumonia, there had been little choice but to take the children with them. Which was why Radcliffe had Billy, Mrs. Hartshair's son, on his lap, while she held her daughter Lucy on her own in the cramped confines of the carriage.

"The Fox and Whistle Inn," Beth called out, leaning out of her window on the opposite side of the carriage, glancing back to see Mrs. Hartshair shake her head firmly.

Peering out his own window, Radcliffe began reading the names of any passing inns himself, disheartened each time the cook said "nay." He was becoming seriously concerned that she had recalled the wrong street address when he called out the next name. He glanced back to see her spring to attention like a soldier.

"That's it! The Cock and Bull. That's it, I tell you!"

Hearing her excited cry, Stokes pulled over at once and Radcliffe quickly set young Billy on his feet in the carriage so that he could disembark. Tomas was right behind him when he stepped down from the carriage, but paused to frown at Beth when she, too, followed.

"Nay, Beth. You should wait here with Mrs. Hartshair and Stokes."

"But, dressed as I am, they may think I am Charlie and talk more freely."

"We do not even know who Charlie was meeting here."

"All the more reason to take me with you," she argued staunchly. "They may give themselves away when they see me."

"She may be right," Radcliffe murmured when Tomas opened his mouth to refuse her again. When the younger man nodded reluctantly, Beth was off at once, leading the way to the inn. They entered.

"No one seems to be reacting," Tomas pointed out, his gaze moving narrowly around the room as the three of them paused inside the door to allow their eyes to adjust.

"Aye. Let's talk to the barkeep."

Once again, Beth led the way. The moment the beefy barkeep spied her, they knew they had hit pay dirt. His jaw dropped so far that it almost hit the floor. "What the devil are ye doing back here? Ye should be well on the way to—"

He caught himself just in time, but cried out in the next moment as Radcliffe stepped around Elizabeth, caught the beefy man by the throat, and dragged him halfway across the counter. "Well on the way to where?"

His eyes bulged in alarm, but his mouth stayed firmly closed until Radcliffe made a fist with his free hand and brought it up to the man's face. "You were saying?"

"Gretna," he blurted out.

"Gretna Green?" Radcliffe's hand clenched tighter on the throat he held.

Turning blue in the face, the man choked out an affirmation, and Radcliffe released him to whirl toward the exit with Beth and Tomas hurrying after him.

"That must be where Carland and Uncle Henry were headed when we ran into them," Beth murmured worriedly as they reached the carriage. "Were they the blackmailers."

Nodding, Radcliffe opened the door. "Come along, Mrs. Hartshair. I shall give you some money and you may hire a hack to get you and the children back to the townhouse."

"My lord!" Stokes cried, even as Beth gasped. "You cannot simply dump the lady and her children here unattended."

"This *is* a rather nasty neighborhood, Radcliffe," Tomas murmured reasonably.

"You are right, of course. Stokes, you stay with them and see them home. Tomas and I shall take turns heading the horses for this journey."

A concerned murmur from Beth made him glance at her to see her staring at her husband's stoic face.

"I shall be fine," Mowbray assured her quietly, but she shook her head.

"My lord, Tomas and his driver took turns driving to Gretna Green and back. It is how we managed the journey so quickly. As it is, the two men were so exhausted last night that we decided to rest the night at an inn. Of course, after hearing Carland and Uncle Henry's discussion, we had to give up our room and hurry home. He has had very little sleep the last four days and nights. I fear he is not up to sharing the duty."

"I will manage it," Tomas reiterated firmly, but Beth shook her head apologetically.

"If this concerned anyone but Charlie, I would be willing to risk it, Tom, but—"

"She is right," Radcliffe announced with obvious frustration. "We cannot risk it with Charlie's future at stake."

When he turned to survey the woman and children peering at him uncertainly from the carriage, Mrs. Hartshair offered him a hesitant smile. "My babies will be good, my lord. They tend to sleep during long trips."

Radcliffe threw up his hands in defeat. "Very well. Everyone back into the carriage. We shall all have to go. Stokes and I shall take turns at driving. Tomas, you rest up so that you may be of assistance later." He knew better than to suggest the man stay here. He would not stay behind without his new bride, and Beth would not allow him to ride off to Charlie's rescue without her.

* * *

"Oh, my."

"Oh, m'lady," Bessie murmured, eyeing her with concern. "Are you not well?"

Charlie ignored Bessie's question, doing her best to concentrate on anything but how she was feeling. "Oh, dear."

"Are you all right, m'lady?" Bessie moved anxiously closer, staring at her face with a half-horrified expression.

"Oh, Lord." Charlie groaned, closing her eyes and trying to concentrate on bright sunny days in the park. On fresh green grass . . . nice firm, unmoving grass that a body could stand on without feeling as though they were pitching about in a small, tight, airless carriage that was bouncing along a rutted road.

"Yer lookin' kind of green."

"Oh, God!" Charlie grabbed desperately for the door, thrusting it open in a panic.

Crying out in alarm, Bessie grasped her arm, keeping Charlie from leaping out of the moving vehicle right away. By the time she had shaken off the maid's hold, the man riding on the footman's stand at the back of the carriage had spotted the open door, shouted a warning, and the carriage was slowing to a halt. It had nearly come to a stop when Charlie stumbled weakly out onto the roadside. The villain from the back of the carriage was there at once, solid and stern before her, blocking her path. Charlie covered her mouth and tried to step around him, but he mirrored her movement, determined to stop her from succeeding at what he thought was an escape attempt.

Charlie tried one more time to avoid him as her stomach roiled dangerously, but he remained directly before her. There was little she could do to prevent what happened when her stomach refused to stay down and he refused to get out of the way. Charlie tossed her stomach's contents all over the man's feet and lower legs.

"Oh, gor! Putrid damn. . . . Ugh!" The man stumbled several steps away, trying to escape the fowl stuff, but as it was on him, he couldn't possibly succeed. Charlie felt a moment's embarrassment at what had happened, but soothed herself with the fact that she had done all she could to avoid the event. . . . Besides, he *was* a villain.

"They were here, my lord."

Radcliffe straightened from examining the new horses the stable master was harnessing to the carriage in trade for the original four, to eye Stokes questioningly. "Charlie?"

"Aye, my lord. It seems she was taken ill. She had . . . er . . . passed up her breakfast on one of the fellows. They stopped here to trade horses and let the fellow clean up. They also purchased some laudanum. Presumably they are hoping to make her sleep the rest of the way so that she causes them no more trouble."

"How long ago was this?"

"They apparently arrived nearly six hours ago, but had trouble finding and purchasing the laudanum so that they only left four hours ago."

"If we leave right away, we will have gained two hours on them," Tom said with excitement.

Radcliffe nodded, but wasn't quite as excited by the fact. They were still four hours behind them, and with Charlie in a laudanum-induced sleep, there was little likelihood she could slow them down further. Their only hope of catching them before reaching Gretna was if the other carriage lost a wheel or something.

A roar went up from the man in the back that was quickly echoed by those at the front as they glanced around to see Charlie swaying in the open door of the carriage. They managed to bring the hack to a halt just as she leapt to the side of the road.

Sinking to her knees, she proceeded to toss up the latest dose of laudanum she had been given. Actually, she did not mind being sick this time and hadn't since the first time they had forced the laudanum on her. She'd had every intention of sticking her finger down her throat to bring up the drug the first time they had forced it on her, but had hardly needed to. They had barely set off in the coach again when she had felt her stomach roil. They had just made it around the first bend in the road when she had felt it charging up her throat. Just as the tincture Beth had given her on the way to London had refused to stay down, so had the laudanum. Charlie had been getting sick at regular intervals ever since, forcing them to stop repeatedly, much to their captors' disgust.

It was a shame Bessie was not right and that Radcliffe wasn't chasing after them. Then at least, this bout of misery she was having to endure would be working to their advantage by allowing him to catch up to them. Unfortunately, there was no way he could know that they had been kidnapped and where they were headed.

"Not much farther now."

"Aye. But will we be in time?" Radcliffe rubbed a weary hand over his face.

Tomas was driving again. Stokes was in the cabin with Beth and the Hartshairs, resting. They had been taking turns, one man sleeping, one driving, and one keeping the driver company. Every six hours of the last nearly forty hours they had switched roles. Now they were not even an hour away from their destination. Radcliffe would have been relieved to have the nearly two-day trip done with were he not so terrified that at this very minute Charlie might be being forced to marry Carland. That worry made the last hour of the trip pass like days for Radcliffe. By the time they arrived, he was so wound up that he was off the carriage before it had even come to a standstill.

Striding into the stables, he quickly found the man in charge, learned that no one fitting Charlie and Bessie's description had arrived at his establishment, arranged for the care of the horses, then hurried back outside. "They did not stop here. We shall have to ask around."

"M'lady?"

Charlie opened her eyes slowly, and groaned. The world was still rocking. Was this hell not over yet?

"M'lady?" Bessie repeated, bending to peer down at her.

They were once again on the floor of the carriage. Actually, the floor of the carriage was where Charlie had spent the last night and day of this trip. It was where the men had deposited her after her last bout of sickness, and Charlie, too weak and miserable to bother moving, had stayed there. Bessie had joined her in an effort to make her more comfortable. Charlie was positive no one in England had a better maid than Bessie.

"M'lady? I think we are nearly there."

Charlie raised her head to peer out the window, her gaze finding a small grove of firs in the near distance. She had heard enough to know that that was the landmark to look for. "Aye. We have arrived."

"What are we going to do?"

Charlie peered at her through the pre-dawn darkness. Unfortunately, Charlie had no idea what they would do, but as she had gotten the girl into this mess, she tried to rouse herself to some sensibility. Pushing herself weakly to a sitting position, she then dragged herself up to sit on the bench seat and sighed as fresh air blew in the open window to brush soothingly across her face.

"We will await an opportunity, then make our escape," she said with more bravado than faith. Weak as she was, it would have to be one wing-ding of an opportunity for them to escape.

Bessie either had more faith in Charlie than she deserved, or was too polite to show her doubt. She said nothing as she shifted from the floor to sit on the bench seat opposite her mistress.

"What news?" Beth asked anxiously as the three men finally returned.

"Nothing," Radcliffe admitted unhappily. "We—"

He paused as a carriage rolled quickly past, the clip-clop of the horses' hooves too loud to talk over.

Surrounded by the three men, Beth peered toward the carriage through an inch of space between Tom and Radcliffe, then clutched at her husband's arm, a choked gasp slipping from her throat.

"What is it?" Tom asked worriedly.

"Charlie," she breathed, staring after the carriage. It was heading north. The only direction the men had not yet checked. "I saw Charlie in that carriage," she explained, then frowned. "She looked ill. She was terribly pale."

Turning soundlessly, Radcliffe was after the carriage like a shot. Tomas hesitated long enough to glance toward the stables. "Trade our horses for new ones and have them harnessed to the carriage, Beth. Then follow us," he instructed, only to frown when he turned to glance at his wife and found she was gone, running down the street behind Radcliffe, her pert little behind jiggling with each step she took in the tight breeches.

"I shall take care of it, my lord."

"What?" Tom glanced at Stokes blankly, then blinked and nodded. "Oh . . . oh, fine. Good. Do that. Thanks." Then he was gone, too, chasing after his wife's jiggling behind.

"M'lady?"

Charlie blinked her eyes open weakly, startled to find that she had fallen asleep again, and sitting up! How on earth could she sleep at a time like this? The answer was simple enough, she realized unhappily. Nearly two days of heaving with no water or food being offered could do that to a body. Her gaze slid to Bessie's worried face and she sighed. "Never fear, Bessie, once they realize that you are not Beth, they will let you go."

Biting her lip, Bessie shook her head. " 'Tis not me I am worried about, m'lady."

All Charlie could manage was a grunt at that. Then she turned and peered out the window to the inn they had stopped before. The inn where her uncle and Carland waited, no doubt, she thought with despair. It was beginning to look as if she would be marrying the brutal bastard after all, and she shuddered at the thought of the wedding night ahead. She imagined Carland touching her as Radcliffe had—Nay. Not like Radcliffe. Carland had no gentleness in him. He would touch her in the same places, but in a far different manner.

Maybe she would be lucky and he would beat her to death early on in the marriage, she thought fatalistically. If she had been feeling better, Charlie would have been ashamed of such thoughts, but she wasn't feeling better. She felt half-dead. She was weak, exhausted, dry as dust. She also felt terribly sorry for herself. And to think she had been furious just the morning before that Radcliffe had wanted to marry her out of pity and guilt. That morning and her arrogance now seemed a lifetime away. Today, she would have taken him had she had to pay him. Come to that, she'd pay the nearest farmer to allow her to marry one of his pigs to avoid marrying Carland.

Raised voices drew her gaze to the man who had

approached the inn. He was returning with another man, this one still in his night rail. Charlie recognized him at once as Symes, her uncle's man of affairs.

"Put your veil back on, Bessie," she murmured as they drew near. She would keep the girl with her as long as she could.

Charlie had never had much use for Symes, having witnessed several of the petty cruelties he had inflicted on the rest of the staff over the years, so she did not bother greeting him when he peered through the carriage window. His glance slid swiftly over Bessie in her veil and gown, then stopped on Charlie, eyes widening at her male garb, then narrowing on her pale face and sunken eyes. Pulling his head back out, he turned on the men. "What the deuce did you do to her? She looks half-dead!"

"She don't travel well," one of the men snapped. "Now, where's our money?"

"You will have to wait until His Lordship wakes up."

"What?"

Charlie nearly laughed at the dismay on her kidnappers' faces as they heard that. It seemed they didn't know the sort of man they had done this dirty deed for, or perhaps they worked for the blackmailer and were just picking up the payment for goods delivered. Aye, that made sense, she guessed. Otherwise the men would have realized that Henry liked his pleasures to excess. He drank, ate, and gambled to excess. He also slept to excess and had been known to take his riding crop to anyone foolish enough to try to disturb his sleep . . . for any reason. Even a matter like the arrival of his runaway niece and the need to pay off her kidnappers would never be allowed to intrude on his rest.

Uncle Henry never got up before noon and it was barely dawn now. He had probably only been abed for an hour. Charlie supposed that meant that she had several more hours of freedom left. . . . Unless Carland was an early riser.

She hoped not. She fervently hoped that he had caroused with Henry throughout the night and would rise just as late.

"You heard what I said," Symes said shortly. "You will have to wait until he awakens."

"The devil take that!" the big-nosed man snarled furiously. "Go wake the bugger up."

"I am not waking him up. And I strongly suggest that you do not either," Symes added sharply as the beefy man turned determinedly toward the inn. "Not if you wish to get paid."

That brought the man up short. Whirling back, he eyed Symes narrowly. "Yer damn right I want to get paid. We've brought the girls and he'll pay for them."

"You brought the girls *late*," Symes corrected pompously. "You were supposed to arrive at least six hours ago. He was up then and would have taken them off your hands and paid you gladly for them *then*."

"That one was sick. She kept leaping off the carriage to puke by the side of the road," the man complained. "It slowed us down."

Symes shrugged. "That is your problem. Now, you will have to wait."

"Well, what in Hades are we supposed to do with her until he gets up?"

"That is your problem, too. But I strongly suggest you don't lose her." Turning on those dry words, Symes returned to the inn and his bed.

Chapter 17

*T*HERE it is," Tom said as he came to a halt beside Radcliffe.

Their being on foot, it had taken them several minutes to catch up to the carriage. Radcliffe had cursed himself for a fool a dozen times a minute as he had raced along. He should have kept the horses harnessed, then they could have followed right behind them. But he had expected to arrive after his quarry, not before.

This explained why they had not heard news of the other carriage during the last day of their travels. They had questioned people each time they stopped to change horses, hoping to learn if they were gaining on them, but had learned nothing. No one had matched the descriptions they had given with that of any group that had passed through. Radcliffe had thought they were merely choosing different inns to stop at to trade horses. Now, he realized that they may have been doing that at first, but somewhere along the way, they had ridden right by them.

His gaze slid over the three men standing by the carriage and talking. He had stopped quite a distance from the carriage and the inn it sat before, not wanting to alert the kidnappers to his presence. But he was close enough to tell that the three men were agitated about something.

"Have they taken her in yet, do you think?"

Radcliffe frowned. "I do not know. I thought I saw someone entering the inn as it came into view, but I could not tell who it was or if they were alone."

"Well, if they have not, we could rush them when they do."

"Aye. That may be the best idea," he agreed, glancing around as Beth joined them. With his longer strides, Tom had passed her some distance back. "Where is Stokes?"

Beth shook her head breathlessly and Tom answered the question. "He was to follow with the carriage and Mrs.—" He paused as the hack rattled into view. Stokes and Mrs. Hartshair shared the driver's bench while her children both hung out the windows, helping to keep an eye out for them.

Stepping into the street, Radcliffe raised his arms over his head and waved until he was sure Stokes had spotted him, then gestured for Beth and Tom to follow as he walked to meet the carriage.

Bessie raised her head and opened her eyes. She had been sending up another prayer. Just in case the first five hundred or so had been misheard. Now, she glanced worriedly at Lady Charlie, taking in her pallor, the smudges under her eyes, and the dead slumber she was in. Her mistress needed sustenance, as Bessie had told their captors after the nasty man had gone back into the inn, but they had ignored her pleas even for water. She supposed they were too annoyed at having to cool their heels to care about Lady Charlie's welfare.

"Surely the women are not still inside the carriage, Radcliffe? They must have taken them inside the inn as soon as they arrived."

"Aye." Radcliffe sighed unhappily at Tom's words. The seven of them had sat cramped inside the carriage for well over an hour. He, Mrs. Hartshair, and Stokes were wedged on the bench seat on one side, and Tomas, Beth, and the two children crowded onto the other. They had been watching the three men play dice beside the carriage for the entire time. Not one of the men had even glanced at the carriage. Charlie and Bessie must already be inside. Which merely made things more difficult.

"What are we going to do, my lord?" Beth asked anxiously.

"We will have to find out where they are and get them out."

"They will be guarded," Beth murmured. "And that guard would most likely be Symes." At their questioning glances, she explained, "Symes is my uncle's man of affairs. He is only about my size, but he is a dead shot and he is never without his flintlocks. He probably sleeps with them under his pillow."

"Then there are Carland and Seguin to consider," Tom said. "And Lord knows how many men they may have brought with them."

"What are you suggesting?" Radcliffe snapped furiously. "That we give up? Just leave Charlie to Carland?"

"Nay. Of course not," Tom assured him. "We just need a plan. We shall get her out and save her."

"We may not need to get her out to save her," Beth murmured. When Radcliffe turned on her questioningly, she added, "I was recalling on the way here how Charlie and I used to switch places all the time. Most often it was just for fun, but sometimes it was to get out of doing something we did not wish to do."

"I do not see how that is relevant here, Beth," Tom said gently.

She turned to peer closely at Radcliffe. "You said in London that the two of you were to be married?"

Radcliffe winced as he recalled his arrogance while making the announcement to Charles, but nodded.

"Well, if you were married to her, Carland could not do so."

"Exactly. So we must get her out—" he began, pausing when she shook her head.

"Not if we made the switch again."

"Now hold on!" Tom cried in dismay. "The idea here isn't to get Charlie out of danger and put you into it."

"I would not be in danger," Beth assured him calmly.

"You had best explain," Radcliffe said, feeling as confused as Tom looked.

"You could marry me—" Beth began, but Tom's head nearly hit the roof of the carriage as he sprang upright in his seat.

"The devil you say! I will do many things to save your sister, but giving you up is not one of them. You are *my* wife."

"Aye, but if he married me as—"

"As Charlie" she had meant to say, but Tomas didn't give her the chance before interrupting irately. "Now see here, I have heard just about enough of this talk. You are married to me, and that is that!"

"Er . . . my lords, I believe you may be misunderstanding what Lady Elizabeth is trying to say," Stokes said quietly.

"Misunderstanding?" Mrs. Hartshair snorted in disgust, then took it upon herself to explain the matter. "She's saying she could marry His Lordship as Lady Charlie."

When Tomas and Radcliffe stared at the cook blankly, she shook her head. "Look at her. She is wearing the same clothes as Lady Charlie. She looks like Lady Charlie. She even sounds like Lady Charlie. She could pretend to be Lady Charlie while you, Lord Radcliffe, marry her. She can say 'I do,' sign her name—" Pausing, she glanced worriedly at Beth. "You *can* copy her signature?"

When Beth nodded, she relaxed and continued, "Then, once the ceremony is over, you can walk straight into the inn and demand your *wife* back."

"My God." Tomas sank back on the seat, wonder on his face. "It may work."

"I do not know." Radcliffe frowned, then shook his head. "Nay. They already have Charlie, and the wedding will be registered with today's date. They will know that she could not have married me."

"That will not matter if she is me," Beth pointed out, and both men immediately looked confused again. Realizing that they had not quite grasped the concept of switching, she explained patiently. "If after the wedding, I continue to pretend to be Charlie and we confront Uncle Henry claiming that Charlie is me, Beth, it will work."

"Oh, I see!" Tomas exclaimed. "We will tell them that Charlie is you; and since you and I married four days ago, they cannot force her to marry Carland. And since Charlie, whom you will be playing, will have just married Radcliffe, they cannot force you to marry Carland either. You will both be safe."

"Exactly!" Beth smiled at him widely.

Though his head was spinning, Radcliffe was hopeful. "Will Charlie know to pretend to be you?"

Beth nodded firmly. "She and I have done this sort of thing often enough that she will catch on at once to what is happening."

"Shall I take us to the priest, my lord?" Stokes asked.

"Ah, well, he is not a priest really. Well, perhaps he is, I am not sure," Beth murmured uncertainly, and Tomas covered her hand and squeezed gently as he explained, "You will be taking us to a fisherman, Stokes. He performs the marriages around here."

Radcliffe accepted that news with equanimity. He had sustained so many shocks in short order that he felt sure he was now immune to them. . . .

Until he got a good look at the fisherman. A portly fellow, wearing a blue dress coat of indiscriminate age, he eyed them solemnly at first, pushing a huge gob of tobacco about inside his cheek until he understood that he was to marry Radcliffe to Beth . . . who, of course, was still dressed as Charles. The man nearly choked on his chaw.

"Oh, nay! I'll no' marry ye to a boy. 'Tis a sin aginst God and all creation. Marriage is a sacred rite between a man and a woman, not something to be twisted by yer sort."

Radcliffe flushed with embarrassment as he realized what the man was thinking. Tom appeared consumed with the effort not to laugh. Stokes was looking nonplused and quite unsure how to handle this situation, and Mrs. Hartshair was busy soothing and rocking her son, who had stumbled getting out of the carriage and scraped his knee. That left Beth to set the man straight. "I am a woman, sir," she announced dryly, whipping the wig from her head with a great flourish that did not impress the man at all.

"What, and greasy hair is to fool me into thinkin' yer a girl?"

Beth's hand raised to her hair in alarm. She had not had an opportunity to bathe since the night they had planned to spend at the inn on the way back to London from Gretna Green the first time. Bathing was the first thing she had done on reaching the inn, doing so even before joining Tomas for a meal below.

Thank goodness, she thought now, for she had spied her uncle on returning below. Luckily, he had not spotted her, and she had quickly hurried back upstairs, sending a note below with a maid explaining the situation to Tomas. Intelligence being one of the things she loved about Tomas, he had used his and done a bit of eavesdropping on Uncle Henry's conversation with Carland before meeting her in their room to relate what he had heard. Their plans to rest the night at the inn had been put aside at once for the need to warn Charlie. Beth had not had an opportunity to bathe since.

Sighing, she plopped the wig back on her head and

glanced toward the tall, thin woman who had answered the door to their knock and who may or may not have been the man's wife. "Is there a room where we may have some privacy?"

When the woman looked uncertain, the man scowled. "What are you wanting with her?"

"I am going to prove that I am a woman," Beth explained patiently.

"And how wid ye be plannin' on managin' that?"

Beth flushed, but raised her chin and announced with great dignity, "By showing her my breasts."

The rude little man burst out laughing at that as his gaze dropped to the area in question. "What for? I can see plain as day ye havena got any."

"They are bound," Beth choked out with no little embarrassment.

"Sure they are," he muttered with patent disbelief. "You can show her well enough there in the corner."

When Beth hesitated, he sneered again. "What? Changed your mind now that you canna threaten her into sayin' what ye want?"

Tomas lost his temper at that and grabbed the man by the front of his shirt, preparing to punch him. The man merely smiled and shrugged. "Hit me if ye like, but see if ye can get anyone to marry yer friends here that way."

"Tom," Beth murmured in a strained voice. "Mayhap you could give your cape to Mrs. Hartshair. She can hold it up for privacy for me."

Reluctantly releasing the man, Tomas shrugged out of his cloak and handed it over, and Mrs. Hartshair followed Beth to the corner the man had indicated and held it up for her as the woman followed.

She waited patiently as Beth quickly and with as little thought as possible shrugged out of her doublet, vest, and shirt. The woman's eyes sparked with interest when she saw the cloth binding Beth's chest, but she said nothing until Beth had unwound the cloth, freeing her aching breasts.

"Oh, my," she breathed with amazement.

"What is it?" the fisherman asked, taking a step forward that stopped short when Tomas stepped in front of him with a deadly expression.

"She's breasts a'right . . . and a fine pair they are, too," the woman announced. "Huge."

Radcliffe could hear Beth's groan of mortification and felt sympathy pinch his patience. "Will you marry us now?"

The man hesitated. "Maybe I should just be sure and see fer mesel'f—"

His words were cut off by Tom's sudden hand at his throat.

"Her word is enef, I guess," he squeaked out, his eyes bugging. "I'll marry 'em."

Tom didn't release the man until Beth was rebound and dressed, and the three people had returned. Then he gave a little squeeze before releasing him. "Get to it, then."

"Lady Charlie? Lady Charlie!"

Blinking her eyes open, Charlie sat up abruptly, swaying with dizziness as she peered around at the alarm in Bessie's voice. "What is it?" Her voice was a husky croak, but Charlie hardly noticed when she spied Bessie's veiled face. "What's the matter?"

"Something is going on. Another carriage has

arrived and—" Her voice died abruptly as the door opened and she turned to peer at it. One moment she was there. The next she was gone. It happened so fast that Charlie almost missed the hands that had reached in and snatched the girl out.

"Bessie," she cried, moving forward only to sag weakly against the closed carriage door as it slammed in her face. Charlie blinked out the window to see the young maid being dragged away toward another carriage. It took her a moment to recognize the crest on the side.

"Seguin," she breathed with dismay, then, "Nay! She is not Beth! She is not!" Her cry ended on a fit of coughing as her dry, sore throat caught on the cry. By the time she had recovered, the carriage was gone and Bessie with it.

Cursing under her breath, Charlie watched the men make their way back to her carriage and move to the side facing the inn. Sliding along the seat, she peered out to see that they were settling back into a game of dice. She watched for several minutes and when they hadn't glanced toward the carriage once in that time, she decided they must think her too weak to cause them any trouble . . . And five minutes ago they would have been right. But that was before Bessie had been taken. Now, knowing she had got the girl into this mess, Charlie was determined to save her. Determination could give strength to the weakest body.

Turning away from the men, Charlie slid back along the seat to the opposite door, opened it, and slid out.

* * *

"What do you mean, she got away?" Symes cried in alarm.

"There were three of you supposed to be watching her. *Three* of you could not keep one girl from escaping?"

"We only turned our backs for a minute. She was weak as a kitten. I don't know how she managed it."

"Telling me that she was weak as a kitten is not improving my opinion of you allowing her to escape," Symes snarled.

"My men are searching for her now. They'll bring her back."

"They had *better*, and they had best come back with her ere my lord comes out."

"They should be back any minute with her. If you hadna come back out early ye ne'er would have known. Why are ye back anyway? Ye said 'til noon."

Symes heaved a sigh. "Lord Carland is an early riser and insisted on my lord being awoken when I told him that you had arrived with the girl. Of course, now my lord is in a foul temper, one he will most like take out on you should your men not return ere he comes out, or—"

"Symes! Where is this carriage you said Charlotte was in?"

"Damn," the beefy man muttered. It was a sentiment echoed by Symes as he turned with resignation to face Henry Westerly.

"Did you hear that? She has escaped!" Mrs. Hartshair crowed happily.

"That is my Charlie," Beth murmured with pride.

Radcliffe pounded on the wall of the carriage

behind the driver's seat and the carriage pulled off. Once they were a safe distance away from the inn, he thumped on the wall again, then got out when it stopped and crawled onto the bench seat. "Did you hear?"

"Aye, my lord," Stokes said. "Am I right in assuming that we are going to try to find Lady Charlie ere they do?"

"Aye, you would be right. Keep your eyes open."

Nodding, the older man urged the horses forward again.

Charlie nearly fainted with relief when she spotted Seguin's carriage. She picked up her pace and hurried forward. She had been walking around for what seemed like hours searching for it while trying to dodge her pursuers. Oddly enough, the longer she walked, the stronger she felt. She suspected it was the fresh air that was doing it, that and the water she had scooped from a pail in the stables when at one point she had ducked in there to avoid her kidnappers spotting her.

"There she is!"

Glancing over her shoulder, she spotted the two men running toward her. Cursing roundly, she ducked into the building, spotting Bessie at once. The maid stood before a man in a blue coat, and beside Seguin who held her arm firmly with one hand while he bent to sign something with his other.

"Wait!" Charlie cried hoarsely. "Stop! Bessie, do not sign it!"

"You again!" The man in the blue coat scowled as she hurried forward.

Charlie hardly noticed, her attention on Seguin

and Bessie as the lord straightened from signing his name. "You cannot force her to marry you. She is not Elizabeth."

Seguin rolled his eyes impatiently. "Who the devil are you? Never mind, I do not care and it does not matter. I shall not fall for your tricks. She tried the same argument with me already, boy. Besides, 'tis too late, 'tis done. The ceremony is over and we have both signed. She is my wife."

"He *made* me sign," Bessie wailed miserably just as the door crashed open behind Charlie.

"Grab her!"

Charlie was just beginning to struggle against the hands that suddenly arrested her when the door crashed open again and Uncle Henry's voice rang out. "I see that you found her. At least you had the sense to bring her here."

Charlie sagged in defeat as she was turned to face her uncle, his man Symes, and a grim-looking Carland who now sauntered toward them. "You see, Carland, I told you all would be well. You can marry the chit now without delay."

"Nay. He cannae," the fisherman snapped, drawing all eyes. "I'll not marry her to anyone else today."

"The devil you say." Uncle Henry beetled his eyes at the man.

"The devil I *do* say. I canna marry someone who's already married, and she is already married."

"You mean to say that *that* is Charlotte?" Seguin gasped, grasping the implication of what the fisherman was saying. "Why, she looks like a boy." His lecherous old eyes moved to his bride with new possibilities shining in them. "Do you wear breeches too, my dear?"

"She is *not* already married," Uncle Henry snapped impatiently, ignoring Seguin's lascivious wonderings.

The fisherman's eyes narrowed, his mouth firming into a straight line. "Aye, she is. I presided over it myself not more than twenty minutes ago."

Charlie gave a start at that, her eyes widening incredulously. He must be talking about Beth, she thought. But that made no sense. Her sister should have been married several days ago and be back in London by now.

"Henry?" Carland murmured in a threatening tone.

"Well, it just is not so," her uncle gasped. "It cannot be."

"Can it not? Twenty minutes ago is about when we learned she had escaped."

"Aye, but—" He was sputtering in his panic. "Who could she have married?"

"Me."

Charlie gaped at Radcliffe who now filled the entrance to the little building. What was *he* doing here? And why did the man in blue think—? Oh! Of course. He had paid the man off, she thought, then noticed with surprise that Tomas and Stokes were flanking him. She caught a quick glimpse of a slender lad behind them.

"That's him!" the fisherman agreed. "I hitched these two to each other not a quarter of the hour ago. It's registered right here all good and proper."

"Henry," Carland growled.

Blanching at the cold fury on Carland's face, Henry turned to Charlie. "Why, you little—" he began, raising his fist to hit her.

Radcliffe was there before he could finish either

action or words, grabbing his fist in his own much larger one and startling the older man into silence. "You will not speak to my bride that way."

Henry reacted first with alarm, then a certain craftiness entered his eyes and he even managed a conciliatory smile as he glanced toward Carland. "All is not lost. They may have married, but they could not have possibly consummated it yet. We can take her back to London and have the king dissolve what was done. Then you can marry her yourself."

"You will not be taking her anywhere," Radcliffe corrected, crushing the hand he held. "And the wedding was consummated before the fact. She is no longer a virgin."

Uncle Henry must have already been paid and spent the money Carland had promised for the privilege of marrying her, Charlie decided when her uncle winced in pain. Still, the man continued to plead with Carland. "He is lying. He must be. If you would just call your men and—"

"I need a goddamned heir, Henry. You know that. I'll not take the chance of her carrying another man's brat. I want my money back."

Her uncle was beginning to look quite sick with panic when Symes suddenly moved forward, tugging a sack from his doublet. "Lord Seguin gave me this as agreed when he collected Lady Elizabeth, my lord."

Uncle Henry nearly fell upon the man with relief. "Oh, Symes! How clever of you to think of that now. Here you are, Carland." He took the sack from his man of affairs and handed it over. "Seguin was paying the same amount for Elizabeth that you were for Charlotte—so it should all be here."

"It had better be," Carland said coldly, pocketing the bag.

"Did I hear my name?"

Charlie turned to find Beth now standing in the entrance. She was dressed in the lavender gown Charlie had packed away in the satchel for her to be married in. If it had been her sister she had glimpsed dressed as a boy earlier, she must have changed faster than she had ever done before in her life. Still, that didn't startle Charlie nearly as much as the fact that her sister was backed by Mrs. Hartshair and her children. Good Lord! Was everyone here?

"Elizabeth." Uncle Henry breathed the name in horror.

"Elizabeth?" Seguin gaped from her to the veiled woman he had just married. "Who? Who are—"

"I tried to tell you," Bessie wailed.

"So did I," Charlie murmured archly. "Seguin, meet your bride, Bessie . . . my lady's maid. Though, I guess she is a countess now."

"L-lady's maid?" Seguin choked, clutching his upper arm as if it pained him. "L-lady's maid?"

Finally released from the cruel grasp he had had on her since collecting her from their kidnappers, Bessie ripped the veiled hat from her head, revealing her red hair and powderless face.

"Do not panic," Henry cried earnestly, talking as fast as he was thinking in an effort to get out of this mess. "We can clear this all up. Your marriage to the chit cannot be legal if she signed Beth's name. We can still marry you to Elizabeth."

"Nay. He cannot. I married Elizabeth right here in

this room not four days ago," Tom announced with satisfaction.

"Aye." The fisherman nodded in verification, then glanced down at the papers both of the newlyweds had signed. "Besides, she signed the name Bessie Roberd. Is that yer name?" When Bessie nodded miserably, he shrugged. "'Tis all legal, then. You two are married."

"But I thought she was Elizabeth!" Seguin cried, rubbing his arm faster. "It was under false pretenses."

The fisherman shook his head. "She told ye her name twice or three times ere I commenced the ceremony. I heard her tell ye. There weren't no false nothin'. 'Sides." His eyes narrowed. "Ye had to threaten her to get her to marry ye in the first place, ye'll not be cryin' off now."

"H-Henry, you b-bastard! This is all your fault." Seguin gasped, staggering a couple of steps toward the pale man with murder in his eyes before pain replaced it and he suddenly switched the hand that had been clutching his arm to his chest. Swaying briefly, he growled another curse, then collapsed on his face.

They all stared wide-eyed as Radcliffe stepped forward and rolled the man over. After bending to press an ear to his chest, he straightened and shook his head. "Dead."

Carland gave a harsh laugh at the pronouncement. "You are the luckiest bastard I know, Henry."

When the other man merely peered at him blankly, Carland hefted the sack of coins he held. "Now you do not owe him *his* money back." Pocketing the sack, he turned and sauntered out of the building.

Chapter 18

"M MMM," Charlie murmured with pleasure as the warm, silky water closed around her body. It felt like days since she had been clean. It *had* been days, she realized with a sigh, but firmly turned her mind from such thoughts. She did not want to think of her kidnapping, that horrid carriage ride, or the scene in the fisherman's hovel. She had been more than happy to turn her back on Gretna, literally. Charlie had left Gretna Green mounted before Radcliffe on a horse. He had purchased the animal for the return trip at the livery where he had changed horses upon arriving and, much to her relief, had insisted that she ride with him. Aside from her nasty reaction to traveling, there simply had not been enough room in the carriage for everyone. Even with just Tomas, Beth, Bessie, and Mrs. Hartshair and her children inside it had looked terribly crowded.

They had had to travel for nearly the whole day before coming across an inn with enough rooms to accommodate them all.

This inn. She tilted her head back on the rim of the bath and peered around the room. It was sparsely furnished with just a bed and, at present, a tub. The room was small, but it was clean. Besides, next to the carriage that she had spent the past two days in, it resembled a chamber in the finest palace.

The opening of the door made her stiffen and peer about as Beth slipped into the room. She and the others had still been filling themselves on the hearty meal the innkeeper's wife had supplied when Charlie had left the common room. Her stomach, still tender after the traveling sickness she had suffered, Charlie had managed only a few bites before retiring to their room to take a bath.

"My, that looks lovely," Beth sighed, eyeing the bath a bit enviously as she approached.

"It is," Charlie murmured, then began cleaning herself. "I will hurry, but you shall probably need fresh water when I am through. I really needed this bath."

"Oh, do not worry. There is no need to hurry. I have a bath being prepared for me in our room."

"Our room?" Charlie raised her eyebrows. "Are you not staying in here with me?"

"Nay. Tomas and I have the room next door." She blushed prettily, but Charlie hardly noticed as she frowned.

"But I thought—I mean, Radcliffe could only hire five rooms here."

"Aye."

"Well, Mrs. Hartshair and her children are in one, are they not?"

"Aye."

"And Bessie has one?"

"Aye."

"Then Tomas and you have one, I have this one, and I presume Stokes—Oh! Radcliffe must be bedding down with Stokes," she realized and relaxed, unaware that Beth had stiffened.

"Charlie?"

"Aye?"

"Radcliffe will not be bedding down with Stokes."

She tilted her head up curiously. "Well, then where is he staying? Oh, surely he has not stuck Stokes in the stables?"

"Nay, Charlie . . ." She hesitated, then plunged on. "He will be staying here . . . with you. You are married now."

She blinked at that. "Married? Nay, Beth, Radcliffe just said that to prevent my having to marry Carland."

Beth shook her head. "You are married."

"But I never married Radcliffe."

"Aye, you did."

"Beth, I think I would recall something like that. I never married Radcliffe."

"Nay," she agreed. "I did in your place."

"What?" She peered at her sister blankly, not quite grasping her words.

"I dressed up as Charles, married him, and copied your signature to the—"

"What?" Charlie sat up abruptly in the bath, splashing water everywhere.

"He said the two of you were to marry. That you had made love."

Charlie flushed at that, irritation pulling at her expression. "Radcliffe has a big mouth. Besides, both partners must be in love for it to be lovemaking."

"You do not love him?" Beth asked with concern, and Charlie's frown darkened.

"Of course, I love him. What is not to love? The man is a darling. Sweet, generous, adventurous—"

"Adventurous?" Beth gasped, interrupting her. "The man is as stuffy as that carriage we rode here in."

"Nonsense. Just look at the adventures we have had since meeting him."

Beth shook her head with a laugh. "Charlie, *you* are the one who brings about these adventures."

"Mayhap." She shrugged. "But I could not have done so without Radcliffe." When Beth looked doubtful, Charlie sighed. "He took us under his wing and brought us to London. If he had not, we would even now be moldering away at Ralphy's."

"Charlie, *you* will *never* molder. Besides, he only did that out of a sense of duty." When Charlie shook her head, Beth raised her eyebrows. "Nay?"

"Nay, Beth. All he had to do to soothe his sense of duty was warn us, or even give us a pistol. Or he could have dumped us once he saw us safely to London. Yet he did not; he took us into his home."

Beth was frowning over that, never having considered it herself. "Mayhap you are right, but I still have trouble seeing Radcliffe as adventurous. Just look at the fuss he made about the puppies. He *is* stuffy."

"He made a fuss over rescuing Bessie and Mrs. Hartshair as well," Charlie laughed. "But that is just talk, a way to try to hide his true nature. How many times have I told you, never listen to a person's words, watch their actions to see what is in their heart. A person can say many things they do not mean. For instance, Jimmy and Freddy who you said were betting on who could ruin the most girls in the ton; do you not think they said things to those girls that they never meant as they set out to ruin them?"

"Aye, but—"

"There are no buts," Charlie interrupted, then sighed. "All right, look at it this way. Radcliffe made a fuss about Bessie, but when it came down to it, he is the one who announced that she was to be your lady's maid and actually hired her on. Do you think someone like Lady Mowbray would have had her as a lady's maid?"

"Oh, good Lord, no." Beth's eyes were wide. "Bessie had no training. Lady Mowbray would not put out good money for an unskilled servant."

"Exactly. And the same goes for Mrs. Hartshair. Yet Radcliffe hired both of them despite his grumbling. Even taking in Mrs. Hartshair's children. And then there are the puppies. He could have denied me the money to save them and said it was for the best, or even have paid the farmer, insisting he keep them and use the money for their care. But he did not. He speaks like an old curmudgeon, but his actions negate that." She glanced down at the water briefly, then added, "No stuffy old curmudgeon could possess the passion he does, either."

"You *do* love him," Beth said with relief.

"Aye."

"Then you will not try to contest the marriage?"

She gave a bitter laugh. "How could I? Uncle Henry would just try to force me into marriage with someone else, and Lord knows who he would find this time since I would be ruined."

"You do not sound happy," Beth murmured worriedly.

"Would you be happy to be married to Tom, loving him yet knowing he did not love you?"

"Oh, Charlie, he must love you! How could he not?"

"Spoken like a true sister," Charlie murmured wryly, then admitted, "He told me he did not love me."

"He *told* you?" she gasped in horror.

"Well, he told Charles," she explained on a sigh. "I asked if he loved her—me—and he said, 'I do not.'"

"Oh, Charlie." Her sister's eyes filled with sympathetic tears.

Swallowing a sudden lump in her throat, Charlie stiffened her back a bit and glanced away. "You had best get going. Your bath should be ready by now."

Beth hesitated, then seeming to recognize Charlie's need to be alone, she nodded reluctantly and moved slowly toward the door. "Good night."

"Good night," Charlie murmured as the door closed, then heaved a sigh and proceeded to wash her hair.

Radcliffe raised his hand to the door, then paused and drew it back, leaving the door unopened. Oddly enough, he was suddenly inexplicably nervous. This was his wedding night, but it would not be his first night with Charlie—so that was not the reason behind this sudden nervousness. Nay. He suspected the source of it was his uncertainty as to how his new bride was reacting to the knowledge that they were now married. He had no idea what to expect. Was she happy about it? Content? Resentful? She had been silent during the ride from Gretna. And he had been unwilling to ask her thoughts on the subject. Was she angry that Beth had married him in her name? Would she greet him with a shy smile, or whip something heavy and nasty at his head as soon as he entered the door?

Radcliffe smiled wryly. He doubted that most men suffered such worries on their wedding night, but then, they did not have wives like Charlie. Beautiful, bold, charming Charlie. He suspected that his calm, quiet days in the country were over. Life had suddenly become an adventure. Even going to his bed now carried some element of peril with it.

Did he wish for those serene times back? Radcliffe recalled the harmonious days that had blended into one another ere encountering Charlie and Elizabeth, then each wild escapade he had enjoyed since their arrival in his life. He chuckled softly to himself. He had thought it amusing when Clarissa had hung all over "the boy" like a limpet. Knowing that she had really been a girl made the memory even more amusing. Then he recalled Charles on the farmer's back, fighting for the lives of those puppies, and he marveled at her courage. Then there was the time when she had been tied to the bed at the brothel with the whip-wielding Aggie straddling her. . . . He began to chuckle aloud again, then blinked with consternation. Good Lord! He had taken his wife to a *brothel*, he realized with dismay. And that was how his wife found him; standing before the door, his eyes wide, his mouth open in a round "O" of alarm.

Charlie had quickly finished her bath after Beth's departure then—with the dirty clothes she had worn for two days as her only other option—had wrapped the bed linens around herself in the Roman style and moved to sit before the fire to work on drying her long, damp tresses. Her hair had been perhaps half-dried when she had first heard the doorknob jiggle.

Her heart slamming against her chest, she had turned to stare at the door wide-eyed. When nothing had happened and the door had remained closed, she had relaxed slightly and gone back to finger-brushing her hair before the fire, only to pause again a moment later as a soft chuckle had reached her through the door. She'd had no trouble recognizing Radcliffe's distinctive laugh.

Thinking he was talking to someone in the hall, Charlie had continued to work with her hair, but when she'd heard no hint of another person's voice and Radcliffe's laugh came once more, curiosity had got the better of her and she had hurried to open the door. Now she stared at his rather horrified expression and frowned uncertainly.

Why was he looking at her like that? Did he find her that unattractive or—

"I took you to a brothel!"

Charlie blinked as that comment exploded from his lips, then relaxed and glanced curiously up and down the hall. "Are you alone, my lord?"

"What? Oh, aye," he murmured distractedly as he stepped into the room and closed the door.

"Then what were you laughing at?" Charlie asked curiously, trailing him across the room, the excess material of the linens she wore trailing behind her.

"I was not—Oh, well . . ." He frowned at her. "Did you not hear? I took you to a brothel, for God's sake."

"Hmmm," Charlie murmured, taking in the pale tinge to his skin. "And a gaming hall too."

He blanched further at that, then his eyes widened to great wide holes in his head "Good Lord, we slept together in the same bed the very night we met!"

"I was above the linens while you were under them, if it makes you feel better."

She had moved to the fire and was holding her hands out toward it as if they were cold, her expression impossible for him to read. Gripping his future firmly in both hands, he murmured, "And is that how you wish to sleep tonight as well?"

She glanced about sharply at that, then followed his gaze to the linen she wore draped around her in what he suddenly realized was a most fetching and seductive manner. After the briefest of hesitations, she met his gaze again, holding his eyes with her own as she calmly reached up and undid the toga-style affair. It dropped to the floor without even a whisper of sound, and she raised her chin defiantly. He may not love her, but he wanted her, and, with her usual gusto for life, she would take what it had to offer.

Radcliffe swallowed. His wife did not say a word. But then, she did not need to. Her actions were answer enough, he supposed as his gaze slid down over her generous breasts with their proudly erect nipples, across the gentle swell of her stomach, along the curve of her hips to her well-shaped thighs and calves before sliding back up to her face.

"My beautiful, bold, charming Charlie," he breathed his thoughts of earlier aloud. Her action, her stance, and her proud bearing seemed to epitomize her personality. Bold and passionate. *Dear God,*

I am the luckiest of men, he thought faintly, then lifted a hand, holding it out to her. "Come here."

When she stiffened, then hesitated, he thought they were about to begin the war of wills that was surely to come, for she was not one who would be ordered about. But instead of standing her ground and demanding that he come to her, she took several steps forward, erasing half the distance between them, then stopped, her eyes challenging.

Her message was clear. She would meet him halfway but that was as far as she would go. Carland would have beat her for her defiance on the spot. Radcliffe merely smiled and removed the rest of the distance between them with a couple of short strides.

Let other men battle for obedience, he decided as his arms closed around her warm soft body. He had Charlie. That was his last sensible thought before his wife's arms slid around his neck.

Chapter 19

CHARLIE peered down at the ring she was twisting on her finger and sighed. Her wedding ring. Radcliffe had given it to her at the inn they had stayed in after leaving Gretna Green. That had been two weeks ago. For two weeks she had lived the life of a *supposed* married woman. She thought of it as supposed because she was not at all sure that their marriage was legal, since she had neither attended it nor signed the register. Despite that, Charlie actually did feel married. . . . And it was just as miserable as she had feared it would be. Not that Radcliffe treated her badly. He merely treated her as she imagined most of the husbands in London treated their wives. He was kind and gentle, even concerned. Unfortunately, he did not talk to her anymore. Not the way he had when he had thought her to be Charles. They'd had grand discussions and debates then. He had discussed various investments with her, listening to her opinions as if they were valid. Now he tended to take on a rather condescending air and humoring attitude with her, no matter what she said. And he simply refused to speak of business at all.

Charlie could not stand it. She thought if he gave her one more of his "What-a-precious-little-creature-you-are" smiles, she would throw something at him. The only place he treated her as an equal anymore was in bed. Unfortunately, Radcliffe seemed to have a problem with concentrating upon financial affairs in bed. He could not be there long without becoming distracted by her less-intellectual assets and in turn distracting her.

"My lady?"

Charlie glanced around to see Stokes framed in the salon doorway. "Aye?"

"Lady Seguin, the countess of Chiltingham, is here to see you."

Relieved to have something to distract her from her thoughts, Charlie hurried forward and flew past him into the hallway.

"Bessie!" she greeted affectionately; then her smile died as she saw the other girl's tear-filled eyes and tightly clenched hands. Rushing forward to clasp those cold, work-worn fingers, she frowned anxiously. "My dear! What is it?"

"Oh, I cannot stand it!" Bessie cried miserably. "They are all a bunch of cruel, nasty vultures picking at me. Talking about me behind my back, and even in front of me, calling me a country cow and—"

Her voice broke on a sob and Charlie hugged her tightly, silently cursing the whole of London society for having behaved so predictably. Elizabeth had been filled with trepidation on the trip back to London, afraid of the scandal that would erupt once the ton knew of their antics. Charlie had assured her sister at the time that all would be well. She had suspected that, with both men being members of the peerage, added to the fact that most of London wished to get in on Radcliffe's investments, no one would say much about their scandalous behavior. And she had been right. Rather than being condemned, they had been touted as romantic heroines. At least openly. Bessie had not been as lucky. Charlie had feared that she might not, and she had been correct in her worry. Polite society would never forgive one of the working class for daring to step above themselves so.

Despite the fact that no one knew that Seguin had married the girl by mistake—both Carland and Uncle Henry had kept their mouths shut to date—the ton would not forgive the former maid for marrying a member of the nobility. Tongues were wagging overtime and rumors were rampant. There were whispers that she had blackmailed him into marrying her. Others whispered that Seguin had married the girl to spite Beth when he had found out that she had married another. And there was even speculation as to whether the family would contest the marriage and try to have it dissolved. But in the meantime, Bessie was settled uncomfortably in Seguin's townhouse, under constant siege by visitors as the curious arrived at her door to inspect her as if she were some sort of animal in a cage.

A knock at the door drew Stokes away from where he had been hovering by Charlie and the sobbing Bessie. She watched him open the door to answer it and caught a glimpse of a small boy on the step; then the lad handed Stokes a message and fled.

"'Tis for His Lordship," he announced, catching Charlie's questioning glance as he turned back. "I shall place it on the desk in the library."

Nodding, Charlie turned Bessie toward the room she had just come out of. "Would you bring us some tea in the salon afterward, please, Stokes?"

When he nodded, she led Bessie into the room, urged her into a chair, and sat down to peer at her unhappy face with concern. "Is it as bad as all that, Bessie?"

"It is simply horrid. I would rather clean bedpans than put up with the nasty old biddies who arrive at my door every day."

"Oh, dear." Charlie patted her hand, trying not to grimace at the idea of cleaning bedpans. The girl was in an awful state. "Why do you not simply instruct your butler to announce that you are not in?" she suggested gently as Stokes entered with the tea tray, then blanched in surprise when Bessie raised a suddenly furious gaze to her.

"I have!" the new countess told her bitterly. "He will not listen. He takes great delight in watching me squirm with humiliation at the tender mercies of those women. No one in Seguin's house listens to me. My lady's maid does not even pretend to answer my summons. The cook will not speak to me, and if I eat at all it is cold bread and cheese slapped down on the table by a surly old woman who is some sort of servant, though I know not what. There does not even appear to be anyone who cleans the place, at least not since I have arrived. The townhouse is cold, draughty, dust is collecting and . . ." She shuddered. "It was all rather unattractive to begin with. As time passes with this neglect, it becomes quite hideous."

Charlie jumped slightly as Stokes, who had come to a standstill at Bessie's outburst, slammed the tea tray down on the table with a crash. Spying the outrage on his face, she knew he was angry on Bessie's behalf and sympathized with him. Stokes had very definite feelings in the matter of how servants should and should not behave. Apparently he did not approve of the behavior of Bessie's new servants. Clearing her throat, Charlie leaned forward and patted the other girl's hand again. "Then you must make some changes."

"What? How can *I* change things?" she asked in dismay.

"For one thing, you must stop thinking of everything as Seguin's. He is dead. The townhouse is not Seguin's home any longer, it is yours," she pointed out gently as Stokes set the teacups before the women, nodding his agreement with his mistress as he worked. "And the servants are no longer Seguin's staff, but yours. If they will not listen to you, you must replace them. Just as if you are unhappy with the gloomy atmosphere of the house, you should change it."

"You make it sound so simple," Bessie marveled.

"It *is* simple," Charlie assured her gently, but Bessie continued to look uncertain.

"But what if his family has the marriage undone? What if—"

"But what if they do not?" Charlie interrupted. "Bessie, you cannot live your life on *if* and *but*. Right now you are Lady Seguin, the countess of Chiltingham, and they are your staff. Only you can do something about the way they treat you."

Unable to contain himself any longer, Stokes burst out, "Lady Charlie is absolutely right. You should clean house. Remove every single servant who will not attend you as you require and bring in new people."

Charlie bit her lip to hide a smile as she considered the change in her husband's valet and butler. Now that he was married, Radcliffe had mentioned expectations to spend a bit more time in London. He had considered hiring on a proper household staff to take the burden off of Stokes and Mrs. Hartshair—who was presently filling both positions as cook and lady's maid to Charlie. Stokes had made his opinion of that suggestion quite clear. While he had no argument with hiring another young girl to act as lady's maid for his mistress and take that chore off of Mrs. Hartshair, he had no desire to have the house filled up with extra servants he would have to chase about. They had Fred in the stable, a woman who came in the afternoons to keep the place clean and tidy, and unless they felt the need to throw a soiree—at which point extra temporary help could be brought in—that was all they needed. He was not so old that he could not tend to his lord's garments and answer the door once in a while too, Stokes had assured them rather huffily.

Charlie suspected the truth was that the man feared losing out on some of the news and gossip he was presently privy to, should someone be hired to assist him. He quite liked things the way they were.

"I believe I know of a book that may help you," Charlie murmured now, turning her attention back to Bessie's problem. "It is a book on how to manage an estate and large staff by a duchess Someone-or-Other."

"Oh, aye." Stokes nodded enthusiastically. "I believe I know which one you mean and I am sure His Lordship has a copy in the library. Shall I fetch it for you, my lady?"

"Nay. I will," Charlie said. "That way I can check to see if there are any other books she may find useful. Why do you not sit down and see if you cannot think of any words of wisdom that may assist her yourself."

Nodding, Stokes sat down with a serious air and faced the young woman, absently reaching for his mistress's unused teacup as he began to lecture her on how a proper staff should behave. Charlie managed to hold back her chuckles until she was out of the room. It was hard for her to recall the rather stiffly upright servant that had been Stokes when she had first arrived with Beth. She had not really noticed the changes that had taken place in the man over time. At least, not until the trip home from Gretna Green. He had seemed to break loose from the shell of propriety that had cloaked him so thoroughly before.

Charlie placed the responsibility for his very definite loosening up at Mrs. Hartshair's door. The man was obviously besotted with the woman. And he positively doted on her two children. Mrs. Hartshair seemed to have a growing affection for the man as well, and Charlie thought it was all rather marvelous. The Hartshairs deserved a good man in their lives after what the late Mr. Hartshair had put them through. Charlie could not think of anyone nicer or more stable than Stokes.

Slipping into the library, Charlie quickly found the book in question. Snatching it off the shelf, she set the heavy tome on the desk and returned to browse the shelves for any other books that may be of service in this situation. Once she had three more books selected, she returned to the desk to collect the first one, only to freeze as her gaze encountered the message that Stokes had placed on the desk where his lord would spot it upon his return. The note had been rolled up and tied with a bloodred ribbon. Just as the blackmailer's missives had been. The skin prickling at the back of her neck, she set the books down gently on the side of the desk, then picked up the message and quickly removed the ribbon, sinking onto the desk chair as she read the words written there.

If you wish to discover the identity of the person who has been blackmailing your bride, come to Aggie's at eleven.

Charlie lowered the note to glance at the bracket clock on the wall by the door. Why, that was in just ten minutes! Radcliffe was not even home. He would never see the message and get there in time to—

Frowning, she shook her head. Why would he need to anyway? They were married now. Besides, the secret of her and Elizabeth's escapades was well known among the ton and had been forgiven. Well . . . most of them anyway, she thought with a grimace and glanced down at the rest of the message.

If you do not show up, I will assume that you will not mind all of London knowing that your wife visited a brothel ere your marriage.

Charlie groaned as she read that. That little adventure was the only one that the ton was not aware of. She could well imagine the furor that would arise should it come out that Lady Radcliffe had been a patron of a common bawdy house.

Crumpling the letter in her fist, she threw it angrily across the room and stood to hurry around the desk and out of the library. When a glance into the salon showed her that Mrs. Hartshair had joined the little advisory discussion around the tea tray and that her own presence was not being missed, Charlie swerved toward the stairs and rushed up them.

Despite her assurances to Radcliffe, Charlie still had one of the outfits she had worn during her stint as Charles. She had not understood on their return home why he would insist that she destroy them all, but had merely murmured her consent and handed them over to Stokes to get rid of as he saw fit . . . except for the outfit she now dug out of the chest at the foot of the bed. She suspected now that it may have been her husband's hope to avoid something like this from occurring. Radcliffe was very good with details and would not have overlooked the fact that the blackmailer who had sold her back to her uncle was still out there and may contact them again. Charlie had not thought of that. She had assumed that now that she was married, she was safe. She supposed that her husband, in his own way, had been trying to protect her. But would he really rather risk her being ruined than to have her dress as a man again to meet a blackmailer and save herself?

Probably, she thought with a wry grimace as she stripped out of her clothes. Men could be so irrational at times! Grabbing up the strip of cloth, she quickly bound her breasts, grimacing at the necessary discomfort. Then she donned the male clothes, tied her hair at the nape of her neck, slid it down the back of her shirt, and slapped the now ratty old wig on her head.

Moving to the small chest on the bedside table, she used the key that hung around her neck to unlock it and quickly scooped out a handful of coins. Charlie then hurried from the room, ran down the stairs and straight out the front door without a word to anyone. They would have just tried to talk her out of going, and she would have had to waste a lot of time convincing them that she was doing the right thing. Charlie did not have that time to spare. She could not risk the black-mailer's giving up on Radcliffe's arrival and going else-where with his information.

She wasn't worried about this information getting out so much on her own behalf. Nay. Her main con-cern was for Radcliffe. The scandal that would erupt should the story of her antics get out would be a hu-miliating price to pay for having tried only to rescue her from a horrible life, or more likely death, with Carland. He deserved better. She owed him better. And she would see that he got it, she thought deter-minedly as she flagged down a hack and climbed in-side after shouting out her destination to the driver.

It was a very short ride to Aggie's. She recalled it as having been longer the first time, but that may have been due to the circumstances. Then, she had been anticipating a night at the club or someplace equally entertaining. She had been impatient to arrive. Today, she was full of trepidation about going there.

When the carriage stopped, Charlie peered out the window at the facade of the brothel, then descended reluctantly and handed the driver a coin.

"I don't think they're open yet, m'lord," the man commented, taking in the silent and still atmosphere around the building as well. It was as if all its inhabitants and even the building itself were sleeping, or waiting. He shook his head. "They are most like all still abed after last night's business. Are you sure you wouldn't rather go elsewheres?"

"Nay. This is fine. Thank you," Charlie murmured, turning away to walk slowly up to the door. She took a moment to inhale a deep breath before knocking, then managed not to shrink when it was opened by a giant who eyed her doubtfully and rumbled, "We ain't open yet."

Clearing her throat, she lifted her chin and announced with as much arrogance as she could muster, "Radcliffe at your service. I am expected."

His bushy red eyebrows rose at that, but he stepped aside at once. Charlie could not be sure whether he doubted her veracity in claiming to be expected, or that he did not believe that the slender young lad before him was Lord Radcliffe. She did not care either way. She simply ignored his attitude and stepped inside, eager to get this business over with and return home to her imperfect, but at least mostly pleasant, life with her husband.

"This way." Turning, he led her across the hall and upstairs. Recognizing the room he led her to as the very one she had encountered Bessie in, Charlie hesitated about entering until she spotted the man standing by the window with his back to the room.

Blowing her breath out on a long sigh of resignation, she stiffened her spine and strode into the room with a false air of bravado, then jumped in surprise when the door slammed shut behind her. The man at the window had not even reacted to the sound. After several moments ticked by and he still had not turned to face her, Charlie gave up her feigned indifference and shifted unhappily. "Well?"

"Well," the man murmured and turned to face her, revealing the flintlock pistol he held in his hand.

A jolt of disbelief ran through her as she stared at the weapon. A second rocked through her when she raised her gaze to peer at his face.

"Norwich!" she gasped, her gaze shifting between his face and the pistol he held as it dropped limply to his side. The pistol looked vaguely familiar to her, though she'd had no occasion to have seen it before now. One hardly displayed guns at balls and soirees, and those were the only places Charlie had ever had occasion to meet up with the brother of the man Radcliffe's sister had married. "What are you doing here?"

He stared at her blankly, then down at the weapon he held and away toward the window, a frown furrowing his brow. "I . . ." He hesitated, then grimaced and gazed back at her, giving a short laugh that ended on a sigh. "You know why I am here."

"A spot of blackmail?" she suggested dryly. "It was you all along, was it?"

He shrugged slightly. "London living is quite expensive."

"How did you know who we were?"

"I have a passing acquaintance with your uncle. I was even at your country estate once. It was a very brief stop," he added when he spotted her doubtful expression. "He owed me some money and I came by to get it. I was not there long enough to be properly introduced, but I did spot you and your sister returning from the village as I left in my carriage." Sighing, he moved several steps to the right to set his pistol on one of the bedside tables, then leaned back against the wall beside it, crossing his arms over his chest and his legs at the ankles in a semi-relaxed manner as he continued. "Still, I did not recognize you at first. It had been well over a year since I saw the two of you. Then, too, it was clever of you to disguise yourself as a boy." He complimented her with a sudden grin that, under other circumstances, she would have found charming. "Very ingenious."

"Not ingenious enough if you recognized us."

"Oh." He waved a hand airily. "That was not your fault, really. After all, it helped that I knew Radcliffe had no relatives. That led me to wonder who you were. And still, I may not have figured it out had you changed your names."

Charlie sighed at that. Their names had been the weakest part of the entire plan. But after having already given them to Radcliffe, they had decided that Charlie and Elizabeth were common enough—as were most royal names—and that they could get away with it. Besides, the off-chance of recognition had seemed less likely to give them away than using alternate names and slipping up by calling each other by their real names, or by forgetting and not answering to the fake ones. Still, if it had not been for the fact that they had never been to London and that few people had ever come to the estate since their parents' deaths, they would never have chanced it.

"You really should have let Radcliffe keep this meeting."

Charlie glanced sharply at him, made extremely wary by the regret and weariness in his tone. "Aye, well, he was not available. He was not even home and the letter did say that if he did not show up, you would tell the entire ton. Besides, why should he pay you off? We had *him* fooled as well."

"Did he really not know you were a woman?"

She shook her head solemnly. "Do you think he would have dragged me off to a brothel had he realized I was a woman?"

"Good point," he said wryly, and shook his head. "This was where I first saw you, you know."

Charlie tilted her head at that. "Really?"

"Aye. I saw you creeping out of one room and slipping down the hall checking each door until you slipped into this one. What were you looking for?"

"Radcliffe," she murmured, recalling that night.

"I realized you were a woman right away."

Charlie gave a start at the claim, then shook her head, not bothering to hide her disbelief. "Oh, aye. The rest of London was fooled, but not you."

He merely shrugged. "It is all in the presentation, I suspect. Had I first met you at the theater or a ball like everyone else, I may have been fooled. But I first saw you in a brothel." When she merely stared at him blankly, he continued, "The women here wear all manner of costume to please their customers, and when I first saw you it was from behind as you backed out of the room down the hall."

She arched her eyebrows. "So?"

"Your hips are far too generous and shapely to be a boy's. Quite pert and attractive, actually, and as I have never found a man's behind attractive, you had to be a woman." He grinned wickedly again as she flushed, but continued, "I thought perhaps you were a new girl playing a role for one of the men."

"I see." Charlie cleared her throat. "Then when we were introduced to you as Radcliffe's cousins—when you knew he had no family—you put two and two together and decided to blackmail us."

"You make me sound quite dastardly," he murmured with a grimace.

"Are you not?" she asked archly.

He laughed without humor. "Not as dastardly as I am going to be," he muttered under his breath, then took up his pistol again.

Charlie's gaze dropped to the pistol automatically, taking in the cut steel stock inlays and the initials on the butt. "The inn."

He frowned at her softly spoken word. "What?"

"That is where I recognize your pistol from," she explained. "An inn on the way into London. The innkeeper showed it to me. He said that he had gotten it off of a fellow who had gambled all of his money away to another patron at the inn and had tried to sneak out on his bill. That pistol looked just like yours. In fact it had initials on it," she recalled, and frowned as she tried to recall what those initials had been.

"R. N."

"Aye," Charlie murmured uncertainly. Radcliffe had told her that Norwich's name was George, after the king.

"The R is for Robert. My brother," he explained. "Robert Norwich. They were his. A matched set, you see. They passed on to me when he died and I kept them for sentimental reasons, which is why I did not simply hand over one of the guns to the innkeeper in lieu of payment, rather than risk the embarrassment of being caught fleeing in the night."

"You must have loved your brother deeply."

"Oh, good Lord, no, I loathed him," he laughed, then scowled at the gun in his hand. "I shall have to go back to that inn and fetch back the other one once I have Radcliffe's money."

Charlie shook her head slightly in bewilderment. "Why? You have just said that you loathed your brother. Why would you want his pistols? And how can you have a sentimental attachment to them if you disliked him so?"

"Because they are what I killed him with."

Chapter 20

CHARLIE stared at the man before her with horror. "You . . . ?"

"Killed him," Norwich repeated slowly as if for the benefit of a simpleton. "Aye. With his own pistols. Can you imagine? It was the crowning moment of my life to date. I can still see the expression on his face as clearly as if he stood before me now." He peered off into space for a moment, savoring the image in his mind, then sighed. "Ah well, that is the trouble with life. Such pleasures are long awaited and sadly fleeting when they finally arrive."

Charlie shifted impatiently. "May we get back to the part about your killing your brother?"

"Oh, were we not finished with that conversation? I thought we were. What is it you wish to know?"

Charlie took a deep breath, trying to sort the questions barraging her mind. "I was told he was killed by bandits."

"Well, I could hardly go riding back to the house shouting 'I shot him, I shot my brother.'" He shrugged. "There had been a bandit working in the area; he made an easy target for laying the blame."

She hesitated. This was the question she found hardest to ask, even though she knew what the answer must be. "And his wife? Radcliffe's sister?"

"Ahhh. Mary. Sweet Mary. Aye, I killed her too."

"How could you?"

He held up the pistol in his hand. "A matched set, remember? Two pistols, two bullets, two dead."

"Nay, I mean, he was your own brother. And she—"

"Actually, he was not my brother."

That brought her up short. "Not . . . ?"

"Nay. The old Norwich was not my father either. He merely gave me his name . . . For a price." He enjoyed her uncertain curiosity briefly, then explained, "My mother was the king's mistress. She became pregnant and he, already being married, paid Norwich to marry my mother and save her from scandal. 'Tis why I was named George. For my father."

He grinned at her wide-eyed expression. "You see, you have the honor of speaking to a man who, under other circumstances, would have been a king, or at the very least a prince."

"And the king paid Norwich to—"

"Aye. A dowry just this side of a king's ransom. Still, I don't think Norwich would have been persuaded even by that if it had not been the king asking. He really had no need of money, and by all accounts he had loved his first wife dearly and was not looking for a replacement. Still, how does one say no to the king?"

"I do not suppose one does," she murmured, eyebrows furrowed as she tried to absorb all she was learning. "Is that why you killed Robert, because he was Norwich's son and—"

"I killed him for money," he interrupted with amusement. "I hated him because he was himself. He was . . ." Norwich shook his head, frustrated by his inability to put his thoughts into words. "He was perfect. Handsome, strong, charming, intelligent. He was the apple of his father's eye. He could do no wrong. Women loved him, men admired him. He always made me look bad." Becoming agitated, he paced a few steps, then turned, exclaiming, "Me! A king's son. Yet next to him I appeared insignificant. Never as good. Never as smart. Never as handsome. Even my mother doted on him. And he inherited *everything* on the old man's death. He became a duke, while I, a king's son, was titleless, landless," he muttered bitterly, then paused and straightened, drawing in a deep draught of air before continuing almost smugly, "But I showed him. Oh, yes. I planned a way to get it all. The land, the title, the wealth. Even his wife."

"You did not—" Charlie clamped her teeth on the question, but he was able to work it out for himself.

"Rape her?" He scowled. "Good heavens, no. What do you take me for?"

Charlie could hardly answer that one. Good God, the man had admitted to murder and blackmail, but she was supposed to know he drew the line at rape?

"Nay, as I said, I had a plan to get it all. Unfortunately, Mary rather messed that up by getting with child." He shook his head with disgust. "I had intended to kill Robert. Of course, I would be there to comfort the grieving widow. Then, shortly afterward, I had intended to kill Radcliffe. Since he had no other relatives, something I had looked into—which is why I knew you and your sister could not be his cousins, by the way—Mary would have been his sole heir. Then, while she was reeling from both losses in quick succession, I had intended on marrying her, making it all *mine*." He heaved a deep sigh and paced across the room. "It was a perfect plan. . . . But then one morning, shortly before my plan was to go into motion, Robert announced that Mary was with child." Pausing at the fireplace, he suddenly swept his hand violently along the mantel sending a pendulum clock and several candleholders crashing to the floor. Charlie jumped, then eyed him warily as he turned to face her.

"An heir would have ruined everything, of course. I lost my temper," he announced with a charming grimace. "And in a fit of pique and fury I decided to kill her as well. Shortly after they left to go to Radcliffe's, I searched out Robert's pistols, loaded them, and rode to a spot halfway between both estates. It was a damp day. Chilly. I remember my hands grew numb from the cold at one point and I feared I would not be able to shoot the pistol. But then, finally, I saw them come around the bend on their horses. They were laughing at something and casting each other loving looks. I stepped from the trees, aimed for Mary's heart, and shot. She did not even cry out. She simply stiffened in her seat, then tumbled to the ground. Robert screamed her name and leapt to the ground to hurry to her side. He lifted her into his arms, rocking her and whispering her name over and over. He did not even look around to see me approach, not until I stood right beside him. Then he raised his head, stared at me blankly, and said in the most pitiful voice, 'George, Mary's been shot.' I said, 'Aye. I shot her.' Then as the realization dawned on his face, I raised the other gun, his other gun, and shot him, too."

He released a deep sigh of satisfaction. "It is a moment I have enjoyed remembering with great satisfaction for years. . . . Still, I do regret that I did not stick to the original plan. Once my temper had cooled, I realized that I could have followed the original plan to the letter, except that once I had married Mary, I would have had to instigate a fall from a horse or a tumble down the stairs to cause either a miscarriage of Robert's child or both their deaths. Either eventuality would have solved the dilemma nicely, and I really could have used Radcliffe's fortune."

"One fortune was not enough?" she asked with disgust.

"As I said, London living is quite expensive. Besides—as you may have guessed, thanks to the incident with Robert's pistol—I do like to gamble. When I win, I win big. But when I lose—" He shrugged philosophically. "Money has gotten a bit tight. The creditors are becoming quite nasty with their threats. That was why I was so happy when I heard that Radcliffe had married you."

Charlie was having trouble following his reasoning. What did her marriage to Radcliffe have to do with his gambling? Unless—

"I realized then that God was giving me a second chance."

"God has nothing to do with this madness!" Charlie gasped.

He eyed her with a solemnity that seemed almost sane. "You are wrong, my dear. The kings of England are direct descendants of Christ. His blood flows through our veins. God takes great interest in what I do. '*Dieu et mon adroit.*' "

If she had wondered about his sanity ere this, there was no longer a need to wonder. The man was mad. Still, she tried to reason with him. "Surely, Norwich, you do not believe that God wishes for you to black-mail us?"

"Blackmail?" He appeared surprised. "I do not in-tend to blackmail you anymore."

Now she was truly confused. "But the letter . . . the demand that Radcliffe meet you here. . . ."

"Did I tell him to bring any jewels or coins?"

"Nay," she realized with a frown. "Then, what—"

"I plan to kill him, of course." When she blanched at those easy words, he smiled. "You are married to Radcliffe. He has no other relatives. When he dies you will inherit all. Then I shall marry you and it will all be mine."

He was looking terribly pleased with himself, and much to Charlie's horror she could see that, had she not learned all she had today, and had Radcliffe been home, received the message, kept the meeting and been killed, she might very well, in time, have been charmed enough by the handsome, engaging man be-fore her and have married him—never knowing he had killed her husband. But now she did know. "You do not honestly expect that if you do somehow man-age to kill my husband, I will be willing to marry you?"

He scowled. "Unfortunately, that is the problem you have created by arriving here in his place today. You were never to know any of this. I fear you have rather messed up my plans. In some ways, it is almost a repeat of the day Mary and Robert died."

Charlie felt fear pierce her clear and sharp. Oddly enough, this was the first real fear she had felt since recognizing that Norwich was the man holding the pistol on her. Now, as she recalled his calm recitation of the way Mary had paid for messing up his plans, she very much feared for her life.

"My lord! Thank God you are home."

Radcliffe turned from closing the door to see Stokes hurrying toward him from the salon with Mrs. Hartshair and Bessie hard on his heels. The expression on the usually placid man's face was enough to raise a responding anxiety in Radcliffe. "What is it? Where is Charlie?"

"I . . . that is . . . I do not know," the servant admitted helplessly. "She went to fetch a book for Bes—Lady Seguin, and she did not come back. When we checked the library it was empty. We searched the rest of the house but she is simply not here. I did not know what to do. I had no idea where you were so could not send word to you and . . ." His voice trailed away unhappily.

Radcliffe stared at him blankly. "You mean she has just disappeared?"

"Well . . ."

When Stokes hesitated, seemingly at a loss, Radcliffe asked, "How long has she been gone?"

"Since before noon," he admitted reluctantly. "I sent a message to Lady Elizabeth to ask if she had gone there, but have heard nothing back yet."

Radcliffe was absorbing all of this information

when the door knocker sounded. Turning, he pulled the door open, relief rushing through him briefly as he peered at the woman on the doorstep, until he realized that she was wearing a pastel gown. "Elizabeth?"

"Aye." Stepping quickly into the house when he moved aside, she took in the worried faces around her. "You have not found her yet, I take it?"

"Nay," Bessie answered, biting her lip unhappily.

"And you have no idea where she could have gone?" she asked, waiting as the people in the hall glanced at each other miserably. Sighing, Beth led the way into the salon. "Come. Let us sit down and try to reason this out. There must be some clue to tell us where she may have gone. Charlie does not run about willy-nilly. Something must have happened to make her leave. We simply have to look at this logically."

Charlie shoved at the window furiously. She had been trying to open it since Norwich had left to consider what he was to do next. She supposed that he was trying to determine a way to let her live and force her to marry him after Radcliffe had showed up and he had killed him. Charlie had not told him that Radcliffe was not likely to show up. She distinctly recalled throwing the message across the library in a crumpled ball. She had seen it roll under a chair in a corner as she had rushed out of the library. Radcliffe was not likely to find it.

Sighing, she gave up her frantic jerking of the window and examined it instead, cursing when she spied the nails that had been used to seal it shut. It seemed the proprietors were taking no chances after

Bessie's escape. Moving to the next window, she checked to find that it too was nailed shut, then walked to the bed and sat on the edge of it. She had to think of a plan to get herself out of there. She had to warn Radcliffe.

"So." Beth peered down at the list she had made. "Charlie spent most of the morning in here. Then Bessie arrived, directly after which a boy came to the door with a message for Radcliffe and you took it into the library?" She glanced at Stokes to see the man nod solemnly before she continued, "She chatted in here briefly with Bessie, then went in search of a book in the library and never returned. But, Stokes, you thought you heard the door close shortly afterward?"

"Aye," he admitted unhappily.

"And a search of the house revealed that she was nowhere to be found, but that several books were on the desk, the gown she had been wearing was in a heap on her dressing room floor, no other dresses seem to be missing to have replaced it, and that the message was gone?"

When Stokes, Mrs. Hartshair, and Bessie all nodded in agreement that this was the basic situation as they knew it, she sighed. "And you do not know who this message was from?"

Stokes shook his head. "As I said, a boy brought it." He hesitated, then added miserably, "It did not have any writing on the outside, it was just rolled up and tied with a ribbon."

Beth and Bessie both stiffened at that. "A ribbon?" they echoed in unison.

"Aye."

"What color was this ribbon?" Bessie asked anxiously.

"Red. Deep red, almost the color of blood."

"Damn." Beth sank back in her seat.

"What is it?" Radcliffe asked.

"That is the way the blackmailer's messages came," she told him grimly, then glanced at Stokes to ask, "You are sure that the message is not still here?"

"Well . . . it was not on the desk," he murmured uncertainly.

Standing, Beth hurried out into the hall and on into the library. A glance at the desk proved Stokes right. The message was not there. She was gazing blankly around the room when a sudden uproar in the hallway drew her attention. Moving to the door, she opened it to see that the puppies were loose and Mrs. Hartshair and her children were attempting to round them up while the pups, thinking it all a grand game of chase, did their best to avoid capture.

"I opened the kitchen door to go check on the children, just as they came in the back door with the pups," the cook explained as she chased a pup past Beth. She cornered the creature at the end of the hall, but when she swooped down to gather it up, it scampered past her, scurrying into the library right past Beth.

"Really," Radcliffe said, "this is hardly the time for such antics."

Turning, Elizabeth hurried after the animal with Mrs. Hartshair on her heels. The puppy led them a merry chase, dashing under the desk, then across the room and under a chair. Each of them taking a side, they blocked the animal in, then Mrs. Hartshair bent to fetch the pup out.

"What have you got there?" the woman muttered, tugging a small ball of paper from his mouth. "Honestly, you little beasties are forever into one thing or another," she chastised mildly.

"Let me see that," Beth said.

Eyebrows rising, the cook handed the paper over and watched curiously as Beth uncrumpled it. "It is not—"

"It is!" Beth cried jubilantly, quickly reading the message. "Radcliffe!"

He appeared in the door as she reached it and she cried, "Mrs. Hartshair found it. It is from the blackmailer. He wanted you to meet him at Aggie's."

"And Charlie went in my place," he guessed, taking the note to read it.

"Oh, surely not," Mrs. Hartshair argued. "A decent woman wouldn't be seen at that place. She would not even be allowed in."

"Nay, but Charles would," Beth murmured, thinking of the crumpled gown on the floor in her dressing room and the fact that no other dresses had been missing.

"Damn!" Radcliffe breathed, whirling to hurry toward the door.

"Wait!" Beth cried, chasing after him to grab his arm and keep him from leaving. "You cannot just show up there. It may be a trap."

"But Charlie is there."

"That is even more reason to go about this cautiously. You may get her killed if you storm in without a plan."

"It is early afternoon, Beth. No matter how I approach it, I will draw attention. All who will be there right now are women."

Her eyebrows rose, an idea taking shape on her face. "Aye. You are right. You would be recognized . . . as a man."

The click of the key in the lock warned her moments before the door opened. Standing abruptly, Charlie put on a brave face as the door swung open, only to sag in relief as Aggie entered. Garbed in a gown of flaming orange that was just as tight, loud, and ugly as the red dress she had been wearing when last they met, the woman eyed Charlie with fascination for a moment, then glanced over her shoulder and gestured to an older woman in the hallway. The servant rushed into the room carrying a tray of food, set it down on the end of the bed beside Charlie, and hurried out.

Aggie pushed the door closed, then turned to examine Charlie once more, her gaze sliding slowly over every inch of her in the male garb. Then she shook her head. "I don't know how you had me fooled into thinking you a lad."

"People see what they want to see," Charlie murmured with an indifferent shrug as she looked over the tray she had been brought with feigned interest, hoping the woman would just hurry up and leave.

"Are you not curious to know what is happening?"

Charlie was silent for a moment, but she finally raised one eyebrow in silent query.

"Himself is writing a letter," the old prostitute announced grandly as if throwing crumbs to the starving masses. "It is for your husband, Lord Radcliffe. He is telling him that we have you and that if he wishes to see you again, he is to come here, alone, unarmed, at midnight."

"And then what happens?" Charlie asked with a feigned calm that made the old whore arch an eyebrow.

"Why, then himself kills him and heads to Gretna Green to marry you."

Charlie gave a bark of laughter, shaking her head with an amusement that was only half-feigned. "Oh, that will work. I am sure no one will comment on that. Radcliffe dead and me on my way to be remarried within moments? No one would suspect that myself or Norwich or both of us had done it. Good Lord, he is insane. Especially if he thinks I would marry the man who killed my husband."

"Oh, you will," Aggie assured her smugly. "You will if you do not wish him to kill your sister as well." When Charlie blanched at the threat, Aggie grinned nastily. "Well, finally some reaction. Is that not interesting, though? The idea of Radcliffe's death leaves you stone-faced, while the thought of your sister's death worries you greatly. Does your husband realize that you care so little for him?" When Charlie did not respond, annoyance flickered over Aggie's face before she turned to the door. "Well, I must get back to work. I have a business to run, you know." Opening the door, she paused and glanced back to add, "You will enjoy marriage to Norwich. If Maisey is to be believed, he is an incredibly vigorous lover. A bit rough perhaps, but vigorous just the same."

Charlie watched the door close behind the woman,

then gave the tray of food a shove that sent it crashing to the floor.

"Oh, my!"

Stokes bit his lip and turned away as Lady Elizabeth's eyes widened on her first sight of Lord Radcliffe. This was no time for levity, he lectured himself firmly. There was nothing the least bit amusing about the situation. Still, the sight of His Lordship bewigged and gowned in Mrs. Hartshair's frilly pink dress was really more than a good valet should have to see. Even helping him into the ridiculous outfit had been beyond the call of duty. Stokes had a new respect for the women employed as lady's maids. Truly, their chore in dressing their mistresses was atrocious. There were zonas and boned corsets with laces that Lady Elizabeth had assured him had to be drawn tight, tighter, and tighter still, despite the fact that His Lordship had been woozy from the constriction. Petticoats and day sleeves, buffens and cuffs, stockings and garters. And that had just been the underthings. Then had come the outer; a stomacher, a bodice with its hook-and-eye fastenings, a waistcoat and skirt. . . . And with all of that, His Lordship still looked like himself in a dress, the servant thought with disgust. It seemed that the dress did not make the woman.

"Umm." Lady Elizabeth managed a rather forced smile and backed toward the door. "I shall return directly."

Radcliffe glanced toward Stokes with a scowl. "She did not look pleased."

"Oh, I am sure she is pleased, my lord," Stokes murmured quickly, afraid the man was simply looking for an excuse to get out of the dress. It had taken Lady Elizabeth a solid hour of talking to convince him that he would have a better chance of rescuing Lady Charlie as a woman than as himself. Then the problem of a dress came into play. Lady Elizabeth and Lady Charlie were shorter than His Lordship by a good ten inches, as was Lady Bessie. Mrs. Hartshair, on the other hand, was only an inch or two shorter than His Lordship. She was also full-figured and round, and while His Lordship was lean and well muscled, he was wide in the shoulders and had need of the extra space in the bodice of the gown.

"Here we are." Lady Elizabeth rushed back into the master bedroom, powder, rouge, kohl liner, and lip color in one hand and a mob cap, Bergere straw hat, and hooded mantle in the other. Dropping the clothing on the end of the bed, she urged Radcliffe to sit in a chair and close his eyes, then set to work.

"Do stop scowling, my lord, you are causing lines in your powder," she muttered several moments later.

"Surely you are done now," was Radcliffe's answer.

"Nearly," she murmured, adding more color to his cheeks, then stepped back and peered at him critically, tilting her head first one way, then the other, then the first way again. Her shoulders fell slightly. He looked even worse now than he had before. He looked like Radcliffe in wig, face powder, and a dress.

"Perhaps the hat, my lady?" Stokes suggested encouragingly.

"Oh, aye." Relief obvious on her face, she whirled back to the bed to grab the rest of the gear she had brought in. Moving back, she set the mob cap over his wig, then added the straw hat, setting it at a jaunty angle, then changed her mind and tilted it forward so that it shadowed his face . . . then further still.

Stepping back, she frowned over him, dissatisfied, until Stokes gave a cough, drawing her attention. When she glanced his way, he gestured toward his own chest behind Radcliffe's back. It took her a moment to read his signals, and then her eyes slid back to Radcliffe's flat chest. Of course, that was why he looked so odd! She glanced around the room, then spied the hose lying on the floor and scooped them up. "Here."

Moving to stand before Radcliffe, she began stuffing the hose down his top, arranging and pushing the material until she had to give it up as a lost cause. She supposed there were quite a few women who had not been in line when God had handed out upper endowments. Tugging the material out, she tossed it aside and took the mantle Stokes now held out, arranging it around Radcliffe's shoulders, pulling it forward to hide his lackluster chest, then tugging the voluminous hood of the cape up to cover his head and hang over half of his face.

"Are you quite through?"

Beth sighed unhappily, but nodded and stepped back. Lord Radcliffe was off the chair at once and striding toward the door. Beth followed quickly, trailing him down the stairs and throwing the women warning looks over his head as Mrs. Hartshair and Bessie turned to see them descending. Catching the warning, both women managed to contain their humor and merely watched wide-eyed as His Lordship stomped down the steps in the tight, frilly, too-short dress. He was at the door to the street when he paused and tugged his skirts up slightly to peer at his feet. Turning back to face them, he frowned. "Shoes."

Lady Elizabeth glanced down with distress at his strong masculine legs amongst so many pink frills and released a choked sound. Whirling away, she fled to the salon. Stokes hurried after her. He thought her distress was over the fact that there certainly would not be one pair of lady's slippers or even clogs in the house that would fit His Lordship, but when he entered the room, far from finding her crying as he had feared, he discovered her laughing into the back of the settee, her entire body shaking with the effort to do so silently.

" 'Tis all right," Radcliffe cried, hurrying into the salon after them. "I shall just wear my jackboots. No one will see them under my skirts."

When Lady Elizabeth's shoulders began to shake even more furiously at that, Stokes promptly positioned his body to hide hers as he turned to face Radcliffe. He barely managed to maintain his solemn demeanor as he nodded in what he hoped would be taken as agreement, then sagged with relief as the Earl of Radcliffe hurried out of the room in search of the boots. Turning back to his mistress's sister, he found her recovering from her lack of decorum and wiping tears of mirth from her eyes.

"He will be noticed at once," she sighed, her humor gone as if it had never been.

"Aye. But mayhap not recognized."

"We must hope not."

"He has a better chance dressed so than as himself,"

Stokes said solemnly. "Mayhap we can just persuade him to try to keep his back to anyone he encounters and to slouch a little so that he does not appear so large."

"Aye," she sighed, getting to her feet.

"I am ready." Radcliffe stomped into the room then, his jackboots peeking out from under the pink skirts with every step. "Come, we have wasted enough time." Skirts flying, he whirled to lead the way out of the room.

Chapter 21

"That is the room they kept me in, if you will recall, my lord," Bessie murmured, pointing at a window on the second floor of the building as the driver directed the carriage down the alley beside Aggie's establishment. "They are probably keeping her in there. From what I heard while I was there, that room is kept for the express purpose of holding unwilling guests."

Radcliffe shook his head. "Nay, she cannot be there, Bessie, else she would have just crawled out the window as the two of you did that night."

"If she was able," Elizabeth murmured with a frown. When he blanched at her words, she quickly added, "They may have tied her up or something, my lord."

"Oh, aye." Relaxing the teensiest fraction, he suddenly yanked his skirt up to check to be sure that his pistol was still in the pocket sack that hung under the petticoats, then quickly tugged it back down with irritation when he saw the women blush and turn away. It was beyond him why women wore what they did. He was laced in so tightly that he could hardly breathe, and weighted down with so much material he could hardly move. Women were a lot stronger than men gave them credit for. Unfortunately, most of that strength appeared to be wasted on carting about their clothes.

"How are you going to get in?" Stokes asked anxiously.

"I shall try the windows first, I think," Radcliffe said with a frown as he straightened out his skirts. "I fear using the front door would be too much of a risk."

"Aye," Stokes said, then, "My lord, you . . . er . . . your purpose may be better served did you try to . . . er . . . keep your face turned away from anyone you encounter."

"Aye," Elizabeth agreed encouragingly. "And mayhap if you tried not to look quite so tall, you might be able to avoid some unwanted attention."

"And if anyone does approach and question you, you might merely cover your face with a handkerchief and titter."

Radcliffe blinked at that suggestion from Bessie. "I do not have a handkerchief."

"Oh!" Whipping one from her sleeve, Beth handed it to him as he got out of the carriage. "Good luck, my lord. I know you shall save her."

"Titter," Radcliffe muttered as he pushed the window open on the first empty room he found on the main floor. "What the devil is a titter? And how the hell am I supposed to try not to look so large?" Shaking his head with disgust, he held the window open with one hand as he sat on the ledge, then swung one leg after the other over the sill and into the room. Standing, he let the window slide closed, then took a moment to brush the wrinkles out of his skirt and yank at the bottom of his bodice to straighten it before hurrying across the room.

Pausing at the door, he pressed an ear to it to listen briefly, then eased it open and peered out. It was early afternoon and yet it seemed the women were all still abed. Slipping into the hallway, he pulled the door gently closed and hurried as quickly as a man could in a dress that kept catching at his boot spurs, toward the stairs. He had just set foot on the first step when a door farther down the hall opened. Cursing under his breath, he rushed silently up the stairs.

"Aggie!"

Radcliffe froze on the fifth step at the shout from below. The voice was a man's and it sounded vaguely familiar. Trying to place it in his mind, he continued up the stairs more warily until he heard the madam's voice answer from the back of the house. "Aye?"

"Send me Little Willy. The letter is ready to go to Radcliffe."

Standing on the stairs, Radcliffe hesitated. He still could not place the voice below and that annoyed him, but what had made him stop was the sudden thought that he could confront the villain right now and have done with it. His gaze moved up the last few steps to the hallway that stretched out before him, however, and he frowned. He really should rescue Charlie first. Once she was safely away from here, he could tend to the man below. If he tried ere seeing her safe and something happened, he would never forgive himself. Nodding to himself, he continued quickly up the stairs and along the hall to the room

Bessie and Charlie had climbed out of so many nights ago.

Reaching for the door handle, he twisted it carefully, not really surprised when it turned easily. Had they locked Charlie in this room, she simply would have climbed out the window as she had when she rescued Bessie. Still, he pushed the door open and peered about to be sure she was not tied to a chair or something. The drapes were closed, casting the room in deep shadow, but from the light spilling through the doorway around him, he did not think that there were any bound and gagged figures in the room. He hesitated, then sighed and slid inside, pushing the door half-closed behind him as he hurried to the windows and yanked the drapes open. Light now filled every corner of the room and still there was no sign of Charlie.

Sighing, he turned back to peer out the window at the alley below, a frown tugging at his brow. He saw at once that he was in the wrong room. The window Charlie and Bessie had climbed out of was the next one over from the one he was at.

Muttering under his breath, he reached up to grab the edges of the drapes, snapping them shut again just as the door squeaked farther open behind him and a voice called softly, "Darlee?"

Radcliffe swallowed a curse at that low rumble behind him, and went completely still, hoping that the dim light from the hallway did not reach him where he stood by the now closed drapes. No such luck, he realized as the man spoke again, sounding closer.

"I did not think you would be back until later.

Lord Ascomb usually keeps you through the night and well into the next when he hires your services."

If anyone does approach and question you, you might merely cover your face with a handkerchief and titter. Bessie's words sounded in his head and Radcliffe frowned. How did one titter? What was a titter? The word made him think of high, twittering sounds. He did not think that he could manage something like that. Then the man pressed against his ruffled backside and rumbled, "Willy's missed ye."

Willy? Radcliffe's eyes widened incredulously. This was *Little* Willy? Good Lord! He had thought the "little" part had referred to Willy being a child. He should have known better. This *was* a brothel, after all. It probably referred to the size of his—Radcliffe's thought died as the man slid his hands around his waist and began to slide them up toward his nonexistent bosom. That was too much for Radcliffe. He was not about to stand around being groped by a fellow named Little Willy.

Tugging sharply away, he whirled to face the fellow, prepared to do battle, but the size of Little Willy brought him up short. The man was half a head taller than Radcliffe and at least twice as wide. At least he looked that large in the dimness of the room. He also was not hampered by a woman's skirt, Radcliffe thought gloomily, preparing to be soundly trounced. Fortunately, it was dark enough in the room that Little Willy could not make out Radcliffe's features. At least that was what he assumed when, rather than rear back in outrage at recognizing him for a man, Little Willy took on a pouting air.

"Ah, now, Darlee, don't be like that. Ye always return from Lord Ascomb's in a huff and I know he don't use you right, but I'll be gentle as always and help ye forget." On that note, the man tugged Radcliffe firmly into his embrace, ignoring his sudden struggles as he buried his face in his neck and slid his arms around him.

Radcliffe was too shocked at the situation at first to react, but when the man's beefy hands slid down to cup his buttocks through his skirts and squeeze, he suddenly found the ability to titter. At least, the choked sound that slid from his lips sounded like a titter to him. Or perhaps a twitter.

"Little Willy!"

Having been just about to plow his fist into the face of the man before him in a desperate bid for freedom, Radcliffe nearly thanked God aloud for that timely call up the stairway. "Little" Willy suddenly stiffened, then heaved a resigned sigh as the shout came again, more impatiently this time.

"I'd best go ere he wakes up the rest of the house," the man rumbled unhappily. "No doubt he's just wantin' to be sure that I sent his letter with the stable lad, but he won't leave off till I tell him so myself."

Giving Radcliffe's pink-clad bottom a friendly squeeze that made him jump and bite his tongue to keep back the curses on the tip of his tongue, the man pulled away, mumbling, "Yer losing weight, Darlee. Yer bottom's tight as a drum. Ye need to eat more. I'll bring ye a little snack when I come back. Then I'll have to examine ye real close to see where else ye've lost weight," he murmured playfully, moving toward the door.

"The hell you will," Radcliffe muttered as soon as the door closed behind the other man. Hurrying forward, he opened the door a crack to see Little Willy lumbering down the stairs. The man was a giant. His fists were nearly as large as his head, which was admittedly small for his body. Radcliffe supposed he should be grateful that those fists had only squeezed his behind. Had the man hit him with one of them, he probably would have killed him with the first blow.

Radcliffe sighed at his own thoughts. Dresses, he decided, were hard on a man's ego. They affected his confidence poorly. Any other time he would have thought the man was large but slow on his feet and that he could easily have outwitted him. In the dress, all he could think was that he would trip himself up with his own skirts and be lucky to survive. He had to find Charlie, get her out of there, and get the damn thing off. Then he would lecture his wife soundly on never *ever* getting herself in such a dangerous predicament again ... for all the good that would do.

Sighing, he eased out into the hallway and closed the door. He had never found himself in situations like this before Charlie had sauntered into his life, he groused to himself as he headed toward the next room. Ah, well. At least he would never need fear his life becoming boring. Charlie would see to that, and without even trying, he suspected. Pausing at the next door along the hall, he checked the knob to see if it turned, a frisson of excitement running up his spine when it did not. She must be in there.

"Charlie?" he whispered. "Are you in there, Charlie? Can you hear me?"

"Jeremy?" Her heart leaping, Charlie rushed to the

door, pressing her face against it eagerly. "Jeremy? Is that you?"

"Aye. Are you all right? They have not hurt you?"

"Nay. I am all right."

Radcliffe glanced around to be sure he was alone, then hissed, "Why have you not escaped out the window then? Are you tied up?"

"Nay, I am not tied up. But they have nailed the windows shut. I have been trying to pry the nails out with a candleholder, but it is going very slow," she admitted with vexation, then sighed. "I take it you found the letter after all?"

"Aye."

"How did you get in without being seen?"

"I came in a window downstairs."

"Thank you," she breathed through the door.

"Thank you?" he murmured with confusion.

"For caring enough to come and try to save me," she explained. "But now you must leave. At once," she ordered firmly. "Norwich will kill you if you are caught."

"Norwich?" He scowled, now understanding why he had thought the voice below sounded familiar.

"Aye. He was the blackmailer. But this last message was merely to get you here so that he might kill you."

"Kill me? Why the devil should he wish to do a thing like that?"

Her voice was sad yet anxious. "It is a long story, my lord. Suffice it to say that he is insane." She sighed again through the door, then insisted, "Please, my lord, you must leave at once. He really will not hesitate to kill you."

"I am not leaving you here."

"Well, you cannot get me out. The door is locked and the window nailed shut. Breaking through either way would create enough noise to bring the household running. Unless you've brought an army with you, I really suggest you leave right now."

"An army," Radcliffe murmured, thinking of Stokes, Bessie, Elizabeth, and Mrs. Hartshair and her children in the carriage below. They had all insisted on coming, and not wishing to waste the time on arguing, Radcliffe had agreed so long as they all stayed in the carriage.

"Radcliffe?"

"Aye?" He glanced at the door. Her voice had seemed to come from much lower along the door this time.

"What are you wearing?"

His gaze shot down to the keyhole and he knelt swiftly to see her eye peering out. She had a beautiful eye, he thought now. It was odd that he had forgotten that. Both her eyes were beautiful. Large, usually twinkling with some inner amusement, and a deep coal black color that looked like a starry night. "Hello," he murmured huskily.

"Are you wearing something pink with ruffles?" she squawked in disbelief, knocking him squarely out of his gentle musings on her beauty.

Scowling, he stood abruptly. "It was your sister's idea."

"Beth? Beth put you in pink ruffles?"

"It is a disguise," he managed to state with great dignity. "She thought that I might be able to avoid detection longer as a woman than as myself."

"It *is* a dress?" she squawked. "You are wearing a frilly, pink *dress?*"

"It is a *disguise,*" Radcliffe snapped, then frowned at the muffled chuckle that came through the door.

"Now you know why I was the one who came up with the plans." She laughed, then, before he could respond, sighed, "You do care for me, then."

"What?" He knelt at the keyhole again, peering in at her one eye. "What do you mean, I care for you?"

"Well, that is the only reason a man might be persuaded to don a dress. To save someone he cares for."

"That is tripe. Good Lord, woman, I chased you clear across England and into Scotland in an airless little trap with Stokes, Tomas, Beth, Mrs. Hartshair and her children, yet that does not impress you with my feelings? I put on one stupid frilly dress and suddenly you think I might care for you? I do not *care* for you madam. I would not dress so for someone I *cared* for. I love you!"

"You do?"

"Of course I do. Why do you think I married you?"

"To save me from Carland."

"I could have simply bought your uncle off, or sent you to the Americas to achieve that end," he said with disgust. "Tying myself down to you for the rest of my life was not necessary."

"But the morning after we . . . umm . . . 'er'd,'" she said at last for want of a better word. "You told me you did not love me."

"You were not even awake when I left you."

"When you thought I was Charles," she explained. He was silent for a moment, then said, "I recall your asking about love, and my starting to say that I did not think it an important consideration at that point, but stopped to consider my feelings. I was very confused at that time. I had feelings for Charles that I thought wholly inappropriate, and feelings for Beth sometimes but not others. It was not until I learned of the switching you and your sister were doing that I sorted everything out and realized that all of my feelings were for you."

"Then you do love me?"

"Would I be kneeling on the floor in pink ruffles if I did not?"

"Oh, Jeremy, I love you too," she sighed, tears pooling in the one eye he could see. "I wish I could hold you."

"You will," he said firmly. "I will get you out of there, but first I have to—"

"Darlee?"

Radcliffe stiffened at that low rumble and turned to stare over his shoulder at the giant standing over him. He had not heard the man approach.

"Yer not Darlee." Radcliffe saw the fist coming down toward his head like a hammer, but didn't have a chance to duck out of the way before pain exploded in his head and unconsciousness overtook him.

It was cold water splashing in his face that dragged him back to reality. Swimming up through the swirling fog in his brain, Radcliffe blinked his eyes open, closed them, then opened them again to squint at the blurry images around him, attempting with difficulty to bring them into focus. Charlie was the first thing he saw, or Charles, he supposed, taking in her breeches and waistcoat as well as the fact that she was seated on the floor, cradling his head in her lap. Then he saw that she was glaring at the second blur furiously, and he squinted at it until it shaped itself into Norwich, who stood above them. An empty pitcher was dangling from one of the man's hands.

"Finally," the other man sighed impatiently. "Really, the two of you are quite tiresome. First, she shows up instead of you, then you come early. I told you midnight—can neither of you read? Nice frock, by the way," he sneered, turning to stomp toward the door. "You have a little over six hours until midnight. Enjoy them. They shall be the last you have together."

"Bastard," Charlie hissed as the door closed behind him, then turned to look down at Radcliffe with concern. "Are you all right?"

"Aye," Radcliffe sighed, sitting up with her help and peering around, his hand moving automatically to rub his aching temple.

"Mayhap you should stay lying down for a bit," Charlie murmured anxiously, but he shook his head and forced himself to his feet where he swayed woozily.

"I do not have that luxury. I have to figure out a way to get us out of here."

"I shall do that, you just rest," she insisted, taking his arm to steady him.

"Nay. I—"

"Dammit Radcliffe, I am wearing the breeches now. Sit down before you fall down," she snapped.

"You are wearing the breeches? What the devil is that supposed to mean?"

"Whatever you want it to, now just sit down." Charlie gave her husband a gentle push that made him drop weakly onto the foot of the bed, then moved to the windows to inspect her handiwork from earlier. She had been working on one of the nails with a silver candlestick holder when Radcliffe had knocked at the door and called out her name.

"What are you doing?"

Glancing around, she saw that Radcliffe had stumbled weakly over to join her and now stood swaying like a sapling in a stiff breeze beside her. Frowning, she took his arm and urged him back to the bed. "Will you just sit down and let me deal with this? I have enough to worry about without having to keep you from falling on your face."

"I will not fall on my face," he snapped irritably, shrugging her hand off. "And I am your *husband*; you do not order me about."

"Is that right? Well, I have news for you, Radcliffe. You are not my husband."

"I am so."

"Are not. You married Beth."

"She may have stood in for you, but it is your name on the register."

"But not my signature. We are not married."

He was stumped briefly by that, then scowled. "Well, we shall rectify that situation. The moment we are out of here I will arrange a proper wedding."

"Good for you, be sure and send me an invitation, I will see if I can not show up to witness it."

He stared at her in bewilderment, wondering whether the injury to his head had not done more damage than he had initially thought. "What is going on? The last thing I recall before being knocked out was our admitting our love for each other, yet now you seem to be saying you will not marry me. What did I miss here?"

Sighing in frustration, Charlie rubbed her hands over her face wearily and shook her head as she crossed back to the window. "You have not missed anything. I missed it. I love you, Radcliffe, but I am not sure that I wish to spend the rest of my life with a man who treats me like an inferior."

"I would never treat you like an inferior."

"Well, you certainly do not treat me like an equal anymore."

"Oh, that is nonsense."

"It is not nonsense. Ever since you found out that I was not really a Charles, you have been treating me like some sort of hothouse flower that does not have a thought in her head and might expire from the effort should I try to place one in it."

"I have not," he denied hotly.

"Oh, really? Well, when was the last time that you discussed business with me?"

"It is not polite to discuss business in mixed company; besides women cannot understand the intricacies of . . ." His voice trailed away, his face flushing with guilt as he realized what he was saying.

"Funny that I seemed to understand it well enough as Charles, but am not even good enough to discuss it as Charlotte."

"I had not realized . . ." he began faintly, dropping to sit on the bed with dismay.

"What? That you saw women as lacking? That you have been treating me like a tickle-brained jolthead?"

she asked dryly, then moved to pick up a candelabra and positioned herself beside the door. Before Radcliffe could ask her what she was about, she let out a bloodcurdling scream and raised the holder over her head as a key jiggled in the lock. The door flew open, a wide-eyed Little Willy stepped in, and she brought the heavy holder down on his head with enough gusto that Radcliffe half-suspected that she was working out some of her anger at him on the poor man's skull.

When the behemoth crumpled to the floor in a heap, she tossed the holder aside, bent to snatch the keys from his limp hand, then straightened to eye Radcliffe impatiently. "Well? Are you coming, or had you intended to wait there for midnight?"

Closing his gaping mouth, Radcliffe got quickly to his feet and stumbled forward. The moment he had stepped through the door, she pulled it closed and locked it, then pocketed the keys and hurried toward the stairs. They were halfway down them when Norwich appeared at the bottom. Much to Radcliffe's amazement, Charlie continued down even as Norwich stepped back and raised his gun to await them. At the bottom of the stairs, Radcliffe moved quickly to place himself protectively before his not-quite-legally-married-wife and faced the man.

Norwich frowned at him with annoyance as he raised his gun and aimed it, then said, "I do not know what is the matter with you two. Why can you not simply do as you are told? Things would be so much easier if you did so."

"Oh, yes, that would be nice, would it not?" Charlie snapped over Radcliffe's shoulder. "Then you could give nice little orders like *die* and we would just drop at your feet."

Norwich frowned at her, then raised an eyebrow at Radcliffe. "Sassy little thing, is she not?"

"I prefer to think of her as passionate."

Norwich's eyebrow rose further. "Really? Well, I can hardly wait to experience her full passion."

"Not in this lifetime, Norwich," Radcliffe snarled.

"He is right," Charlie said calmly when the man chuckled derisively at the threat. "I am afraid the game is up. Your plan never would have worked in any case. Radcliffe and I are not even really married. Beth is the one who married him in Gretna Green."

"Your sister married Mowbray."

"Aye. Four days prior to our arrival in Gretna Green she married Tomas, then the morning your men rode into Gretna with us, she dressed up as Charles and married Radcliffe. It was not a legal marriage. If you kill Radcliffe, all you will get from marrying me are a couple of paltry jewels. Most of them have been sold and the money invested." When he started to shake his head with patent disbelief, she shrugged. "If you do not believe me, ask Beth. She is standing right behind you."

He laughed openly at that. "If you expect me to believe—" His voice died as something hard poked him in his lower back.

"Well, hello, Lord Norwich. Fancy meeting you here," Beth trilled cheerfully, then nudged him a little harder in the ribs with her weapon. "You will give up your gun to Lord Radcliffe, will you not?"

Radcliffe took the pistol as it suddenly hung limply

in the other man's hand. Beth waited just long enough for him to point the weapon at the villain, then rushed around him to hug her sister. "I did it, Charlie! I saved you. *I* saved *you*. And I did it with a candlestick," she half-laughed and half-gasped, pulling away to hold up her weapon. "Oh, it was marvelous. What a rush of sensation! I have never felt so frightened or so truly alive. Do you know, I do not think I shall ever be afraid of anyone again," she said, then laughed and hugged her again. "I *did* it."

"Aye, you did." Charlie smiled at her widely. "Where are the others?"

"Right here, my lady," Stokes said, pushing a bound-and-gagged Aggie down the hallway toward them with Bessie and Mrs. Hartshair following.

"But how did you know they were all here?" Beth asked Charlie in amazement.

"I saw you all climb out of the carriage and crawl through the first-floor window from the room upstairs," Charlie explained. "I was trying to decide at that point whether 'twould be better to block the door, break the window, and climb out, or lure Little Willy into the room, knock him out, and risk the stairs. Seeing you come in made me decide to try the stairs. I hoped you would arrive in time to help with Norwich."

"And I did!" Beth's face was as bright as a candle flame with pride and Charlie could not help but laugh.

"Aye, you did. You were marvelous."

"I was, was I not?" she marveled breathlessly.

"Aye, and I never again want to hear you say you

are a coward. It took great courage to face him down with naught but a candlestick. You could have been killed. Why, all he had to do was glance over his shoulder and—Beth?" Reaching out quickly, she caught her twin as Beth crumpled to the floor in a dead faint.

Chapter 22

"WHAT time is it?"

"You have asked that question twenty times, Radcliffe," Tomas pointed out with exasperation as he checked his timepiece once again. " 'Tis four minutes after the hour."

"They are late."

"Women are always late. I do not know why you are worrying yourself so. *I* am not worried."

Radcliffe grimaced at that. "You are already married. Whether you go through with the service again today or not, *you* will still be married to Beth. Charlie and I are another matter entirely."

"But the two of you sorted it out. She has agreed to marry you. Has she not?"

"Aye." He looked slightly heartened, but then worry crept across his face again. "But what if something has happened?"

"Something like what?" Tomas asked curiously.

"Who can say with Charlie? She attracts trouble like no woman I have ever known."

"True," Tomas agreed morosely, worry plucking at his own brow now as well. "And Beth has taken on that rather unfortunate trait herself lately. Ever since that incident with Norwich, in fact."

Radcliffe nodded solemnly. It was true; the once quiet and sensible Beth had become more like Charlie, thrusting herself into the path of injustice at every turn and making her husband crazy with it. Much to Radcliffe's amusement, the Mowbray home, too, now sported an array of waifs and strays she had rescued from one predicament or another. Though he would never reveal his secret amusement to his friend. And Tomas was correct in saying that it all harked back to the incident with Norwich and her disarming the man with naught but a candlestick. It seemed her words of that day had been true, despite the faint that had followed the incident; she truly was no longer afraid of anyone.

As for Norwich himself, the last they had seen of the man was when the authorities had taken him and Aggie away. He had been squawking that he was the son of a king at the time. What had happened to him since was anyone's guess. Aggie had suffered a heart attack in prison and had not survived to stand trial, and when Radcliffe had made inquiries about the prosecution of Norwich, he had been told not to worry, the matter had been handled. He had heard various rumors, but suspected that the man had been locked away in Bedlam where he could cause no further embarrassment to the royal family.

"Damn," Tomas muttered suddenly, drawing Radcliffe from his thoughts. "Now I am worried too."

Exchanging gloomy glances, the two men began pacing the front of the church under the watchful eye of the minister and the four hundred restless guests cramped into the church. Every single member of the ton had wanted to be present at this "renewal of vows" between Charlie and Radcliffe and Beth and Tomas. They all thought it terribly romantic. Of course, none of them realized that it would be the first time Charlie would get to say her vows and that their earlier marriage might not be quite legal.

Charlie had insisted on it being one year to the day after their supposed marriage at Gretna Green, just so that there would be no confusion over wedding anniversaries. Beth and Tomas had understood and agreed to the date. Of course, that had been before they had learned that Charlie was pregnant and that her due date was just a week after the date set for this "renewal of vows." Radcliffe had tried to convince her that they should push up the wedding date. There was no way he wanted the child born prior to the wedding and possibly being a bastard because of it. Still, Charlie—charming, exciting, sweet, *stubborn* Charlie—had said nay. They would continue as planned and hope the baby did not come early.

"How *did* you convince her to remarry you?" Tomas asked curiously, drawing Radcliffe from his thoughts.

Making a face, he admitted, "I had to draw up a contract stating that I would never again condescend to her. That I would discuss business with her on a daily basis were she interested, and . . ."

"And?"

He sighed unhappily. "And that I would take her to my club dressed as a man."

Tomas gave a start. "What?"

"Shh," Radcliffe cautioned, glancing nervously

around to be sure that they had not been overheard. No one seemed to be paying attention to them. Most of the guests were casting expectant glances toward the back of the church, hoping to spot the brides who should have been there by now. Glancing back to Tomas, he nodded. "She was quite adamant about seeing the club. It seems she was jealous of Beth's getting within those 'hallowed halls'—her words, not mine—and she was determined to see inside for herself."

"Have you taken her there yet?"

"Nay, nay. I managed to put her off for quite some time, and then by the time she lost her patience with my stalling, she was with child and did not think the smoky atmosphere would be good for the baby. I am hoping by the time it is born and she is up and about again, she will have forgotten—" A faint shriek from outside the church made him pause and stiffen in alarm. "That sounded like Charlie."

Turning, he hurried toward the back of the church with Tomas on his heel. Crashing through the church doors, they both froze at the top of the steps and gaped at the spectacle taking place on the street below. Charlie and Beth, in all their wedding finery, were in the midst of attacking what appeared to be a street vendor. Flowers were flying through the air as they both pummeled the man with their bouquets and shouted at him furiously.

"Have I mentioned, Radcliffe, how little I appreciate the effect your wife has had on mine?" Tomas murmured suddenly, and Radcliffe glanced at him with amazement.

"My wife? Good Lord, Tomas, you cannot blame Beth's sudden change on Charlie. They grew up together, for God's sake. After twenty years of influence, she was not like this."

Tomas frowned. "I had not thought of that. What do you suppose did it, then?"

Radcliffe grinned slightly. "The only new thing in her life is you."

Tomas was gaping over that truth when Stokes slipped out of the church to join them. "Oh, dear. Lady Charlie and Lady Beth are hardly in the condition for that sort of behavior."

Radcliffe and Tomas glanced back to the activity in the street. The man had turned away, it seemed, and tried to climb up on the bench seat of a wagon, only to have one of the women launch herself at his back. She appeared to be attempting to climb him like a mountain, and despite her advanced state of pregnancy, was doing a bang-up job of it. Meantime, the other "bride" was now stomping on his toes, kicking him in the shins, and yanking his hair for all she was worth. The vendor was squealing like a pig.

Both men started forward at once, grim determination on their faces. Radcliffe went automatically for the woman on the man's back, unhooking her from the vendor and carrying her several steps away to set her down. When she turned to face him, he blinked in surprise. "Elizabeth?"

"You are letting him go. Stop him!" Beth cried, running forward even as Charlie slipped from Tom's grasp and rushed toward the man.

Cursing in unison, Radcliffe and Tomas hurried forward, latching onto their wives' arms and urging them away before grabbing the vendor by his arms as he tried to climb into his wagon once more. Dragging him back to the ground, they turned him about to face the panting women.

"Now." Radcliffe frowned over the women's disheveled and breathless state. "What is going on?"

"He was beating that child," Charlie gasped furiously, reaching up to straighten her veil.

"What child?" Tomas frowned, and his wife answered.

"The boy in the back of the wagon."

Leaving the vendor where he was, both men moved to the wagon to peer in at the child cowering there. There was no mistaking the marks he bore as anything but bruises from a vicious beating. Radcliffe reached in to lift the child off the filthy strips of leather he lay on.

"Here now. Put him back. He's mine." The vendor rushed forward.

Radcliffe arched a brow coldly. "Yours?"

"My nephew, I got him when his parents died. I'm apprenticing him. Teaching him to be a cobbler and he's mine to deal with as I see fit. Besides, he deserved the beating. He done gone and run off on me. O'course I beat 'im when I spotted 'im here and caught him back."

"I would run off, too, if you beat me," Charlie snapped. "Not all those bruises are new."

Radcliffe and Tom peered from each other to the face of the miserable child Radcliffe held. The boy was thin, too thin, bruises old and new decorated his pale skin, and he had a hopeless expression on his face that no child should have. Shifting impatiently, Radcliffe glanced at the cobbler. "I will buy him from you."

"Radcliffe," Charlie gasped in horror. "You cannot *buy* a child."

"Aye, he can," the cobbler said quickly. "How much?"

"We shall discuss that in the office of my solicitor tomorrow morning at eight o'clock." While Charlie listened grimly, he gave the address to the man, then handed the child to Stokes, took Charlie's elbow, and started them up the steps to the church. They were halfway up before he realized that Charlie was being unexpectedly quiet. Glancing at her narrowly, he frowned at her tight-lipped expression. "Are you all right?"

"Aye," she said quickly, pressing a hand to her burgeoning stomach.

"You are not—" He paused on the steps as she bit her lip in pain. "You are, aren't you?"

"It will wait until after the wedding," she said determinedly, taking another shaky step.

"Charlie, are you going into labor?" Beth asked anxiously as she and Tomas joined them on the steps, her own gown burgeoning with the girth of a child. She was only a month behind her sister in her pregnancy. It did seem the twins liked to do things together. "You are, aren't you? Mayhap we should delay—" She fell silent as Charlie turned on her furiously.

"This child will not be born until his parents are properly wed."

Radcliffe was torn for a moment, then, cursing, he swept her up in his arms and hurried up the stairs with her, leaving the others to follow.

" 'Tis all right, husband, you can set me down, I

think that the pains have stopped," Charlie murmured as he pushed his way through the church doors with her. When Radcliffe ignored her and strode purposely up the aisle of the crowded church, Charlie forced a smile for the benefit of the guests, who had turned as one and were now watching their approach wide-eyed. "Here we are," she called out in feigned cheerfulness. "Sorry for the delay."

"Get to it, Father," Radcliffe said grimly, pausing before the gaping man.

"Set me down," Charlie hissed, and after a hesitation, Radcliffe did so, setting her on her feet just as Tomas, Beth, Stokes, and the cobbler's boy reached their side.

"Father!" Radcliffe snapped impatiently, and the man gave a start, then cleared his throat and began.

"Dearly beloved, we are gathered here—"

"We all know why we are gathered, Father. Please get to the important bit."

"Now see here, young man," he began, then glanced worriedly at Charlie as she suddenly gasped and clutched her stomach. "Are you all right, my lady?"

"She is about to have a baby, Father. Perhaps we could get this over with before it comes?"

"Well, aye, I know she is having a— You mean *now*?" The horror on his face knew no bounds. "Then you must get her home, see her comfortable and—" His voice died on a choked sound as Radcliffe grabbed him by his vestments and eyed him menacingly.

"Marry us first." When the poor man nodded quickly, Radcliffe released him and put a comforting arm around Charlie. Not that she noticed. Holding her stomach, she had begun to pant in a worrisome way.

"Do you, Lord Radcliffe, take—"

"I do," he snapped, and the minister frowned at him.

"At least let me finish—" He paused and swallowed as Charlie released a sudden groan, pain on her expressive face. "Oh, dear Lord," he breathed, then straightened grimly. "All right, Lord Radcliffe takes Lady Radcliffe, and, my lady, do you take him too?" When she nodded, he glanced toward Tom and Beth. "Lord Mowbray, do you take Lady Mowbray? And Lady Mowbray, what about you?"

They nodded as one and murmured, "We do."

"Good, good, then . . . er . . . what is next?" Sweat appearing on his brow, he floundered briefly, then cried, "The rings! Put them on." Once Tomas and Radcliffe had slipped the rings on their wives' fingers, he sighed with relief. "That is it. You are man and wife . . . again. Now kiss them and begone."

Kissing Charlie on the forehead, Radcliffe bent to catch her up in his arms, then turned and hurried down the aisle with her, Tomas and Beth hurrying behind them.

Radcliffe, Tomas, and Stokes were pacing ruts into the salon floor when they heard the coughing squall of a baby's cry. The clock on the mantel read five minutes to midnight. They had been pacing for more than twelve hours.

On arriving at the townhouse, Beth had had Radcliffe carry Charlie upstairs to their room, then relegated him and Tomas to the salon. Stokes had returned from the church shortly afterward with the cobbler's nephew, Mrs. Hartshair, her children, and Charlie's new lady's maid, Maggie, all in Mowbray's carriage.

Leaving the children in Stokes's care, Mrs. Hartshair and Maggie had hurried upstairs to see what assistance they could offer. And that was the last the men had seen of any of them except for the occasional sight of one woman or another flying past the door of the salon on her way to fetch this or that. At least, Stokes at first had had tending to the children to distract him, but then they had been put to bed and he had joined his master and Tomas in the salon to accompany them in their pacing.

Now, hearing the cry from above, the three men eyed each other with a combination of relief and trepidation; relief because it was obvious from the child's lusty cry that he was healthy, but trepidation because now they must await news of the mother's condition. For Radcliffe, the wait was interminable. Charlie's screams had reached them clear down into the salon, and every one had torn at his heart like the claws of a lion. A half-hour passed like a year as the men stood still, their pacing over as they stared at the stairs through the open salon door, waiting. Then Tomas murmured, "What do you suppose is taking so long?"

The question was enough to snap Radcliffe's patience. Muttering a curse, he stormed out of the salon. Tomas and Stokes glanced at each other, then moved as one to follow him up the stairs.

Beth had just finished remaking the bed and was helping Charlie settle back into it when the pounding started on the door. Mrs. Hartshair answered it, and Charlie heard Radcliffe's determined voice quite clearly: "I want to see my wife."

Mrs. Hartshair stepped aside at once, allowing him to enter before closing the door on the anxious gazes of Tomas and Stokes.

"Charlie?" Radcliffe hurried forward, then paused uncertainly at the side of the bed when he saw her. She looked exhausted; her face pale, hair disheveled and lank, and her eyes and expression incredibly weary as she glanced from the baby in her arms to him. She had never looked more lovely to Radcliffe, and he told her so as he eased carefully onto the side of the bed, one hand moving to cover hers on the baby and squeeze gently.

Charlie made a face at the claim, knowing just how bad she must look, then smiled slightly. "Do you not wish to see your son, my lord?"

"Son?" He peered down blankly at the bundle she held. "He's a boy?"

"Aye. Would you like to hold him?"

Radcliffe looked doubtful, but took the small baby. Holding him awkwardly and feeling incredibly clumsy, he peered down at the child and felt something tighten in his chest. He looked oddly like a little old man: his eyes were squeezed closed, his head nearly bald except for a fine feathering of fuzz, his face all squinched up in displeasure and an angry red from the ordeal he had suffered, and he was flailing one chubby little fist about. He was the ugliest little thing Radcliffe had ever seen, and the most adorable. "He is so tiny," he marveled, feeling tears well in his eyes. He and Charlie had made this miraculous new life.

"You would not say that, my lord, had he squeezed his way out of you," Charlie muttered with asperity, and her husband looked briefly stricken, then saw the amusement dancing in her eyes and smiled.

"Actually, he is not small at all," Beth murmured, moving to join them. "For a baby, he is quite large, in fact. Larger than any of the babies I saw born at Westerly."

"Beth has always had an interest in healing," Charlie explained when Radcliffe looked curious. "Back at home, if there was a body that was ill, or a birth taking place, Beth was usually there to try to help."

"Shall I take the baby out to show Tomas and Stokes so that the two of you can have a moment alone?"

"Aye, please." Radcliffe handed the child over to his aunt, then glanced around. The other women had already finished what they were doing and slipped out of the room. He waited until Beth closed the door silently behind her, then turned back to Charlie, bent forward, and kissed her gently on the lips.

"Thank you," he breathed into her hair as he hugged her carefully.

"You are welcome, my lord," she sighed, leaning into his embrace. "What for?"

"For our child."

"I seem to recall your having had a hand in that," she murmured with amusement as she pulled back to lean against the pillows, then heaved a sigh and grimaced. "I am sorry for today, my lord."

His eyebrows rose. "For what?"

"For ruining our wedding. I did not mean to, but when I saw that cobbler beating that boy—"

"You could not help yourself."

"Aye." She bit her lip. "I could not simply turn my head and ignore it."

"And I would not want you to," he assured her gently, and she raised her eyes to meet his gaze.

"Truly?"

"Truly. Your compassion for the weak, and disgust for injustice are two of the things I love most about you. Though," he added wryly as she relaxed, "I am grateful that in your condition you were not the one to jump on the man's back as you did with the farmer over the pups. I was quite relieved when I pulled who I thought was you off the cobbler's back and found it was Beth."

"I was attempting some restraint," she said with dignity. "It is something I am learning from you."

"Then we are each learning from the other. For I have been learning to live again from you," he murmured, and realized that it was true; even his guilt had left him.

Charlie had told him all that she had learned of Mary and Robert's murder from Norwich as soon as they were safely home that night. Learning this news had removed a world of guilt from him. There was nothing he could have done to save his sister. Even had he convinced them to take the carriage, an armed guard, or an army, Norwich would have killed them another day. He could not have protected her from him. Even Robert could not have. None of them had suspected his intentions. He'd been quite mad.

"I am so happy and content just now, Radcliffe," Charlie murmured suddenly, and Radcliffe smiled and stretched out on the bed beside her, holding her gently.

"So am I, my love."

She was silent for a moment, then asked, "Radcliffe, would you really not change me for the world?"

"Not a bit," he assured her solemnly.

"Beth says there was no tearing and I should be up and about in no time. You know what that means, do you not?"

Radcliffe blinked at what he thought to be a change of subject, but tried to follow it gamely. "What does it mean, my love?"

"It means we can go to your club soon."

"Oh, Charlie," Radcliffe groaned, then started to laugh as he hugged her. "I should have known you would not forget about that."

"Oh, come now, Radcliffe. It will be exciting."

"Oh, aye, it will be exciting all right," he agreed wryly. "Especially when someone recognizes you as Charles, and knows Charles is really Lady Radcliffe, and I am thrown out of my club. That will be most exciting."

"That will not happen. Beth and I have devised a disguise we are sure will work."

"A disguise, hmm?" he murmured doubtfully, his gaze fixing on the excited gleam in her eyes.

"Aye. And just think of it, husband. Me in my tight breeches. You the only one knowing 'tis I." Her eyebrows waggled suggestively. "Mayhap we could find a room or a closet unoccupied and . . ." She shrugged slightly as her voice trailed away, and Radcliffe wasn't surprised to feel excitement stirring within him. It seemed like forever since they had made love, though it had only been the last week or so that they had stopped for fear of hurting the child. Her suggestion now was raising a great deal of interest in him. Only Charlie would consider the possibility of making love under the noses of the ton.

"When did Beth say she thought you might be up to that sort of thing?" he asked in a growl, and Charlie beamed at him brightly.

"I always knew you had the soul of an adventurer, my lord."

HIGHLAND ROMANCE FROM
NEW YORK TIMES BESTSELLING AUTHOR

Lynsay Sands

Devil of the Highlands

978-0-06-134477-0

Cullen, Laird of Donnachaidh, must find a wife to
bear his sons to ensure the future of the clan. Evelinde
has agreed to marry him despite his reputation, for the
Devil of the Highlands inspires a heat within her
unlike anything she has ever known.

Taming the Highland Bride

978-0-06-134478-7

Alexander d'Aumesbery is desperate to convince the
beautiful and brazen Merry Stewart that he's a well-
mannered gentleman who's nothing like the members
of her roguish clan. But beneath it all beats a heart as
intense and uncontrollable as hers.

The Hellion and the Highlander

978-0-06-134479-4

When the flame-haired Lady Averill Mortagne braves
an unexpected danger at Highland warrior Kade
Stewart's side, she proves that her heart is as fiery
as her hair. And he realizes that submitting to their
scorching passion would be heaven indeed.